AVENGING DEVIL

PART 2

Satan's Devils MC - San Diego Chapter #4

COPYRIGHT

Published 2021 by Trish Haill Associates

ISBN: 978-1-912288-95-3

www.mandamellett.com

Disclaimer

This is a work of fiction. Names, characters, businesses, places, events and incidents are either the products of the author's imagination or used in a fictitious manner. Any resemblance to actual persons, living or dead, or actual events is purely coincidental.

Warning

This book is dark in places and contains content of a sexual, abusive and violent nature. It may not be suitable for persons under the age of 18.

PRODUCTION ACKNOWLEDGMENTS

Cover Design by Wicked Smart Designs

Edited and formatted by Maggie Kern @ Ms.K Edits

Proof reading by Darlene Tallman

Photographer: Golden Czermak of Furious Fotog

Model: Curtis Presley

CAST OF CHARACTERS

SAN DIEGO CHAPTER

Officers
Lost – President
Dart – Vice President
Grumbler – Sergeant-at-Arms
Salem – Enforcer
Scribe – Secretary
Bones – Treasurer
Blaze – Road Captain
Hard Token – Computer Expert

Patched Members
Brakes
Deuce
Dusty
Keeper
Kink
Niran

Pennywise
Reboot
Snips

Prospects
Connor
Curtis
Wrangler

Old Lady's and Children
Alex (Dart's): Tyler, Isla
Patty (Lost's): Beth, Connor
Mary (Grumbler's): Alicia

Club Girls
Cindy
Eva
Pearl
Tits

Members Out Bad
Bastard
Crow
DJ
Rattler
Tinder

Deceased Members
Bird (ex-Prez)
Gator
Kid (Prospect)
Poke (ex-SAA) Dispatched to Satan
Shark
Smoker

CAST OF CHARACTERS

Snake (ex-Prez) Dispatched to Satan

ARIZONA CHAPTER

Officers
Drummer – President
Wraith – Vice President
Peg – Sergeant-at-Arms
Blaze – Enforcer
Joker – Road Captain

Patched Members
Bullet
Lady
Rock
Slick
Viper

COLORADO CHAPTER

Officers
Demon – President
Beef – Vice President
Thunder – Sergeant-at-Arms
Mace – Enforcer
Sparky – Road Captain

Patched Members
Buzzard
Ink
Pyro

LAS VEGAS CHAPTER

Officers
Red – President
Crash – Vice President
Indian – Sergeant-at-Arms
Twister – Enforcer
Shadow – Road Captain
Keys – Computer Expert

Patched Members
Hammer
Rope
Sarge

UTAH CHAPTER

Officers
Snatcher – President
Thor – Vice President
Preacher – Sergeant-at-Arms
Swift – Enforcer
Rascal – Treasurer
Road – Road Captain
Stormy – Computer Expert

Patched Members
Bolt
Cowboy
Duty
Gears
Goofy
Grinch

Honor
Mystic
Piston

Prospects
Igor
Brute

SATAN'S DEVILS MC

CHAPTER ONE

Niran

I don't have to ask the identity of the man who's calling the shots, there's only one person who'd burst into Saffie's apartment and talk to her using his fists. The infamous Duke.

Time seems to freeze as the man called Slit holds a gun to my head and my mind fills with rapid-fire questions.

How the fuck did he find her? Why didn't I know he was close? Why had all the warnings we'd put in place failed?

Instead of my life, it's the last few minutes that flash before my eyes. Kid entering, all light-hearted and smiling, carrying those pizza boxes that now lie ruined on the floor next to his dead body.

Kid, the young man with so many hopes and dreams, and yet who'd been given no time to achieve them. I hadn't been quick enough. If I'd been faster, nimbler, maybe I could have got the drop on them, but my fuckin' leg had given way, sending me crashing to my knees. Vulnerable, Slit had been able to overpower me. Some fuckin' saviour I am. I can't even protect the woman I vowed to, nor the prospect who'd barely begun to live his life. The only mercy was his death had been quick, and I doubt Kid had time to consider his impending doom.

Now I'm staring at the wrong end of a gun, seething at the senseless killing of the prospect while Duke uses his fists on Saffie. I can barely contain my rage, but control it I have to if there's to be any chance of helping her now. A clear head is required to come up with a plan, though it's a long shot to find anything that might work. The one aim I have left in life is to fulfil my promise of bringing every man present as painful a death as I can make it.

But the gun to my head suggests getting my vengeance may require me crawling up out of hell. So be it. I'll be bringing the Devil back with me. One thing's for certain, they are not going to escape what's coming to them. I'll fucking haunt them for the rest of their miserable lives.

Closing my eyes momentarily, I apologise to Kid for putting him in this situation, and then reopen them, knowing I'm going to put on the performance of my life, and that I've got to sound convincing. I'm no use to Duke, it's Saffie he's come for, and once he takes her, her life isn't going to be worth living.

They've already killed Kid without blinking an eye, not even bothering to ask his name. I'm facing the same sentence unless I come up with something fast. I can't afford to die, can't lose my chance to make Duke pay for all the times he's hurt her, both then and now. Every blow, every punch, every kick, every pain he ever caused her will be paid back with the type of interest that would make any loan shark blink.

He'll wish he was dead long before I end him.

But I've got to get on his right side first, and even then, there's a high risk my plan won't work.

When Saffie's curled up in a ball of pain, he loses interest in her, and now turns his attention my way.

"Who the fuck are you?" he asks me directly. "Why are you with my ol' lady? You fuckin' her? Oh fuck it, I don't even care." He nods at the man holding the gun to my head. "Just kill the fuckin' nigger. I don't want him breathing the same air."

I hear the gun cocking and know I have a split second for him to change his mind. "Hold up," I speak fast. "Let's not be hasty here. I'm the reason you found her."

From her position on the floor, Saffie, horrified, stares at me. I force my eyes away from the horror and betrayal in hers as I take the calculated gamble that someone's either been feeding him information, or could have dropped clues for Grit to find— the man who Duke seems to look to for information.

At least I've got his attention. Duke holds up his hand, indicating a stay of execution, but I don't get elated. There's no guarantee anything will work. At his raised eyebrow, I give him more, starting by answering his questions.

"The name's Niran. I ride with the Satan's Devils MC."

He eyes me suspiciously. "Where's your fuckin' cut?"

I nod to the back of the door where I'd automatically hung it when I'd walked in. Saffie's triggered by that piece of leather, so I'd taken it off to help her see me as just a man. Now Duke walks over and examines it.

"Satan's Devils wouldn't help the Crazy Wolves," he murmurs, half to himself, but loud enough for me to hear.

I treat it as a question that needs answering. "Maybe not," I agree. "But *I* would. The Devils are a fuckin' pansy club. I should never have joined them." Sneering, I add, "They don't deserve to wear the one-percenter patch. Fuckin' club's all about legit business."

"And you want easy money?" Duke doesn't sound impressed.

"I want an interesting fuckin' life. One where I can act like a fuckin' man."

Duke snorts. "I don't believe you. It wasn't you I got my information from, was it, Grit?"

The man named Grit, who up to now has done and said nothing, shakes his head. "Nah, VP. It was a bitch."

A bitch. With those two words, he's given me more information than I could have hoped for. Duke didn't stumble across Saffie by accident, and not through any efforts of his own or faults of hers. Betrayal burns in my gut, as the gender limits who the traitor could be. It's either the woman who wants me as her old man, or the woman that's supposed to be on my side. *My own fucking sister.* I discount the sweet butts who wouldn't dare cross the Devils.

Susie or Cyn. Whichever it is, they're dead. Fuck, I hope it wasn't Cyn. The knowledge that it could be threatens to send me off track, when having my head firmly in the game is the only thing that might save me. Garnering all the acting skills I possess, I huff, which isn't easy with Slit still weighing me down, and roll my eyes.

"And where do you think she was getting her information from? Don't know about your club, but women in ours don't get to know club business."

I think Slit wants to shut me up. I sense a taste for bloodlust coming from him as he leans onto my neck, making me choke and struggle for breath. Even in my fight to survive, I feel, as much as see, Saffie's dismayed eyes burning into me. But I keep all emotion from my face. It's best if she believes me. Only half an hour ago I'd been devastated to learn she trusted me so little, but hopefully that mistrust I'd tried so hard to assuage will play into my hands now.

While Duke's processing my words, I try to come to terms that if I die today, the fault lies at only one of two people's hands. Out of the two, I'd put money on it being the bitch who all but raped me. Cyn? Nah, I can't believe it was her. Or maybe I just don't want to.

Sparing one glance at Saffie, my gut clenches as I see the look of hatred on her face. Unable to give her any support or compassion, I turn my attention to the man she's still, unfortunately, married to.

Duke is looking at Grit—the man who I knew by hearing his name was the Wolves' equivalent of Token—their computer and information expert. Grit, who's standing casually with his hands in his pockets, shrugs, not giving a confirmation or denial.

"You want me to believe it was you?" Duke shakes his head, but his pause suggests he's giving me the chance to prove it.

Taking the gamble that, even if it was Cyn, she hadn't mentioned me being her brother, I snort. "How the fuck else did the bitch get all the information? The woman gags for my cock. Getting her to do what I wanted was too fuckin' easy." I wince again at Saffie's blatant look of disgust tinged with disappointment, but I can't offer her solace. Me having a chance to save her depends on getting on Duke's right side, even if it means I land on the worst side of hers.

I'm right to allude to Susie as a bitch. Duke grins as though I'm speaking his language. "Yeah. Most women will do anything for a good dicking." He pauses and kicks out at Saffie again, and again I have to suppress my wince and ire. "Most," he emphasises with a twisted expression.

Mentally apologising to Saffie, I press my case. "Your ol' lady ran away. Fuckin' obvious you'd want her back. Heard her fuckin' sob story, and knew the Crazy Wolves were a club to whom I could relate. I kinda hoped you'd return a favour for a favour."

"You want money?" Duke raises his eyebrow.

"Nah." Money would do fuck all to help Saffie. The only way I'll have a chance of looking out for her is to get them to take me with her. "The Wolves sound a lot more to my liking than the fuckin' Devils I currently ride with."

"You want in on my club?" Duke's eyes widen, while the man pinning me down snorts. Their computer guy covers his mouth and chuckles, while the man who so remorselessly killed Kid laughs loudly, earning him a rebuke. "Shut it, Croak."

Glancing down at Saffie, obviously seeing she's in pain and immobile, Duke seats himself on the couch, spreading out his arms over the back. He regards me carefully.

"You fucked my ol' lady?"

"Fuck a bitch who's carrying another man's baby?" I widen my eyes deliberately. "Not fuckin' likely. That's not my kink."

His eyes narrow, as if my words haven't satisfied him, and says deceptively calmly, "So you encouraged her to get rid of my kid?" Damn, I didn't realise my words could have had a different meaning.

I inject shock into my voice. "For fuck's sake, man. Kill a man's baby? That's all fucked up. I tried to fuckin' stop her, but the club got me doing shit and I got there too late. Can't fuckin' trust bitches." I sneer at Saffie. One half of me focuses on this important conversation—one wrong word could end my life—while the other wonders how he seems to know everything. I decide to stick as closely as I can to the truth. "I got to the hospital as fast as I could when our guy got the information she was booked in for the procedure. Only," I grimace, "I wasn't in time. That's fuckin' shit, Brother. A man should have a say in his kid's future."

"You don't call me brother," Duke snarls, his face blazing with rage. I file away that information. Then, as fast as the storm arrived, it recedes. "You're right. That was my kid in her belly, and she fuckin' killed it."

"Hospital records show it had anencephaly," the guy with the info reminds him, letting me have some answer at least. Duke's had access to her medical history.

"But he still might have been born alive, Grit." Duke's hands clench together. "He might have survived on fuckin' life support or something."

As Saffie gasps, I try to piece it together. Why should a

living child be so important? I don't take Duke for the caring sort and proposing to keep the baby alive hooked up to machines is absolutely sick when there's no hope for a positive outcome.

"I tried, man. I tried." I impress my supposed efforts on him, shaking my head, hopefully sadly.

"You failed!" Duke throws at me in a burst of rage. Then his expression becomes calculating. "Why didn't you get news to me sooner? It's been a month since the operation."

Damn this is hard. Still pinned, I try to give a dismissive shrug. "I'm just a member. I get told shit. Only the officers know deets. I knew she was property, she told me herself, but she wouldn't say anything about your club. I'm a fighter, I don't use no keyboard. It took time to learn you ride with the Crazy Wolves. When I did, I got the info to you as fast as I could. I'm just sorry, man, that it wasn't earlier."

His narrowed eyes show he remains suspicious. "Why use the bitch? You scared of a fuckin' phone?"

I let my eyes widen. "Our computer guy has all that shit locked down. I, er, I don't think they fully trust me. I know they keep track of the numbers I call. Hence, I used her. She'd do anything for cock, man." I give a lewd sneer. It's not too much of a stretch. Knowing Susie, she probably would. *Could have been Cyn,* I remind myself. Fuck, but I hope not.

Duke considers me carefully. "So you got me here, but I'm in no mood to give thanks. Shouldn't have had to traipse over half the country to get back what I own. Give me one reason I shouldn't just let Slit kill you?"

At least he's asked. The stakes are sky high, and it's time I plead for my life. But I'm not one to beg and know that wouldn't impress him.

"No reason at all. I suspect your man here is right." I jerk my head up as I refer to the comment Slit had made about neighbourly concern in Saffie's apartment block. "Probably no one would give a damn about a gunshot in this building. But there's a chance they might, and that's an inconvenience you don't need if the cops get called and turn up." I pause for a beat. "Thing is, I'm a man looking for a new club. And I might be just the man you want."

"You think so?" Duke snorts and sits forward, his raised eyebrow challenging me. "And what makes you think that?"

As much as I can with Slit sitting on me, I puff out my chest. "I'm a Marine. I'd still be serving if I hadn't lost half my leg. I'm a munitions expert, sharpshooter, and can build a bike from fuckin' scratch with one hand tied behind my back."

"Marine, huh?" Duke pulls at his short beard. After staring at me for a moment, he looks over my head. "What d'you reckon, SAA?"

Another thing learned. Slit is their sergeant-at-arms.

"We didn't replace Jude," the man remarks. "And he's a Satan's Devil with no reason to stay loyal."

"Good points." Duke looks at me, calculating. "I don't tend to trust niggers, nor men who turn their backs so easily on their clubs. And, as you've seen, Croak has no problem killing a man with his bare hands. No need to get the cops involved." He finishes with a kind of 'there you go' smug grin.

I ignore the racial slight, it's the least of my worries right now. Having the sense this isn't going well, I decide to stop taking it all lying down. I'm no stranger to working out, have had to compensate for my missing leg, and kind of got hooked on going to the gym. To counterbalance my missing limb, I've tons of upper body strength. While I've been talking, I've also been assessing the weight of the man leaning on me, and I'm pretty sure he's more fat than brawn.

Tensing, I bunch my muscles. Rolling swiftly to take him by surprise, I hook my good leg around his, forcing him to stay on the ground. Now it's me pinning him with my bodyweight as I grab the gun from his loosened grip and turn the tables on him.

When he raises his hands, I stand, but keep the weapon firmly pointed at his head.

"Seems like your sergeant-at-arm's life is in my hands," I tell Duke coldly. By now, Duke, Croak and Grit have all drawn their pieces. I'm gambling on how much they value this man's life.

"Impressive," Duke remarks. "Maybe you should just shoot Slit now, seeing as he couldn't hold you down."

"Not many men can," I respond, continuing to sell myself. "And if you need a new sergeant-at-arms, then I'm your man. Stood in for ours when Grumbler came off his bike."

"Can't see that's a recommendation, seeing as it's a pussy club," he sneers.

"Yeah?" I find an extra weapon in my arsenal and don't hesitate to use it. "But it's a pussy club who was keeping your property away from you, and they're the pussies I know everything about."

"VP?" Slit sounds hesitant, as though he doesn't really trust Duke to stop me from shooting him. A situation I can understand. I find nothing attractive about him myself, and wouldn't, even if I wasn't aware of Saffie's history.

"Oh, for fuck's sake." Duke barks a laugh and holsters his sidearm and indicates the other two men should do the same. "Let the man stand and give him his gun back. You might be a man I could use." He considers me carefully. "Need to start at the fuckin' bottom, of course. You'll need to prove you're not going to step out on us like you have with the Devils."

I shrug. "It's not like I don't know what I'm stepping into. But have no doubts, I'll prove myself."

Now released, Slit walks over and speaks into Duke's ear. Duke grins and in a way I really don't like. He chuckles and turns to me.

"Slit's just reminded me it's time to get moving, Boy." He chuckles when he uses the slight. "Just in case those Devils of yours have more backbone than you've described and start trying to locate their missing member." Which is obviously what I've been hoping, of course, but luckily Duke can't read my mind. "Bring the bitch and make sure she does nothing stupid." He tilts his head to one side, as if wondering whether I'm going to obey.

I have to. I have to jump to his every command as though I really am a new recruit desperate to prove myself. *If only I could take her and run.* But having given Slit his piece back, I'm unarmed and faced with four men wearing guns.

I harden my voice, and even smirk, an expression of which I know Duke will approve. "I'll keep her quiet." Knowing she's going to hate me, or even more than she already does, I walk straight over to her and jerk her up roughly by one arm, ignoring her wince as I must have touched a bruise. "You gonna behave?"

"Fuck you," she spits.

I could admire her spirit, but Duke wouldn't like it. Knowing what's expected, I twist the arm I'm holding painfully behind her back. When she yelps, Duke looks on in approval.

Never, ever have I hurt a woman before. My own behaviour sickens me. The only justification I can use is that at the end of the day, keeping her safe is all that matters. And I've achieved my first objectives—to stay alive and at her side.

"Behave, bitch," Duke tosses at her. "You, my little socialite, are coming home where you were always meant to be."

She makes a valiant effort to struggle out of my grasp, but I've got hold of her with a tight grip. She kicks my ankle but gets the prosthetic instead of flesh. I shake her and say sharply, "Fuckin' behave, woman."

"Fuck you! Fuck all of you," she spits out again.

Saffie, I'm so fucking sorry. We should have protected you from all this. But outwardly, I laugh as though I find her tussling with me amusing. Inwardly, I'm hoping like fuck the Satan's Devils will figure out what's wrong and come after us. Until then, she's only got me to protect her, and I can only do that if I stay alive. Which means doing anything these fuckers ask, even causing her harm if I have to, though I'd be dying inside.

She's kicking and screaming, but in this block it won't matter. Nevertheless, once outside the apartment, I stoop, elbow her in the stomach, making her breath leave her in a whoosh, and toss her up over my shoulder in a fireman's lift. Once again, I get Duke's smirk and sharp nod.

This time she doesn't take into account my prosthesis, nor does she relax or do anything to make my life easier. She kicks out, tries to bite, and does anything to make my task difficult. While harbouring an internal sense of pride and hoping my leg will stand up to the punishment, carefully I make my way down the stairs.

I'm praying someone will open their door and see this situation is all kinds of wrong, that a woman is being kidnapped right off her doorstep. But of course, no one interferes, and the only shouts of disapproval I hear are those directed at Saffie, telling her to keep her screaming down.

Even the drug dealers seem to be absent, and the parking lot is empty except for vehicles. To my disappointment, no Devils are waiting in sight. Not that there's any reason they should be, but I'd been optimistic. There is, however, a big truck. Slit speeds up to get ahead, then opens the door and points me to the third row of seats, the ones with no doors beside them. Then Grit sits in the middle row along with the Kid-murdering-Croak, and Slit takes his seat beside Duke in the front.

Grimacing, feeling it like a kick to my stomach, I notice Kid's bike beside mine, waiting patiently for its owner who will never return. *I'll avenge you, Kid,* I silently promise him. *I'll make them fucking pay. I'll make them regret the day they were born and every day of their life since.* It's a vow to a dead man, but one I'm determined to keep.

"I hate you," the woman beside me whispers, her voice

hoarse from the shouting which had had no results. She spits in my face.

Stoically, I wipe the spittle away as the words echo inside my head. She can't hate me as much as I hate myself.

Not my fault, though, thinking about who actually betrayed her. It had to be Susie, that jealous, manipulative bitch. My mistake was not jettisoning her from the club long before I had. But I had had no idea just how badly she was going to fuck up, nor how twisted her mind really is. Or, it could have been Cyn. Am I blaming Susie, as I don't want to think my sister would be so cruel? Whichever, I'll be finding out. And whoever it is, I don't give a damn she's female. For what she's done, she deserves death. Even my sister.

Duke and Slit exchange words in the front seat, but quietly so I can't hear what they're saying. I suspect we're heading back to Nevada, but I'm curious as to how we're getting there? Are we driving all the way?

What's become obvious is that they didn't bike down. We'd been wrong. All of us had been assuming they'd make the grand gesture and ride their motorcycles. No wonder we didn't get warning that the Wolves were on the move.

Still, it's a long drive. Maybe there'll be an opportunity to escape, or at least get Saffie away. If we make a stop for gas, or at a rest stop, I'll lull them into a false sense of security, then make my move. It will take last-minute planning once I see what I'm working with, but I'm resourceful, and certain I can make it work.

But our route takes us out of the city in the opposite direction from the road I expected. An hour later, their reasoning becomes obvious as an airfield comes into sight, not unlike the one which houses our compound. But this one's very much in use.

Okay, so my initial plan's a non-starter. I swallow down my disappointment. A Marine is always prepared to work on whatever presents itself. I eye my surroundings with care, scanning for someone who might recognise some sort of distress signal, but there are few people around, and those that are don't seem bothered by a truck steaming toward its destination, a plane ready for takeoff. A sight, which for some reason, has Saffie tensing. *Does she not like to fly?*

When Duke draws up alongside it, she screams out, "That's my father's plane!"

Looking back over his shoulder, Duke snorts a laugh. "Yeah, good of him to lend it to us, wasn't it? But then, you are his only daughter, Sapphire."

The bored looking pilot is waiting and doesn't blink an eye when I drag a struggling woman out of the truck. A mechanic is making final checks, and he too, ignores the sight. Being a distance from the rudimentary terminal, I resign myself to the truth. Whether or not we want to go, Saffie and I are headed to the lair of the Crazy Wolves.

CHAPTER TWO

Grumbler

"Y ou doing okay?" Gently, I place my hand against Mary's face, wondering the same thing I do every day. *How the fuck did I get so lucky to have this woman as my wife?*

Nuzzling into me sleepily, she murmurs, "I'd be better if your son wasn't using my bladder as a trampoline."

I chuckle. "Need help getting up, Momma?"

"Nah. I'll be okay for a few more minutes. You go and do your stuff, old man."

"I'm *your* ol' man, and don't you forget it." Leaning over, I give her a kiss, pausing to lay my hand against her swollen belly. The baby's certainly lively this morning. *My son.* My heart feels full to bursting at what my life has become. A gorgeous woman by my side wasn't something I'd ever expected. Add on the promise of a child in just a couple of months' time, and everything's just about perfect.

Or will be.

The pregnancy is going well, but nothing in life comes with a cast-iron guarantee. Both my age and Mary's are against us. So far, we're beating the odds, but there's a long way to go before we hold our baby, and still time for things to go wrong.

"You get off to work, Grumbler."

Assessing her, I see no adverse changes. Her pallor is what it should be. Her eyes, though bleary with sleep, are bright and alert. If I had the slightest fear something wasn't right, I'd stay right here with her. It's the same mental checks I go through each morning.

"For heaven's sake." Mary lightly punches my arm. "Stop worrying about me."

Hmm. Perhaps I'm not so circumspect about my morning inspections as I thought I was. "Anything—"

"If anything changes and I don't feel right, I'll call you, okay?" She rolls her eyes.

It's the same reassurance I need from her each morning so I can feel at peace during the day.

Swinging my legs out of bed, I rest my head in my hands.

When Mary had first gotten pregnant, it had come as a shock to us both. At forty-seven, she was pushing the limits of conceiving naturally. Despite being warned of what might lie ahead, we'd decided to let nature take its course. If the baby was meant to be, we'd be happy. If not, well, that was the way the cards would fall.

Despite being more tired than she had been during her first pregnancy eighteen years ago, Mary's been happy and healthy, and all the checks show the baby is just where he should be.

That things could go wrong had been brought home to us recently after a chance meeting with Saffie.

Saffie's seventeen years younger than Mary, yet she had to terminate her pregnancy when her baby had no chance of being born to live any kind of life. Being faced with the horror of what could go wrong has been hard on both Mary and me, forcing such problems into the forefront of our minds.

Saffie was devastated when she lost her baby, and who could

blame her? But hearing about her from Niran, who'd witnessed her pain, had brought home exactly how hard it would be. However pragmatic you think yourself, however much you think your eyes have been wide open the whole time, means fuck all when it actually happens.

If Mary loses the baby, or fuck it, if I lose her, I don't know how I'd survive.

"You're thinking too loud," Mary grumbles, as she manoeuvres herself over onto her other side. "Go to work."

I pat her arm, then get to my feet, and in preparation to do as instructed, start my morning routine.

With Mary in the hospital, my brothers give me some leeway. It's late in the morning when I'm walking into the auto-shop which I kind of manage on behalf of my club, the Satan's Devils MC. I say kind of, because we're more of a team, with no one actually being termed the boss. I suppose it's my age that gives me the rank.

I bump fists with Snips and greet our civilian employees—all vets who we give a helping hand to by giving them a job, and who repay us in spades. Two of whom, Ross and Gibbs, are at the coffee machine.

"Grab one for me, will ya?" I request, walking past.

"Sure, Grumps."

Grumps? "You fuckin' what?" I spin around, only to see Ross doubling up and pointing his finger at Gibbs.

"Wasn't me." He singsongs like a child.

Inwardly chuckling, I show them my finger.

I drink my coffee made just the way I like it, then do a stock take, checking we've all the parts we're likely to need, ordering where we're running low. Then I go give Ross a hand tracking down a fault of a newer model car. Diagnostic tools are okay, except when they give vague results. Sometimes I wonder whether Token should be working here, as it's more often computer work than mechanical nowadays. Give me an old-fashioned engine and I'll be satisfied.

I suppose it must be a couple of hours later that I realise Niran's not come in. It's not that we keep strict working hours—members share the profits, so we all put in the time—but Niran's a creature of habit, and normally appears at the day's start.

"Hey, anyone heard from Niran?"

My shouted query addressed to no one in particular gets only shrugs of shoulders or the odd, *Dunno*, in response. So thinking it's best to go straight to the horse's mouth and call him, I take out my phone.

Damn. It goes straight to voicemail. "Hey, Brother. Give me a shout, yeah?" Message left, I put my phone away.

"Grumbler? That exhaust come in for the Indian?" A head appears around the office door.

"Give me a sec, Gibbs. I'll go check."

It seems that it hasn't and should have been here yesterday. I waste a good few minutes on the phone to the supplier chasing them up.

Ending that call, my phone chimes with another. Picking it up, I expect to hear Niran and answer accordingly. "'Bout fuckin' time, Niran—"

"Nah, Bro. It's me, Token. I now suspect you won't be able to help me. I'm trying to track down Niran. I take it he's not there?"

"No, and I've been trying to call him myself."

"Damn phone of his. Battery's fucked. I keep meaning to give him a new one."

I know all about that. I've heard Niran moaning about it enough. "Whatcha want him for? Can I help?"

"I got some info for him. Shit he might want to know."

"Like?"

"Like get your ass over to the club if you want to find out. I think I need to bring Prez in on this."

"Wanna tell me the headlines?" I drum my fingers against the top of the desk.

"Crazy Wolves might be making a move."

I suck in air. This is indeed something Niran should be in on. Knowing there's no point asking Token for more when he'll only have to go through it all again, I end with, "I'll see you in twenty, Brother."

Leaving the office, I just give a shout, "Heading back to see Prez."

Damn Niran and that phone of his. I've lost count of the times I've tried to call him to get no response. He's got an older smartphone, and the battery life can be fucking erratic. I've heard him complaining about it for weeks, but the stupid fucker hasn't done anything about it.

Being far from the first time I've been unable to raise him, I know I should have fucking insisted. I am the sergeant-at-arms for the club.

Crazy Wolves might be on the move. If it's in our direction, there's only one reason they'd be heading for San Diego, and that's to retrieve their VP's woman—the same Saffie as I was thinking about earlier this morning.

Fuck it, but that girl's already got far too much on her plate. I know Niran fucked up with her. His solution was to bring her into the club and under our protection as his old lady. But Saffie had good reason not to want to be club property again, and didn't appreciate the suggestion.

While as far as I know, she's kicked him to the kerb, he indeed needs to know this new information. The plans to move Saffie out of state should be enacted immediately.

It's only when I near the club that I start to wonder whether Niran's phone did die on him, and whether there's another reason we can't contact him.

Backing my bike into its familiar spot, I extract the key and listen for a moment to the engine ticking. *Where the fuck are you, Niran?* My guess at this time of day would be the clubhouse or the shop, and as Token's based here and called me, he's not at either of those. When my phone vibrates, I take it out, and glancing at the screen see Token's just sent a group text.

Token: Anyone know where Niran went?

There's no need for me to respond. He already knows I don't. I pull my leg over the seat and head on into the building.

Token looks up from his laptop as I stick my head around the door to his office, then gets to his feet.

"Anyone respond yet?" I demand.

"Cool your fuckin' tits. Give 'em a minute. Only just sent the darn message. Let's go see Prez."

Lost looks up sharply as I rap on the door, then push it open. As Token walks in behind me, Lost peers past us as though expecting someone else.

"Thought you wanted Niran here?"

"Can't raise him, Prez. His damn phone's on the blink again." Token takes one of the seats in front of Lost's desk.

"This about Saffie?" Lost has clearly put two and two together fast. "You got new info, Toke? Her papers ready to go?"

"Her new ID's been set up. Just waiting for confirmation on accommodation. But it's not about that." Token leans forward and places his laptop on the desk but doesn't open it. "Stormy's a clever fucker, you know?" His comment about the brother from Utah is clearly rhetorical, so neither Lost nor I answer. "We've got eyes out for Crazy Wolves heading our way on bikes. Stormy went one step further. He's looking at all routes. He discovered a flight plan was filed earlier this morning from an airbase near where the Wolves are located to San Diego. Private plane registered to a Bartell Enterprises."

"And what's that got to do with the Wolves?" Lost presses. "Stormy think they were on board? What's he got to go on?"

"Winston Bartell is Saffie's father," Token declares, in such a way as I suspect a *ta-da* to come after it.

My brow creases and I sit forward. "What?" I'm confused. "If she's got parents, why the hell didn't they get her away from that bastard?" Frowning, I continue, "Could it be the father coming to get her, and nothing to do with the Wolves?"

"If she had a loving family, wouldn't it have been them she'd run to?" Lost asks, perfectly reasonably, but looking perplexed.

I haven't lived the life that I have without being aware of the seedier side. "Not all family is loving. Shit, they might have traded her to Duke to pay off some debt. Can't assume rich folks are on the up and up." In my experience, not following the straight and narrow was how they often became loaded in the first place.

Lost grimaces. "You're right, of course, Grumbler. But I'd like more than that before we assume we've got a pack heading for us."

Token slides his laptop toward him and flips it open, then turns it to face me. "That good enough? Stormy hacked into the security footage."

Leaning over, I focus my eyes on the image. There are four bikes parked up close by a plane that yeah, is emblazoned with the name he'd just told us. On at least one of the motorcycles a decal denoting the Crazy Wolves MC can be seen clearly.

"Good enough for me." I push the laptop around so Lost can get a closer look and slip into my sergeant-at-arms role as if putting on a comfortable cloak. "Is this a battle we're fighting, Prez?"

Lost stares at the screen, but his eyes lose focus, as if he's mulling things over in his head. It takes a moment before he speaks. "Niran claimed Saffie. In our books, is there anything that says that's aborted if the woman doesn't say yes?"

Token snorts loudly. "Not that we'd ever enforce it, but you're right, of course, Prez."

Damn straight we wouldn't enforce it. I tilt my head up as if to better listen to what Lost says.

"Then it's our fight," he pronounces.

"There's no way they know her address," I tell them. "They can only be on a fishing expedition."

Lost narrows his eyes. "I wish I could be so fuckin' certain. Who flies to San Diego for no damn reason? They've hardly come to visit the zoo, world famed though it is."

He's got a good point. "What do you want us to do?" I ask.

He's tapping his chin with his fingers. "Get ready," he starts, then expands, "Saffie is Niran's, she's club property. We need to keep her safe. And just four Wolves roaming the streets of San Diego?" he muses aloud. "We've got the numbers. I don't mind taking them on and letting them know they'll not find their lost mate in my fuckin' town."

Now that's what I want to hear. I exchange a fist bump with Token, whose laptop pings at the same time. Taking ownership of it again, he suddenly straightens. His jaw tightens.

"Kink just responded to the group text I sent. He says, and I quote, 'If Niran's got any sense after what I said last night, he'll have gone around to see Saffie.'"

All a sudden I'm not so sure of my assertion they can't know where she lives, and equally wondering again whether I was too fast to blame Niran's dodgy phone's battery.

Token's already tapping on his phone. As he does, he says, "I'm calling Saffie. I've been communicating with her about the paperwork." When I go to speak, he holds up a finger. I can hear the ringing tone coming from the device.

When the voicemail comes on, he shakes his head, and gets back onto his laptop. Within moments, he's rubbing his cheek, and saying quietly, "Fuck."

"Toke?"

"Prez. Saffie's phone's at her apartment."

But she's not answering.

Prez goes completely still. "And you said you can't get a hold of Niran?"

"He's not answering his phone," I tell them.

"Can't even ping it," Token adds.

Lost stands. "Kink thinks he's gone to see Saffie. We can't raise either of them on the phone. If the fuckin' Wolves have learned her location…" Lost lets his voice trail off, before commencing again, saying firmly, "Let's get over there, Brothers."

CHAPTER THREE

Grumbler

I'm first out of the office. Entering the clubroom, I see Salem deep in conversation with Dart. Both men's eyes narrow as they see us determinedly striding out.

"Whatsup?" the VP demands. "You still looking for Niran?"

Lost quickly sums up where we're at. "Kink thinks he's with Saffie and we can't raise either of them. We've received intelligence that we've got Wolves on the prowl. They're in our town."

Salem, stripping out of his overalls, simultaneously speaks into his phone, "Pennywise, get your ass over here now. And bring hardware."

Yeah. Too right we're going in armed. My piece is in a concealed compartment at the bottom of my saddlebags. Knowing Lost and Token, theirs will be as well. It's not good for members of an MC to be caught carrying in California.

Before we can exit the clubroom, the prospect, Connor, comes running up. "Prez? Fuckin' Kid didn't turn up this morning. I still can't track him down. He's been missing for hours." He looks put out, and I assume he's been landed with some shit job Kid's managed to evade.

But is it too much of a coincidence to lose track of a member

23

and a prospect in the same morning? Could there be any connection? "Hey, Prospect!" I yell at his retreating back. "You tried calling him?" The roll of his eyes tells me he has. "Know his last fuckin' location?" When Connor looks down at the floor, managing to look both irritated and reluctant, I add for encouragement, "Spit it the fuck out."

Connor grimaces. "He was fuckin' a woman in town, was staying with her. Last text I had was around lunchtime. He said he had something to do for Niran but would be here soon."

Jesus Christ! That certainly links him with our missing member, and he's uncontactable as well? From the expressions on the faces around me, it's not just me who thinks this doesn't bode well.

"Let's get moving." Lost raises his chin to his stepson but doesn't enlighten him on where we're going or whether it's got anything to do with Kid. Prospects get used to not being told shit and from Connor's lack of concern, he's not reading anything into it.

With Lost in pole position, Dart and I right behind him, followed by Salem and Token with Pennywise bringing up the rear, we twist our throttles hard to get to our destination.

I thought I was prepared when Niran and Mary had told me the locality around Saffie's apartment block left much to be desired, but seeing it for myself, shows they'd underestimated, probably to save me nightmares. It's an absolute shithole. Riding up, I decide when I find Niran I'm going to tear him a new one for allowing Mary to come here, not once but fucking twice. My temper hasn't improved when we pull up behind Kid and Niran's motorcycles and I hear a crunch as I put my foot down. Looking down, it's a fucking discarded syringe. My jaw clenches. *Mary should never have been anywhere near here.*

Glancing around, ostensibly to see whether the prospect or Niran are miraculously anywhere in sight, I take in the cars resting on bricks, some down on their hub caps, more discarded drug paraphernalia, a stroller lying on its side, and garbage sacks sprawling open with their contents scattered around. At least one, I notice, is moving. *I fucking hate rats.* If I'd known this was where Saffie was living, I'd have demanded she return to the clubhouse myself. I wouldn't allow a dog to live here. *What was Niran thinking?*

Then I think of my Mary, stubborn as a fucking mule at times. Maybe all Niran could do was keep an eye on Saffie. Short of kidnapping her and tying her up, what could he have done? Especially considering her justifiable fear of men who ride motorcycles.

"This place is a fuckin' dump." Lost is surveying the area much like I am. "You got her apartment number, Toke?"

"Yeah. Four-twelve."

Dart starts heading toward the doorway with us trailing behind him. Inside the hallway stinks of urine, and if I'm not mistaken, that's human faeces in the corner. I eye the elevator with distaste, but even more so when Salem stabs at the button which remains unlit, and my ears catch no sound of moving machinery.

With shakes of our heads and a couple of 'fuck that's' we move toward the stairs. Each floor we pass is an education on the seedy side of life. I swear I see a drug deal going down on one, a prostitute plying her wares on another. On the third a door busts open, and some poor sucker comes tumbling out, an angry female throwing his clothes after him.

My Mary subjected herself to this? I'm gonna tan her ass. Well, maybe I'll have to wait until our son is born. By the time I reach Saffie's floor, I'm doubling up on that promise. I, myself am puffing, and she's seven months' pregnant for fuck's sake. *She should have been looking after herself.*

"Fuck." Lost, in the lead, pulls out his weapon and waves us to stop. He points down the hallway to where a door is busted and is hanging off centre on its frame.

Mentally, I do the calculation. Yeah, apartment four-twelve would be right about there. *Fuck, Niran. Are we too late?* Already rethinking my desire to beat his ass when I find him, I veer more now toward hugging. *Just let him be safe.* That's all I ask.

We approach the door in cautious formation. I hear shouting from above, but this floor is eerily silent. Dart and Salem take positions to the left and right of the entrance to what I'd correctly guessed is Saffie's apartment, and cautiously ease their heads around the door, guns held in front of them.

"Oh shit," Dart says with feeling, causing my heart to damn near stop, then, signalling Salem to cover his back, he steps inside.

As sergeant-at-arms, I should be up front. I push past Salem and enter after Dart. Immediately, I see Kid prone on the floor, his head at an awkward angle, two boxes with liberated pizzas lying next to him.

Motherfucker!

Falling to my knees, I check optimistically for a pulse. I don't find one. He's dead. There's no helping him. I'll grieve for him later. Most importantly, what else will we find? Hand signalling to Salem, Dart and Pennywise, I indicate we should start searching. Spotting each other, we go to the kitchen area, glancing down at the empty floor, then check the one bedroom and bathroom. Apart from Kid, the apartment is empty.

I open cabinets and drawers, finding what looks like all Saffie's clothes and personal shit still here, making me suspect she didn't leave of her own accord.

Fuck. I say it under my breath. Pennywise swears out loud.

Back in the living area, Salem, who'd been on his knees, gets to his feet. "His neck was broken," he announces, staring down with almost a look of defeat on his face. "Kid didn't have a fuckin' chance." He indicates the spillage around him. "Looks like he was bringing food and maybe got jumped and followed inside."

"Was Niran here?" I stare around, looking for signs. The amount of food wasted would lead me to suspect that he was, but had he gone on an errand, and has yet to return? Nah, I'm grasping at straws. The one thing he wouldn't leave was his bike, and that's still outside.

Lost, clearly not relishing us being seen here with a dead man in plain sight, tries to pull the broken door closed behind him. As he does, something catches my eye. It's Niran's cut, hanging on a hook.

"Niran wouldn't have left voluntarily without that." I state the obvious, while pain fills my gut. That we've not found Niran's body doesn't mean he's still breathing.

"Got blood stains here." Salem points to a patch on the floor.

Assessing it quickly, due to the amount, I dismiss it as being from a fatal wound.

"Are we assuming it's the Crazy Wolves?" Dart asks to no one in particular. "Given this apartment block, it could have been a home invasion."

"They'd need numbers to overcome Niran," I remind them sharply. "This was no street kids' crime. Saffie's shit is all in her bedroom, including her purse and wallet." I meet Lost's eyes, seeing his reading of the situation is the same as mine—that Saffie has fallen back into the wrong hands, and from his abandoned bike outside, Niran as well.

"Call Utah," Lost instructs tersely. "Get Stormy to see if and when a return flight plan was filed."

"Want to head straight for the airport, Prez?"

"Which fuckin' one, Token? They would hardly drag a kidnapped woman and man through the terminal at Lindbergh Field." It's not the time to remind him that the San Diego International Airport has a new name now.

"They could be driving," Pennywise suggests. "What's their journey time, five or six hours?"

If they drive… Getting an idea, I share it fast. "If they're on the road, they might still be travelling. Can we talk to Red, Prez? The Crazy Wolves are based north of Vegas, and I15 is the direct route. Can we get him to ambush them on the road?"

"Long shot, Grumbler. We don't even know if they're driving, or what vehicle they're in if they are," Pennywise points out.

Dart shrugs. "Worth a try?"

Prez spares him, then me a glance and immediately takes out his phone. Token does the same, each walking to opposite corners of the room. Various phrases such as *motherfuckers,* come from Lost's direction, and a lot of *fucks* come from the other.

Token's first to finish, and immediately crosses to Lost, shaking his head furiously, and points to the phone he's holding. When Prez passes it across, we all turn and shamelessly listen.

"Red? It's Token here. I've just been speaking to Stormy in Utah… Yeah, the asshole. He's done a quick search. They're flying. The return flight plan was filed a couple of hours back. Winston Bartell's private jet is due to land any moment… Yeah, I'll tell you the significance, Bartell is Saffie's fuckin' father… Nah, Brother. Though I'd love to say that she's returned into her loving father's arms, that's not how we read it. Stormy's fairly convinced the Crazy Wolves have some hold over the family… Yeah, I'll give you back to Lost now."

Lost takes the phone. "Only heard that the same time as you, Red… I think it's safe to say that the Crazy Wolves are taking Saffie, and hopefully, Niran, back to their compound… You can't get to the airfield in time?... Yeah, Brother. I know you would if you could… Yeah, I would be fuckin' grateful for any info you've got… Appreciate the offer, Red. Yeah, they killed one of our prospects as I just told you, and not only that, Saffie's under

Satan's Devils' protection—she's Niran's old lady... Thanks, Red. Let me get my troops together and update the mother chapter prez. Speak soon, Brother."

I raise an eyebrow in his direction as he ends the call. He grimaces, then lets out a long sigh. "Looks like the war isn't coming to us. Satan's Devils are going to have to go to the Crazy Wolves."

Too fucking right. What they've taken is ours. There won't be one brother complaining or protesting otherwise.

"Let's get back to the compound," the VP suggests. "No point hanging around here, and they'll soon have gone to ground. We need to start planning." He looks down, his mouth twists, and pain fills his eyes as they settle on the body. "I'll send Curtis and Connor to bring Kid home. Doubt anyone will ask questions about an incapacitated man being carried out of this fuckin' shithole."

Kid. As my eyes fall on him, I silently vow vengeance. He'd shown promise, and in time, I'd expected to call him my brother. What a fucking waste of a life.

"They're going to pay, Grumbler." Lost sounds like he's making me a promise.

I give him a raise and dip of my chin.

In time, we'll arrange a Satan's Devils funeral with full honours for the prospect who I suspect will be posthumously patched in. Without needing discussion, though, I know it will have to take its place in the queue. Our first duties are to those hopefully still in the land of the living.

"You still got that contact at the funeral home?" Prez asks me.

"Yeah." At least Kid can be stored somewhere that will treat him as he deserves. "He won't ask questions, Prez." I make a mental note to make the arrangements immediately. Me and my contact go back years to Snake's days when corpses unfortunately built up. For the cost of a few dollars, an extra body would be added into the incinerator, or, as in Kid's case, cared for and kept on ice until we are in a position to respectfully deal with it. While we don't often have the call for such niceties nowadays, I've maintained the connection.

Closing the door as well as we can, we make our way back down the stairs. Gratefully, I step out of the apartment block of horrors. In silence, we go to our bikes, and without wasting time, are heading back to the compound in the same formation as how we'd arrived.

Niran. Where the fuck are you, Brother? Are you safe? Nightmare scenarios flow through my mind. Why had they taken him? I can't guess, but hopefully they see a use for him. Otherwise, there's a chance he was tossed out of the plane en route or murdered and dumped on the way to the airport.

While I hadn't seen him do it, Prez must have sent a general *all-hands-on-deck* call out text, considering the amount of bikes already parked up as we arrive, with only a few stragglers following us in.

"Church!" Lost yells as he enters the clubroom and doesn't break step as he marches straight across. Once in the meeting room, he barely waits until asses are on seats before commencing his one chilling announcement. "Niran's missing. Either the Crazy Wolves have him, or he's already been taken out."

A stunned silence greets his words before everyone starts talking at once.

"The fuck you talking about?" Blaze roars.

"You gotta be fuckin' kidding," Kink shouts.

And a more to the point, "What we fuckin' sitting around here for?" comes from Dusty. "Why aren't we out getting his ass back home?"

Lost bangs the gavel, loudly and repeatedly a few times. "Kid's dead." This time deathly quiet descends allowing Prez to continue, "Way we read it is Crazy Wolves came to our fuckin' territory, killed Kid, then took Niran and Saffie. They've got the use of a private plane, so by now, they'll be back in their lair."

"Prez, we've got more problems." Token's voice sounds loud, for him. He breaks off from rapidly tapping at his laptop and looks up with an expression of horror on his face. "Stormy's just informed me the Crazy Wolves are into that white supremacy shit. They ain't going to treat Niran kindly."

I glance at the VP, then at Salem, and judge they're thinking the same way as me. This isn't going to be a rescue mission, it's more likely we'll be retrieving a corpse.

CHAPTER FOUR

Saffie

"Why..." *slap...* "did you fuckin'..." *punch...* "do it, Sapphire? Why the fuck did you get rid of my kid?"

Curling into a ball, I try to protect myself from the blows which keep raining down. I'm crying and gasping for breath, trying to understand how it is I'm back in the Crazy Wolves' clubhouse, though it's hard to keep my mind straight when every part of my body is screaming in agony.

How did everything go to shit? Fucking Niran, that's how. *He'd played me from the start, from the day we met.* He must have known who I was somehow.

The first time we met I was wearing a disguise. It clearly hadn't worked. He'd known who I was even then. *But that doesn't make sense.* How could he have been fooling me for weeks? It must have been after that.

It had taken time for me to admit I'd met bikers before. Maybe that was what had raised a red flag. Maybe it was only then Niran had decided to use me for his own gains. That must have been when the betrayal had come, when he'd learned I was property to one of his brothers in leather. My only solace is that won't do him any favours. He might have been brought along with us for now, but Duke won't tolerate a man like him for long.

I hate Niran with every fibre of my being. Almost as much as I despise Duke.

"Are you fuckin' listening to me, Sapphire?" A vicious kick to my stomach makes me retch.

I know where I am only too well. I'm back in an all-too-familiar room in the clubhouse, the one where I've been imprisoned before. When I was first dragged in, I'd tried to reason with Duke, but he started using his fists, and while he's asked questions, he's not given me an opportunity to get a word in.

Something he must realise and rectifies now, or maybe it was the whispered words from Slit.

"She won't be able to talk soon, VP."

Duke pulls his punch, turning to put his fist through the wall instead, before turning back and glaring at me balled up on the floor. "Speak to me, Sapphire. Why the fuck did you abort my kid?"

Now I have the chance to state my defence, I don't want to take it. I don't want to speak about my beloved baby, not to him. It's like tainting his memory. But weak as I am, when I see those fists poised again, I cry out, "I didn't have a choice, Duke. He didn't have a chance." I sob the words out between painful gasps. "He would have died if he'd been born. He could have been in pain. I couldn't handle that."

"You couldn't handle that?" he roars and backhands me again.

With one eye swollen shut already, I try to peer out of the other, then close that one too. Duke has murder in his eyes. It's signalling it's me with no chance now. If death's coming, I'd rather not see it. With nothing to lose, it makes me reckless.

"Just go ahead and kill me and be done with it." I've no reason to live. No baby, deceived by yet another man who'd wormed his way into my trust, and trapped back here with the one I despise with every bone in my body, life holds nothing more.

He grabs me by my hair, lifting me inches off the floor, my scalp screaming in agony. "You think I wouldn't kill you in a flash and be done with it? You think I want you anywhere near me, you snivelling little bitch? Oh yes, that's what I'd fuckin' like to do, but unfortunately for you, you're not going to get that wish. You're staying here in a living death, and you'll be my fuckin' brood mare—" He breaks off, spits at me, then continues, "All those years when you had me fooled you were an infertile cunt, it turns out you were taking the pill the whole time. Christ, I passed you around my brothers just in case I was firing blanks. But it wasn't me, was it? It was all you. And when you did fall pregnant, you go and kill my kid."

Duke's really missing the point. I'm going to enrage him, but if it drives him over the edge, so be it. I don't want to live.

"I was pregnant before, Duke. You killed that baby in my womb. If you really want me to have your child, you'll have to stop beating me. You'll have to stop passing me around to your disgusting brothers who are probably riddled with STDs and stop feeding drugs to me."

He draws back his fist. I tense for the killing blow, but it doesn't fall. Instead, he snorts a laugh. "I didn't want to be saddled with a kid hanging around for years before I needed it. Things change. I don't *want* you to have my fuckin' kid, Sapphire, I *need* you to. Hell of a difference. You think I want to fuck your scrawny ass? Hell, whores, fuck that, sex dolls are more responsive than you."

He needs me to? Bewildered, I state, "I don't understand."

"No, you don't fuckin' understand anything. You're useless, you know that, Sapphire? You couldn't even breed a healthy kid. And you went and fuckin' killed him. That was my son, Sapphire!" He seems to be getting enraged all over again.

Before he explodes, I scream out to explain, "He wouldn't have survived!"

"He might have on life support or something!" Duke screams at me. "He only had to live for maybe a year..." He shuts his mouth, but he's said too much.

I can't let that go. I have no hopes of an explanation, but I ask for one anyway. "What do you mean?"

His body is taut, his jaw tight as he stares down at me. "You have no fuckin' idea how much I want to kill you, Sapphire. I don't think I've ever detested anyone so much. You were fun to play with to begin with, but when you walked out? That was the final straw. No one leaves me, understand? No one. Ever."

I didn't exactly walk out. As I remember, I was wheeled into the hospital, and wheeled back out by the good folks from the Freedom Trail. But I've some sanity left, so I don't elaborate on that.

"I'd kill you right now, but I need you healthy. This is how it's going to go, my little socialite. You're going to stay here, locked in this room. You're never going out, which sadly means I can't have the fun that I want as I can't risk you going to the hospital again." His expression and raised eyebrow almost suggest I should feel sympathy for him. "I'll have to fuck you, but you getting pregnant is all that I want. I don't even care if it's fuckin' fathered by one of my brothers. I'll accept paternity. No one would question it as you're my wife."

He's given voice to my absolute worst nightmare. When Duke says fuck, he means it. He's rough, violent, and always makes me hurt. That's bad enough, but some of the other equally perverted members can be worse. It's a death sentence if only for my mental well-being. He's talking about me being raped, repeatedly. I don't know if I can stand it.

I'm still struggling to comprehend why it's so important to him when he adds, "When you're pregnant, you'll stay right here, as I can't trust you, can I, Sapphire?"

Of course he can't. That goes without saying. The first chance I get to run, I'll be taking it.

"Why bother, Duke? You don't even like me." I try to appeal to him. "We can get divorced. You could get another wife if you want a child so much." That's the reasonable approach, isn't it?

He looks at me snidely. "Oh, there'll be no divorce. I can't dispose of you for a while, however much I want to. Another woman wouldn't be you, would they, Sapphire?"

What difference does that make? He doesn't even like me, he's admitted as much.

He chuckles as he sees my look of confusion. "Another woman wouldn't have the family connections you do."

"My father disowned me," I tell him flatly. But why did he allow Duke to use his plane? There must be more to it. Try as I might though, I can't imagine my staid father in league with a man like Duke.

"Your father did what I told him to."

What the hell? Uncurling myself, wincing as I do so, I draw myself up on my knees, my desire for information outweighing my concern for making myself a target for his fists.

"What are you talking about?"

"You're your father's heir, Sapphire. An heir to a fuckin' fortune."

"He wrote me out of his will when I married you." I know he did, or at least, that's what he threatened to do.

"Oh, my dear Sapphire." He shakes his head as though he's sad, but I don't buy it for one minute. "It was all too easy to convince you that your father cut all ties with you. When actually, he's been paying me to keep you safe. All the money he owns will go to your brat when he dies. My heir will inherit everything."

My father's been paying him?

"Perhaps it's time you learned some facts of life," he mutters, almost to himself. Then directly to me, he says, "See, Sapphire, your daddy dotes on you. Sure, he threatened to cut you off if you married me but having one of those fits of the rebellion you're prone to, you became mine. It was then I took over communications. Your father's been working with the MC for a very long time. We do most of his money laundering for him."

My dad's no criminal, he has to be wrong. My disbelief must show on my face.

"The idea of using you came when he refused me a loan. It was part how to get back at him, and part how to increase the money coming into the club. He knew to stay away from you. All I had to do was keep him updated with proof of life. Those photos you were gullible enough to model for me? Well, those were sent to your dear old dad."

I gasp. Sure, there had been times he asked me to dress in all my finery, and of course I did so. To refuse would be inviting his fists. But I also did so in the hope Duke would treat me like a proper wife. I never dreamed there was an ulterior motive.

"I don't believe you. If Dad cared enough, he'd have moved heaven and earth to get me back."

"Now, now, be sensible, Sapphire. He cares about you, but he'd acted outside the law—a law we kept him breaking. All he needed was one hint we'd get the feds involved, and he was running for cover. Also, he's got no fuckin' army, and that's what he'd need if he wanted to take you back. Why do you think I had you guarded so carefully?"

"What about over the last few months? You couldn't prove I was alive during that time. You didn't even know where I was. Did he know I was gone?" I ask, dying inside, wondering if all this time I'd believed my father would slam the door in my face, he would have welcomed me back with open arms, and helped me escape had I gone straight to him. Hid me and refused to give me back. Given me money to start a new life. Yet Duke had had me believe he'd totally washed his hands of me.

"He knew I was looking for you. We were watching him, too.

That's where I thought you'd run to be honest, but it seems I did my job convincing you too well. When your nigger boyfriend got me your location, I commandeered his plane."

My gut twists at his mention of Niran, and hatred for him sweeps through me again. But I push that out of my mind, focusing on what's more important. "I want to see my father."

"That's not part of the bargain. But, Sapphire, dearest, once your face is respectable again, we'll have another photo session. By then, hopefully, your belly will be round with my baby."

"I need time to recover, the doctors said…"

His hand slashes through the air. "No time, Sapphire. I want you pregnant as soon as I can."

And I have to find some excuse to delay. The thought of Duke's hands, or worse, his dick, near me makes me want to vomit, never mind any of the other Wolves. "What's the rush?"

He grins as if he's about to deliver good news. "Oh, I didn't tell you, did I? Your dad was diagnosed with cancer last year. It's become quite aggressive now. He's got a year, maybe less, maybe a little more, and then he'll be gone."

I cover my mouth with my hand. I'd had no idea my dad was even ill, yet alone terminal. I swallow hard, trying to come to terms with conflicting thoughts—hopes that we're not as estranged as I'd expected and that I might see him again, then having that chance whipped away by Duke's cruel words. Knowing I'll need to process that with my other numerous burdens later, I force myself to stay on track. I can't follow Duke's logic. "If he dies, everything goes to Mom."

He shakes his head. "Your money's old and tied up in red tape. The bulk of his inheritance is held in perpetual trust, and always goes to the next in line, not someone who's married in. He may be able to leave her a sufficient amount to live on, but not all his assets, and that's where his money is."

"But doesn't that mean, me?" Duke controls me, he'll control my money. There's no need to bring a kid into the mix.

"No," he disputes firmly. "As your husband, I'm not blood, but if it goes to my son or daughter, then I'll be the guardian. If it goes to you without you having any children, you'd have to sign off on everything."

Surely, he'd just make me do what he wants? "What if I die without a child? Doesn't it come to you then?"

He shrugs dismissively. "I'm not blood. It would go to some distant cousin you've probably never even met."

"If I'm worth so much to you, Duke, why did you try to kill me?" The man is stark-raving mad. "You nearly succeeded last time."

"Nah," he refutes. "I always stopped. I just liked the thought of you believing I held your life in my hands. That's why you went to that fuckin' hospital, to make sure you survived."

If he was so worried, he wouldn't have hurt me at all. But like a penny dropping, it all falls into place. Duke wants me pregnant, but once I give birth, I'm no use. Getting pregnant again is a death sentence, though this time for me, and not my child. *Maybe it's what I deserve.* Maybe so, but I'll be damned if I don't fight to the teeth to prevent giving Duke what he wants. I definitely don't want to give birth to his child. Not when it sounds like I won't be around to protect it. It's the money he wants, not a daughter or son.

But one thing still puzzles me. "If I'd given birth to a disabled child…"

He actually grins. "Wouldn't have mattered. We'd have proved his birth. If he was that disabled, Grit's a fuckin' expert with computers as you know well. We'd have sent him away for specialist treatment, then after a few months, reappear with him alive and kicking. Didn't even have to be the same baby. Grit's paperwork would have been indisputable evidence a miracle had occurred. A retarded kid would have suited my purposes, as guardian I'd have complete control. But you, my dear, you'd be superfluous. Now, it appears, as you precipitated matters and got rid of the child, I'll have to keep and torment you for a little longer."

He takes out his phone and looks at it, frowning as he reads a text. "Now, Sapphire, I'm going to have to leave you for a while. I hope you don't miss me too much. I've got a new prospect to break in." His eyes view me sharply, his gaze calculating, as if assessing just how much damage to inflict. "What was the relationship between you and that Black?"

Oh how I want to drop Niran in it. He betrayed me. He's the reason why I'm here. My eyes flash sparks as I tell him, "Obviously, he wasn't the friend I believed. It was all a trick to get information to you."

"You fucked him?"

My eyes widen. "No, I did not." I don't know whether he'll believe me or not, and if the latter, I don't care. Niran deserves everything coming to him.

"How long did you know him? Any chance you're carrying a fuckin' Black kid?"

That wouldn't suit his purposes. He could get away with a white kid, but not a half-Black baby. If he thinks there's a chance that I am, I wouldn't be going to the hospital for any abortion, he'd kick it out of me. Now I've got reason to convince him on my behalf.

"I didn't fuck him," I say as forcefully as possible. "I was pregnant, Duke, then I had the termination. I wasn't in a state to want any man near me. Niran just befriended me, presumably to find out what use I was to him. I met him a few weeks back." Times and dates are getting muddled in my throbbing head. *When was it Niran knew I was going to leave again? Had he come around this morning to make sure I stayed put until Duke turned up? Was that why he'd told me Duke wasn't close to finding me?* In my befuddled mind, that makes sense. "He must have been buying you time to come to get me. That's why he was in my apartment today." My mouth fills with saliva. I spit it out, wishing it was onto Niran's face.

He eyes me carefully, something akin to mirth in his eyes. "You really fuckin' believe that, don't you?"

"Give me a gun and I'll kill him myself. I hate him, almost as much as I hate you!" I scream. And, oh hell, my tears start again. I heard the news about my dad without crying, discussed the loss of my son without shedding a tear, heard my death sentence pronounced as though it was happening to someone else, but the thought of Niran's betrayal cuts so deeply it wounds me the worst.

Duke gives another of his snorted laughs, then I hear his and Slit's footsteps, the door opening, closing and being locked behind them.

At last, I'm alone.

CHAPTER FIVE

Niran

I'm alive. I've got to be thankful for that. Staying breathing means I have a chance of getting Saffie out of the jaws of the Crazy Wolves. I'm not an idiot, it won't be easy, may not turn out to be possible at all. I'd played a long shot, and it had paid off. Instead of lying dead alongside Kid in her shitty apartment, I've been transported across state lines and into their den.

I'll need to keep my cool and make the most of any opportunity afforded to me. One thing I can't do is think Duke is a fool. There's a reason he's brought me here, and it's not because he believes me. *I'm Black in the heart of a white supremacist club.*

So why did he let me tag along? Even if Duke thinks my story holds water, even if I have skills that he might want, I openly admitted to betraying my club, something MCs take very seriously.

A man prospects to earn the patch, to prove his loyalty to the brotherhood. What they'd see looking at me is a man who either lied or changed his mind. A trust gained and given so lightly is worth fuck all to any club, whatever type of operation they're running. If the Satan's Devils hadn't been a good fit for me, I would have seen that while I was on probation. An honest man wouldn't have deceitfully taken their patch.

Honour among thieves to us isn't just a saying, it's the way we live.

Duke must have seen something that he considers useful. Or I'm some sort of entertainment for him, like a mouse to a cat. If the latter, I don't hold out much hope for my chances. The question is, how long will I be of use to him before the claws come out and I'm ripped to shreds.

I only need long enough to save Saffie.

As I pace from side to side in the room I've been locked in ever since I arrived, I try to come up with some kind of plan, but it's like playing a game where I don't know the rules. One thing I know, even to save my life, or Saffie's, I'd never betray the Satan's Devils MC. If I were of that mind, I doubt the Crazy Wolves would be interested. Our nearest chapter, Vegas, might be in the same state, but we don't have any dealings with each other, and are literally hundreds of miles apart. If they want info on Vegas, I'm not the man to give it. I don't know that chapter well enough.

My entrance to this club had been illuminating, if I'd needed to be enlightened that is. As I'd been marched through the clubhouse, I'd kept my eyes scanning around, noticing that the expressions on the faces of the assembled members had spoken volumes. I'd interpreted some anticipatory glances viewing me as fresh meat to be tortured, others somewhat confused, but the majority looked on with utter disgust. It was those unhidden looks of repugnance which gave me an uneasy feeling.

But if Duke wanted me dead, he's already had ample opportunity to kill me. For some reason, he wants me alive. And whatever that reason is, I don't think I'm going to like it.

Fuck, I hate knowing how much Saffie must loathe me. Right now, I expect her to be thinking about me with disgust. I don't doubt she believed me, everything fit too neatly. The number of people who knew where she lived was very limited and known only to me and members of my club.

The more I think about it, the more I'm convinced that I was betrayed by Susie of all people, maybe helped knowingly or not by Cyn. Two women who selfishly want what I can't or won't give them. *But how did they know her address?*

I pace, pondering it. *A note pushed under Saffie's door, words designed to make her flee...* Damn it. The answer comes to me. Trigger an exit and then wait to follow her home. Tracking a distressed woman would be easy.

Hell hath no fury like a woman scorned. I snort. It's a bit too late to remember that. I take a certain twisted pleasure in knowing if Susie thought getting rid of the competition would draw me to her, me losing my life would certainly not advance her agenda.

While I know it's highly likely my remaining time will be short, as long as I'm still breathing, I vow I'll find some way to help Saffie escape. Even if I die before she knows the truth about me. I'd had no option but to lie, and I don't regret it. It wasn't to preserve my own life, but so she doesn't lose hers.

I'm here, presumably in the same building as she's being held. Maybe there's some way I can see her and offer her some hope.

The only positive is that my brother Devils will move heaven and earth to find me. Hopefully they won't arrive too late to save either me or her.

Bracing myself, I practice deep breathing, keeping my heart rate calm and oxygen feeding my brain. I'll need every one of my wits about me to live out this day, let alone any that come after.

With no phone or watch, and no convenient clock, I measure the time passing only by the light filtering in from underneath the door, the room being windowless. It gradually darkens, then lights suddenly, with a different hue than before as electric lighting replaces the dying sunlight.

More time passes, and rowdy sounds reach my ears. Where I'm being held can't be far from their clubroom. I hear laughter, shouts, voices raised in argument, then cheers as if a fight has been won. More than once, I hear a woman's scream, and not one of pleasure. *Not Saffie, it can't be.*

Knowing I'll go crazy if I interpret the cries as hers, I blank my mind and focus on differentiating voices. I try to get an idea of numbers. When I'd walked in earlier, there had been about a dozen men. Now it sounds like there's more of them.

Listening avidly, I don't miss the footsteps approaching the door, nor the key turning in the lock. Pulling back my shoulders, I take a deep breath, preparing myself for whatever I've got coming.

Duke enters, which I expect. What comes as a surprise is the woman he's dragging in with him. He throws her at my feet. "I hope you appreciate this. It was some trouble to get her here."

It's Susie. My eyes widen in disbelief while simultaneously I feel relief that at least it isn't Cyn. But how did they get her here this quickly, and what does she think she's doing?

Whatever, no good would come from anything out of her mouth. It's up to me to take the initiative. Thinking fast and reaching down my hand, I pull her to her feet. "You did good, Susie. I'm proud of you."

Though my words to her wouldn't make sense, like I hope, my appreciation makes her beam.

Duke's brow creases and he looks like he's been knocked off balance. Pulling Susie around to face him, he demands, "He told you to contact us?"

Susie looks at me and flutters her eyelids. "Well, not in so many words, but I always know what he means."

As she turns back to Duke, I raise my finger to my head and circle it—the universal sign suggesting she's got a screw loose—

and I'd had to work to get my point across. For good measure, I roll my eyes.

His brow furrows further, as he continues to probe. "So you got the information that Sapphire was mine and contacted the Crazy Wolves?"

"Well, yeah. Duh." She glances at me and winks as if to show how clever she's been.

Taking a chance, I jump in before he has a chance to pose the question himself. "Tell him how you located his club, sweetheart." I have no idea how she had. She knew the info about Saffie from Cyn, but even I wouldn't have been able to contact Duke without relying on the services of Token, and I sincerely doubt Susie's got computer skills.

She giggles. "My second cousin of course. He's with the feds."

And how didn't we know that? Christ. Token is supposed to conduct background searches on hangarounds who come around regularly. In this instance, he clearly hadn't gone deep enough. Even the Satan's Devils wouldn't have entertained someone with a connection to the feds. As for the Crazy Wolves? From the look on Duke's face, she's just signed her death warrant.

I only fleetingly care. Susie's betrayal cuts me deep. The only mercy I'll show her is a wish Duke will make her end quick.

Duke shakes his head, and I can almost read his thoughts. I told him the Devils were a bunch of pussies, and now he must think we're in with the feds.

I decide to take advantage, saying angrily, "You can see how that club's not for me. Fuckin' security checks my ass."

His gaze now goes to Susie, then back at me. "What's your relationship with this one?"

"She's a fuckin' sweet butt who's got her sights set on becoming my ol' lady."

Slit, standing behind him, snorts.

Susie's beaming like the cat who's got the cream. "Now Saffie's gone, I can be, can't I, Niran?"

"You want her?" Duke's grinning widely as though the whole thing's a joke. Which to him, it probably is.

But how should I answer Duke's question? If I have any inclination to try save her life, maybe I should keep her with me. Problem is, I couldn't stand her before. Now, I actively hate her. She deserves everything she's got coming to her. She's the reason Saffie and I are probably going to die. I can spare no thought of mercy for her.

"Never did," I state forcefully. "She was a means to an end."

Susie, waiting for me to declare my undying love, takes a moment to process my words. Then she turns and hits me. "You're a fuckin' animal. You tricked me."

Crossing my fingers, I hope that Duke thinks she means in the past, and not in the conversation that we've only just had, where she had, in truth, decided not to contradict me.

But whether or not he trusts me, he has more faith in a man than a bitch. When Susie changes her attention to him and starts to scream, "He wants Saffie! He ditched me for her. He's lying to you," it's me Duke chooses to believe.

"Take her out, Slit. The brothers will appreciate a stunner like her."

When Slit takes a firm hold of her arm, Susie looks scared to death, especially as his hold is so tight, it looks like it will bruise. "I helped you. Let me go," she begs Duke.

"Doesn't work like that," Slit informs her. "You're here to stay."

"What are you going to do with me?" Her voice is shrill, her eyes are wild, and she's hyperventilating as the enormous mistake she's made sinks in.

Duke turns and smirks. "Good-looking bitch like you? I'd guess you like sex. Well, let's just say you're going to get very,

very lucky." He pauses a beat for that to sink in, then adds to Slit, "Just make sure you tell them she's related to a fed."

I force a grin on my face as she walks out, though I have to fight back the bile rising in my throat. She deserves a bullet for what she's done, but not to be tortured to death.

Saffie, I repeat over and over in my head, watching Susie leave without saying a word in her defence. *I have to focus on the one woman who deserves to be saved.*

"How did you bring her here?" I force myself to sound like I don't really care.

Duke chuckles. "I called the informant's number back, and surprise, surprise, I got her. And you know what? She jumped at the fuckin' chance to join you in your new club." For the first time, I see something akin to a look of respect on his face. Then, as fast as it arrived, it disappears. "You might even fit in here, Niran. Just like us, you don't think bitches call the shots."

I feel bile rise in my throat at the thought he believes I've anything in common with him.

As the weeping of Susie starts to fade, another man enters to take Slit's place. This one carries an air of authority which makes me stand up straight.

While his eyes roam over me, Duke greets him with a respectful chin lift and one word, "Prez."

The man's stare pierces me as if trying to see into my soul. I return his gaze steadily, not wanting to cower in front of him. He's a man in his forties who's kept himself fit. A man who normally I'd be wary of. His hair is greying, but his eyes are sharp, His lips are thin, and there's a cruel twist to his mouth. Part of his left ear is missing. I suspect lost in a knife fight.

"So you're the man who wants to prospect for us," he says at last. "I'm mystified as to what the hell you think someone like you can offer the Crazy Wolves." He catches his VP's eyes and smirks.

"Loyalty to the type of club I want to ride with," I say,

managing to keep any irony out of my voice. "I reunited your VP with his woman. Kind of proves I respect the fuck out of a club's property. Not like the rest of the brothers I used to ride with."

"Ah, yes. The Satan's Devils. I've heard of Drummer, of course." He would, he's the prez of our mother chapter. "Heard they're into legal shit, but still fuckin' wear the one-percenter patch."

Yeah, just because we earn money legitimately doesn't always mean we stay on the right side of the law. As he'll find out soon. That's if I'm right, and the Satan's Devils are coming.

"As I said to the VP," I incline my head toward Duke, "they're fuckin' pussies." I sigh, heavily. "You found me without a piece. They don't like us riding tooled up, just in case we're stopped by the cops."

In truth, we'd learned that the hard way. My weapon is hidden in its secret compartment on my bike, a bike now left abandoned outside Saffie's. I've resigned myself to not finding it in the same state I left it in. That's if I find it there at all.

Duke nods. "I wondered why you weren't armed."

Their prez still regards me thoughtfully. "When the Devils find you gone, they going to declare you out bad?"

"They might." I shrug. "You going to have a problem with that?" He'd catch me out in a lie if I said they would not.

He shakes his head. "Not on the face of it. We have nothing to do with the SDMC. But whether we give you a home is something we need to discuss."

"I'm willing to prospect."

"What are you thinking, Knife?" Duke asks, giving me the name of their prez. *Knife for the knife wound that took his ear?* Maybe, but I've more to worry about than how the man got his handle.

"I'm thinking we're short one prospect. Jude's dead and we haven't replaced him." Knife pulls at his short beard thoughtfully.

"Fuckin' Jude," Duke spits, making me wonder what the poor prospect did, or what was done to him, which makes my fists clench as I remember what happened to Kid. Life's certainly cheap around here.

As will theirs be in time. These two men standing in front of me are as good as already deceased. They just don't know it yet.

"I know what prospecting's about." I add my bit for what it could be worth. "I've done that shit both with the Marines and with the MC. Whatever might be asked of me doesn't faze me one iota."

"I hear you're missing a leg. That give you any problems?"

"Put me in the ring, I'll take any man down." It's a boast and one I hope I can live up to. It's maybe rash seeing as I don't know the men in this club.

Knife chuckles. "I've heard of a club where prospects earn their way in with a fight to the death. Last man alive gets the patch. You'd be up for that?"

I'd be a fool to say yes. To say no would make me look weak. While I stay silent, letting the rise and fall of my shoulders be my non-committal answer, I feel an unfamiliar trickle of unease as I get the feeling it might not be an MC he's heard about, but that it happens here. Still, being given a literal fighting chance has to be better than a bullet to the head.

"Let me be straight with you, Niran." Knife pauses and gives a twisted grin. "What's that, anyway? Some nigger name?"

"Fuck knows." I shake my head. "Seems I was born with it." That trickle becomes a fast-moving stream. *I'm in a White supremacist club and they're doing a great job of reminding me.*

"Well, Niran. You've run out on your club, and that means you broke their trust. Seems like you'd have a long way to go to earn ours. You spat on the patch you were given. Who's to say you won't betray us? No, Niran, we're not letting you prospect. You have to prove yourself to us before we even take that step."

I don't know why they're wasting time talking to me. All this is only pretend—on my part and theirs—that they'd ever consider letting me patch in. My skin's the wrong colour. Still, I'll play the game. It's not like I've anything else to do.

"What are you suggesting, Prez?" Duke asks, sounding bored, as if he couldn't care one way or another. "Hangaround?"

Wondering why they're continuing this ruse, I raise my chin, letting them know if that's the way in, I wouldn't refuse. Standing stoic, I let them decide.

Knife looks me up and down, his gaze starting at my face, going to my feet, then back again. It's as though I'm being stripped naked. After a moment, he raises his chin. "This is the one and only chance I'm going to give, understand? You do the fuckin' grunt work around here, answering to everyone including the prospects, yeah? The nitty gritty, so to speak." He pauses to chuckle, then adds, "If we tell you to dance a jig, you'll do it with a fuckin' smile on your face. You'll be our *boy.* You got me?"

Oh yeah, I got him. *Loud and fucking clear.* As I breathe in, I have to work hard not to let my nostrils flare, and struggle to keep my fingers stretched out. With those few words, they've let me in on exactly what type of club this is and what they expect of me. They said *boy.* They might as well have said *performing monkey.*

If I refuse, I've no doubt they'll kill me, and get some enjoyment out of my demise, probably marked as some kind of experiment to see if my blood runs red. Whatever way they choose, at the end of it, I'll be dead. If I'm not here, Saffie will be on her own. Though I still can't see what I'll be able to do to protect her, if I keep breathing, a chance might present itself. That alone is worth jumping through their hoops.

Boy, nigger… If I'm honest, I've been called worse before. I swallow my pride but don't let them off scot-free. They might think me a fool, but even an idiot wouldn't give in blindly. I make a counteroffer. "I'll be your boy. I'll let you see you can trust me. But let's give it a time limit. One month, and then I'll be wearing a prospect patch." Heaven help me, I'll have killed myself before then, even if they don't do it for me. *Ride with the Wolves? Call them brothers?* Never.

"You're in no position to bargain, but hey, I'm a generous man." Knife stretches his arms above his head and attempts a friendly grin. It doesn't work. "If you work hard, prove you're a man we can trust, in one month you'll get a prospect patch. Now I can't be fairer than that, can I, Boy?"

Reminding myself we called Kid, Kid, because of his deceptive youthful looks, I try to tell myself that my new name has no worse connotations than that. But it does, and it fuckin' hurts. I don't give them the satisfaction or show they've gotten a rise out of me. For now, I'll focus on the prize while promising death to them later.

For Saffie, I'll put up with one hell of a lot, the least being racial slurs.

Words, I remind myself, *don't hurt.*

CHAPTER SIX

Niran

I'd been through the worst of hazing as a Marine recruit. Then, I went through similar when I joined the Satan's Devils MC. I thought I'd seen it all and could put up with anything.

I'd barely scratched the surface.

When Duke had taken me out of the room we'd been talking in and into the crowded clubhouse, he'd whistled loudly, and waited until he'd gotten everyone's attention.

"Listen up, fuckers! We've got a new hangaround. Answers to Boy."

A stunned silence had greeted him, then Knife had come up to my side. "Let's show him what we're made of, Brothers." Having delivered those ominous sounding words, he yelled, "Asslicker, come show Boy here the ropes."

A man wearing a prospect patch comes over at a run. "Prez!" He salutes, and then sneers at me, his eyes widening with shock. "He's a prospect?"

"Less than that," Knife answers. "Got to prove himself before he thinks of even putting on a prospect patch." He gives me a dubious look. "I'm not convinced he's going to be able to do that. Been riding with some wannabe assholes." This is directed to the patched members rather than the prospect. "The Satan's Devils."

"Devils?" One man with fewer teeth than Snips steps forward, lisping through the gaps in his mouth. "I heard they were going straight."

"This fucker know what type of fuckin' club we are?" someone who I can't pick out shouts, and is immediately hushed by his neighbours. Hmm, yeah, I think I've got a pretty good idea by now. It's not my face that doesn't fit, my skin is too dark for them.

"Rules." Duke snaps his fingers, getting my attention back to him. "You're the lowest on the totem pole. You do what you're told by anyone, the only exception being the club whores, and you don't even speak to them. Got it?"

I nod my head while tensing my jaw. I fucking got it.

For the next couple of hours, I'm run ragged. There are three prospects here—Asslicker, Tony and Ruddle—who seem to think all their Christmases have arrived at once with someone they can order around.

The club keeps two guard dogs, and guess who's sent to clean their shit up? Apparently, it's a job no one likes doing, and it showed. There was tons of crap. Then I'd been sent to clean the heads, and fuck, it wasn't that it wasn't anything I didn't expect. Get a group of men together, and there's piss all over the place. It was the sight I'd walked into that caused me surprise—a man clearly enjoying a blow job. Not that the woman had any say in the matter, he was forcing her head onto his crotch, holding her so tightly, she was gagging and trying to breathe.

He'd just spared one glance at me, then went back to what he was doing.

I went about my work, cleaning what I could, while trying for the sake of my sanity to keep my eyes off the couple. *Can't make waves,* I repeated to myself. *Not if I want to save Saffie.*

When he'd finished with her, he let the gasping girl fall to the ground. When the door had closed behind him, I went over to help her up, handing her some toilet paper to clean her face.

"This ain't no life for you," I tell her, gruffly. "Anywhere's got to be better than here."

Sad, tear-filled eyes, look up at me. "You think I've got a choice?" When my eyes narrow, she continues, "Women don't get away from the Crazy Wolves."

The door opens behind us, pushed so hard it slams against the wall. "Boy, you in here?"

Swallowing my crazy desire to shout back, *yes Massa*, I offer a simple, "Yeah."

"Duke's got a job for you." His eyes fall on the woman who's splashing her face. "Bitches ain't for you, Boy," he sneers as if I was the one who'd gotten her in that state.

"I'm aware," I reply, pulling off my rubber gloves. "Where do I find Duke?"

"In his fuckin' office, of course."

When he shows me his back, I know I'm going to have to find that for myself.

It's a strange club, and one that doesn't welcome me or my kind. As I make my way through the clubhouse, evading legs stretched out deliberately trying to trip me, I notice everyone seems to be made from the same mould. All White, a few shaven bald, and many sporting swastika tats. Inwardly I shudder, knowing I'm lucky to be alive, while wondering why I still am.

When you're part of a minority, you develop a hypervigilance, which becomes part of your life. You wear your difference like a second skin. Privilege can be found in many places, where the majority is the normal and where you at the least, don't fit in, or worse, could be in danger. Whether it's because you're a sole woman in the room, a gay amidst a bunch of straights, or as in this case, a Black in a roomful of White supremacists.

It's not me being hypersensitive when I believe, given half a chance most of these men would tear me limb from limb. Duke's toying with me, I know it, and the question is why. Clearly there are obvious benefits for me in this game, the top one being, I'm still alive. I wish I knew the rules though, knowing one wrong move could see me lose. This den of snakes would be all over me, and I don't see any sign of a ladder.

Consequently, I'm wary of approaching any of the members and asking to be directed to the VP's office, so I head for where I see Asslicker serving beers. When he's got a free moment, I lean over the bar.

"Duke's office?"

"In trouble already?" he sneers but points the way.

Not yet, I hope, I think to myself, as politely I weave my way around the milling members. One waves a knife in my direction, another slaps my back so hard I almost stumble, and yet another mimes cutting his throat. *Message received and understood.*

The only plan I've come up with so far is getting to a phone and making contact with the outside world. I'm sure as fuck the Satan's Devils will have done the right addition and their two and two will add up to them coming to find me, and I'll be on the inside to help.

If they know I've been taken, they will. They've had my back before as I've had theirs.

I'm fucking certain.

It's only this place playing with my mind that's making me wonder whether they too think I don't fit in and won't be riding to save me.

I growl at myself. I prospected. I was a patched member. Stood in for Grumbler and never once was I made to feel I was an outsider. *Fuck the Crazy Wolves,* they're fucking with my head. The Devils will figure it out and *will* come for me. My task is to stay alive and try and keep Saffie that way until they turn up.

Simple.

But Lost hadn't been pleased when I said I'd thought about turning my patch in. Would he just give me up? Blame me for Kid's death and assume I ran off with Saffie? *Surely not.*

Still, getting to a phone would reassure me, though I suspect that won't be easy.

Approaching the room to where Asslicker had hopefully correctly directed me, I knock on the office door, and open it when Duke's voice barks for me to get the fuck inside.

His eyes narrow as they land on me, and he doesn't point me to a seat. I stand, back straight, legs apart, and hands firmly clasped behind my back.

"Got a job for you, Boy."

I raise my chin in response.

"I'm assigning you to look after Sapphire." He pauses a beat for that to sink in. In my head, my brain is screaming, *trap.* "You'll deliver her food and stand guard outside her door."

"Keeping people out or her in?" I ask him to clarify.

There's a flicker in his eyes as he replies, "Her in." He examines my face as though looking for something. I ensure I don't so much as twitch. After a moment, he sighs. "You let no one in other than a patched member. Sapphire destroyed my trust when she ran away, taking my son with her. She'll stay in that room until she's regained it."

I don't point out she's still trying to mentally recuperate, if that's even possible, from the worst thing a woman can have happen to her in her life. An idea occurs to me. One which might gain time for her and benefit me personally. I have to bank though, that Duke won't know what happens to a woman who's gone through a termination of a pregnancy.

"She needs supplies," I tell him.

His eyes sharpen. "What you fuckin' talking about?"

"She's still bleeding," I allow myself a look of disgust, "and will be for a while. It's a result of the op. She needs women's things." I'm crossing my fingers that firstly he believes me, and secondly, hoping none of the fuckers here will want to be seen dead in that particular aisle, maybe he'll allow me to go buy them. Once off the compound, I can get to a phone and satisfy myself I haven't been forgotten. "She'll need painkillers as well." Doubly so, remembering how she was beaten at the apartment, even if Duke hasn't touched her since.

"She's not getting any fuckin' painkillers. She brought this all on herself. But I suppose she'll need the other shit." He rubs his hand over his forehead and then tugs at his chin. "Tell Tony or Ruddle what she needs, and they'll go get them."

It's on the tip of my tongue to say I don't mind going, but I don't want him thinking I'm showing my hand.

"Is that it?" I ask, still trying to keep my face impassive. I don't resent the task I've been assigned. At least I'll be able to satisfy myself that she's alright, well, as much as can be when she's been kidnapped by her psychotic husband and held against her will. As well as continuing to come to terms with the pregnancy that in my view, she so rightly ended.

"No questions?"

He seems surprised, so I just shrug. "As a…" I can't say prospect, so change it to, "new recruit, I do what I'm told. Not my place to question orders."

He chuckles. "Oh, I bet you were a good little soldier boy, Boy. Now get the fuck out of here and go guard my wife. Just one thing, you don't fuckin' speak to her. Not one word. Got me?"

After giving him a sharp nod, I do, with pleasure, leave, unwilling to spend much time alone with him. It's not much better out in the clubroom. As I'm crossing to the bar, another foot shoots out to topple me. My prosthetic makes me stumble, but I manage to stay upright. I don't say a word, or even pause to give the man a glare, just continue in the direction I was heading while mentally promising myself at some point, I'll get retribution.

As I expect, both prospects Duke had pointed me to raise objections about their task. From the way they react, we could be back in Neanderthal times when a woman bleeding was something to be feared. But while I take a punch to my gut for my audacity in asking, Tony eventually agrees to the task when I suggest he take his objections up with his VP. Duke, it appears, is a person they don't dare cross.

I ask where Saffie is being held and am surprised by the looks of relief on their faces as I explain my new role as her jailor. I pick up on one word, *Jude,* and a mumbling of *rather him than me,* and wonder what that's all about. They've done this before, and at least share what's expected of me. After leading me upstairs and through a maze of corridors which I assume house the brothers living here, almost ceremoniously, Asslicker passes me a key ring, and indicates the closed and locked door. He leaves me alone immediately.

An hour, two perhaps, pass, then Asslicker appears again.

"Food," he states unnecessarily, nodding at the tray as he hands it over. "And this."

Without checking, I assume the bag contains the supplies I'd requested, and take them. Supplies Saffie no longer requires and which I wasn't allowed off compound to buy. Hopefully she'll take it as a sign her needs remain at the forefront of my mind. And if Duke thinks she's bleeding, maybe he'll give her more time.

Asslicker turns away, takes a step, then turns back. "Oh, tell her we all hope she's feeling better."

An innocuous request, but one that has the hairs on the back of my neck rising. *Duke had given me specific instructions not to talk to her.* Deciding this must be some sort of test, a permission to break my promise to their VP, I know I have to keep my mouth zipped shut. But I give no indication that I'm on to him, simply offer a raise of my chin.

Instead, I wait until he's out of sight, then take that key from my pocket, and apply it to the lock.

My gut twists as I push the door open. My stomach roils. Saffie's been subjected to Duke's not-so-tender mercy yet again. Her face is swollen, not just with tears, but clearly as a result of his fists. One eye's completely shut, the other blackened but just about able to open. Her mouth is red and looks tender, and the way she's holding herself, she's probably bruised everywhere else. I want to rush to her, hold her in my arms and promise no one will ever hurt her again. But I can't touch her. My heart breaks at the woman sitting on a cot which passes for a bed, broken and beaten. *How dare Duke touch one hair of her head!*

He's going to die painfully, begging for his miserable life to be spared, then he'll start begging for death. Once again, I vow I'll have my revenge. Nothing will placate me until he takes his last breath.

Oh fuck, Saffie. How can I get you out of this? The magnitude of my task confronts me. I'm only one fucking man.

I stand, waiting for her to acknowledge me. I can't risk speaking to her, in case someone has eyes on me, or happens to pass by the door. Not after the strict instructions given to me. But it's hard for me to stay silent, to not offer comfort to her. Though what could I say? Any assurance everything will turn out okay will fall on deaf or unbelieving ears. *She hates me.*

Slowly, at last, she looks up. When she sees it's me, she immediately goes on the attack.

"You're as bad a monster as Duke. I fucking believed you!"

What can I do? I can't defend myself. By misleading Duke, I misled her.

Bravely, she stands up straight. "Why are you here? I thought you'd be back in San Diego fucking Susie by now."

In my defence, if I hadn't lied to get Duke to bring me along, I'd not be capable of fucking anyone. And if I was, it would be anyone but that traitor. Unable to put her right, I simply shake my head, put down the tray on a small table, then go to the door, hating taking the steps which take me away from her, wishing I could pull her into my arms instead.

I knew she wouldn't greet me like a friend, and had thought I'd be prepared for her animosity, but I'm not. Every word she throws at me hits its target as painfully as a bullet to my chest. But I ignore her and refuse to react.

Dropping the bag I've been holding by the door unobtrusively, I let my eyes survey the room. It's only just adequate. She's got the barest of facilities, but at least a bathroom for her own use. And there, up in the corner, just as I had suspected, I see an almost invisible camera.

Is the room bugged as well as watched? I can only assume that it is.

CHAPTER SEVEN

Saffie

When Duke leaves, I sit on the bed, dropping my head into my hands and again letting the tears fall freely. As so often in the past, I catalogue my latest injuries. That I can still see out of one eye, I count as a victory. My mouth is swollen, but I've still got all my teeth. My legs, arms, stomach and back will be blackened with bruises, but there's nothing broken at least.

My whole body throbs in pain, but around Duke, that's nothing new.

I'll heal. Just as I've always done in the past, only for Duke to repeat my torture all over again.

Now, though, it's different. Now I've got answers as to why Duke went through all the pretence, acting so out of character five years ago. Why Duke had asked me to marry him, when it soon became obvious I meant nothing to him.

I was a means to an end.

What a stupid fool I'd been, believing what Duke had told me. But he hadn't needed to try hard. I'd been more than ready to accept my father had washed his hands of me after I'd so stupidly married a man of whom my family did not approve. I must have been crazy. It had never crossed my mind that it had all been a ploy to get his hands on my family's fortune.

Duke was playing the end game and reaping rewards along the way. My survival depended on my father obeying whatever demands Duke asked of him. *My parents must hate me.* Or still love me perhaps, doing the only thing they could to keep me safe —keeping Duke happy.

I should have run to them for help. Dad's got money, and once out of Duke's clutches, he'd have kept me that way. He'd have been able to protect me, wouldn't he? I hate that I can't be sure.

A whimper comes from inside as I realise for the first time in our marriage, Duke's been honest with me. Which means, my father is dying. *I'll never see him again.* I know Duke won't let me.

No, I'll be kept here like a brood mare until I give birth to a child for him. The only comfort is that this time, maybe he won't be so free with his hands. If a pregnancy is so important to him, once pregnant, he can't afford to hurt me. Until I give him a child.

Then, I'll no longer be of any use to him.

Like I have so many times over the past five years, I strain my mind, wondering what I ever saw in him. How was he able to pull the wool over my eyes and convince me he was my forever? I'm so gullible, so naïve.

There must be something missing in me, some sense of self-preservation, some gene of judgement others have but I lack. I can't overlook how Niran also had me fooled.

My lips twist cruelly. I might not have known Duke then, but I know him now. And a man like Niran has no place in the Crazy Wolves MC. He's been thrown to the wolves, quite literally. *I hope whatever they do to him hurts like hell. And only when he's in utter agony will he meet a gory end.*

Oh God, is this really me? Condoning torture and death?

But Niran only repeated what Duke had done first. Sucked me in with a persona that didn't exist, before mockingly coming clean to me.

He deserves everything he gets.

Fuck the man. He had to have been playing me from the start. Conveniently, I discount he can't have known who, or what I was, when he first met me. Whatever, once he found out, he betrayed me.

I never thought I'd be thankful that I terminated my pregnancy, but now I am. My child would have been used as a pawn. Born alive, he might have been kept as a vegetable living only with the aid of machines. Born dead or dying, he'd have been substituted with another child. At least my innocent baby has escaped that… for now. But what of Duke's plan to get me pregnant again?

I shudder and shove my hand into my mouth to stifle a wail. What hope has any child of mine once he falls into Duke's hands? What can I do to prevent conceiving again? I'm hardly going to get access to birth control pills this time. Unfortunately, without them, I seem pretty fertile.

My hand trembles as I brush back my hair, seeing no hope, no escape, only continued torture. Duke's fucking is brutal, lacking any semblance of love or tenderness. His one purpose is to get off, and now I know the reason, it all makes sense. He didn't even have to enjoy it. *He was trying to get me pregnant.*

And there's nothing I can do about it. Glancing around the room I've been kept in before, I already know the windows are barred. There's no way out except through the locked door, and that's only when my jailer turns the key. Even if I was able to overpower whoever opened it up, I'd never get through the clubhouse.

Wailing, I fall prone, beating my hands against the meagre mattress, knowing I've nothing to live for, and Duke would ensure he left me no way to kill myself.

Unless I push Duke too far. Get him to hit me and not stop. But even then, with his end goal, that plan might not work.

Rhythmically, I bang my fist into my palm, searching for options, but knowing I've got none.

Surely people like Patsy and Mary weren't involved in a plot to return me to my husband? I can't believe they were. Niran and Susie, or even maybe Cyn, must have been working together unbeknownst to the rest of the Devils.

But even if the others weren't involved, they won't care that I'm gone. I'll be a problem resolved. *They'll think Niran and I have disappeared together.* They're probably breathing a sigh of relief even now, thinking we've just pre-empted my move from San Diego.

However I look at it, I'm fucked, or will be, when Duke has his way with me.

Hours pass, hours during which I hope I've been forgotten, while knowing I've not. Every minute will be Duke's calculation, another punishment forced upon me. At least there's a small adjacent bathroom I can use, and don't have to be escorted to one of the filthy communal ones.

I'd rather be left alone.

I'd rather not be here at all.

Is there any lower to go when my only option to escape is enraging Duke to the extent he loses control and kills me?

Why did I trust Niran? Why didn't I run when I first knew Duke was closing in on me?

Because I'd just lost my baby. I thought nothing worse could happen to me. *I was wrong.*

Eventually, I hear the sound of footsteps outside the door. *Is it Duke coming to make good on his threat already?*

Or will Duke let me wallow in my misery, and, just like before, send a prospect to deliver food to me?

As I hear a key turn in the lock, I pull myself into a seated position, wrap my arms around myself and stare at the floor.

Whoever it is, I won't talk to them. Not Duke, who no words I could use would stop him abusing me. Nor any prospect. Not when I got Jude in mortal danger before.

The door opens, and a dark shadow falls over me. *It's not Duke.* Somehow I can tell, the scent of evil he brings with him is missing.

Motorcycle boots stand in front of me. They don't move, and the owner doesn't deign to speak.

Despite myself, curiosity makes me look up. *Oh hell, no. It's Niran.* A blinding rage comes over me.

"What the fuck are you doing here?" I spit out as I rise to my feet. I'd thought Duke would have killed him by now. *I'd hoped.* I never wanted to see his lying face again. Him, I'd gladly get killed.

Once he's got my attention, Niran doesn't respond, just goes to the small table and deposits a tray on it. I note the contents are the same as many times before—a plate with a cloth covering it, and plastic cutlery.

While I don't know this man at all, especially after he betrayed me, I never got a vibe that he would physically hurt me. So I let my rage come out, take a pace closer, and open my mouth.

"I hope you're fucking pleased with yourself." My chest heaves as I draw oxygen in. "You're as bad a monster as Duke. I fucking believed you!"

The bastard shrugs. He inclines his head, but I take that as a sign he's listening to me. "Why are you here? I thought you'd be back in San Diego fucking Susie by now." That's my lie. Duke would never have let him leave.

A shake of his head, then he marches to the door and steps out.

Without really knowing what I'm doing, I take the plate of food that was left, pick it up and throw it with all my might against the wall. The plate smashes, and the food falls to the ground.

The crash pulls me up, then I grin. *Maybe that's my way out? I'll starve myself.* Or, I sit up straighter, *could I use the broken shards as a weapon?* While I envisage me stabbing Duke, I'd only have one chance at killing him. Then I'd have to get away from his brothers. *No fucking chance.* Their treatment of a woman who'd murdered their VP doesn't bear thinking about.

Fuck Duke and double fuck Niran.

I fume. What the hell is Duke up to? They'd never accept a Black man into the club. I'm surprised he's still breathing, let alone acting like a prospect, obviously given the job the prospects had performed before.

Oh, Niran was a good little boy, following orders just as he'd been told. He hadn't spoken, as he'd probably been instructed. Not even to point out to me I was a stupid girl and that I'd played into his hands, allowing myself to be taken in by him and his fake caring routine.

Grrrr, I'm so angry, I could scream with frustration. That he sent Niran in had been another of Duke's games. Rubbing my stupidity in my face, that's all he's doing.

Well, he's not going to achieve anything. I already know I've got zero sense when judging a man. First Clive, then Duke, now Niran.

But angry as I am, my rage is battling with the pain inside me. For weeks I thought Niran had been my friend. For some reason, his betrayal hurts as much, if not more, than when I first found out the kind of man Duke was.

Duke had been too good to be true. If I'd described my ideal man, Duke would have measured up to that and then some. When he'd first brought me here and the scales had fallen from my eyes, I felt like I'd always been waiting for the other shoe to drop.

Niran? Well, he was nothing like anyone I'd have gone

searching for, but he wormed his way in despite my efforts to keep him out. He'd always been there when I needed a shoulder to lean on. Even in the beginning, Duke had never offered that, and with him, I'd done all I could to prove I hadn't needed one.

I still can't believe Niran's act had all been a ploy. He deserves an Oscar nomination, hell, to win the darn thing.

I start to pace, wondering how I misread all the signs. Niran had seemed a good fit for his club from what I'd seen. Their sergeant-at-arms had trusted him with his woman, and his brothers had seemed to hold him in good stead. It just doesn't make sense that he betrayed them as well.

But he has. The evidence is right in front of my eyes in that smashed plate and scattered food.

My pacing takes me to the door, and to a bag lying just inside that I hadn't noticed before. *More food?* Curious, I reach down and pick it up. Peering inside, I suck in a breath.

Sanitary napkins.

What? My op was a month back, I don't need them now. And even if I did, Duke would never have thought to get them, and despite us being husband and wife, I'd never have asked.

It's a message from Niran.

I frown. *But what message?* Is it a sign he's still looking out for me as he did before? How does that gel with a man who returned me to a monster he knew would make my life a misery?

That it doesn't is a conundrum I can't understand right now.

CHAPTER EIGHT

Niran

My non-reaction enrages her, but I let her words fall from me like water off a duck's back. Hating myself for not being able to reassure her, I leave as I came in. Stoic and unresponsive.

As I close the door, the crash of the plate smashing reaches my ears. Inwardly, I grin. *Saffie's broken but not defeated.* If she'd just given in, then I'd probably have more difficulty getting her to take a chance on an escape attempt should one present itself.

Locking her in and me out, I take up my position playing sentry again, wondering whether I'll be relieved later, while knowing I'll happily stand here for twenty-four hours as long as it means I'm the one to protect her.

As the question of where I'll be sleeping hasn't been addressed, I wonder whether they want to test me, see how long I'll stand here. A cold feeling inside of me warns it could be because they don't expect I'll live out the day. Dead men need no accommodation.

It's already late in the evening. My life might already be

measured in hours, but if that's the case, I'll go out fighting, and hopefully take Duke with me.

I stand, after a while abandoning my military stance, using the wall at my back to support me and to relieve some of the pressure on my stump. Whatever's ahead, I'll need to be at full strength.

Those keys to her room are burning a hole in my pocket. I want to use them. I want to go inside and check her injuries for myself. Comfort her, explain how bad I feel at hurting her, that I only said those despicable things to sure, keep myself alive, but mostly so she wasn't brought back to Duke on her own. Then I'd assure her I'd sacrifice my life if it meant she could get away.

My fingers itch and seem to inch toward the metal in my pocket, needing a conscious effort to pull them back. So close at one point, it takes footsteps on the stairs to bring me to my senses.

When the Crazy Wolves' member reaches the top, he stares straight ahead as he passes, leaving me unprepared for the fist in my stomach that has me inhaling sharply and bending over. He walks on, not even a glance spared. And like a good hangaround, I bite my tongue and make no protest. I just mentally add him to my growing list of people who'll eventually feel my wrath.

That I'm putting up with this shit for Saffie makes me admit I've been fooling myself. From the start I'd thought I was doing her a favour, that I was reacting to a damsel in distress, her knight in black leather armour, riding in on my metal steed to rescue her.

Now, with hours with nothing to do but think, I finally admit that it wasn't just for her, it was as much for myself. I've always wanted her.

The realisation pulls me up as I question how she's become so important to me. It's not her looks or her figure, I've barely seen her without red-rimmed eyes. And when I first met her, someone else's baby was inside her. It's not what's on the outside, it's the inner strength I see within in her, along with the fragility I want to protect. Kink might have been right. Something within her calls to me as if only I can fix her.

It's crazy, but since I was forced into claiming her, I consider her my old lady, even though I doubt she'd ever say yes. My claim, I fully believe, trumps that of Duke's. Half of me wonders whether he has an inkling putting me so close to her is the greatest torture he could inflict.

Only a door separates us, but it could be a million miles. I can't rush in like a hero in a movie, even though I've the means to undo the lock.

What is an undisputable fact—Duke doesn't trust me and the men in this club don't want me here. That they're pretending I've a chance at getting a patch is all a trick. They're fucking with my head, making me suspect there's hope, when there's none to have. They'll kill me, they have to, if only to tie up loose ends.

I'm not personally scared of that outcome. Hell, I've served. Though a Marine doesn't go on a mission with that result in mind, it can't be totally disregarded. Signing on, there's an acceptance that though you'll fight to avoid it, an unseen roadside mine, a stray shot, or an act of deliberate hostility could cut your life short. It fuels the adrenaline that makes us try to do better.

When I joined the Devils, I accepted the patch knowing I'd exchange my existence for that of any of my brothers who required it. *Ride free or die* is the motto I live by.

I'm no use to Saffie if I allow Duke to take me out. I can only help her by staying in the land of the living, which means I can't use that key. And if by staying aloof and refusing to talk to her I fuel the hatred she has, there's nothing I can do about it.

Not now. But hopefully one day, when we're out of here and free, I'll show her that the real me was the man she first met, and not this current stranger.

Just as almost everyone does, I have a desire to be liked. It's not in my nature to actively make someone dislike me. But that's what I've got to do if either of us have a chance to survive. And if she's the only one who's going to make it out of here, I'll go into this like any other mission. The end justifies the means, even if it turns out that to free her, I'll have to die.

As I did back in those early days as a Marine when I was on guard duty for lonely hours on end, I scan left and right constantly, ears alert for any sound. When I hear weeping from behind the locked door, I clench both my fists, but stay exactly where I am.

Wolves pass by occasionally, and except for the first, they totally ignore me. Eventually, I hear what I've been waiting for as the sound of more purposeful footsteps approaching reaches my ears. My head swings in that direction, and I see Asslicker again coming down the hallway. It's then I notice the light has changed, and the sounds from the clubroom below are diminishing.

"Brought her more water," he tells me.

I take it from him. He turns and leaves without waiting.

Once again, I unlock the door and enter. This time, she's lying on the bed. When she spies me, her eyes narrow and meet mine for a second with a puzzled expression on her face.

Then she gives an abrupt shake of her head, and turns over, presenting her back to me.

I leave the water and exit without speaking.

When the club room downstairs goes completely quiet, I take it no one is coming to relieve me, and that I won't be offered a place to sleep. There's a big part of me that's happy they seem to have forgotten about me. I'm right where I want to be—watching over Saffie.

She might not know it, but her every move is being watched. If it weren't for me spotting that camera, I might have been tempted to go in and speak to her, now everyone else appears to be asleep. If that's what they're waiting for, they're going to be disappointed. I've too much self-control to risk everything now.

The room I'm supposed to be guarding is opposite me. At my back is a door, with another adjacent to it. Right at the end is a fourth, just before the corridor kinks to the left and heads off somewhere else. I'm curious what the rooms behind me are used for. A few brothers have walked past, but they've bypassed the doorways. *Storerooms?* Perhaps. I'm tempted to check it out in case there's a handy weapon around, but that's probably wishful thinking.

As if to stretch my legs, I start to pace casually up and down the hallway. While keeping my head turned to the ground, I peek up through my eyelashes. Try as I might, I can see no more hidden cameras. I'm comfortably sure they haven't got eyes on me.

Shall I look behind the other doors? Or will I be caught? If I step one foot out of line, it will give them the excuse that they need, and my days will be ended.

A good prospect will always follow every instruction and never deviate from any course given. That the closed doors are tantalisingly close could be them putting temptation in my way.

When it's been deathly quiet for more than a few minutes, my curiosity gets the better of me. I'm just about to investigate when I hear footsteps coming up from my right.

With a feeling of relief that I hadn't given in to the impulse to explore, I stand at attention when Duke comes into sight.

I'm about to greet him politely when there's a commotion behind him, and I hear a female cry.

"Please, no." The girl's voice is shrill and piercing. "Please, let me go."

When she comes into sight, her pretty face is made ugly with tears streaming, and crease lines showing that the man dragging her along has her in a painful grip.

Duke swings around but offers no commiseration. "Bring her," he instructs.

Without a glance in my direction, as if I was invisible, he proceeds to the room at the end and opens it with a key. Sneaking a glance I get a glimpse of a well-appointed bedroom, which I take to be his.

The tattooed biker drags the unwilling woman past me. She sees me and shoots me a look of appeal, but I can do nothing to help her. Although it makes bile boil in my gut, like a guard on a base, I ignore anything that's not a threat to me, and let them move past without making a move or requesting an explanation.

At the doorway ahead, Duke stands back, allowing the other biker to push the girl in. The last sight I see is her sprawled on the floor, before the door is closed and it's only me and the Crazy Wolf left in the corridor.

As he walks back down the way he'd approached, he pauses to wink at me. "The VP's gonna have fun tonight. He always likes breaking a new girl in."

As agonised screams begin to float down the corridor, I start hoping that Saffie's room is soundproofed, while knowing that's unlikely. It's probably wrong and I should have more compassion for the poor girl, but all I can think of is with him occupied, it's not Saffie being subjected to his attentions. Perhaps it was a good ploy to suggest she's still bleeding.

I can't help but wonder who the girl is. Her clothing was torn, but from what I could see of what remained, it was nothing like a sweet butt's. It wasn't expensive, cheap but smart looking, as though she'd been picked up off the street, maybe on her way home from a job in an office.

My fists clench and I'd give anything to be able to intercede. But I can't save everyone, and it's Saffie who's important to me. Even if I could break up Duke's fun night, I wouldn't be able to get the girl off the compound or find a way to let her go free. Killing Duke with my bare hands might give me satisfaction, but it wouldn't help me or save the girl. And where would that leave Saffie?

Is Saffie important to the MC, or just to their VP? If I killed Duke, she might be even worse off.

As the sounds lower to a constant sobbing, I gather Duke's occupied for now. Apart from the background of the girl's distress, I hear no one else around. Inching up the hallway, I place my back against one of the doors that remain a mystery.

Reaching into my boot, I take the innocuous weapon that hadn't been removed from me—a bent piece of wire—and have that door unlocked in three seconds flat. Pausing again to make sure Duke hasn't finished with his toy, I crack the door open and peer in. A large cabinet meets my eyes, but on inspection, unfortunately it holds no weapons. Otherwise there are a few mattresses piled up, and worn-looking bed linen, but nothing else. Just my luck. I step back out and lock it back up.

After checking, I can still hear no movement and that the distraught sobbing from the room at the end is continuing, I try the next door. In here there's a bed, unmade and dishevelled, but not much else. Nothing personal to indicate it belongs to any of the men, but the scent of sex and weed is strong. *A crash room? Maybe.*

Taking a deep breath, I step inside, checking for cameras but there's none I can see. My objective is finding a weapon, something with which to defend myself, but that would be too easy.

Still, I search, reaching my hand under the bed, opening the drawer in the bedside table, moving aside boxes of condoms which seem more than any one man would need. The variety of sizes and types suggest I was right. This is a place the men would take women for casual sex.

It was a vain hope I'd find a gun or a knife. While I'm to be disappointed in my search, I'm not surprised. Looking back toward the door, I see a bolt on the inside. *Huh. Seems some people around here do like their privacy.*

My brain registers that the sounds from Duke's room have died down. Believing he'll kick the girl out rather than allowing her to share his bed for the night, I exit quickly, hesitating before relocking the door. *Might be useful if I quickly need a place to hide.*

Now positioned leaning against the wall opposite Saffie's room, I let my body slide down until my ass is against the floor. I bow my head, resting it on my knees.

I'll be able to doze, knowing my senses will remain alert.

Only a few minutes later, I hear footsteps on the stairs. Jerking fully awake, I jump to my feet and regain my sentry pose.

The member who passes shoots a death glare at me but proceeds to the door at the end. He knocks. It opens. A naked, bloodied and almost comatose girl is pushed into his arms. With just a chin lift, he hefts her over his shoulder, slaps her ass, and hauls her away, walking back past me without even a glance my way.

Duke sees me, grins, lifts his hand in a mock salute, then disappears back into his room.

"This is taking too fuckin' long." In my anguish, I slam my hand down onto the tabletop. "They've had them both for twenty-four hours." At least we know Niran is, or was, alive. Stormy had hacked into the security camera footage at the small Nevada airport again and had provided evidence that both he and Saffie had disembarked from the plane.

"Duke wants Saffie alive," Lost says in a reasonable tone. "Otherwise, why take her back to Nevada?"

"And Niran?" Standing so fast, my chair rocks back and falls to the ground with a crash. Placing both palms on the table, I lean forward and all but snarl in his face. "They don't want a man like Niran in their fuckin' White club. So what's the point in keeping him alive? Sure, he arrived, but that doesn't mean he's still breathing." I have visions of him being taken to the equivalent of our brig, the place where we interrogate those hostile to the club.

"We have to hope that he is," Salem shoots back, a man who knows better than most about torture, as he's normally the one to dish it out. "We can't give up, Brother."

"Every hour he's left there is an hour too many," I shout. "They won't be gentle if they're questioning him about our club."

"Which they'll do if they want to understand what might be coming for them," Pennywise puts in, looking between me and Salem.

"Or they might not expect us to worry about a lost brother, not when he's Black," Dart points out, his mouth twisting with distaste. If he wasn't married to Alex, a woman of the same colour skin as Niran, I'd consider that statement racist. But coming from the VP, I know it's not. Satan's Devils don't give a damn about the wrapping, it's what's on the inside that counts. And Niran is as good a brother as I've ever come across.

"I agree with Grumbler. I can't understand why we're not already on the road," Blaze complains.

Token clears his throat. "I'm waiting on an update from Stormy—"

"Fuck Stormy," I round on him. "He was quick off the mark when it came to taking out Alder. He didn't wait then."

Prez bangs the gavel. "Grumbler. Will you sit the fuck down? We can't just ride to Nevada without getting intel. It will be signing the death warrants of at least some of us. If you go off half-cocked, it will be me explaining to Mary why her man isn't coming home."

I wouldn't want my old lady to hear something like that. "So what are we doing other than sitting around with our thumbs up our asses?" Begrudgingly, I pick up and right my chair, and then sit back down.

To me, Niran's not just another brother, he's a friend, and a good one at that. We'd grown close when he'd taken on my duties when I was banged up. If I step down from my sergeant-at-arms role, I know no man here would have any hesitation voting him in to take the vacated slot. Giving myself a mental slap, I realise every man around this table must be hurting. Begrudgingly, I realise Lost is right. Charging in without knowing what we're heading into could leave a number of us dead, and maybe even get Niran killed in the process. If he's still alive, that is.

Lost's phone rings. He takes it out, glances at it, then places it on the table. "You've got Lost."

"Hope I'm in the right place, Brother." A chuckle comes down the line.

"Red," Lost breathes out, referencing the Vegas Satan's Devils' prez. "Thanks for getting back to me. We're in church. I've got you on speaker."

"I've got Crash and Indian here at my end." I know they're the Vegas VP and sergeant-at-arms, respectively.

"You got anything?" Prez asks, barely hiding the impatience in his voice.

"Yeah. We know of the Crazy Wolves. They hole up about an hour and a half from here. We know they're into some bad shit, but as long as they kept that out of Vegas, we kept our distance. After your request, I sent Twister and Hammer to carry out some surveillance." He pauses, but it's only to take a breath. "They're based in a compound out in the country. Hard to approach unseen, though darkness would help. They've got guard dogs and have patrolling sentries. Whatever they keep inside, they want it to themselves."

"Our brother is resourceful. Any chance of him making it out?" This is from Dart.

Red doesn't answer immediately. There's a murmuring of voices at the other end. "Keys has been speaking to Stormy and running through the members they have. Some are ex-military, and of those, most didn't leave voluntarily. A lot are just thugs off the street. Knife, the prez, has got connections to a white supremacist organisation. What's worse for us, Stormy's found links to a prostitution ring they're running in Vegas." He snorts. "Seems like you're going to have us on your side, and not just because a Devil is missing. We'll be behind you to take these fuckers out. Vegas is *my* town and no one shits on my territory."

"Thought prostitution was the bread and butter of Vegas," Kink puts in.

Red growls in his throat. "Yeah, but not when the girls are forced into it and kept caged for the *gentleman's* pleasure."

Okay then. I can see why Red's all for taking them out.

"Are we any clearer on numbers?" Lost asks.

"More than expected. Seems they've accepted a few more into the ranks. Twister tells me he counted a couple of dozen bikes…" his voice trails off.

"I've got seventeen men ready to ride," Lost states. "And Drummer said he'd help." I nod at the news. Getting brothers from Tucson would be good.

"I have men," Red offers. "I've spoken to Demon." He references the Colorado prez. "He's willing to get involved, as will Utah. But how many Snatcher can spare depends on what they're working on. Snatcher at least has offered the plane to ferry us around."

"We can ride, Brother," Lost decides. "You're close, we can make it in four hours, and Drummer's boys in six give or take. But Demon might appreciate the offer to fly."

"I'll offer up the clubhouse," Red says fast. "You'll have to bring sleeping bags and be prepared to sleep rough, but we'll get you housed."

"Twister have any ideas about how we get onto the compound?" I ask, earning myself a chin lift from the VP.

"He reckons explosives. I know Demon's got Pyro who's handy with bombs. You got anyone there?"

"We did," I offer grimly. "Niran."

"What about Curtis?" Dart asks. "I thought he specialised in munitions?"

"Man's near getting his patch," Lost observes. "And he's close to Niran. I reckon he'd jump at the chance to come along for the ride."

"Drummer's got Slick," Dart observes. "He'd be good to have onside."

"Tucson's also got a construction company," Lost comments, tapping the table. "Be interesting to know if Viper and Bullet are as good at bringing shit down as they are at putting it up."

"Wouldn't be surprised," Red agrees.

Lost raises his hand to scratch the side of his nose. "Okay, I'll update Drummer and explain what we need. One thing, Red." Prez's eyes find mine. "We need to get this shit moving. Niran hasn't got much time."

Red allows a few seconds of silence, and I read he's considering it may already be too late. Then he states, "Whether it's a rescue or revenge, Brother, they're coming down. You feel me, Lost?"

"I feel you and I'm right there with you."

The call's ended, and the room is deathly quiet. All eyes look to Lost who's rubbing at his eyes. For a moment no one speaks, all giving our prez time.

"Grumbler, what protection do we need to leave here?"

Forcing myself to think of the club and not just one man, I give his question consideration before I reply, "There's nothing particular on the radar, Prez, but if Curtis is coming along for the ride, that leaves only Connor if we all go." I grimace, having reminded myself we've lost Kid.

Prez nods. "I want three brothers to remain here."

His not unexpected words cause a rumble of discontent to go around the table. No one wants to be left behind when it's a case of rescuing a brother. All eyes are staring down as if a glance up would be taken for volunteering.

An idea occurs to me. "Ross has mentioned prospecting a few times. He could be backup for Connor."

"He can't ride," Pennywise objects.

"He's recently got a new hand," I tell them. "Not as fancy as Utah's member, Bolt, but he's been eyeing up one of the electric bikes and as long as he can hold the handlebars, he should be able to ride. Not saying we immediately make him a prospect, but he's got military experience. How about we bring him in as a hangaround? I reckon he'd be up for it."

"Yeah, he'll be handy to have around." Snips laughs at his own joke, but he's the only one who does.

"Ask him, Grumbler. That sounds like a plan." Lost nods at me appreciatively, then looks around. "But I still want brothers here. Snips, Scribe and Keeper, I'm leaving you behind."

"Prez—"

"Nah. Not up for discussion." Lost glares at the men who he's named, who return various expressions of disgust. But as he stares them down, reluctant acceptance washes over them. "I'll make my phone calls. Blaze, can you check all the bikes are ready to roll? If everything falls into place, we can set out in a couple of hours and get to Vegas tonight. Tomorrow, we'll attack their compound and get this over with."

"You think we ought to hitch a plane ride?" Dart asks. "I'm not happy us riding with all the firepower we need. Especially if we'll be taking C4 with us."

Lost grins at his VP. "If I'm not mistaken, that's one area where Utah will be able to help us and fly the heavy gear in. All we'll need is to have our sidearms, and most of us have places we can hide them on our rides. Curtis can drive the crash truck with the rifles." The crash truck has a handy hidden compartment for this exact purpose.

That would help. We'll pass muster on a lighthearted traffic stop, but not a serious one. But from the way Blaze is glaring around, as road captain, he'll be making sure we ride steady. The only reason the cops will have for stopping us is the number of bikers on the road at the same time.

As Lost wraps up the meeting, I make a mental list of what I need to be doing. Checking everyone has sufficient ammunition for a start. I realise how much I've been relying on Niran and wish he was here with us. Though if he was, we wouldn't be planning a war.

When Lost bangs the gavel for the final time, I get to my feet. It's impossible to stop worrying about my brother. I wonder whether he's already been tortured for hours, and what state we'll find him in. I refuse to consider our forthcoming trip may see us returning with a body.

It's been years since the San Diego chapter went to war. Sure, a number of us have ridden across to Arizona to help pull the mother chapter's irons out of the fire on more than one occasion, but the whole club riding out to rescue one of their own, well, when we last did that is long in my rearview. Before Lost's time, and never in the couple of years Snake was head of the table. It was in the previous prez's day, many moons back.

The buzz, the thrill, never fades though. I hate to admit I'm excited, though half of me is terrified, but not on my own behalf. If it was only me I was worrying about, I wouldn't be scared of not returning. No, it's my heavily pregnant wife.

As I exit the meeting room, as if I've conjured her up, I hear Mary's laugh. Steeling my features, I cross the room over to her. She's laughing at Isla who appears to be doing her best to run Alex ragged. Seeing an eighteen-month-old trying to copy her mother's moves on the pole would be funny if I was in the mood for amusement.

Mary's face grows serious as I approach.

"Niran?"

I shake my head, letting her know there's no news. Of course we don't share club business with old ladies, but there's no hiding he's not around. Even if we tried to come up with a rational explanation, neither she, Patsy or Alex are stupid, and would quickly see through any excuse just by observing the brothers' sombre expressions and downhearted behaviour.

"What are you going to do about it?"

As I look into her trusting eyes, I know how much the younger biker means to her. They'd clicked from the time I left him to protect her in her house. Alicia, her, *our* teenage daughter, likes him as well. To be honest, Niran's one of the good guys, and most people who meet him would feel the same way.

I just wonder if she knows what she's asking. Sure, we'll move heaven and earth to get Niran back, but there'll be a cost to pay for it. I can only hope it's not too much and that I can come back to her.

"We know where he is." Since we've gotten together, there's not been a night when I haven't slept beside her, so however much I want to hide my involvement, it will be impossible to keep it from her. "We're heading to Vegas, probably tonight. Might be away a day or so, darlin'."

She bites her lip, drawing my attention to her face, noting now I'm less focused on Niran and more on her—how tired and pale she's looking. I put it down to worry for our missing brother, and hope bringing him back if it's humanely possible will return a smile to her face.

"You do what you've got to do," she semi-whispers, and as she broadens her shoulders, I know she's trying to be brave.

"Hey, Grumbler old man."

I reel from the slap on my back that Dart's just placed on it. "Just been talking to Alex. She's suggested Patsy, Mary and Alicia go over to our place and have a girl's sleepover."

Mary gives a half-hearted grin. "Girls?" she queries.

"Mary, you beauty. You'll always be a girl to me." Dart places his hand over his heart dramatically, while I elbow him in the ribs.

"Oomph," he exclaims, glaring.

"I think it's a good idea, Mary." I'd prefer her not to be

alone. Heaven forbid anything happens with the baby while I'm not there to help her. Alicia's a good kid, but might miss some signs. All three women she would be staying with have had babies before.

"Alex would appreciate the help with the kids, and Isla there will remind you what you've got in store," Dart adds, as though it's encouragement.

Mary chuckles softly. "I can get in some diaper changing practice at least."

"So you're coming?" Alex appears with Isla's hand now firmly in her grip.

When Mary nods, Alex curls her free arm around her. "It will be good to have some female company for a change. We'll watch movies, drink wine... or at least Patsy and I will, and watch movies with Alicia while you refamiliarize yourself with looking after kids." She winks at my old lady who rolls her eyes.

"I'm rethinking this," Mary replies to her laughing, then she frowns. "Oh, what about Cyn?"

My eyes widen. *I'd forgotten about her.* "Damn it." I bounce a fist off the palm of my other hand a couple of times.

"Take her with you. She'll buy the suggestion it's a girls' night. Say we're off on a ride, that Niran's gone ahead if she asks for him." Dart's thinking quickly. "If she wants details, say it's club business."

"You think she'll accept it?" I ask him, wondering what Niran's kid sister would do if we returned without him.

He shrugs. "She's not got a choice, has she?" Then he taps my shoulder and jerks his head. Knowing he wants to discuss club business, I step away and follow him.

"Can you get the ammunition and rifles stored in the crash truck?"

"That's what I was about to get started on VP. After I've given Ross a call."

Dart's eyes focus behind me. "Mary okay? She looks a bit pale."

Grimacing, I answer, "I think so. She's close to Niran, and she's worried about him."

The reply seems to satisfy him. "So are we all, Grumbler. So are we fuckin' all."

CHAPTER TEN

Niran

When Duke's finished with his entertainment for the night it all goes quiet. After a while, I again sink back to the floor and try to relax my body at least. Having seen the evidence of what Duke is capable of, my resolve only strengthens. *I've got to get Saffie away.* But I'm relying on my brothers riding to help me. I can think of no other plan. On the face of it, it would be easy to unlock Saffie's room and lead her down to the now quiet clubroom. But that's too obvious, and I have no doubt that someone will be waiting for me, and that's if they haven't got someone monitoring the camera feed in real time. For now, I'm stumped as to how to come up with a plan.

Darkness finally breaks, and daylight starts to invade from the window just before the turn of the hallway. The clubhouse begins to wake slowly like a slumberous beast—a few clatters, the thudding of boots on the stairs, a shout, a groan, a frustrated, *fuck off.* And then members appear from the corner and start to file past me.

The sun's moved into view and has completed a quarter of its journey into the sky before Duke's door opens. He passes without speaking to me, only pausing to bang loudly on Saffie's door, shouting loudly, "Good morning, Princess." Then he leaves.

Jesus. Behind that door, I know Saffie will be quaking, anticipating the door opening and Duke going in when he'd had no such intention. *Mental torture.*

Once again, the key burns in my pocket, and again I leave it untouched. Soon, surely, they'll bring some food to her. As my stomach growls, I know I could do with some sustenance myself.

At last, Asslicker appears carrying a tray. It serves my purpose to ask him to relieve me for a few minutes while I, well, relieve myself. I've a strong bladder, but hey, I've been standing here for hours.

Showing he's got at least some semblance of humanity, he tells me where to go. Once I'm out of sight, I start to worry he might carry in Saffie's tray himself, and deprive me of the chance of seeing her. I empty my bladder as fast as I can, willing the stream that seems never-ending to dry up.

When I get back, feeling one hundred times better, the food and the prospect are still there. Well, of course they are, the darn key's still in my pocket. I laugh at myself. *I needn't have worried.*

He leaves, I check the tray. There are two plates—more than enough food on them to feed both her and me. *At least they're not trying to starve me.*

Taking a breath, hating that I'm going to be facing her animosity, unable to do anything about it, I brace myself, open the door, and step in to perform on camera.

It goes about as well as last time, though overnight she's chosen a few choice words, sayings that hit me right in the gut. Sentences aiming to hurt. *Black bastard,* other taunts about my ancestry, slurs on my career and suggestions why I'm no longer a Marine. Outright accusations I'm a coward and a liar.

At first I feel pain, anguish I'm unable to protect myself, but then I block those feelings out. At least she feels safe enough to insult me. Even in this situation, she believes I'm no threat. And probably more important, she's holding on to her spirit. She's not giving up.

If there's going to be any chance of escape, those are two important factors. She's got to trust me enough to follow my lead and be prepared for us to fight our way out.

No, a meek and mild Saffie wouldn't be a good thing. This side she's showing is one she hasn't revealed before.

Of course I can give no indication of the pleasure her attitude gives me. Instead, using my hands, I stoically sweep up the food that she wasted yesterday. My nod to the plate, a silent admonishment that she needs to eat is met with disdain, though I note she doesn't make a move to throw the fresh plate at me.

Then I leave, insults still being hurled at my back.

That's my girl, I think, locking the door again.

I eat what was on the second plate and leave the detritus of last night's meal and the tray by my feet. Then, once again, I take up position, hoping they send no one to relieve me.

It might be a false impression, but by being here, I feel I'm helping keep Saffie safe.

Wolves come and go, passing me without a word, but their expressions speak volumes. *No one trusts me or wants me here.* Sooner or later, I'm going to discover Duke's end plan, and I very much doubt that it's going to involve a prospect patch.

Still, I'll pretend to be ignorant. I'll raise my chin and stand all polite as if becoming one of their number is my highest fucking priority. And if I scowl at their backs after they pass, who's to know?

The sun's just past its zenith by the time the monotony is broken.

Slit appears, striding along the corridor. I stare ahead, minding my business, expecting him to past. Instead, he stops.

"Boy, open the door."

Growing cold, I realise he's going in to see Saffie. But what can I do? I'm hardly in a position to protest.

But I try. "She looks a bit peaky this morning." That's a lie. In her fighting mode, she was looking her best.

"Don't give a fuckin' damn," he states, ominously. "Duke might get queasy with a bit of blood, but hey, as far as I'm concerned, it's extra lubrication."

I breathe in sharply. *Duke's possessive, isn't he? He wouldn't let his sergeant-at-arms… would he?*

If I'm wrong, what can I do about it?

"Open up, Boy!" Impatient, Slit jerks his head pointedly at the locked door. Unable to arouse his suspicions and hoping like fuck he's only going to have a conversation, I pull the key from my pocket, place it in the lock, turn it, push the door open for him then step back.

He slams it behind him.

How can I do this? How can I stand here and listen? I'm certain he's going to hurt her, even if not physically, but with words. How can I say I'm a man and do nothing?

If I race in, he's sure to be armed. One shot and I'll be dead, and what use will I be to anyone then? But if I could take him down, I could be armed. *Then what could I do?* I've no plan, no way out. Just running blindly would be us committing suicide even if I took one or two of them with us.

Perhaps they'll just talk.

Fuck. Mental torture? I don't know the meaning of it, not until I start to hear raised voices, and the distinct sound of someone being slapped, and I doubt it's him.

My hands form fists, my jaw clenches as their voices become louder.

"Get away from me, Slit!" A man's chuckle, then, "Slit! No. Noooo!. Duke would never—"

"Who the fuck do you think sent me here, slut? Duke wants you pregnant, and he doesn't care by whom."

"Slit! Get off me!" There's another round of flesh meeting flesh, and an agonised wail as something hits the ground. Feeling sick, I suspect it's Saffie.

How can I stand here and bear it? The only way not to hear the woman I care for being raped is to cover my ears. *But if I rush in, I'm dead, or any chance we had to escape is gone.* I'm so fucking torn, barely holding myself back from charging at the door.

Another scream, followed by a crash and Slit's roar and I can't help myself. My legendary control gone completely, throwing myself at the door, I dive in.

Saffie's crouching with her arms over her head to protect herself. Her t-shirt is torn, exposing her bra. Shards of a broken plate litter the floor, and an enraged Slit has blood over his face, and is poised to launch himself at her.

In a split second, I've summed up the situation, diving for a sharp fragment of porcelain and sinking it deep into his neck. Gurgling, clutching at himself, glaring lethal daggers at my face but unable to stop his lifeblood pouring out, Slit drops to the floor.

He may still be twitching, and he might not know it yet, but he's only got seconds of his life left.

"Come." I grab for her hand. She pulls away. "Saffie. For fuck's sake. Here's our chance to escape." We might not succeed, but we have to take it.

"Get away from me." Scrambling back, she evades my touch.

"We don't fuckin' have time for this," I growl, "Just come with me." Our likelihood of getting away is slim to none, but I've just killed their sergeant-at-arms, and she initiated the attack by smashing the plate over his head from what I could gather. We're both dead unless somehow we can get clear. Especially if the cameras are being monitored right now. I can only hope Slit asked for privacy.

Saffie's still backing away, her eyes flicking between me and the prone body. "You *betrayed* me, Niran. Why the fuck should I go with you?"

Speaking as fast as I can, I hiss words at her. "I had to lie to them, else they'd have killed me. Getting them to believe I was the one who led them to you meant they'd bring me too, and I'd have a stab at finding a chance for us both to escape."

"I don't believe you. You could have said something last night. It's too late for your lame explanation."

"Saffie," I snap, pointing over my head. "There's a fuckin' camera up there. I couldn't say anything. I don't even know now if Slit had it turned off before coming in. If he hasn't…" I don't bother finishing that sentence. If someone has seen their sergeant-at-arms meeting his maker, they'll already be on their way. I haven't heard boots storming up the stairs yet, but that doesn't mean they're not coming.

Her eyes narrow, then they glance up above my head and widen. Then the Devil proves he's with one of his own, as she accepts the inevitable, that for now she has to trust me. *Thank fuck.* She swallows fast then simply asks, "Which way?"

Taking her hand, I pull her out of the room, and now hear footsteps in the distance. Praying as I haven't since I was a gullible child, I quickly lock the door, thrust her over to one of the rooms I explored last night, push her in and shoot the bolt.

"Under the bed," I hiss.

Let Slit have turned off the camera wanting some private time with his VP's woman.

Let them assume it's me who's on the loose and they'll start searching.

Let them think this room has always been locked.

Let me fuckin' think of a way to get out of this.

As it stands, we're trapped like sitting ducks.

CHAPTER ELEVEN

Grumbler

By the time we arrive in Vegas, my previously injured leg is protesting, and so's my ass. In my youth, I could ride for hours, but now over four hours of being on the road has taken its toll. Pulling up in the already crowded parking lot outside Red's clubhouse, I cross my fingers that when I put down the kickstand, my busted leg doesn't give way.

Luckily managing to stand on two feet, I arch my back, putting my hands to the small of it and stretching.

Lost catches my eye and grimaces himself, rolling his neck to get the kinks out of it.

"Long ride, Brother," he commiserates as he comes across.

"It's nothing, Prez. Just we're getting older."

"Welcome, San Diego!" Red bellows to no one in particular, then, catching sight of the prez and myself, comes across. He takes Lost's hand, locks thumbs, then pulls him in so they can exchange hefty back slaps.

Indian, my counterpart in the Vegas chapter, follows his prez and he and I exchange similar man hugs.

"Welcome, my brother, Grumbler. You need our help getting your missing man back?" His voice is a rich baritone.

"That we do, Brother." I give him a chin lift.

All around me, brothers are greeting brothers. As Indian pulls back, I scan the milling throng of bikers around me. The one thing uniting us all is the Satan's Devils patch. I recognise most of them though I might not be able to put the right names to everyone, and quickly surmise there's more than just Vegas here.

Taking a few steps forward brings me in front of Thunder, the Colorado sergeant-at-arms.

"Well fuckin' met, Brother," I greet him heartily. When he gives me chin back, and pulls me in and thumps my cut, I start to wonder whether my back will survive tonight intact. Thunder, like me, has a history with the MC going way back, and we've shared more than a few drinks before. More than once, we've fought beside each other. Comfortable, I therefore nudge him and asks quietly, "Who're they?"

Thunder twists and gives a quick glance to where I'm pointing. "Ah, I've only just met them myself. The big man's Thor. He's Utah's VP. Snatcher's around here somewhere. I've already forgotten most of their names, oh, except for Swift, their enforcer."

Now I spot Utah's female member, I recognise her, of course, and there's Bolt standing beside her. I'd met them both when they'd come to San Diego to help us out when my Mary had gotten herself into a situation. Not far away is another Utah man I recognise, but that was from when he was with Tucson. It's Road, who I've heard is a fucking brave man, being that he's Swift's partner. The others are unknowns to me, and I eye them with interest.

Far from being the country bumpkins we'd all been led to believe, the Utah chapter has become renowned for their military and data expertise. They're a close-knit bunch and are tending to stick together. I'm unsurprised. All other chapters look on them with suspicion. No one likes being lied to, and not when that lie has been perpetuated for years.

But they've turned out to come rescue Niran, and from what I now know, I reckon they'll be good men—and woman—to have on our side.

Thunder taps my arm to get my attention. "Their sergeant-at-arms is their pilot. After flying us here, he took off immediately to go to Arizona to pick up Tucson."

"They're not riding in?" I'm surprised.

Thunder snorts. "Viper, Bullet and Slick aren't. They're bringing some toys. Drummer and the rest are biking it."

Toys. I grin. Yeah, the more of those the better.

A sharp whistle pierces the air. Voices fall silent as Red once again bellows, "Brothers! Beers and food are available inside. Standing room only." We all give dutiful laughs. "Drummer's about half an hour out. When he arrives, we'll have an officers' only meeting, but until then, please partake of our hospitality."

As men start moving past me, a hand falls on my shoulder. "Hey, Grumbler. How's your old lady? Pregnancy going well?"

I turn to shake Bolt's hand, marvelling not for the first time, how real it feels in mine. "She's doing good, Bolt. Only another couple of months to go." Thinking about Bolt's prosthesis makes me wonder about asking him if there's any advice he can give Ross, who just before we'd left had readily agreed to be our new hangaround. Although we'd probably not be able to afford the experimental model like he has, maybe he knows someone who'd be able to help.

"Bad business about Niran. I was impressed with him in San Diego." Bolt eyes me seriously. "We'll do whatever it takes to get him back."

Thoughts about Ross immediately forgotten, I return to the business at hand. "We've gotta move fast, Bolt. That's if..." I can't even voice what I'm thinking.

His hand squeezes my shoulder. "We've had some ideas on the way across. And Preacher's got a few surprises up his sleeves. Stormy's making his own way here. He's driving a command centre. We'll get him back, Grumbler."

I fucking hope so. I raise my chin, wordlessly showing my appreciation, and realising Utah is good to have on our team.

It's utter chaos inside as I make my way through, finally getting a beer in my hand. Vegas members are behind the bar helping the prospects to keep the line moving, and buffet tables have been set up overflowing with food.

"Your old ladies done good," I remark to Crash when I pass him.

"Old ladies?" The Vegas VP barks a laugh. "Nah. Rosa's got more brains than that. She and Tiffany got in touch with a catering firm that does outdoor events."

"Only two old ladies?" I eye a couple of excited-looking, scantily clad women, and jerk my head in their direction.

Crash chuckles. "That pair are a couple of our sweet butts. Hey, Pixie," he shouts out. "You behave yourself. You'll have plenty of time to enjoy the visitors later."

The sweet butt he's addressed sticks her tongue out at him, then goes back to surveying the newcomers as if she's just been presented with one of Las Vegas' finest all-you-can-eat buffets.

When Crash moves on, I spy Blaze and start walking across to him. As I do, I see Curtis helping out behind the bar, and detour in his direction.

"Good call," I lean in and say softly when I've got his attention.

"You've got a good one here," Rope, a Vegas member serving beers, claps his hand on the prospect's shoulder. "Didn't wait to be asked."

"I've already been asked to transfer to Vegas," Curtis informs me cheekily.

"No poaching," I warn Rope, pointing my finger.

The door opens with a crash, causing me to swing around to see Demon, the Colorado prez, followed by Beef, his VP, stepping in, followed by Thunder, their sergeant-at-arms. Behind them come several of the Colorado members, Pyro, Mace, Buzzard and Ink if my memory is correct. Red waves them in, points to the bar and I step back to clear a space, watching Curtis being run ragged again.

Before I can think of who I should greet next, there's more commotion from the entrance.

"Make way," a loud voice yells. Spinning around, I spy Peg, my counterpart from Tucson. He's such a big fucking man. He towers over the crowd.

Drummer comes in behind him, followed by other familiar-looking men. Like the Red Sea parting, brothers briskly step aside to let the mother chapter members in.

One enters, pauses and surveys the room, then yells, "Fuckin' shiny side up, Brother!"

I turn in the direction of the response when I hear an equally loud, "Dirty side down." Then watch with a grin as I see a man break from the bar and stride fast to the speaker. The two men shake hands, then cling on to each other.

Rock and Beef, I remember from visiting Tucson, were always best of friends.

I make my way over to where Deuce, Reboot, and Wrangler are standing, looking slightly awed and out of place. Apart from Swift and Bolt, I doubt they'd met many here before, and those they have, only on the odd run.

I take a moment to shoot the shit with them, to reassure them it's been more than a minute since we've had a gathering such as this. Normally it would be something fun like a charity ride. It's been a while since we rode with the other chapters in anger, and well before they were patched in.

When I leave the group, I feel a lump in my throat. I just hope Niran knows how respected he is, if in some cases only by reputation. He's got the whole damn MC coming for him, none of the chapters hesitating in offering their support.

Hang on, Brother. Devils are riding to save you.

"Hey, fuckers!" Another loud shout reaches me, as I again turn, seeing two men walking in—a tall slender one's arm resting on the shoulder of a brawnier brother. *Joker and Lady if I recall correctly.* The two Tucson men who came out. "How's it swinging?"

A roar greets the ex-Vegas members, and they're quickly surrounded. I notice only one man standing back with a frown on his face. His name I can't quite remember.

But the general reaction makes me smile to myself. Yeah, Satan's Devils are inclusive. Then, as my eyes land on Swift from Utah, my thoughts make me snort. *We most certainly are.* My amusement is swiftly tempered by the knowledge that unlike us, the Crazy Wolves have strict restrictions on membership, and that they've got in their clutches a man who they'd despise, and certainly wouldn't think worthy of wearing their patch.

That's why we're here.

I know we're shortly going to get down to business, but for now, members who haven't crossed paths in years seem more interested in catching up. I grow impatient, hoping they remember what we're here for, and that this isn't a fucking reunion.

"VP." I step in front of Dart when he walks past. "When are we going to get fuckin' started?"

His eyes are full of understanding. "Soon, Brother. Soon." Then, showing he's as guilty as the rest, he continues his path toward where Rock, Beef and Road, his ex-Tucson brothers, are standing.

Suppressing my exasperation, what else is there to be done? I drink my beer, go to the bar and grab another, well, riding is thirsty work, and down some fried chicken to keep me going. I'm just wiping off my fingers, when that damn ear-piercing whistle comes again, and Red suddenly comes into view, pulling himself up so he's standing on the bar top.

"Officers to our meeting room. The rest of you, fuel your-selves up."

At fucking last.

I finish my second beer fast, spy Lost, and follow him, ending up in a room just like ours where we hold church. I take a seat at the end of the table.

Red goes to the head of the table, but instead of sitting down, offers the chair to Drummer. The mother chapter prez pauses, then takes it. When Red sits on his left, Lost takes the seat on his right, and Demon places himself next to him. Snatcher positions himself opposite Red.

Drummer bangs the gavel, and the room goes quiet. "Okay," he starts, looking around. "Introductions first. Let's make sure we all know each other. With me, I've got Wraith, my VP, Blade my enforcer, Peg, sergeant-at-arms, and Joker, road captain." He points to each as he introduces his officers, then indicates to Red.

"I'm Red, you all know me." He grins boyishly. "That's Crash, there. He's VP, Indian, my sergeant-at-arms, Shadow my road captain and Twister who doesn't say no to torturing anybody. For the good of the club," he belatedly adds.

Lost is next up. "Lost, San Diego. Dart, my VP, Salem, enforcer, Blaze, road captain and Grumbler back there trying to hide is my sergeant-at-arms."

"I'm Demon," a long-haired man informs us. "Colorado. My VP's Beef, Mace my enforcer, Thunder my sergeant-at-arms, and Sparky who gets us where we should be going."

Then, all eyes fall on the last man. "Snatcher, Utah. Thor's my VP, Swift is my enforcer, and Preacher, sergeant-at-arms-come-taxi driver." That's followed by a dutiful laugh as he names the pilot who flew three chapters here. "And our RC of course, Road."

When Swift was introduced, I saw a few curious eyes land on her. I was doubtful myself until I'd met her, but now I know she's worthy of the Satan's Devils' patch, and with Drummer's own endorsement, I doubt any man would say anything against her. When I see the hard-nut Blade salute her, I realise she's been accepted by the club.

Introductions over, Drummer tugs at his beard. "As if any of you need an update, I'll sum up fast. Lost here has lost a member and his ol' lady, and Red's found out another club is stepping on his territory and in ways he doesn't like. This has become Satan's Devils' business." He pauses, then uses that steely gaze for which he's famed. "We're going to war, Brothers. If any chapter thinks this isn't their fight, you're welcome to stand up and get out."

Demon lazily stretches back on his chair, his long arm reaching out so it rests on the back of the adjacent seat. "Wouldn't be here if we hadn't already decided you weren't going to leave us out. Been far too quiet recently." Leaning forward and reaching around with his free hand, he bumps fists with Beef.

Snatcher, his posture contradictory and not at all relaxed, sits forward. "We might not have always played nicely with other chapters, but we're changing that. We're one hundred percent with you, that's if you want us."

"Need you, more fuckin' like," Lost states. "I'm kinda hoping that plane of yours has come stocked."

"Sure has." Preacher grins widely. "Got a whole bunch of toys you might find useful." He nods at Drummer. "Got Tucson's shit here as well. We've got enough explosives to blow the fuckin' Pentagon up."

"Along with our expertise," Swift puts in matter-of-factly. "May I, Drummer?"

The mother chapter prez looks a bit flummoxed by the request from the only female at the table, but his mouth quirks, and he raises his chin in permission.

Swift opens her laptop. "The Crazy Wolves compound is housed in an old religious retreat. We were able to find some floor plans of when it was in use. There's a large central building. The ground floor was used for worship, refectory, recreational area and kitchens which we assume the Crazy Wolves use as their clubroom. The upper floor was a dormitory, and probably used for similar purposes now. It's laid out in a quadrangle, and has an odd little quirk that was some sort of tower where we think there are more rooms. There are out buildings, but we don't know…" she pauses, taps at her laptop, stares at the screen, then taps again. Then she chooses to enlighten us. "Got more info coming in. Stormy went straight to the locality and arrived a few minutes ago. He's already sent up a drone. We're just trying to analyse the imagery."

"Want our IT experts in on it?" Drummer offers.

"Yeah, later, perhaps," Swift says offhandedly. "We've got it for now."

Snatcher leans over to her and says something under his breath. She looks surprised, then shakes her head. "There are several outbuildings in various states of repair. One, looks like their garage. Stormy's seen wheel tracks. One of the barn-like structures is interesting." She uses her fingers to enlarge the screen and studies it. "There seems to be a guard standing outside of it."

I sit up sharply. "Does he think that's where they've got Niran and Saffie?"

Swift looks up and meets my eyes, and there's a flash of recognition in them, tinged with sympathy. "Could be Niran. But with Saffie being the VP's property, it's likely she'd be housed either with or near him."

"It's the middle of the fuckin' night," Red observes. "How the fuck can you see? Or is this old shit?"

"It's real time," she confirms. "Stormy's using a drone equipped with night vision."

"So they're guarding something twenty-four hours," Peg puts in. "Something they don't want getting free."

"My money is on that's where we'll find Niran." Mace shares his view which coincides with mine. I send him a chin lift. "That's what we should aim to hit."

"I'm not so sure," Swift contradicts. "It seems too easy."

"I prefer multiple points of attack," Thor offers.

"I agree," Beef says. "But apart from rescuing Niran, what's the game plan? We doing an extraction, or taking the bastards out?"

Drummer raises an eyebrow and looks toward Red who's waggling his fingers indicating he wants to talk.

Red glances first at Crash who gives him a nod, leading me to guess they've already discussed their approach. He takes a breath. "Satan's Devils and Crazy Wolves haven't much crossed paths. They keep themselves to themselves. But learning they're forcing women into prostitution, and in my town, is something that doesn't settle easy with me."

"Or any of us," Crash reinforces.

"That'll be one whole barrel full of bad apples," Snatcher observes. "Crazy Wolves are a fuckin' dirty club."

"Yeah, and we've got a chance to wipe them all out. Question is, are we going to take it?" Red raises an eyebrow.

Drummer raps the table with his fingers, and gives a sharp nod acknowledging what Red had just said. "To some extent, we might not have a choice. But in the event we've got options, Brothers, what's the fuckin' preference? Go in on a dedicated mission just to get Niran and his woman out. Make it clean and quick if we can with collateral damage only, or take out the officers and hope the rest of the club falls apart—"

"Or," Swift interrupts. "We put down the whole damn nest of vipers."

When Drummer's eyes meet hers, he gives a smirk as if not used to being cut off mid-sentence, and is quite amused by it, then he raises his chin.

"You want twenty deaths or more on your conscience?"

Demon lazily asks, seemingly more out of interest than actually raising an objection. "Some of the members could be persuaded there are better ways of life."

"Will we have a choice?" Lost poses the question, which Drummer had just alluded to. "With their numbers, even a well-planned in-and-out operation is risky. I'd be happier if we discussed every scenario."

"Plans A to Z?" Salem quips with a chuckle.

I smile myself. That's our prez for you. Mind you, his attention to detail has saved our asses before.

Blade spins his knife on the table, the movement catching all our eyes. When he sees he's got our attention, he stops the spinning action with the blade pointing at Swift. "You were in the SAS?"

"Not quite," she confirms with a grimace. "But I qualified."

"Went through all the training?" At this she raises her chin before dipping it again. "Hostage extraction from hostile territory?" She shrugs as if of course she has. "Then I'm happy if you give us your ideas."

"You're advocating putting Swift in charge?" Drummer challenges, his eyebrows knitting together as he stares at his enforcer.

Blade grins widely. "Kinda ironic a woman taking a bunch of misogynistic white supremacists out. I'd fuckin' love to see their faces."

His comment attracts a few snorts and more than one laugh.

Drummer exchanges meaningful glances with Red, Demon and Lost, then drums his fingers once more. "Okay, Brothers," he says, leaning forward and clasping his hands. "In true Devils' fashion, we thrash everything out. Plans A to fuckin' Z if that's what it takes." He raises his chin to Lost, showing he approves of his approach. "Then once we've settled, Swift takes the lead and directs all resources on the ground." He pauses to wipe a hand over his beard. "We need someone who can react and react fast, and someone who can multi-task, a virtue us poor males are said to be lacking. Anyone against?"

Again, there are snorts of amusement, but none of derision.

I grin, momentarily thinking of telling this story to any future grandkids I'm lucky enough to have. *And that, kids, is how a woman came to lead the charge of the Satan's Devils and take the Crazy Wolves out.* And, of course, all to rescue a Black member.

Satan's Devils have changed over the past few years and all for the better.

The next hour is spent going over how we might approach mission, *free Niran and Saffie*. I don't think we end up with twenty-six plans, but we're not far off of it. Swift's on her toes, knocking ideas down if they have no merit, and sifting through those that have. Her experience and insight is fucking useful, and I doubt I'd be the only one to admit that. I'm also grateful that she's on our side.

Finally, when we all have some semblance of what's expected of us, we call it a night.

Drummer bangs the gavel. "Alright. That's it for now. We leave first thing in the morning. Get some rest, Brothers. Fuck, drink, make merry or do what the hell you like."

He doesn't need to say it, but this might be the last night for some of us.

CHAPTER TWELVE

Niran

"We're trapped." Saffie hisses. "Is this your plan? 'Cause at the moment, I don't think much of it."

I have no time to mollify her or admit to her I haven't got the faintest idea how I'm going to get us out. All I know is Slit was going to rape her, and I had to stop him. Now, anyone coming to check will find a dead body and both her and I missing. Fuck.

"Stay here, throw the bolt and lock the door after me."

"Where are you going?" Her eyes widen. "You can't leave me here alone, Niran. Sooner or later, they'll come looking for Slit, find his body and…" After a pause, she continues, her voice shrill but still hushed, "They'll tear me limb from limb. Slit's their sergeant-at-arms."

"You'll be okay," I try to impress on her. "No one would think to search here. The room's locked and you wouldn't have a key. Hide under the bed. If they do come in, they'll only give it a cursory look to confirm it's empty." I cross my fingers behind my back. It sounds flimsy even to me.

Unconvinced, she challenges me. "And what will you be doing? Saving your own ass?"

Her mistrust in me is chilling. Hissing myself, I approach her, backing her against the wall. "You don't fuckin' know me at all, do you, Saffie? I'm a fuckin' Marine. I *never* leave a woman or man behind." I wait a beat for that to sink in. "I'm unarmed, I need a gun. I need to find a way to get you out of here. I'm going out, but I will be back."

How I'm going to do that I have zero ideas at present. I might be a Marine, but I'd slipped up. In my haste to get Saffie out of the room, I'd forgotten to search Slit for weapons. I need to go back, and before someone comes looking for him. When they open that door, they'll be out for blood. I'm banking on having whatever time they'll allow for Slit to take his pleasure. I'm unable, of course, to be able to rank him on his past performance or guess how many minutes they'll give him. That they haven't come already means the security camera isn't working, or that no one's checked the footage. But if it's the latter, time's fast running out.

Still unconvinced, Saffie's eyes shoot to the door. "Take me with you. I know the clubhouse and where the exits are."

"I can't do that." I'm growing frustrated. "Hell, Saffie. What excuse could I offer for walking you about? And I'm fuckin' unarmed."

"My clothes are torn," she says fast. "It could look like Slit's finished with me. There's a barn out back where they keep girls before moving them on. Tell them Duke's going to make a whore of me. Most would believe that."

It's more than I've come up with. "Will that work?"

She grimaces. "It depends who we see. There's no chance if we meet Duke, or Knife, Slit, Croak and Grit, who know how important I am to their VP, maybe even to the whole club. I'm a fucking money cow it seems. But I don't know about the other members. They might believe."

"It's too risky," I respond fast, grimacing at the long list of names. "Or at least, until I'm armed."

She hisses like a cat. "If you go, I'll follow you. You're not leaving me here like a sitting duck."

"Just let me go find a weapon first," I plead with her. I can't even guarantee Slit walked into her room armed. He might not have as a precaution. All I know is I feel naked as a fucking newborn baby without a gun. I'm not afraid to use my fists to defend myself, but that's only one-on-one. I'd be a fool to think I could take on the whole club.

Her face is set. It looks like no amount of pleading will help. I eye her carefully. Her face is red, blotchy with weeping, and the eye which was closed yesterday but open earlier is swollen shut once more. If Slit wasn't already dead, I'd kill him again, and this time take my time over it.

I'm just about to capitulate when heavy footsteps sound right outside the door. Putting a finger to my lips, I unnecessarily admonish her to be quiet.

The footsteps start again and move away. I hear a knocking from a distance, and then a voice calling out, "Duke? You in there?"

A pause, then the footsteps return. Saffie's eyes widen as they again stop, and we hear a heavy rapping on the opposite door.

"Slit?" Then after a pause, "Sapphire? Bitch, answer me. Slit still in there?" Heavy knocks sound again, then what I interpret as a kick. "Bitch, I take it he's gone. You staying dumb ain't going to do shit, just sayin'."

The footsteps move away, back down the corridor, but halt far too soon.

"Hey, anyone seen the nigger? He's s'posed to be here."

"What you need, Croak?" a muffled voice shouts up the stairs.

"I'm looking for Slit. Knife wants him." the man at the top calls down.

"Slit's probably still in with the bitch. Duke told him to take his time." My hand covers Saffie's mouth before her indignant gasp escapes.

"Nah, well I knocked, but no one fuckin' answered."

The man he was speaking to presumably climbs the stairs, as his voice is clearer now. "Bitch probably wore him out. Perhaps they're taking a nap."

"My fuckin' knocking would have woken the dead."

"Well, go in and look."

"Fuckin' hell!" the first man roars. "Whatcha think I want the nigger for? He's got the fuckin' key."

Damn, damn, and fucking damn. I should have taken her and run. We might have lost our chance now. One thing she was right about is here, we're trapped.

Knocking begins again on the door of the room she was kept in.

"She's either fuckin' dead or refusing to talk." I identify Croak's voice again.

"I think we should break the fuckin' door down and check," the other man says.

"Yeah, Slinger?" Croak barks a laugh. "Then we'd have to go to the bother of fixing it up again. Fuck, she's probably passed out from enjoying too much of Slit's attentions. You know how he likes to choke a bitch."

There's a snort. "Didn't think of that. You're probably right."

There's nothing for a second, then, "She's got to still be in there. He's hardly likely to take her out for exercise like a fuckin' dog."

"Who knows with Slit?" Slinger replies. "He's a crazy fucker, 'specially with bitches."

Croak's the one to snort now. "You can say that again. Come on, Sling, let's get downstairs and ask if anyone's seen him. Knowing him, he probably beat the shit out of the VP's ol' lady and now he's taken the nigger off to have some fun with him."

"Yeah." Slinger's voice sounds brighter now. "In that case, let's see where he's at. I've got a few lessons I want to teach that Black fucker myself."

Croak laughs loudly. "Can you fuckin' believe he thought we'd let him patch in?"

As their voices fade, a few more insults at my expense come to my ears.

"Guess you know now," Saffie says drily. "The Wolves are a Whites-only club."

"You think?" Relief the danger has passed for now, I wink. "I kinda came to that conclusion myself." Quickly, I get back to business. "It's only a matter of time until they come back. We need to try to get out, Saffie."

"So I can come with you now?" She rolls her eyes.

"Jeez, woman." I can't leave her here, though I've doubts about us getting successfully away. "You gonna be able to run if we need to?"

She gives me a determined nod even though I know she still must be sore from the beatings she received yesterday and on top of that, whatever Slit did to her earlier. But she confirms it with words. "I can run."

Knowing our situation's far from ideal, I've no plan and no information to formulate one, I have to rely on her. "Okay. Tell me what you know. What's the best way to get out?"

Her brow creases. "Not down the main staircase. But there's a fire escape the other way."

That sounds promising if we can get to it. I ease to the door and put my ear against it. When I hear nothing, I crack it open. *All clear.* When I beckon, she steps up close behind me, but tugs on my shirt, making me look down.

"I'd rather die than stay here." Her expression, the set of her eyes, the determination in the way her jaw is clenched, makes me believe it's not a casual statement. She truly means it.

I fully comprehend. On my part, I'd rather be killed escaping than tortured to death like their new plaything. I respond with an up and down of my chin, and a look of understanding passes between us. Taking the lead, I step out.

My body is tense, my muscles prepared for anything. We reach the corner I've not yet searched around. Craning my head, I rectify that now. At the end is a door with glass panels, and beyond I can see the fire escape that she mentioned. Better still, there's no one standing between us and it.

I don't need to tell her to be quiet, as we make our way over to the exit. Rather than immediately reaching for the bar and pressing down, I check for signs of an alarm. Relieved when I don't find any, I open it.

It's a metal staircase, so I take it cautiously, even so my weight makes it knock and clang against the building.

Scanning the area around the bottom, I notice a window to the left, so ease down to the right of it. Reaching back to take Saffie's hand, I pull her to join me, then take a moment to get the lay of the land.

In the distance, there's a tree line, but a large area of scrubland is between us and it. To the right of us are old farm buildings. Just as I'm deciding to run for them first to use as cover, a man rounds the corner of the building.

He looks as surprised to see us as we are to see him. Both he and I react fast, but he's the one with the gun. Stopping midstride, I've no option but to put up my hands.

We've no chance. We're going to be captured. I'll die, and Saffie will be tortured for the rest of her life. Remembering our pact made moments earlier, I give her the only instruction I can—the one chance to make it out of this life one way or another.

"Run, Saffie!" Inside I'm screaming, knowing her chances are next to none.

I try. I fucking try. The next few seconds seem to happen in slow motion. I launch myself at him, she runs, he aims, I deflect his shot and it goes wide. He tosses me off and takes aim again.

"No!" Uncaring about the danger, I twist my body in midair, my one thought to stop him shooting her long enough to give her a chance to get away.

But this man is fast, military trained if I'm not mistaken, and not one of the slow overweight members I'd seen in the club. He tackles me. I fight back, him trying to keep and me trying to gain possession of the gun. He kicks and hits my prosthesis. It flies from under me, bringing me down. Then he pistol-whips me for good measure.

He fires before I can recover. To my horror, Saffie falls to the ground and lies unmoving.

Stunned, I can't believe what I'm seeing. *Saffie's gone.* I try to tell myself it's what she wanted, but that's no consolation. My brain's having difficulty processing what's in front of my eyes, failing to acknowledge I've lost my chance to hold her, to touch her, to kiss her and make love. I'll never speak to her again for the rest of my probably short life. The shorter the better as far as I'm concerned. Maybe there is an afterlife, and we can be together.

I've failed. Fuck, how I've failed. Instead of saving her, she's dying or dead. Dazed and distraught, I lie stunned, quickly losing my chance at moving when the gunman drops his two-hundred-and-fifty-pound weight onto my chest.

Kneeling on me, holding his pistol to my head, he yells for help.

I hear multiple pairs of boots running toward us, and an exclamation from a voice I recognise. Croak, one of the men who'd been talking outside the room we were hiding in and the man who'd killed Kid.

Shading his eyes from the sun with his hand, he gazes toward Saffie who'd managed to run a fair distance away. "Is she dead, Slinger?" he asks, disinterestedly.

The man kneeling on me, Slinger, shrugs. "I aimed for the head."

He sounds so confident of his marksmanship that that, together with the fact I hadn't seen her moving, takes away my last hope. Oh Saffie. *At least she's at peace.* No one can hurt her now. And it's better than her lying injured as no one seems to be checking.

Next, he turns his attention to me. His eyes narrow, then he shouts to someone else. "Go check the bitch's room. Find Slit, now." Then he looks down at me. "You leave him alive, you filthy motherfucker?" When I don't answer, he shrugs. "Well, I guess we'll soon find out." His eyes go to the top of the fire escape where some of his brothers have just climbed up. After a moment he straightens, and just like Croak had previously done, shields his eyes from the sun.

"Slit's dead," a strangled voice cries out.

Slinger looks down at me, his face contorted with rage. "That's your fucking death warrant, nigger."

That was never a question. What matters more is Saffie. "Sapphire." I use the name they know her by. "Please check her." I still can't accept that she's gone. If she had, wouldn't my own heart stop beating? I hang on to the thought that she's injured instead, and hopefully not fatally. But if so, someone needs to help.

"I went for a fuckin' head shot. I never miss." Slinger scoffs, brimming with confidence and no remorse that he shot an unarmed woman and is leaving her for dead.

A new voice enters the equation. *It's their prez.* "Leave the bitch. I'm fed up to the teeth with her. She's the VP's. He'll have to deal with her when he gets back. If by a slim chance, given she was shot by Slinger, she's alive, she won't get far, and certainly won't reach the perimeter. You, on the other hand." He kicks viciously at my leg. "You've got a fuckin' lot to answer for,

Boy." Then to Slinger, Knife says, "Get him up and bring him along."

The man pinning me down slowly gets off, dragging me up with one arm. As I'm vertical, blood starts to trickle from a deep cut over my eyes. But they don't care I'm half blinded as someone else grabs my other arm.

I dig in my heel and try to balance on the prosthesis that's been kicked out of true, but I can't stop them from starting to drag me away.

Croak hangs back. He seems fascinated with Saffie. "Just in case, Prez, want me to let the dogs out?"

Knife scoffs. "Can't hurt. If she is, they'll bring her down if she tries to get away."

No, no, no, and no. Half of me hopes Saffie's dead and out of this misery already, but the other half won't give up on the hope that she's still alive. But in any event, she's been shot. She'll have no chance unless she gets medical help right now. And they're setting dogs on her.

I struggle, futilely trying to get free if only to run over to her and see if she's in the land of the living, but they're equally determined not to set me free. Twisting my head shows me she's lying face down, but there's no detectable movement, and she's making no sound.

Inside, a rage rushes through me, but the men holding me are too strong. I bellow her name, no longer having to pretend she means nothing to me.

"Saaafffffiiiieeee!"

With my head thrown back, my eyes are caught by an object glinting in the sun. I look back down immediately, my brain recognising it as some kind of drone, and not wanting to draw attention to it.

Would this club have one patrolling its own ground? Possibly it's one of Grit's toys, but unlikely. If it was, Knife could have used it to check on Saffie. What's more likely to be on the cards is that it's Devils coming to rescue me.

But they're too fucking late. Although I want to deny it, Saffie is gone.

I heard the shot, saw her fall, and since then, there's been no movement.

Fuck. My Saffie. My old lady.

CHAPTER THIRTEEN

Grumbler

By the time Drummer had wound up the meeting, it was late in the evening. Though my initial impulse was to wait no longer and head straight out to rescue Niran and Saffie, most of us had been travelling all day, and to be at our best, needed to reboot our bodies and get a good night's rest. I knew that myself. My leg was aching, and the yawns I couldn't suppress betrayed my own tiredness.

I caught up with a few old friends, traded stories with Thunder, Indian, Peg and Preacher. Whatever state we're from, being a sergeant-at-arms is fairly standard fare, and our complaints are all similar. Preacher came in for a bit of a grilling, but apart from the fact he pilots the Utah plane, his role is surprisingly familiar.

True to our role, most of us spend the night glancing around, checking on our own club members, but none of them seem to be drinking too much. Mind you, having the five of us glaring on is enough to put most people off overindulging.

Sleeping bags are brought in and start being laid on the floor. I bid my fellow sergeant-at-arms a goodnight and start walking across the clubroom to collect mine off my bike. I pause once outside in the dark, stare up at the star-studded sky and think about my old lady. I'd called her when I'd first arrived, of course, as I didn't want her worrying, then again straight after the meeting, knowing she'd be waiting for my goodnight call, and not wanting her to stay up late on my account. In both she'd assured me she was fine.

I told her I loved her, and during the second, that I'd see her tomorrow, or failing that, no more than a day later. As I'd ended the call, it felt good having a woman like her waiting for me. Both her and my baby. While I can't influence fate, I'll take care like I'd promised and try my fucking hardest to return to her.

Shaking off thoughts of what could go wrong, I collect my sleeping bag and return inside.

"Grumbler."

I turn at Lost's voice.

He leans in close. "Prezes have been given a room. Want to share?"

And spend the night on a mattress and not a hard floor? Fuck, yeah. "What about Dart?" As VP, his claim is prior.

"Dart's suggestion," Lost offers. "He said us old-timers should bunk down together."

Another time, another place, and I'd have bristled about having my age pointed out, but hell, I am old and tonight feel my age, and I'm not too proud to admit it. These old bones would likely let me know all about it come morning were I to sleep on a hard floor.

The bed's at least king-size, more than enough for me and the prez to each have our space.

"Miss Mary?" he asks, as he turns off the light.

"Like fuck. You Patsy?"

"Like I'm missing a limb, Brother." Lost sighs and pumps his pillow, trying to get comfortable.

"Do me a favour, Prez?"

"Yeah. What?"

"Just don't reach out for her in the night, Brother."

Lost snorts. "G'Night, Grumbler."

It's hard to sleep in an unfamiliar bed, and with a man who snores. I try not to toss and turn, which seems to make matters worse. When noise awakes me, it feels like I've only just dropped off.

The clubhouse doesn't come to life with a quiet murmur, it bursts into it with a roar. From downstairs comes loud sounds of voices, shouts, bursts of laughter, and many pairs of feet stomping past our door.

Sitting, balancing back on his hands, Lost glances at me. "This is it, Grumbler."

"Yeah." I scratch at my chest, then start pulling on my pants. "Let's go get our brother."

Rosa must have called catering in again, as a breakfast feast is already laid out when I get downstairs.

The mood is one of anticipation—men bouncing on their feet, eager to get underway and go rescue their Satan's Devils' brother. Last-minute plans are discussed, copious cups of coffee are drunk, and the place thrums with the sound of cutlery scraping against plates.

As I stand, chomping on bacon, Red comes up alongside me.

"Niran and you are particularly close, aren't you?"

"Can't deny it." I raise my chin at the Vegas prez. "He stepped up when I had to step back. He's a good fucker, Red. He deserves this." I wave my hand around the room. "He deserves all of us."

"As any of us do, Brother." He winks. "Which seems to be my cue."

Another of his ear-piercing whistles that makes me wish I wasn't standing so close, then, when he's got everyone's attention, he launches into a rousing cry. "Ride Satan's Devils. Satan's Devils Ride together."

The battle cry immediately taken up from all sides makes my rheumy eyes water. As men thump their fists over their hearts, I remind myself, *this is what this life stands for.* We ride and live free, and when necessary, we all come together.

While forty or so riders travelling together is certainly not unknown, we decided to depart Vegas in smaller groups, not wanting to arouse suspicion nor the attention of the cops. Especially not since we are armed to the gills. As for the two crash trucks, well, I'd been mightily impressed by the toys Preacher had brought in his plane, along with Slick's and Viper's. I wasn't the only sergeant-at-arms to have his eyes glistening with excitement, not having seen such heavy artillery or explosives since I gave my all to Uncle Sam. They've even got a fucking grenade launcher.

Drummer takes pole position, and, as the most interested parties, Lost and Red head out with the first group, along with their officers, me included. The first to arrive, I waste only a moment rubbing my leg before dismounting my bike and heading for the truck that Stormy had driven in yesterday from Utah.

The back doors open, and Drummer, Lost and Red step inside. Without asking permission, taking the "forgiveness later" route, I, too, push my way in, immediately enthralled by the high-tech interior. *Token's going to go ape when he sees this.*

"Hey, I'm Stormy." The man sitting behind a row of monitors spares just a second to twist his head around. "This is Gears." He indicates the man beside him. Whether he hears the reciprocal introductions I have no idea, as he doesn't acknowledge them, just focuses his attention to the front once again.

I don't mind rudeness if it finds us Niran.

The sound of motorcycles roaring then sudden silence alerts me that the next group have just ridden in.

"Storm, whatcha got, Brother?"

As I'm jostled, I make way for Snatcher to squeeze into the tight space behind me, then find I'm flattened against Lost's side as Preacher loads himself up as well.

"Got two drones up," Stormy talks without turning. "Gears has mapped what we think are weak spots, and places we may gain entry. We think," he points to the middle screen in front of him, "that most of the members are here, in the main part of the clubhouse."

"Two men rode out earlier this morning, they haven't come back. No other comings and goings since daylight," the aforesaid Gears remarks. "If they work, it looks like it's all onsite."

So it sounds like they're all in their lair, except for the two who had ridden out. Lucky for them, they could be the only survivors.

"Easy money trading in women and guns," Preacher snarls. "Doubt they earn legit, and most drug dealing is done in the evenings."

Ignoring that comment, Drummer asks, "What about the outbuilding that you said was guarded?"

Now positioned so I have a sideways view of Stormy's face, I see him wince and his jaw tighten. "They got a delivery last night. Two girls were dragged kicking and screaming from a truck that pulled up in front of that building." Stormy adjusts the screen so the one he mentioned is in plain sight. "After that, there was a steady stream of members going in and out."

Snatcher curses. "They're trying out the new girls? Making sure they're ready to get to work?"

Stormy gives a grim nod. "That's my reading of it. Or just using them for their own entertainment."

"You think Saffie's being held there?" The thought makes me feel sick, but I still have to ask.

Again, Stormy grimaces. "Can't say one way or another. She's supposedly Duke's, but who knows with perverts like them, he might..." His voice trails off but I easily fill in the blanks.

"It doesn't matter," Snatcher says. "We're getting all the

women out. It will make our job easier if she's not in the main building."

"Sure," Preacher says enthusiastically. "We can just blow that shit up."

"Not with Niran inside," I snarl.

"No sign of him as yet," Gears says moving a mouse, switching from screen to screen.

"Last group have just come in," a man states from behind me.

"Make way, give me some space," a voice behind him demands.

Turning, I see Demon, and try to make myself smaller, not wanting to be chucked out. But it's actually Red who gives up his place to him.

No one seems to know what to do when Swift is the last to squeeze herself in, but she doesn't give us a moment to feel awkward about crowding her.

"Preach," she asks. "You got your equipment sorted?"

"Will have in a moment." Last night, I and the other sergeants-at-arms had all agreed to let the Utah sergeant-at-arms take the lead. He knows what his equipment is capable of. "Gears, come outside and help me get shit unloaded."

There's a bit of jostling as we move to let him out. I feel like I should leave too to make some room, but on the other hand, want to stay here in the thick of things.

"Lost…"

"Stay," my prez tells me, his eyes meeting mine. "You know Niran better than any of us. We might need your insight when formulating a rescue plan."

Or body extraction, echoes in my mind.

Drummer's studying the screen. "We go with the original plan. Plant a few firecrackers to get their attention, show them we've got the upper hand."

"Then, if possible, Swift will start the negotiation," Snatcher completes for him, catching first my eye, then hers. "We'll get the girl and brother free, then move in and take them down."

I raise my chin, having developed a respect for Swift, but I've one thing to mention. Gesturing generally to the screens in front of Stormy, I explain, "Don't forget they're a bunch of fuckin' misogynists."

Turning briefly, Stormy grins at me. "And that's the point. They won't know how to deal with Swift. They'll believe they're running rings around her."

"What's that?" At Drummer's words, Stormy's attention snaps back to one of the screens.

"Well fuck." Stormy leans in closer, and I try to peer over his shoulder. *Is that…?* He continues, "Looks like they're rescuing themselves. I take it that's Niran?"

My heart rate speeds up. "It fuckin' is," I confirm, watching the pair inch down the fire escape. "And that's Saffie."

"There's nowhere for them to go," Swift observes, pushing in closer. "There's no fuckin' cover. Bloody hell, what are they thinking?"

"We're not in fucking place yet." Snatcher sounds agonised. "Preacher's setting it up now. They've moved too soon."

I think we're going to have a swift change of plans and one we hadn't anticipated. "Then we go in all guns blazing, now." Even as the words leave my mouth, I know it's useless, as unbeknown to Niran, he'll be spotted any moment by a man who seems to be doing a circular tour of the main building. *Why didn't you wait, Brother?* I scream internally. We haven't even got snipers on the ground.

It's like a nightmare. Everything seems to slow down and to happen in slow motion, yet at the same time in a blur. The man comes upon Niran, Saffie runs, a gun is raised. Niran leaps and there's a fight for the weapon, but Niran goes down. The man aims, fires, and Saffie hits the ground.

Stormy hovers the drone, but she's lying, face down, unmoving. After a collective gasp goes around, he repositions the drone to focus on Niran. Other men now surround him, and he's being dragged away. He puts up a good fight but is heavily outnumbered. His prosthesis is kicked out from under him, and when he falls to the ground, he's punched, kicked, then carted away.

"Where the fuck are they taking him?" Drummer, having pushed his way back to the front, leans his hands on the back of Stormy's chair. "Follow him, man."

Despite a visual clenching of his jaw, Stormy doesn't protest that he knows what he's doing and it's exactly that. We follow Niran's progress until they disappear into the clubhouse.

"He's dead unless we go now," I observe, bouncing on my heels. My elation at seeing Niran alive was short lived.

"Is the girl dead?" Red asks.

Having lost sight of Niran, Stormy again moves the drone back to where it was. "She's not moving, and no one's gone to fuckin' check her."

"Confident bastard who took the shot," Red observes.

"Or," I say coldly, "they don't care whether she's dying or dead. Oh fuck… what's that?"

"Fuckin' dogs," Snatcher confirms, then sighs heavily. "Fuck but I hate shooting dogs."

Said dogs are now hovering near Saffie, presumably making sure if she's capable of moving, she's no option other than to stay in place.

Preacher suddenly appears behind us. "Take these." He begins to pass earbuds out. "Two-way communications, on separate channels for different teams. Stormy will handle the comms and patch through as necessary. He'll be able to keep us updated…"

But the man in question stands, reaches out his hand and, opening and closing it, demands one of the earbuds for himself. "Gears is taking over. I'm on the front line, Brother."

Snatcher rolls his eyes but doesn't protest.

"That kid know what he's doing?" Drummer asks sharply, staring at the man who's now in command of the monitors.

"Gears is as good as Stormy," Snatcher reassures him. "He'll be fine as our eyes."

"Hey," Gears says as he takes the seat Stormy's just vacated, pointing again to the middle screen. "Check out the girl."

"She hasn't moved," I tell him dismissively.

"Nah, and she won't if she's got any sense. Not with the canines they've got on her." Gears gives a quick grin over his shoulder. "But no one's bothered to check her, and I can't see any blood." He zooms in closer. "See? No entry or exit wound on her back or head."

Doesn't mean she wasn't shot, but even so, my heart starts beating faster.

Lost gives me a quick glance before stating adamantly, "If she's breathing, we'll be getting her out."

If she's alive and is playing possum, we might. Though I have my doubts as to whether she is. If she's alive, what's her plan? To wait for dark and make a run for it? She must know even the Crazy Wolves won't leave a dead body lying around for long.

"She's fuckin' moving," Drummer suddenly snarls, lurching forward. "Goddammit! Will you look at that? One of the fuckin' guard dogs just licked the hand she held out."

She's lived on the compound for five years. Among this lot, I wouldn't be surprised if she'd made friends with the dogs. "You think they'd protect her?"

"Can't tell, Brother, but I don't get the vibe they regard her as lunch."

As I continue to watch, I tend to agree with Drummer. Then, I hold my breath as she moves slightly. Only an inch or two, but it's toward the perimeter. "Looks like she's planning to try and crawl her way out."

I'm just amazed and thankful we've seen both of them

breathing. It makes me think there's a chance of this rescue working.

"We've got to go there now!" I shout. I turn, catching Swift's eyes who nods at me.

She doesn't waste time. "Comms open? Right. Group one. Hostage extraction—wait for me. Group two. Distraction. Get in place now. Group Three, head for the woman. Group four, sniper team and covering fire, confirm you're in position."

The speaker in front of Gears bursts into life with the confirmation.

That Saffie's alive, though maybe not uninjured is the miracle that spurs us on. Almost comically, we squeeze our way out of the truck, fitting the earbuds into our ears. All at once, I get a cacophony of sound and I take it straight out again and look at it in disgust.

"All mics are currently open," Stormy comes over, holding his device. "Gears will be handling the comms along with Igor and Brute." He points to two prospects climbing into the truck we've just exited. "After that, it's only the team leaders who'll be able to transmit and receive, unless we need to hear from someone else. Give them a moment to sort it." He looks back inside the truck, narrows his eyes and watches for a moment, then turns back and says with a nod, "Try again now."

This time, it's only Preacher's voice I'm hearing.

With my mind off my ears, I start looking around, seeing men forming teams. I head Dart's way to join the team that's providing the distraction as has already been decided. I'd lost my wish to be in the vanguard myself, heading the charge to get Niran out.

Stormy prods my arm. "Change of plan. You're with me and Peg. Swift wanted a second team to go in. And don't forget this." He hands me a Kevlar vest. Putting it on, I realise I'm the last man not sporting one.

I'm ecstatic with the change of plan. I toss him a grateful

look, but add in a growl, "Still fuckin' suspicious of you, *Brother*."

Stormy snorts seeming unoffended, then leads the way to where Peg is standing.

Peg must notice me favouring my left leg. "You okay to walk? We'll drive in as far as we can but may well have to traverse some ground."

Knowing Peg himself has a prosthetic leg, I'm determined not to show myself up having two made of flesh and blood, even if one's not working great right now. "I'll be fine. Got stiff riding yesterday," I reassure him. And I'd crawl if it meant Niran and Saffie will soon be safe and sound.

"Then let's get fuckin' moving," Peg calls out, pointing to the bikes.

As I mount up and move to join them, I realise I know fuck all of the plan as this wasn't supposed to be my team. Swift's voice sounds in my ears, and presumably those of everyone riding.

"Explosives team. Slick, Pyro, Viper, Bolt, and Curtis, you ready to get into position?"

"Yeah, just waiting for covering fire," or various versions come from five voices.

"And we," ahead I notice Preacher, taking his eyes off the road for a moment, turning and grinning at the men behind him, "will soon be starting the attack."

"Right behind you," Peg says.

"Right with you, Brother, snipers and covering fire about to get into place." That's Thor's voice, I'm certain.

Gears must be having fun toggling the comms channels, but as we ride, I get the gist of the amended plan. With time being of the essence, now Niran's walked straight into their hands, we won't be needing Swift for her negotiation skills. Time for talking has passed. The first attack will be fuckin' mortars firing, getting the Crazy Wolves to keep their heads down. Then the explosives will be planted, set strategically to seriously damage the clubhouse, but hopefully not bring the whole place down. Just enough to get the wolf pack filing out, right into our loving bullets.

Utah is in charge. They've done this before.

But Niran? Fuck. We're taking a chance that he won't be blown up or used as a human shield.

"We know what we're fuckin' doing," Preacher's voice growls into my ear, and I take it that's in answer to someone else's enquiry. "Yeah, Drummer. We've taken that into account. Our assessment is they'll use Niran as a bargaining chip to leave at least some of them alive."

I can only hope they are right, and that Niran won't suffer for any wrong calls of judgement.

I spare a thought for, and send a mental apology to Mary, waiting at home for me to return. This is a war I'm going into, and one battle I might not be able to walk away from. *Forgive me, sweetheart, if I don't return. Just take care of our baby. I love you both.* I send my prayer on the wind.

About to take on the Crazy Wolves in their lair, we'll be lucky if we go home with as many bodies breathing as we've had riding in.

Mary, if I don't survive, just know that I tried. I wouldn't willingly leave you and our baby.

Leaning my weight to the right, I kick up my stand.

CHAPTER FOURTEEN

Niran

As soon as they knew their sergeant-at-arms was dead, I knew my life would be measured in minutes or hours at best, and those last moments of my life would be painful.

While I'm being dragged into the clubhouse, I remind myself I'm already living on borrowed time. If I hadn't lied to get them to bring me with Saffie, I'd already be dead.

I've failed. I deserve everything I have coming to me. My one reason of stealing those extra hours of life had been with one purpose, to protect Saffie, and now she's dying or dead. They didn't even blink an eye at her body or go over to see how badly she was hurt. Though I hate to think of her no longer breathing, I hope it was fast. The thought of her bleeding out in agonising pain is one I can't stand.

I don't plead for my life, I plead for hers. "Please, check Sapphire."

It's not the first time those words have come out of my mouth, nor the first time they've been ignored either. Instead, Croak just rechecks the bindings he's tied around my wrists, making sure they're tight. The fact my hands are going white should have given him a visual clue.

"Shut up talking about the bitch," Knife drawls lazily. "I doubt she survived. Slinger here is a crack shot. As for you, you're going to have more things to worry about."

"Yeah." Croak chuckles, a sound mimicked by several of his brothers. "Like how much pain you'll be able to take, and how long you'll survive. What d'ya reckon, Brothers?"

"He'll pussy out. He'll beg for a bullet," someone puts in, conversationally.

"Ten says he won't last five minutes." Slinger holds out his hand, and people start dropping money into it.

"Nah," another biker looks on, "he was a Marine. I think we'll be able to play with him longer before he taps out."

"What's the bet?" A different voice asks. "When he'll croak, or when he begs for mercy?"

"Mercy," Slinger clarifies. "He'll beg for death within minutes. But hey, I want to see how long a Black motherfucker can last."

I growl in my throat. "Longer than any of you bitches." I know it's not a good idea to provoke them, but I'm not having them insinuate that the colour of my skin makes me any less of a man. Croak and Slinger might look like they'd give me a run for my money, but most of the rest I could take on with one hand tied behind my back. Unfortunately, having two restrained to the arms of the chair does compromise me a little.

"Should we wait for Duke?" Croak asks.

Knife kicks something on the ground. "Fuckin' Duke, he'll be gone a few hours yet. He's gone to Carson City to work on a new drug deal. That's what he should be fuckin' concentrating on."

"He wanted her alive."

"Pah." Knife only spares him a glance. "Stoat, the VP's blinded by fuckin' pussy. There's more than one way to get the money from the Bartell estate. He's been off the rails for months trying to find the bitch when it would have been easier to take a contract out on her. We off her, then the cousin, then Duke's the only legal beneficiary. Blood line or not, he can fight it in the courts. We'll win one way or another."

"He won't be happy she's dead," Slinger warns.

"Fuck him," Knife says. "I'd have put odds on he'd have killed her himself before impregnating her. Man's fuckin' loco. Anyway, it's the nigger's fault. We'll just have to mess him up enough so Duke's satisfied."

"What do you want us to do here, Prez?" Croak asks, eyeing me up. "Want me to get info from him on the Satan's Devils?"

Knife snorts. "I know all I need to about that pussy-ass club. Weak leaders, weak men. You know they've accepted a woman as a member in one of their clubs?" Snorts of derision go up around him. "As for people like him?" He spits in my face. "They're not even worth worrying about."

"We don't need trouble with the Wretched Soulz," Slinger states warningly. "I know the Satan's Devils mother chapter prez is thought highly of."

Knife stills. Suddenly he whips around and snarls, "You fuckin' questioning me, Sling?" He stares the man down for a moment. "What trouble are we going to cause? This fucker's Black, who's going to give a damn?"

My club, I think to myself, remembering the drone. That had to be them. Maybe they're planning a rescue right now. I've just got to hang on.

But Saffie's gone. And so has my will to survive.

How the fuck did she become my reason to live in such a short time? I never had a chance to show her she was important to me. These last couple of days I'd done more to persuade her she was not. *Did she hate me at the end?* Or had I redeemed myself by getting her out? *Only to get her shot.*

Knowing how I'd fucked up, she must have hated me in

those final moments. In despair, I let my head fall forward.

"We boring you?" Knife yells, forcefully grabbing hold of both of my arms which are tied to the chair.

As he screams into my face, it brings me to my senses. *I can't die. Not while Duke's still alive.* I've vowed to kill the man, to make him suffer just like he made Saffie. It's the last thing I can do for her. Spurred into action, I jerk my head back, smashing it forward hard to connect with his nose. Knife yelps and leaps back, his hands trying to stem the flow of blood.

"You're fucking dead, nigger!" he shouts.

I want to laugh. *He thinks that's news?*

With his nose misshapen and swollen, his watering eyes grow dark. "Get him out of his clothes."

His men leap to follow his command, but they don't untie me. No, they use their sharp knives, some accidentally on-purpose slipping and cutting, making my skin slippery with my own blood. I'm roughly handled, pushed, pulled and shoved until finally I'm as naked as the day I was born.

Knife's eyes go to my groin, and he starts to laugh. "See? It's all rumours. Even mine's longer than his."

My cock, quite sensibly, is particularly shrunken today. And while it's the current focus of jeering and comments, as long as the abuse is verbal, it doesn't matter to me. In the scheme of things, sitting with my parts on display is nothing. And I'm a grower, not a shower, but I don't point that out.

I straighten my shoulders and try to ignore them.

"Get that thing off of him."

My prosthesis is ripped away, and not particularly carefully. I wince when someone stomps on it, shattering the cup, but I don't give my feelings away.

My silence and lack of reaction annoys them. Knife looks at me for a moment, then nods to someone behind me. After that, he steps closer, but learning from before, unfortunately not close enough. "I think you're a man who likes to know what he's up against. So I'm going to tell you exactly how this is going to go down. You killed our sergeant-at-arms, and for that you've earned a death sentence. But you're not going to go easily." He accompanies his words with a punch to my face.

My head reels back. Recovering fast, I just stare at him. What does he think I expect? They're hardly going to pat me on the back and offer me a cup of coffee. They're going to hurt me. I knew that from the moment I was caught. Knowing what's coming can't make it worse, can it?

Knife chuckles. "You see? We're going to break every bone in your body. Every single fucking bone until you're just like fuckin' Humpty Dumpty, and no one's ever going to be able to put you together again."

"He'll flop like a fuckin' fish."

"Here, fishy fishy."

Knife waves his hand to get the bikers around him to shut up, as he continues his mental torture. "But we ain't going to do it fast. We're going to take our time. Every single bone you'll feel break. How many bones in the human body, Weasel?"

"Two hundred and six. But that includes thirty-three or so in the spine. I suggest we break that as one, and leave that to last, else he won't feel the pain."

"Yeah, we can start small and lead up to it. You ready, little fishy?"

"Can we have a go at him first?" Slinger asks, almost petulantly.

Knife snorts and waves him forward. I'm pummelled, kicked, and generally used as a punching bag for a few moments, until Knife calls a halt, stressing he wants me conscious.

A man emerges into my line of sight, and despite my resolve I can take anything they throw at me, I shudder internally at the wooden block he's holding, and the sledgehammer and various other implements he has tucked under his arm.

Knife sees I've noticed and grins with delight, then his

eyebrows knit together and he snarls, "Each blow will be retribution for Slit, you hear me?"

Without further ado, he jerks his head, and two men step forward, taking my one remaining flesh and blood foot. I try to rip it away, but it's tied too tightly, and all I can do is scrunch my toes.

It doesn't help. The block is quickly positioned under it, and a hammer falls without further ado.

Christ that hurts. I swallow my scream as my big toe is shattered. *Fuck, fuck, fuck, fuck!* The pain from stubbing your toe always seems out of proportion to the injury itself, and this is a hundred times worse.

But it's not pain I'm afraid of. My main fear is the damage they'll do to that appendage that's so vital to me. Unless they leave something to repair, I'll be totally crippled.

It won't matter. They're not going to let me live anyway.

I hold it for the second and third toes, the additional agony of the fourth and fifth don't add much more to the pain blasting its way up through my foot. Just when I think it can't get much worse, they swap the hammer for the mallet, and giving up on finesse, bring it down my metatarsals, crushing them all at once. This time I can't hold back the exclamation which serves nothing but to get them excited.

The unnamed man wielding the mallet gets over-excited and strikes my shin. I hear my bones shatter.

"What the hell was that, Spike?" Knife admonishes him. "It was his ankle next."

"Sorry, Prez," the man mumbles, then prepares again.

I brace myself for more pain to come, but before the mallet reaches the zenith of its swing, four explosions go off simultaneously, filling the clubhouse with smoke and dust. The building groans ominously, and parts of the ceiling begin to fall.

"What the fuck?" Knife, hit by a piece of plaster brushes himself off. For a second, he's stunned, then, as flames start licking around the old wooden panelling, he screams out, "We're under attack! Get ready to defend!"

"Defend fuckin' what?" Croak yells, his voice full of panic. "This whole fuckin' place is coming down."

Other Wolves aren't waiting. They're rushing for the door, almost stampeding each other in an effort to escape.

"Calm!" Knife yells, but uselessly. Still, he tries. "Get the motherfuckers, Brothers. We're better than anyone who's coming for us."

As soon as the door opens, gunfire sounds. The doorway is a confusion of men trying to get out to escape the flames and those trying to get back inside.

Another boom sounds from the rear of the building, and all of a sudden, the back wall completely slides down.

I grin, knowing it's the Devils who've come to my rescue, pleased that the Crazy Wolves will be taken out, but sad in the knowledge it will come too late to save me. The way this building is coming down, I'll be buried and smothered if the flames and smoke don't kill me first. *Hold on, Saffie. Wait for me.*

I can go with a smile on my face. Knife and his band of white supremacists have reached the end of the line. If the Devil is coming to get me, I can go out with a smile.

Saffie, my only regret is I didn't avenge you.

Jesus, there's another explosion behind me. In a blind panic, Knife and his Wolves desperately try to make it out. The doorway becomes a bottleneck.

Suddenly, a whole crowd of bodies and body parts come flying into the room, splattering me with blood, and a disembodied hand hits my face. Hell, someone fired something substantial at them, *a mortar, perhaps?* But where the fuck did the Devils get that kind of artillery?

The smoke and dust are getting into my lungs. My leg and foot are throbbing with pain so intense it would be easy to give in and pass out, but I struggle to stay conscious, macabrely wanting to stay alert to see how this plays out.

I'll die happy if I see Knife die painfully.

The president of the Crazy Wolves doesn't seem to know which way to turn. Belatedly, he realises his men are sitting ducks trying to get out the front. Failing to make his voice heard above the gunfire, screams, and shouts, he resorts to physically pulling back his men and turning them around.

Windows at the sides of the building start to be smashed out. Half a dozen Wolves make it through, then rapid gunfire sounds. Their falling bodies serve as a caution for others trying to take that way out.

Despite my discomfort and my imminent death, I take great delight in the massacre going on around me, hoping I'll stay alive. So far, no bullet has come near me, but it's only a matter of time. If I'm not caught by a friendly bullet, some of the Wolves cast glances my way with murder in their eyes, showing they haven't forgotten me.

Crashes and smaller explosions, which make what's still standing of the building shudder, sound from the rear once again. Turning my eyes from the men trying to get out, I twist my head to see what's happening behind me.

Men in leather are swarming in, but not in the haphazard formation of the Wolves. No, these are like some well-oiled machine. A front line of body-armour-clad men carrying rifles drop to their knees allowing the men behind to fire over their heads. Despite the hysterical random firing coming their way, the attackers aren't wasting bullets.

The line is approaching as more and more enemy bodies hit the ground. Not all the attackers are safe though, as I watch in horror more than one man fall to the ground. One, I see, clutching his leg. Not men from my club, they must be from another chapter. I hope he's not hurt too badly and am relieved when he gives a quick shake of his head.

The organised men wearing Kevlar armour continue coming in, handling weapons as though they were an extension of their arms. *We're the best in the business,* I think proudly. Devils have many vets to call on, and in true brotherhood fashion, hadn't lost their skills. Some Wolves might have had the same training, but had become lax with easy money, or the reason for their discharge meant they hadn't possessed the same proficiency in the first place.

They can't get organised, rushing around like headless chickens. Knife might be a leader when it comes to capturing helpless women, but he's got no idea about assembling a fighting force. It's every man for themselves as a killing machine approaches them. Wolves firing blindly, Devils make the most of each shot.

Someone I don't recognise catches a bullet to the shoulder, but he just moves his rifle to his good hand and continues on, taking out the man who shot him, and another after that.

I wince seeing Ink, who I know as he's married to Patsy's daughter, take a bullet to his chest, causing him to double over. Even wearing armour, that will have hurt, but as he falls to his knee, another replaces him.

Wolves run outside, seemingly into an ambush, while those inside continue to drop. *Knife's down. Finished,* I add to myself, seeing his rolled up vacant eyes. I sigh with relief.

Now my attention is caught by two men I do recognise, Pennywise and Salem. Pennywise is a sniper with a record for an impressive long-distance kill shot, but he's equally good at close range I decide, as I watch him accurately putting a couple of the Wolves down.

Then, suddenly Salem is running my way.

"You breathing?" He tosses the words at me over his shoulder as he takes up a position which shields me from the front.

"Yeah. Free my hands and give me a fuckin' gun," I demand.

But to do that means giving his back to the Wolves who now

knowing they can't escape are fighting for the right to survive. Salem himself reels back with a snarl, and red billows on his left arm, while his right continues to return fire.

It seems to go on forever, but slowly Salem is joined by the rest of the attacking line, and I'm now behind instead of in the middle of the confrontation. Shots slowly become more sporadic, and then can be counted in ones not in dozens.

"You okay?" I recognise Pennywise's voice, and moving my head, see the question's not directed at me, but at Salem.

"Winged and fuckin' furious, but I'll live."

Then, at last, I see a knife flash in Pennywise's hands and the zip ties holding my hands fall away. Then, gently, almost tenderly, he does the same to the ones around my thighs and my ankle. Although he tries to be careful, the accidental rotation of my damaged foot makes me lose consciousness for a moment. When I come back to my senses, I see him only wearing his cut over his bare chest, and looking down, see his t-shirt covering my body, stretched down to hide my junk.

Pennywise is crouched, staring at my foot. Sensing I'm back with him, he glances up and winks as he sees me eyeing my new modesty. "Can't have you making all of us jealous." He goes back to examining my injuries. "Fuckin' bastards."

Suddenly my foot becomes the least of my problems. "Saffie," I start, then my voice hitches. "Saffie…" Somehow I can't get out the words that she's dead.

"Saffie?" Pennywise holds up his hand to his ear for a moment. "Yeah, I got Niran. He's got a busted foot. Looks like the fuckers broke all the bones in it. They've got his leg as well… Yeah, I'll tell him."

He meets my eyes again, and grins. "Saffie? Yeah, we got her. She's fine. Covered in dog slobber, but uninjured."

On the verge of losing consciousness again, I narrow my eyes and open my mouth to tell him he's not making sense.

Dog slobber?

CHAPTER FIFTEEN

Saffie

*S*lit had been going to rape me.

I'd tried to tell him I was Duke's, but he didn't give a damn. Seemed like Duke was already making good on his threat to let all his men have me. Duke would have been bad enough, but at least I knew his ways and what he wanted from me.

In the past, Duke had shared me, but he'd always been there watching them defile me as though it satisfied some deviant kick of his. But this is new. Just sending one of his brothers to my room means he's treating me like nothing more than a whore.

It's going to be worse than before.

I'd rather be dead.

Maybe I'd have just given in, let Slit have his way and taken the route of self-preservation if it hadn't been for the feeling I've nothing more to lose, that there wasn't much of me that wanted to go on living. Niran's betrayal had been the final straw.

Instead of complying as he'd expected, I'd chosen the route of standing up to him, hoping if I provoked the burly sergeant-at-arms, he would lose his temper and mercifully end this life that now offers me nothing.

First, I'd tried to evade him, dodging out of his reach, but in the small room there was nowhere to go. With no lock on the bathroom door, it was useless trying to hide in there. I ducked and dived, managing to get under his outstretched hand, but his other had reached out and reeled me in. With one hand cruelly twisted into my hair, he'd ripped my clothes. I knew there was no point appealing to the better nature he didn't possess.

He punched me, making my eye swell all over again.

Scared, knowing I'd lose in a straight fight, with the one eye I still could see out of, I spied something I could use. Twisting my head and throwing my body, ignoring the pain as I lost a chunk of my hair, I'd fallen, but had gotten my hand on the plate still covered with food I couldn't face eating. My hand had grasped it almost without my brain issuing an instruction, and I'd thrown it straight at his head.

I'd surprised him. He hadn't time to raise a hand to deflect my improvised missile, and it scored a direct hit on his face. Enraged, he'd launched himself at me.

This was it. The end.

Go ahead, kill me, I'd silently challenged.

Time seemed to stand still in those moments. Him poised, one fist raised, the other trying to wipe the congealed mess from his eyes. I took pleasure in seeing blood on his face.

God had deserted me despite all my prayers for a healthy child. There was no point pleading with him now. But I sent up my wish anyway. Just make it fast.

Out of the corner of my eye, I saw the door opening. When I recognised Niran, my heart broke once more, knowing he was entering to support Slit, and not to rescue me.

Seconds passed like hours. Slit's eyes narrowed and focused on me. His fist drew back... Simultaneously, his movements blurring so fast in comparison, Niran launched himself, picked up a shard of broken plate, and had it in Slit's neck before his arm could complete its swing.

He wasn't dead, but he soon would be. Ignoring him, I stared wide-eyed at Niran, not knowing what to believe.

Niran had saved me.

Niran had betrayed me.

I didn't, couldn't, trust him.

But the words that he'd said didn't gel with the fact Slit was right now dying by his hand with one last gurgle and one final twitch.

If the colour of Niran's skin hadn't already been a death sentence for him, killing the Crazy Wolves' sergeant-at-arms had made that a certainty.

What did I do now?

I hated Niran. But even with my poor instincts, I couldn't reconcile the image of Niran as a betrayer with the man who'd killed to protect me.

What could I do when he held out his hand?

Stay here with Slit's body? Put the blame where it belongs? But then I'd be Duke's plaything again.

Take the chance of escape? Take the risk Niran hadn't meant one single word that he'd said?

It would take a long time for me to feel even a fledgling of trust for him, but I knew he was right. Unless I wanted to wait for Duke's retribution, which would land on me even if I hadn't dealt the killing blow. I had to get away, and before Slit's body was found.

One thing was for certain, I wasn't going to be left in that room where he wanted to hide me. Once the Wolves came looking for their missing man and found Slit's body, they'd leave no stone unturned to find Niran or me.

And there's that lack of trust between us. If Niran got away, would he really come back? Or did he prefer to run, unencumbered by the woman he'd just saved? All he could offer me were assurances that I couldn't believe.

It's not the first time I've tried to escape the Crazy Wolves, but I'd never been successful, not on my own. Could having someone with me be the charm I'd needed?

I knew the clubhouse far better than he and of the handy fire escape that wasn't far away. For a moment, once we were descending, my heart beat faster as I thought we might have a chance to get clean away.

But how? There was open land all around, and it would be an impossibility to cross it. We were trapped in the open just as badly as we'd been trapped inside.

When Slinger had rounded the building, I knew we were both dead. Or, more likely, that Niran would soon be, and that an even worse fate would happen to me. I'd be forced to stay here only to breed. If Slit had gotten his way, that might have happened today.

So when Niran told me to run, I knew I had to escape or die trying. They were the only two options I allowed myself to think about.

Since I lost my baby, my thoughts have not been about taking care of me. I've not once thought of getting my body back into shape. I used to run but haven't for years.

But ignoring my muscles that immediately protest, and my lungs which don't seem to want to work, I propel myself forward like a bullet from a gun with a speed I didn't know I possessed. As it was, I'd gotten further than I expected.

My lungs burned, my bare feet hurt, but I pumped my arms and legs and literally ran for my life.

But this was no athlete's track. This was rough, unkempt biker land, full of rabbit holes, stones and rough ground. A gunshot reached my ears at the precise second my ankle twisted and gave way, but my momentum carried me on. I crashed to the ground wondering why I was still alive, and why death hadn't come immediately.

I must be fatally hurt.

I lie still as the past hour passes through my mind. Slit's

dead, Niran got me out of Duke's clutches. I hadn't lied when I said I'd rather die. And now, it seems, I've got my wish.

My ankle is throbbing. My hands smart from where I put them out to prevent my face crashing into the ground. I'm winded, it's hard to breathe. My head hurts from the jolt it just received. The strange thing is, I can't tell where that bullet hit me.

A mortal injury. It has to be. *Slinger's a marksman. He wouldn't have missed me.*

I lie in a strange state of mind as I wait for death, smelling the damp grass under my face, feeling the warmth of the sun on my cheek and the throbbing of my various aches, and tasting the blood from where I'd bitten my cheek.

My ears still work. In the distance, I can hear men shouting at Niran. I continue to breathe while the shouts telling me they've found Slit reach me.

Niran had tried to help me. Had he been helping me all along? Lying to get brought here with me? *Maybe.* If so, he doesn't deserve the kind of death I know he'll now receive. It won't be merciful.

Run, Niran, take your chances. Be shot like me. After all, I can confirm, it doesn't really hurt.

I'm vaguely conscious of the voices moving away.

Good. No one's coming to check on me, meaning I can just lie here, waiting peacefully for the grim reaper to take me.

So I lie still, my face mushed into the damp grass. With no shouting to distract me, I try to concentrate on the birdsong, the last thing I'll hear in my life.

Closing my eyes, I wait for the end to take me.

The ground starts to tremor under my cheek—not much but enough to let me guess someone's coming to me. *Someone eager. They're panting.*

Someone who's planting their wet nose into my face.

Wet nose? And a tongue licking me? As a rapid breathing

reaches my ears and slobber drips on my cheek, I begin to laugh, silently.

Reaching out my arm, I touch Fang's fur. "You're a good boy," I tell him, then raise my head. "K-9?" I ruffle his ear and chuckle again. "You been sent to finish me off?"

The thought is ridiculous.

I'd been on the compound five years. Not allowed off, but as long as I stayed on the grounds, I had enough freedom to make friends with the only living beings who didn't torture me, and who were kept prisoner much like myself. Gaining their trust had been a challenge, sneaking them food, gradually taking the chance to get close.

If their masters gave the instruction to attack, I'm not sure who they'd obey, but turning my head slightly to the left, I can glance behind me. *There's no one there.*

Only the dogs for company as my soul leaves this earth.

Fang nudges me, moving down my body, none too gently shoving his nose into the pocket of my shorts where he knows I often kept treats. *None today, boy.*

When his whiskers meet my bare skin, exposed courtesy of Slit, it tickles, and I try to move away.

I can move.

Gingerly, I try my arms and limbs. My ankle hurts, my wrists throb, but nothing else seems wrong. Belatedly, I realise I've been in shock, and that maybe I wasn't actually shot.

I can't stay here.

Raising my head, I see the club's boundary line. It's far too far away.

Now rather than giving up, my brain kicks into gear. Right now, Niran will probably be being tortured. It's unlikely he's dead yet. Knowing Duke, he'll make his pain last for days. All because he killed Slit to save me.

If I got free, I could contact his club.

The perimeter looks miles away. The chances of me making

it are bleak, but knowing the Wolves, they'll be focused on causing Niran pain, and possibly not watching me. What have I to lose? Only my life, and I'd already given up on that today. On the other hand, I have much to gain.

"Shall we do this, boys?"

K-9 yawns widely, then settles down by my side.

"Would you guard me? Or stop me from trying to get away?"

They might do the latter if I get up and run.

But if I inch away? I give it a try, doing an approximation of the leopard crawl I've seen soldiers do on films, dragging my aching ankle behind me.

As I move slowly forward, I realise it's down to Niran that I have even this slim chance to escape. That shout to run had been the trigger I'd needed. *I owe it to him to survive.*

I gain another inch, more determined this time.

What would my life have been like if I'd met Niran before Duke?

Even now he's helping me. The Wolves' hatred of him is buying me time.

Oh, Niran. I'll try to get help, but it's unlikely. He won't get out alive, and while I'd wish him a quick and painless death, that isn't the way of the Wolves.

How far can I get until someone looks out and realises my body has shifted?

I move forward again, this time gaining a foot, and then freeze, terrified and listening for shouts, but I hear nothing except for a whirring sound that seems to come from above me. Twisting my head to the side, I risk looking up.

It's a drone. I'm certain it is—a weird small body with four arms and rotors. There's no gun on it, so it's not overtly a threat to me. *Is it one of Grit's new toys?* Are they monitoring me?

Feeling my heart rise into my mouth, I go still and play possum once more. K-9 again flops down beside me, while Fang sits on his haunches with his tongue lolling out, as if expectantly waiting for me to get on with this game.

The whirring above me starts to fade and eventually moves off.

I can hear no shouts, no voices, and turning my head the other way, see no signs of movement from the clubhouse. But I can't get that damn drone out of my mind. *If it isn't Grit's, whose can it be?*

Law enforcement? How would I know?

But one thing's for certain, I won't gain anything by staying here. I crawl forward again, then wait. When I glance around, I can't see the drone. So I do it again, and again, wondering how soldiers manage to make it look so easy when it's killing my elbows and knees.

The tree line doesn't seem to be getting any closer, and the clubhouse no further away than when I started. I begin wondering whether I should just get up and run, when suddenly four massive explosions go off, making me yelp and turn in the direction the sounds came from. The dogs leap and start to bark excitedly.

I roll to my back, propped on my elbows with my head raised, and look in disbelief as all four corners of the clubhouse start to drop away. As I stare, flames start to lick on one side. I can't see the front of the clubhouse from here, but as increasing levels of shouts come to my ears, as well as rapid gunfire, I see men run and fall to the ground.

My God! There are loads of men swarming the clubhouse. The way they're moving is different to the more familiar style of the Wolves. They're far more competent and organised.

It looks like war's broken out, and the attackers are not on the side of the bikers I hate.

I must be a bad person as I inwardly cheer at every Wolf I see go down. Then my instinct of self-preservation sees those flames getting higher. Every Wolf in the clubhouse is going to come running out soon. If I'm going to take my chance, I've got to go now while I still can. *And risk the dogs bringing their prey down.*

Dubiously, I eye Fang and K-9, then take a gulp. "Come on, boys."

I get to my feet and launch myself forward, this time taking more care where I run, seeking out holes and obstacles that could trip me, not wanting to injure my ankle again. As the tree line comes closer, I'm aware of the dogs galloping next to me, thoroughly enjoying this new game. Then in the periphery of my vision, I see a couple of men running parallel to me. But when I falter, they wave their arms, encouraging me on. They're not Wolves, so I follow their lead.

A man who's limping heavily emerges from the treeline in front. In a lopsided run-jog, he comes to greet me.

I stop, my hands signalling Fang and K-9 to stand down, just as I'd seen the men do. To my joy, they obey me, but low rumbles come from their throats, as if waiting for the attack signal from me.

Friend or foe? Is it a case of out of the frying pan into the fire?

I'm shaking, hyped up on adrenaline, my vision blurry with tears, but whether they're of joy, freedom being so close, or fear of what else might happen to me, or worry about Niran, it's hard to tell.

Blinking rapidly, my vision clears. When I get a glance of the man who's approaching me, limping heavily, I have my answer. I recognise him, recognise that smile, can read the words of encouragement on his lips and as I draw close enough, despite that he's a biker, despite that he's a sergeant-at-arms, I throw myself at him.

Grumbler's arms tighten around me. "You're safe now, Saffie. I got you. You're safe, you hear me?"

I can't help the wave of relief that goes through me, but it's tempered by the shudder that follows. "Grumbler, they've got Niran."

"Not for fuckin' long," he growls. His sound is mimicked by two canine versions, which draw his attention. I feel him tense as he asks, "Can you get those fuckin' dogs to stand down?"

CHAPTER SIXTEEN

Grumbler

We'd been getting ready to go when my fuckin' leg had let me down. Four hours of riding yesterday had proved too much for me. I'd ignored the pain, but when I tried to get on my bike, I kicked up the stand and my right leg had folded, bringing the heavy motorcycle down on top of me.

Frustrated I was delaying my brothers, I'd waved their help off, but they'd lifted the bike off of me.

"Go." I was mad as hell, but if I tried to follow, I'd hold them up. They've got too much to do without watching out for an old codger like me.

Angry with myself, and decidedly acting like my name, I stayed in the truck with Gears and the prospects, with nothing to do but watch the action playing out on the screens.

They had three drones flying around feeding back information. The Utah crew seemed a well-oiled operation, and seeing they knew what they were doing and how to feed information to Swift and the teams, I had little to do but grumble that I'd been left behind.

"Hey, Grumbler. You see that?" Gears suddenly asks. He's hovering a drone over the body of Saffie lying on the ground.

But as I stare where he's pointing, I see Saffie is moving again. This time, the two dogs are moving with her. Belgian Malinois if I'm not mistaken—one a rich fawn and the other a deep mahogany.

"They're sticking with her," he points out needlessly. "Clever girl. If she gets up and runs, they might bring her down."

The drone is no longer above her, but is hovering high above, sending back scenes from the clubhouse, but in the periphery, I can still see her.

Gears is already talking into a microphone.

"Got any men who can go give cover to the woman?"

"I'll go." I make the decision fast. "She knows me."

"I can spare Buzz, he's in my second line."

"Joker's there too."

I'm already on my feet, offering up silent thanks to Drummer and Demon. Outside I get on my slightly scratched bike, this time raising the stand more carefully. With determination driving me, I head down to the edge of the compound Saffie's making for.

Two bikes have made it ahead of me and two Devils have already dismounted. I wave Joker and Buzzard on, favouring my worthless piece of shit leg as I try to catch up.

The two men spare a glance for me, then break away, cutting a hole in the fence, then pushing through, rush ahead, rifles guiding their way to protect her flanks.

Four explosions go off simultaneously. I can see Saffie roll and look back. For a moment, she stays hugged to the ground, then as the bullets start to rain down, taking out Wolves who have flooded out from the clubhouse, she gets to her feet and starts running. I watch the dogs, taking careful aim with my gun, but I'll be fucked, they're not giving chase, just loping alongside her.

Joker and Buzzard are out to her side waving her on. Both brothers keep looking around, ready and poised to take out anyone who's a threat to her.

The sensible girl is running for the tree line, and, without knowing it, directly toward me.

She needs to see someone she knows. Without hesitation, I push myself through the broken strands of wire to meet her. She recognises me when she's close enough and when we meet—me at a stumbling run, her at a more respectable pace—she throws herself into my arms.

"You're okay," I tell her. "We've got you. You're safe." I'm elated she's alive. For a moment, I had really thought she was dead. That's half of our mission completed, now we've just got to save her old man.

Saffie sobs, "Grumbler, they've got Niran."

I know. I offer some platitudes, then hearing a warning growl, eye her companions and ask, "Can you get those fuckin' dogs to stand down?"

She draws in a shuddering breath, then looks down uneasily. "I don't know."

Gingerly, I reach out my hand. The fucking dogs growl at me.

"K-9, Fang," she says hesitantly. "Stop. He's a friend. Sit. Stay."

"Hey," Joker appears, approaching cautiously. He's aiming his gun the dogs' way who for the moment have obeyed her, and now have their asses on the ground. Their eyes, though, they're alert, and their bodies vibrate in readiness. "Get her back behind the fence, Grumbler."

Carefully, I move her back with me. When we're through, Buzzard follows, and Joker, still with his eyes on the guard dogs, gets clear.

Gun exchanged for fingers, he knits together the broken strands of wire, then rasps out, "Get her clear, now."

Moving as fast as I can, I get her back to where the bikes are parked.

"She can come back with me." Joker's eyes flare in amusement. "I don't care about a bitch riding with me. Lady won't be bothered as long as she doesn't have man parts."

Buzzard snorts and I bark a laugh, but quickly recover. "Alright, sweetheart?" I ask her gently, knowing it's me she knows and not him.

She pales when she eyes the motorcycle, but casting a look behind her seems to make up her mind, as she shivers, then states, "Just get me out of here." Her fist goes up to her mouth. "Niran…"

"Niran will be fine," I offer, not having a clue whether or not that's the truth. But fuck me, it's all I can let myself believe.

The ride is short. When we're back at our temporary base, with my arm around her, I lead her back to the truck and set her on the tailgate. "You hurt?" I examine her with my eyes, remembering how we thought she was shot. Her face is swollen as though she's been beaten, which makes my gut clench.

Emotions flit across her face. Relief that she's safe, her teeth worrying her lip as she's probably thinking about her old man, but overall, she seems to be holding up okay. Considering the couple of days she's had, I wouldn't be surprised if she soon comes crashing down. Even now I can see her shivering though Gears has lent her his coat. Her adrenaline rush is fading.

"You hurt?" I repeat.

She glances at me as if she's lost in her head. Then, like me, she ignores her injuries from the abuse I assume she'd received at the hands of Duke, and gives me the update from her escape. "I twisted my ankle, that's all, I think. I-I'd thought they'd shot me."

So did we. I raise my eyes to the heavens, giving silent thanks that wasn't the case.

"Hey." Brute swings around, a beaming smile on his face,

yelling back at us excitedly. "They've got Niran. He's alive. They're just taking out the stragglers and then they'll signal us to go down and get him."

As Saffie drops her head into her hands and lets out a deep breath, I query, "He okay?"

At that, Saffie raises her head again and pays attention.

It's obvious Gears isn't as happy as Brute. His grimace says it all when he, too, turns. Something that's picked up by Saffie.

"Is he hurt badly?" Her face pales as she jumps awkwardly down.

Seeing she looks distressed, I pull her back into my arms. "He's alive, Saffie. Your old man's going to be fine."

"He's not my old man," she hisses, her eyes flaring.

It's Gears who gives the appalled look I feel, and he snarls, "Why do you think five chapters have come and risked their fuckin' lives to get you out of there? Because you're fuckin' Niran's that's why. Because he claimed you, we came to get both you and him out."

Saffie tenses and I want to punch Gears. She's got such a fear of bikers, he's not helping now. But to my surprise, she stands up to him. Pulling out of my grasp, she slides down to stand on her own two feet. "Niran told Duke he betrayed me." She stabs at his chest with her finger. "Last night, he acted as my jailer. He wouldn't even talk to me. Then Niran stopped Slit from raping me." Brushing back her hair with her hand, she shakes her head. "Then he told me to run, and they shot me." Again, there's that full body shudder. "I don't know what to believe. I don't know who Niran is."

Glaring at Gears, he shrugs, and moves back inside the truck. I harden my voice. "Now listen here, Saffie. Niran had fuck all to do with Duke finding you, you hear me? The only fuckin' reason he's here was to try to help you escape. Which he's done." I pause, waiting for some reaction. When I get a hesitant shiver, I carry on. "Sure, it might have not been the way he'd wanted it.

Yes, you were shot at, but you survived. By making sure he didn't let Duke take you alone means Niran was fuckin' prepared to give his life for you. You going to walk out on him now?"

Niran wouldn't have done half of what he had if he didn't care for her. And, he'd claimed her. Once he'd done that, he'd have moved heaven and earth to keep her safe.

Saffie doesn't look quite so indignant. She twists her mouth then covers her face with her hand. After a moment, she looks up and says again, "I don't know what to believe, Grumbler."

"Believe Niran was, is, and will always be on your side. The question is, are you on his now? Choice is yours, Saffie. You say the word, and we'll have you out of here."

Mentally I'm crossing my fingers. I don't know what state Niran's in, but if she leaves, I've got a notion it will break him worse than anything the Wolves could have done. But if she's at least not going to try, it's best to pull that Band-Aid off now.

I don't know what the fuck happened. I don't know why Kid was killed, nor why Niran was captured along with her. Taking her hand, I pull her away, out of earshot of anyone else.

"You've not much time for bikers, have you, Saffie? I can understand that." I pause, letting my sympathy show. "Thing is, Saff, my boy is still fuckin' in there, and he's hurt. Hurting because of you."

"I didn't ask—"

"Whether you asked him or not, you think he'd have stayed back when the Crazy Wolves took you? Fuck, you must know Niran better than that." I take a breath to calm myself. "Saffie, you've just escaped something dreadful. We're ending the fuckin' Wolves, right here, right now. You'll never have to worry about Duke ever again." Again, I halt, waiting to see if my words have sunk in. "Just do me one favour, okay? Hang around, stay with Niran, and give him a fuckin' chance."

"I don't want to be an old lady," she stubbornly whispers.

I sigh deeply. "Then can you let him down gently? Niran must have come here knowing he'd be fuckin' lucky to leave with his life. Give me that, will you? Don't rush off immediately."

"Will you stop me?"

I jerk my head toward Gears who's shamelessly come to the rear of the truck and has been listening in. "Gears is a Devil, just like me. We're in the business of rescuing women, not holding them fuckin' captive. Choice is yours, Saffie."

"Niran's going to need to go to the hospital," Gears interrupts. "Preacher says he's hurt pretty badly."

Saffie's gasp shows how she reacts to that. I press my advantage. "Niran was there for you, sweetheart. It sounds like it's him who needs you now."

"Oh hell." Joker's pronouncement has me swinging around to see the two guard dogs from the compound coming up to us fast.

"In the truck, Saffie." I pull at her arm, as Buzzard and Joker jump up, guns at the ready.

But her eyes are on the dogs. "Sit. Stay," she experimentally calls out, seeing if it will work again.

And I'll be fucked if those dogs don't come to an emergency stop, almost skidding to a halt, then their bums hit the ground, tails wagging wildly.

She looks shocked.

"You get friendly with them, Saffie?" Gears asks quietly, just loud enough for his words to reach her.

She shrugs, wipes tears from her eyes. "Seems that I have." Kneeling, she widens her arms, and calls them to her. They amble up, sit down beside her, letting her tangle her hands in their fur.

Gears jumps down. Going behind her, he stretches out his hand.

"Friend," she says softly.

And fuck me if one doesn't move forward and lick at his fingers.

"Grumbler. You want to see this?" Brute yells from inside the truck.

Seeing as Gears seems to have things under control, I pull myself up and go forward. There I'm treated to a front-row seat as I watch the drama play out.

Putting on headphones, I hear the sounds of sporadic gunfire, but it seems to be less frequent now. We're getting good feedback from the drones positioned over the destroyed clubhouse.

There are a dozen or so dead bodies fallen outside, and Satan's Devils have started dragging them back in. My attention is caught by another screen, the outbuilding that had been covered by a guard. I see Mace from Colorado take off his cut and then enter. Within moments he comes out, vomits onto the ground, then speaks rapidly to Demon, his prez.

Then there's another explosion, much louder than the rest pulling my attention back to the clubhouse which is now just a raging ball of fire.

I see Pyro, the man known for starting fires as well as putting them out, position himself between the buildings, watching the flames until he seems to be satisfied.

"Recovery," Preacher's voice sounds through the speaker. "All targets eliminated. Niran needs transport."

I pull the mic toward me. "Is he—" Brute reaches across, flicks a switch, then nods at me to continue. Raising my chin at him, I begin again. "Is he going to make it?"

Preacher's silent so long I don't know if he's heard me. I'm about to ask Brute if the mic is working when the Utah man clears his throat. "He'll live. But he could have life-changing injuries. Get here as soon as you can, Brother."

Fuck.

Brute stands and is obviously going to go get one of the trucks.

"I'm coming with you," I tell him. I want, need, to see Niran for myself. *Life-changing injuries?* That sounds bad.

Outside, Gears is running the dogs through some commands, rewarding them by feeding them bits of a sandwich he must have carried in his pack.

"We're going to fetch Niran," I tell him, giving a pointed glance toward Saffie, letting him know he's to make sure she stays put.

But Saffie surprises me, standing and challenging me with a look. "I want to come with you."

Briefly I close my eyes, then open them and shake my head. In the few minutes I'd had, I've calmed down and revised my opinion. If she doesn't want Niran, she shouldn't be forced. If she'll be leaving, she shouldn't make promises she can't keep, especially in whatever state he's in. "Nah, Saffie, you're free now. Despite what I've said, the decision is yours to make about whether or not you want to be his. It's not fair to give him false hope."

Gears' jaw tightens, but he doesn't speak.

Saffie glances at the dogs now lying at her feet. That she's been able to control something, even if it's two creatures each with four legs, seems to have put some spirit back into her. She breathes deeply then says, "I don't want to be anyone's old lady, Grumbler. And I don't even know if now the danger has past, he really wants me to be his. But I'm the reason why Niran got hurt. I can't walk away from him now, not when he might need me. Not when he was the reason for freeing me from Duke."

Her eyes plead with me, while I wonder whether taking her with me will be a mistake. She clearly wants nothing to do with any man, and given her past, who could fuckin' blame her? But Niran's my friend, and over the past couple of years, we've bonded. I understand how he ticks. Once he took responsibility for Saffie, stepped up and claimed her, in his mind, I'm pretty damn certain, he'll see her as his. Why the fuck else would he be here if not to stay close to her? Even if he hasn't admitted it to himself yet, he cares deeply for her.

Any of my brothers would see she's alright and get her to wherever she wants to go. She can return to San Diego now the threat's over or move somewhere else.

Would Niran be upset if she left without speaking to him? Fuck yes.

Would he understand she wanted to remove herself from a life she never chose to enter? Again, a resounding yes.

Would it be worse if she comes with me, and he misreads her intentions? A thousand times yes.

"Please, Grumbler, I need this." Saffie looks at me imploringly. "If Niran hadn't been there, I'd already have been raped, and Duke would have kept me until I was no longer useful to him and then I'd be dead. I owe Niran."

"Perhaps you owe him truth and honestly," I counter. "You don't like this life. I can understand that. You don't want a man at your side, get that too, honey. But I tell you this, Niran's heart will leap when he sees you and for all the wrong reasons if you don't reciprocate his feelings. Can you answer truthfully whether you're doing this for yourself or for him?"

I hate having this conversation. I'm only giving her time as I think it's important.

She bites her lips, then turns away. *She's going to leave.* That's for the best, isn't it? After a moment, her shoulders rise, and her spine straightens as she turns back.

"Niran was there when I needed him. If he's hurt, he himself may need someone now. I won't turn away from him. Either you take me, Grumbler, or I'll find some way to him myself."

"And if he misreads the situation?"

Suddenly she snaps. "Perhaps I can read him better than you. Niran knows what I've been through, knows I need time. Heaven knows if I can get past all that's happened, whether I'll ever be comfortable coming around the club. But one thing's for certain, Niran understands."

I stare at her for a moment, then without knowing if what I'm doing is for the best, heaven help me, I agree.

Two minutes later, I'm in the passenger seat while Brute's driving the four-wheel-drive truck, virtually retracing the route she'd taken on foot. The clubhouse is a roaring inferno, and anyone left inside will only be identifiable by teeth. That's if anyone bothers looking. This place is so out of the way, no one's coming to investigate the flames or the smoke.

Still unsure whether I'm doing right by bringing Saffie to him, my thoughts turn to my injured brother instead, off balance by Preacher's suggestion his injuries while not life-threatening, were serious.

It's Swift who waves to me when she sees the truck approach, running up and calling through the window, "He's over there with Preacher and Lost."

"A woman member?" Saffie breathes beside me, turning around as we drive past and catching sight of Swift's three rockers on the back of her cut.

"Haven't you learned you can't judge MCs by what you know of the Crazy Wolves?" I ask her, rather abruptly.

"I'm surprised you let women join, that's all." She huffs.

"Nothing prohibiting it, but she'd have to be special." And Swift's certainly that.

Then my attention is captured by the group in front, and we pull up to park next to what looks like a makeshift stretcher.

I fling myself out of the cab. I'd hoped to see Niran standing, not lying down. Doing my drag hop to his side, I crouch, hearing my knees pop. My eyes scan for injuries.

His face looks swollen, but I'd expected he'd take a punch. He's obviously naked, going by what I can see, but his dignity is preserved by a couple of t-shirts. Fresh blood covers him, and I wonder where from. His prosthetic leg is missing, but his other foot? Well, that's cradled on another t-shirt and looks misshapen. More blood covers it, and fuck it, there's even part of a bone protruding. The leg above it is swollen and doesn't look straight.

"What the fuck have they done to you?" I growl, reaching out my hand, then withdrawing it, uncertain whether he's conscious or not.

"He's got various stab wounds, lost a fair amount of blood." Lost pauses, then adds grimly, "They busted the bones in his foot." When I glance up and catch his eye, I can read the implication in his expression.

"Will they be able to save it?" Fuck, the man's only got one leg as it is.

Lost gives a frustrated shrug.

"If it's humanely possible, they'll do it. If I've got anything to do with it," Preacher snarls, pushing Lost out of the way, and checking Niran's pulse. "I gave him a shot of morphine. He's out of it for the minute. Needed him still for transport."

"Well, let's get him loaded up." I turn to beckon Brute to bring the truck closer.

"Nah." Preacher turns back to me. "I'm calling in a favour. Got a helicopter coming in. It's not a LifeFlight, but it's as close as I could get. One of my old Air Force buddies is bringing a medic. They'll get him to a hospital. If his foot can be saved, he'll need treatment fast."

"I'm going with him." Saffie's come up beside me. Her face is set, and her jaw is stubbornly jutted.

Now there's something different about her. Her compassion isn't for herself, it's for the man lying prone at our feet. Falling to her knees, she gently strokes his forehead.

Lost pulls me away. Reluctantly, I leave my brother. "Worst thing they could have fuckin' done. Preacher's not convinced he can feel a pedal pulse. If it's there, it's weak."

He doesn't have to tell me. Niran was bitter when a careless driver ended his career in the Marines, but he'd come back with the help of the Satan's Devils. Losing his one working foot would be devastating and a massive set back.

A hand slaps down on my back. "They'll fuckin' save it, Brother. If not," Bolt waggles his impressive fake hand, "we'll get him to the fucker who makes these. He'll be riding again, one way or another."

A whop whop sound fills the air. As I look up, Preacher's already in place, signalling where his buddy should land. The next few minutes are taken up with the medic checking Niran's vitals, setting up an IV and then, after applying some splints which Preacher had been hesitant to use, his foot and leg are immobilised. After transferring Niran to a proper stretcher, he's loaded in.

Saffie, to my surprise, announces shakily that she's his old lady and won't be parted from him. Dart, pulling rank, also goes along for the ride. I wanted to go myself, but there's no room for anyone else inside.

Then, less than a quarter of an hour after it arrived, the helicopter lifts into the air. My eyes follow it until it disappears from sight, and only belatedly I ask, "Where are they taking him?"

It's Preacher who answers. "A hospital in Utah. They're already prepared to receive him."

"We've got to get moving." Drummer appears, marching alongside Snatcher. "There's a barn full of women who need to be attended to."

Jeez. I'd forgotten about them. "How many are there? Are they okay? What's the plan? Have you freed them?"

"Far too fuckin' many," Wraith, by Drummer's side, answers. "And nah, we're not doing a thing. We've been watching to make sure no sparks were going to set light to the building, but the fire's dying down enough now so it's safe to leave them."

"Didn't you think they might want to know they're safe?" My eyes widen.

Snatcher stares at me and shakes his head, then indicates the burned-out shell behind me. "Forty plus Devils are here, Brother. Fuck knows how many Wolves we've killed. Can't afford those women to say anything about who's rescued them. Soon as we're out of here, we'll call it in. Anonymously."

Drummer exchanges a glance with his sergeant-at-arms before turning to address Snatcher. "I concur, Snatch. The Crazy Wolves haven't exactly made friends, and hopefully the cops won't look too closely. As long as you're sure Stormy's set it up to look like they got careless with explosives, we shouldn't be linked to this."

"And the bullet holes in all the bodies?" I roll my eyes, wondering how that would fool anyone.

Drummer's steely eyes land on me, making me stand straighter, while internally I'm shrinking. "Ammunition lying around is unpredictable in fire, Brother. And, they'd have to do autopsies to discover the bullet holes. With the Crazy Wolves, do you think they'd bother?"

Personally I think they'll be grateful that their job's been done.

Snatcher, halting his private aside conversation with Swift, joins in. "We might just let it slip it was a mafia hit, just to deflect attention."

My phone vibrates in my pocket. I pull it out and frown, wondering why Connor's calling me. If it was about the club, his instructions were to call the prez or VP. Moving away slightly, I take the device out and press the green key.

"Grumbler."

"Mary needs you. She's been taken to the hospital."

My world feels like it's stopped turning. "What the fuck? What's happened?"

"I don't know. Something about blood pressure and the baby. Can you get here fast, Grumbler?"

I can't breathe, can't speak. All my fucking fears I've been suppressing for the last eight months come hurtling back to me.

We should have ended the pregnancy. We both knew the risks. God forbid, I lose Mary or the baby. And here I am, stuck four hundred miles away. I'd been worried about not returning to them. I never thought they might not be there waiting for me.

"Brother?"

I turn my leaking eyes to Lost. "It's Mary…"

It's all I have to say.

Devils, from whatever chapter burst into action around me. I'm pushed into a truck with a Vegas member called Sarge driving, and Preacher in the passenger seat. I'm only half aware when we speed past the bikes and into open country, then meet up with an interstate.

I'm focused on trying to call someone who could help me, but Connor knows no more, or has nothing useful to tell me. Alicia's not answering her phone, and I haven't the numbers of the other old ladies. One by one, Snips, Scribe and Keeper try to explain to me, but all they know are the headlines Connor's already told me.

It's only when I reach the airport that I realise their intention. I won't be riding home, I'll be flying.

Right now's not the time to tell anyone I fuckin' hate being on a plane and will do anything to avoid it.

I need to be with my old lady. I'll walk through the fires of hell if need be.

I can only hope I'm in time.

Hang on, Mary, I'm coming.

CHAPTER SEVENTEEN

Niran

"**W**here are you hurt, apart from the obvious?"

"Everywhere," I gasped, unable to believe in the nick of time I'd been saved. Better yet, I'd heard those glorious words, Saffie's alive. Fuck knew how. The Devil must have been watching over us today, decided he didn't want us, and left us both in the land of the living.

A man I didn't know dropped to his knees and began assessing my injuries. His eyes looked at the bloody wounds from where they were none too careful when removing my clothes, some deep and blood flowing freely, but when his gaze followed my leg down, the grimace on his face told me all I needed to know. It must look as bad as it felt.

"Lost," I called out, my tone urgent and desperate as I saw my prez approaching.

"Brother?" He quickened his step, squatting down beside me. Like the other man, his mouth twisted.

"My foot. Don't let them take my foot."

"Niran, fuck—"

"Preacher," Lost snapped angrily, then to me, said, "We'll do what we can, Brother. I promise you that."

Fog swirled in my brain. It was hard to stay conscious or to open my swollen eyes, and I wasn't sure if the words escaping my mouth were coherent. "I can't lose my foot, Lost. I just can't. Don't let them take it. Please, Prez." I was conscious. I was starting to beg.

I was safe. My brothers were here. I tried to tell myself that's what was most important. In my head, I was telling them on repeat not to let my foot be amputated, but whether I actually uttered the words, I had no idea. It was my worst fucking nightmare. It wasn't just the disability, the inconvenience of having a missing limb, it was the things people who are whole didn't realise—the phantom pains, the itches that were impossible to scratch because there was nothing there, the learning to cope in an able-bodied world. I didn't want to go through that again. That couldn't be the legacy of getting entangled with the Crazy Wolves.

From that point, I didn't have much memory about getting out of the Crazy Wolves' clubhouse. What I did remember was a haze of pain and however gently my brothers tried to move me, my foot, my leg and all the way up my spine was ablaze with pain.

With Preacher poised to shove a needle into me, I screamed again at him, or maybe it was only in my mind, "Don't let them take my foot."

Then I remembered no more.

The first thing I do when I come around is to raise my head and look down. Letting out a heavy sigh, I see a contraption keeping the sheets raised over where my foot should be. The frame looks familiar, as does the sound of the beeping of the monitor next to me. *I'm in the hospital.* I'm groggy, my throat feels sore, my mouth is dry. All symptoms of having had anaesthesia and an operation.

It's gone. Rolling my head back, I try to fight off the sense of loss that slams into me. *It's happened again.* It's like a rerun of an old program on television, a repeat. I'm waking up in a hospital all over again, to find I'm missing a limb.

"Niran? You're awake. How do you feel?" The gentle tone immediately calms the panic flooding through me.

Saffie. She's with me? I didn't expect that. I thought she'd lost all trust in me after the lies I'd told Duke to get him to take me to Nevada.

Duke. Something is niggling at the back of my mind, but I just can't bring it forward. Something important.

"They've saved your foot." Her soft voice gives me the words I didn't expect to hear.

I feel lightheaded with relief, or maybe that's the aftereffect of the anaesthetic. "They did?" That's a fuckin' miracle.

She chuckles. "Yes. Well, I don't think they had much choice after Dart stood over the surgeon, threatening a painful death if he didn't do his best to save it. Though apparently, there's so much steel in there, you'll set off every metal detector in the vicinity."

I breathe in deeply, trying to come to terms with the knowledge the worst hadn't happened. I hadn't been relishing lining up for another prosthesis. Closing my eyes, I let that sink in for a while. I've no doubt I have a long recovery ahead, but I've still got a foot. And, it seems, the woman I value more than any limb is here beside me.

Am I still dreaming, still high on drugs? Is she a figment of my imagination?

Turning my head toward her, she looks very real. Her face is still bruised and battered from Duke's and Slit's attentions. "Saffie, why are you here?" In the real world, surely she'd have gone as soon as she knew she had her freedom. *I'd destroyed all her faith in me.* Had I told her the reasons? I think I did, but at the time, she'd only half believed me.

She winces and glances down at her hands. "Your brothers

kind of expected me to stay with you. And when I thought about it, I couldn't leave you. Just as you couldn't leave me."

That why she's here is because of my brothers' expectations, rather than any desire of her own, rings warning bells, even in my befuddled brain.

"You're not here as my ol' lady, are you?" I don't pussy around, wanting to know where I stand. Or crawl, as right now I'm crippled.

"I'm here as a friend." She now looks at me. "Can I get you anything?" she asks brightly.

Only you. What's the point of saving my foot if I'm going to lose Saffie? I'd sacrifice anything for her to be my old lady for real. I rest my head back and again close my eyes, mumbling, "I'm okay for the moment."

I know that I've fallen for this woman sitting beside me, fallen hard. She's been the yin to my yang from the very beginning. Starting perhaps like Kink had suggested, someone who called to a dominant, protective streak inside me. She'd been broken, I wanted to fix her. Then it morphed into more than that when I saw the strength inside her. When I got myself taken to be with her, it was to save her, but only for myself, not so any other fucker could sweep in and take her.

It hits me hard with her few words that she doesn't reciprocate the feelings I have for her.

I should tell her to go. Keeping her around would just be torturing myself with something I'll never have, delaying the inevitable when I finally have to say goodbye to her.

I should.

But I won't. She's here with me now and I'm going to take advantage. Not in the way an able-bodied man would, but as much as I can with one leg missing and the other of no fucking use.

I'm not a Neanderthal. While I'd love to drag her off to my cave, I've come to realise that to win Saffie, I've got to break down her barriers. Which means talking to her, really getting to know her, and in the process, letting her get to know me.

Would she be here if there wasn't just a small bit of her that cares? My brothers wouldn't have pressured her, would have allowed her to leave if she'd insisted. Even a concern for an injured man has to be something I can work with.

Opening my eyes, I let them feast on her again. She looks drained and tired, her face bruised, and her eyes blackened and sore. It prompts me to ask how she's feeling.

She startles and smiles. "I think I should be the one asking you that."

"I'm okay," I tell her honestly. "Spaced out from the pain meds and dreading knowing the prospects for my foot. Talk to me and take my mind off it." I might not have lost it, but will what remains be of any use? Will it be weight bearing, and flexible enough to allow me to ride my bike?

She bites her lip, then does a quick up and down of her head. "Where do you want me to start?"

"Start with how the fuck you're alive," I rasp, a little more forcefully than I intended, and thank fuck, my voice still sounds weak, though it breaks when I add, "I saw you take a bullet." My eyes squeeze shut in a vain effort to wipe that memory from my brain. I know I'll be seeing it in nightmares for the rest of my life.

She giggles, then explains, "Sheer luck. I tripped just as the shot rang out. I honestly thought it had hit me." She laughs self-deprecatingly. "Crazy, huh? I didn't see how at that distance they could have missed. So I stayed put, unmoving, just waiting for death to take me."

"If you'd been hit, you'd have felt it."

"I've never been shot before." She shrugs. "I thought I should have felt something, but then I thought maybe he'd gotten my spine. I was in shock, I suppose. Or that's what the doctor Preacher made me see suggested."

"Why Preacher?" Have I got a rival? I frown as her words register. What the fuck is he doing hanging around? Which leads me on to my next question, "Where am I?" I'm in a hospital room, but that could be anywhere.

"Preacher was the one who arranged for you to be airlifted out. He suggested you come to Utah, to a hospital near their clubhouse. Bolt said there was an expert on prosthetics in the north of the state, so it seemed a good place to bring you. Preacher dabbles as a medic as well as a pilot." She sounds impressed.

But at her words I do remember Preacher being the one to look at my leg, but then I'd been in a pain-filled haze. Trying to get my brain working, I recall he's the sergeant-at-arms of the Utah chapter.

"You're staying in the clubhouse? You're close to Preacher?" As soon as the words leave my mouth, I know I'm an ass. She'd made no promises to me.

"No." Her eyes widen as if I'd accused her of a crime. "I couldn't, Niran. They've put me up in a hotel close to the hospital." While I'm processing that probably means she still hasn't overcome her fear of bikers, even though they were who rescued her, she's back to biting her lip again. "They think I'm your old lady. I didn't contradict them. I don't think they'd have let me stay otherwise."

So my brothers from Utah think she's mine? At least that means she's off-limits. "Good call."

She gives another shrug.

I'm glad she perpetuated my lie. As my old lady she's the responsibility of the club. I give her a sharp look, then agree to keep to her story. "I'm just glad you're here. I'll keep up the pretence."

Shaking her head, she winces. "I feel guilty for accepting your club's help. They're paying for the hotel and my expenses."

"Don't be," I refute fast. "Let's be selfish about this. I'm apparently stuck in a hospital far away from my brothers, having to cope with fuck knows what." They may have managed to weld the bones together, but that doesn't mean I'll be able to walk. Or ride. Both consequences I'll have difficulty facing. "I'd appreciate a friend around, Saffie. I'd like you to stay for my sake." As she opens her mouth, I raise my hand. "As for you, Saffie, you've got one hell of a lot of shit that you need to get straight in your head. Your relationship with Duke was fucked. You were kept captive, and when you escaped, he found you and dragged you back. On top of that, you're dealing with the loss of your baby. Why not take this time to think about what you want to do now you're free to live the rest of your life? We're friends, aren't we? Why not help me, and while you're doing that, let me help you?"

Duke. Why is something niggling at my mind when I think of his name? I shake my head trying to clear it, but all I do is make it hurt again.

Saffie is watching me carefully. "You destroyed my trust in you, Niran. I hated you. Then you saved me."

I was hoping actions spoke louder than words. "If I hadn't lied to Duke, he'd have killed me in your apartment. You saw what he did to Kid." I pause and have to wait for that pain to fade. "Lying wasn't to save my life, but a chance to go with you, to keep you safe. I had to lie to you, Saffie. I had to act the part. Otherwise, I'd never have been convincing." I put as much conviction in my voice as I can.

She grimaces and again stares down at her hands. "It shook me, Niran. All my life I've been taken in by everyone. Even as it turns out, my father. That you're capable of lying—"

"I promise I'll never fuckin' lie to you again, Saffie. I never wanted to deceive you."

"I want to believe you."

But it's clear she doesn't yet. I hate that I've lost her trust.

"Before Duke turned up, had I ever let you down before? Had I ever spoken an untruth to you?"

Her brow creases, then she shakes her head, and a little of the tension leaves her.

I decide to change the subject. "Where have they put you up? Is it okay?"

"Sure. The hotel is comfortable, and a woman called Cat has been speaking to me on the phone. She had some clothes ordered and delivered." She grimaces slightly. "I'm not sure I want to go back to San Diego right now. I'm not ready."

I'm not surprised, not if she's returning to that shitty apartment alone. It's full of memories, and all bad ones.

"You're safe here, Saffie. No one's ever going to be coming after you again. It will take you a moment to stop looking behind you. Just take some time and decide what you want your future to look like. And in the meantime, you can visit and keep me company."

That warning bell tinkles at my mind again. But why? Saffie's safe, all the Wolves are dead. I saw them mowed down myself. And if the bullets hadn't found their mark, I've a vague recollection of the clubhouse burning down when I'd been taken out of it.

I'm wondering how long I'll be able to play the needing-a-visitor card. In my experience, hospitals don't keep you any longer than necessary, and with nothing more wrong with me than my leg being in a cast, it probably won't be long before I'm kicked out.

She stares at me for a moment, then she tries a small smile. "Okay."

Thank fuck. I rest my head back on the pillows and allow the aftereffects of the anaesthetic to take me under again, content in the knowledge that Saffie won't run away, and I won't have to chase after her. Fuck knows how I'd do it, immobile as I am. I haven't even got a fucking prosthesis, or, in other words, a leg to stand on.

I'm woken intermittently so the nurses can check me, and each time I open my eyes, I see Saffie has stayed. When I finally wake and have all my wits about me, she's not alone. Dart is seated alongside her.

Seeing me rousing, he sits forward, giving a weighted sideways glance toward Saffie. "Want anything, Niran?"

His stance suggests he wants me alone. "Yeah. I'd kill for a coffee."

"Take a break, Saffie. Go get yourself something to eat and bring back a coffee for your old man. I'll be right here with him."

She glances at me, and I raise my chin. Then, she studies Dart for a moment before standing and leaving.

I push the button to raise the head of the bed. "Thanks for being here, Brother. Utah's a long way from home."

Dart raises his chin. "Had to leave someone to look after your sorry ass. Salem and Pennywise are here too."

"Brothers treating you okay?"

He snorts. "Utah's a different fuckin' club. No sweet butts for a start. Not that it worries me, but the guys are a bit put out. They'd have preferred to go with the first idea, for you to hole up in Vegas."

I'm sure they would. Lots of entertainment in Sin City. I start to chuckle, but then it fades as something is bugging me. I just can't bring it to the forefront.

Knowing not thinking about it is the best way to bring it to mind, instead I ask, "Any fallout?"

"Nah. Apart from two who went scavenging earlier that day and didn't return, all four-legged rodents were put down. Or that's the assumption. We only got a rough body count before the exterminator went in and cleaned it up. Oh, the girls were found okay."

"Girls?" I ask, then frown. "Ah. The Wolves' stable."

He leans in, lowering his voice to a whisper. "Snatcher put out that it was a mafia hit. A tip-off was leaked to the cops, and they went in and freed the girls. Nothing to lead them back to the club. They don't know the Satan's Devils were there."

"I killed Slit, their sergeant-at-arms." The events of that day are coming back to me now. *Was it today, yesterday, or last week?* "He was trying to rape Saffie. I had no fuckin' choice." I close my eyes, remembering how blind rage had taken me, though I know I'd do it again in a heartbeat.

"We didn't stop for a roll call, but all that were there were taken out." He grimaces. "I know you probably wanted your own revenge on Duke, but we were focused on getting you out, Brother. We might have that pair in the wind, but not enough to resurrect the club. The Crazy Wolves have gone forever."

My mood sours. I'd wanted to tear Duke from limb to limb, but he's already met Satan by now. Well, at least Saffie's in the clear.

"Any of ours lost?" I ask through gritted teeth.

"Salem was winged in the arm. He'll show you his scar if you want. Ink caught a bullet in his chest, but his Kevlar just left him a huge fucking bruise. Same thing happened with Marvel from Tucson. Pyro from Colorado was shot in the shoulder, but it was a through and through with no lasting damage. Oh, and a bullet grazed Bones' leg, but he'll live. Oh, and Curtis? Fuck me, but that prospect can shoot. Let's just say, if you go to the range, never put your money on anyone else." He pushes back his long hair that's flopped into his face. "It was to our advantage that they were focused on you and totally fuckin' unprepared. We were more than a match for them." He breaks off and shakes his head. "What they did to you, Brother." Dart's eyes shutter, as though blocking out sights he can see in his mind. "If we hadn't got there when we did…"

I'd be dead now. I shudder, remembering their threats, how they were going to break all my bones one by one. *Just like Humpty Dumpty.*

Their voices are in my head. I shake it, trying to clear it, wanting to forget all about those threats, but something tells me it's important to remember exactly what they'd said.

Just like Humpty Dumpty. No one will be able to put you back together again.

But all I can think of is the pain. How, despite myself, I'd screamed like a fucking girl. I shudder. The beeping of the monitor next to me starts to speed up as I force myself back to those dreadful hours. From the moment Slit was killed to seeing Saffie, what I thought at the time shot, to being tied to the chair and stripped…

"Should we wait for Duke?" That had been Croak.

Then from their prez, *"Fuckin' Duke, he'll be gone a few hours yet. He's gone to Carson City to work on a new drug deal. That's what he should be concentrating on."*

Suddenly I know what I'd been trying to remember. I sit up, too fast, making that monitor go crazy, but with all my strength, I grab Dart's arm.

"Duke's alive! He wasn't there. He was out on a fuckin' run."

Dart's eyes go wide. Removing my hand, he stands. "Fuck it! You're saying he was one of the pair who rode out? Who was with him?" I shake my head. I hadn't known, and if I'd asked, I doubt I'd been told. "Fuckin' hell. Goddamnit." Dart turns and bangs his fist into the wall. "I've gotta go." He swings around and spits fast, "I've got calls to make."

He has.

Before he's at the door, I rasp out, "Saffie. She can't know." She thinks she's safe. I can't take that from her. I don't want her looking over her shoulder again.

Turning, he gives me a sharp nod, letting me know I don't need to explain. "She's under our protection, Brother. She's yours, she's ours. We'll keep her safe."

Fuck, fuck, fuck, fuck, fuck.

What do I do now? Saffie thinks that she's in the clear with no one coming for her. I'd told her it was now up to her what to decide, what she wanted from life. After all the suffering that she's been through, I can't take her new sense of security away. But that means I'll be lying when I've just promised to be truthful to her.

She thinks she's safe. *She's not.*

I want to see her smile. I want her to move forward without looking back. It's better that she believes he's dead.

Without his club, surely Duke's got enough to worry about. The rumour is it was a mafia hit. He'll think she died in the clubhouse.

As long as I keep her close by my side, and we perpetuate the myth that she's my old lady, there's no need for him to know either of us are alive. We'll have to make sure we find him, and this time, deal with him so he can't come back to life.

"Your visitor been upsetting you?" A nurse comes in, frowns at the monitor, then looks at my chart.

"He was just yanking my chain," I excuse him.

"Hmm." She takes my temperature again.

"Is he alright?" A worried looking Saffie appears behind her with a coffee in her hands.

The nurse turns to her brightly. "Looks like he is." Then adds, a little sternly, "Don't you go upsetting him, like your friend."

Christ, now she's going to ask me what Dart was talking about.

Saffie puts the coffee next to me, then takes the seat she was using before. Her mouth twists. "I didn't think Dart was going to tell you."

Tell me what? Does she know Duke's in the wind and even now she's not safe? Eyeing her carefully, of course she doesn't. Dart didn't get a chance, and I've only just remembered. I'm certainly not going to tell her. She looks more relaxed than I've ever seen her, and I'd hate to take that from her.

Not wanting to smash her newfound security, I prompt her to discover what she's talking about. "What's your take on what Dart told me?"

Her face falls, "Oh God, I hope it will be okay, Niran. Grumbler was falling apart when he left... Which I can understand after what I've been through."

Grumbler. What she's been through? My brain must have cleared as immediately neurons start firing, adding things together. *Fucking hell no. Not his baby.*

"How's Mary?" I ask, fast.

"On bed rest in the hospital. They're doing everything they can apparently."

Grumbler. Poor fucker. I did wonder why Dart hadn't mentioned him. Seems I've got my answer now.

They don't deserve this. They don't deserve to lose their baby. I rest back my head, mentally listing all the problems I've woken up to. My foot is smashed, repaired, yes, but it will be awhile until I can use it again, and the jury's still out on whether I'll regain full movement.

Duke's still alive. On one side, that's good, I still get my chance to wreak vengeance, on the other, if he doesn't believe the Crazy Wolves were taken out by a mafia hit, he could join the dots and come up with the Satan's Devils.

Add in Grumbler, and losing their baby will hit him hard. Damn that I'm laid up. I should be there, supporting and covering for him.

And there's Cyn's role in all this. What it actually was, I need to find out. Susie, I'm presuming, died in the raid on the clubhouse. *Or did she?* What did the Wolves do with their whores? Could she have been saved along with the trafficked women? *Would anyone know?* I can see the wisdom in leaving them to the cops and having the authorities deal with them. No one's to know the Devils were ever involved. But where does that leave us if she's still around?

Damn it to hell.

"You're thinking hard," Saffie observes, quietly. "Do you want me to go?"

Never. And now I've more than one reason to want her beside me. If I have my way, she'll never be out of my sight. She's still married to a motherfucker who's alive and breathing.

My heart rate speeds up.

"Niran?" She comes over and rests her palm on my forehead. "Are you alright?"

"Fine," I rasp out through gritted teeth, then add the excuse I know she'll believe, "I'm just worried about Grumbler."

"It's so sad."

When her eyes start to water, I realise I'm an ass, reminding her of what she's only recently been through. Gingerly, I move my hand, inch it over the bed and lie it on hers. There are no words of comfort I can offer, but I'm making a silent promise. *I'm here for you, Saffie.*

The door opens and a man in a white coat wearing a stethoscope like a badge of honour enters. Saffie moves as if she's going to give me some privacy, but I wrap my fingers around hers.

"You can stay." Old lady or friend, she has as much right to know what my likely prognosis is. Maybe I shouldn't make her stay if it turns out I'll never walk again. Nah, I'm too selfish. I'll crawl after her if I have to.

The doctor begins by greeting me pleasantly, nods to her, then starts going over my vitals. Impatient, I hurry him on.

"My foot, Doc. Will I be able to walk?" What I really want to know are my chances of riding again.

His face is unreadable as he glances down at the notes in my chart. I suck in air, preparing myself for the worst, getting ready to hear I've got to build a new life for the third time. Once I escaped to the Marines, then I became a Devil. Without my cut, without my bike, I have no idea where I'd be. I hold my breath until he starts speaking.

"In layman's terms I'd describe it as a jigsaw puzzle which we had to piece back together. But lucky for us, all the pieces were there. We've done as good a job as we could. It might not look pretty, but in time, you should be able to walk. You'll need to keep the cast on for a few weeks and keep all weight off it." He pauses, then puts delicately, "Considering your other... ahem... problem, you'll be confined to a wheelchair."

Damn it. At least when I lost my leg I was able to get around on crutches. I need to be mobile to search for Duke. What help would I be confined to a fucking chair? I get out my next words through gritted teeth. "What if I get a new prosthesis? Can I use crutches then?"

The doctor shakes his head, but his words are a cautious yes. "Mr. Rogers, your leg isn't the problem. The fracture in your tibia was a clean break. It's your foot I'm worried about. The cast will keep the bones in place, but any jarring will disturb them. You'll have to be careful. If we need to operate again, I can't guarantee I'll be able to save your lower leg. For now, it's best that you're patient, and take the utmost care."

My hands clench as I realise how much my independence means to me.

The hand I'm now holding too hard pulls away, but as I tense, it's only for her to turn the tables, and place hers on top. Now it's hers squeezing mine. "It's not forever, Niran. We'll manage. I'll... I'll stay with you until you're mobile again."

Stay, why? Out of misplaced guilt that she's the reason this happened to me? Or maybe, pity? I turn my head to face her. Her face shows not only compassion, but determination. But that magical pronoun she'd used, *we*, hadn't bypassed me, and whatever motive she has, I'll cling to it, to keep her beside me.

"How long do I have to stay here?"

"I don't see why you can't be released tomorrow," the doctor says. "You've not got any infection, and it's just a case of rest while you're healing. I'll get a physiotherapist to come talk to you about how to cope with a chair, and what you need as you've not got a weight-bearing leg. Of course, you'll have to have suitable accommodation…"

"Leave that to us," a gruff voice says. A man who'd entered the room so silently, I hadn't realised he was there. Bolt meets my eyes a little sheepishly. This is a conversation he shouldn't be privy to, but it looks like he doesn't care. "Just tell us what he needs, Doc, and we'll make sure he has it."

The doctor, also startled at Bolt's quiet approach, recovers quickly. Apparently having run out of things to say, he bids me goodbye and leaves.

I'd noticed when Bolt entered, Saffie had taken her hand from mine and huddled up on a chair. It's not hard for me to understand. Bolt must be referring to us going to their clubhouse, a step very much too far for her and perfectly understandable, given recent events. Not wanting to lose the ground with her I'd gained, I look straight at Bolt.

"I'll go to the hotel with my old lady until Lost can get us home."

Bolt raises an eyebrow, but instead of answering me, he turns to Saffie. He crouches down as if to make himself less of a threat, but Saffie still flinches and draws into herself.

"Hey, little lady," he starts. "Know you've got some issues with bikers, and after what you've been through, who could blame you? Our chapter's part of the Satan's Devils, but our expertise isn't in running auto-shops and tattoo parlours—not that we'd have any issues running such businesses." He adds the last fast and to me with a wink. "Our team is specialised, and what we do is highly secret. But you need to know who to trust, and I've been authorised to share with you some of it."

Saffie's eyes sharpen, but she still doesn't relax.

"The Freedom Trail got you away from the Crazy Wolves, didn't it?" Without waiting for a nod, he carries on. "Well, we work with them a lot. We take responsibility for moving people through our area, and as for the new paperwork, well that's all us. We had set up your new identity, darlin'. Got you that home you moved into and sorted you out somewhere to work."

"Did you see her fuckin' apartment?" I can't help myself. They're not doing a good job if that's where they moved her to.

"I moved," Saffie jumps in fast, sending a calming glance my way and an apologetic version to Bolt. "Duke got my details. He knew I was in San Diego. He must have hacked into your database."

"Not ours," Bolt says fast. "The Freedom Trail had your details, and that's where the security vulnerability was. We've helped them plug it. And as for you moving, that's how it works, and no one's judging you, darlin'. Once a person has relocated, they've a name to contact if they need help, but otherwise they're on their own and free to make their own life. You'd have been safe if the Wolves hadn't had an ex-fed at their disposal."

"Grit," she confirms with a shudder. Then with a little spark of interest, asks, "Is that all you do? Relocate abused women?"

Bolt shakes his head. "No, we do a lot more. Our bread and butter is setting up security. We're also experts in kidnap victim extraction."

"But you're a biker club." Saffie seems confused. "You wear the Satan's Devils patch."

"We are. Like most bikers, we want to live and ride free, but like any club, we need to earn money. Won't say all our methods are legal, doll, and that's where the Satan's Devils umbrella comes in handy. Wouldn't have been able to take out the Crazy Wolves as we have if we were a legit organisation."

Her mouth rounds in an O. She must have seen the destruction which was more of a military affair than one organised by the authorities. Even a SWAT team would have been more circumspect. Devils didn't care and weren't looking to leave survivors. But then she frowns. "You keep whores?" she asks, almost accusatory.

Bolt shakes his head adamantly. "No."

I wonder whether they don't has anything to do with security. If so, they'd be right in that. Just look what happened with Susie. Which reminds me, I need to have a conversation with Bolt, but not while Saffie's here.

Bolt elaborates on his answer. "There are two women in the club. Swift who's a full member and capable of kicking anyone's ass, and Cat, who's Stormy's old lady." He breaks off to chuckle. "And she's no shrinking violet either. Pulls Stormy up on his shit. She's pregnant. That going to be a problem for you?" He's not shy about being direct.

Saffie pales slightly, glances at me, but accepting everyone seems to know her business, gives a sad shake of her head. "Any problem I have will be mine, not anyone else's. It's just all too fresh. Seeing someone having what I lost... I can't lie, it will hurt. But I'll have to get over it."

"No pregnancy's easy sailing," Bolt responds, then looks at me. "Speaking of which, got you a phone so you can check in with Grumbler. He'd like to speak to you."

I draw in a breath. I sit up straighter in the bed, wincing when the action puts pressure on my foot as well as my other injuries.

"What's happened, Bolt?"

To Saffie's credit, her hand has covered her mouth, her eyes widen in shock, and an, "Oh no," is sighed from her.

"Call him." Bolt gets to his feet and hands me a phone. Christ knows what happened to mine. The Wolves had taken it off me. "This is new, set up with the numbers of your club and ours." He pauses and says, "Brother, I know you don't know us well yet, but that's something we hope to rectify. Some of the San Diego brothers are here as you've seen. But if you can trust us, let them go back. They're torn, wanting to be here for you, and there for Grumbler."

He walks to the door, then once there, turns back. "Oh, and, Brother? Dart had a word with me. That situation? We've got it handled."

CHAPTER EIGHTEEN

Saffie

The only time I'd ever had an opportunity to discover myself as a person was in that brief interlude between leaving my ex-husband and being ensnared by Duke. I'd gone from protective parents to my first marriage and moulded myself into the role of a perfect wife.

When I got free of the Crazy Wolves compound, or ex-compound to be correct—there's not much left of it now—all I wanted to do was escape and be me and leave the world of bikers behind. With Duke dead, I could have a fresh start, a new life with no one coming after me.

That I was considered Niran's old lady terrifies me. But if it wasn't for Niran, I'd be living a living death.

It wasn't Grumbler who'd persuaded me to stay, it had been a number of things. Surprisingly, it was the appearance of the dogs that had cleared my mind. They'd followed me, escaped the compound which had been as much of a prison to them as it had to me. Their trust in probably the only person to show them compassion had healed something inside me.

Niran wasn't the enemy, and he'd never been. I'd realised, despite my earlier misgivings that Niran had lied to me, that I was only rescued because he had orchestrated things so he wasn't going to be separated from me. That knowledge was the start of making me have doubts about whether I could just up and leave him. But when I'd seen how broken he was, knowing it was because he'd followed me to the Wolves' lair, well, what person could walk away?

He'd still deceived me, just like everyone else. I wasn't totally sure I'd ever fully trust him, but I felt I owed him to stay.

Niran already only has one leg, and now that's badly damaged, so much so, when I'd seen what was left of it, I'd turned away, wondering how it could ever be saved.

"He begged me to save his foot," a man the others call Preacher stated.

"He unconscious?" Grumbler asked, crouching down at his brother's side.

"Nah. I gave him some morphine, it's knocked him out. Moving him is going to be a bitch."

"Can his foot be saved?"

Again, Preacher answered Grumbler. "Just look at it. It will need a fuckin' miracle now."

My stomach had roiled. Niran could be totally disabled. And all because of me. His sacrifice could be too great, I owed him more than I could ever repay. Grumbler had been right. He needed me.

It was a strange turnaround. From the day we first met, I'd needed him. Needed a friend to lean on, needed his support, without him there'd have been no rescue. Now the tables have turned. In his state, he's nothing to offer me, but perhaps I've something to offer him? Something his brothers can't give. With them he'd need to be strong, with me, I'd allow him to be weak.

I had been trapped in my first marriage. I'd been literally imprisoned by Duke. I know what it's like to be unable to see a way out or to map a path forward.

Niran's not caged by a person but held captive by his own

body. His active mind, his desire for action, restricted by physical limits.

I know what it means to have your life constrained, and just maybe I could help him through. Instead of being a dutiful daughter or a trophy wife, maybe for once I could be useful.

Niran would never hurt me. I know that deep in my bones.

Those thoughts were what had made me insist on accompanying him on his life flight, and my insistence, to Grumbler's obvious surprise, that I was his old lady.

There's a fight going on inside myself. One part is screaming I don't want to be around men wearing cuts, the other reminding me I'm alive because bikers had rescued me. The paradox has me on edge.

I don't understand myself, why I don't take the opportunity and leave, but how could I leave such a broken man? When I was shattered in pieces, he'd been there for me.

I couldn't walk away from him. Not now. And, if I'm honest, as much as I'm here for Niran, I'm here for me. He seems like a lifeline, an anchor I still need, even though I could be free.

I'd been given a room in a hotel close by and hadn't thought about him being discharged or what that would mean for us. I'd been taken aback when the doctor had put it so starkly that he'd be confined to a wheelchair. Duh, I suppose I should have expected that, but I thought he'd have been kept in longer until he recovered.

I'd been living in a bubble. One where I met bikers who'd come in to see Niran, or who'd spent their time in the waiting room, hanging around to be there for him. Some I knew from San Diego, others were from the local chapter.

But tomorrow he's being let out and has been offered accommodation at the Utah clubhouse.

Hell no. I can't do that. Even temporarily the thought causes my heart to beat faster and my palms to sweat. My brain associates bikers with the Crazy Wolves, and I'm not sure anything will ever be able to counteract it.

I had listened outwardly calmly to Bolt's description of what the Utah chapter does, finding it at odds with anything I would expect. Their connection to the Freedom Trail who'd gotten me away from Duke was completely unexpected. I suspected from prior discussions with Patsy that the Devils had had some hand in my getting away, but didn't know it had been Utah, nor the extent of their involvement.

I was shocked to hear the clear regard he has for their female member, and then again in a different way when he confides Cat's condition to me and the sympathy in his eyes. It hurts that everyone knows what I've done, but there was no judgement there.

It would be hard to see a woman growing round and blooming in her pregnancy, that was me only a short time back. I've still not gotten over the misery of the future I've lost, and don't expect to ever do so. But especially so soon, being around someone pregnant would only serve to remind me.

I'm lost in my less-than-charitable thoughts when Bolt instructs Niran to phone Grumbler, and Niran makes the leap it's something to do with his old lady. *What's happened? Is Mary worse? Has she, heaven forbid, lost the baby?* I wouldn't wish that on anyone.

With my heart in my mouth, I watch Bolt hand Niran a phone, then, I watch him go.

"You want me to leave?"

Niran seems intent on making that phone call and ignores my question. Promising myself I'll go if he starts discussing some-thing I shouldn't or don't want to know, things that come under the heading of club business, I stay where I am.

"It's Niran, I got a new phone. What's up, Brother?... Yeah, not too bad. They've saved my foot for now though the road to recovery will be a rough one and the outcome undetermined. What's going on with you?"

Niran's face goes through all manner of expressions as I listen. His eyes widen, his brow furrows, his lips purse and his jaw clenches.

"What the fuck's preeclampsia?"

He might not know, but I do. It's when your blood pressure shoots up in pregnancy, a risk to both mother and baby. *Poor Mary.* Leaning forward a little, I strain to hear more, but still only get one side of the conversation.

"Yeah… Uh-huh… Brother… Yeah. That sucks. Keep me posted with updates… Grumbler, I'm so fuckin' sorry… I'll be back as soon as I can… Yeah." I watch him frown and grimace. "Yeah, Pennywise would be great at that. Give my love to Mary and give her a hug from me…" He smiles slightly and pulls the phone away from his ear. "Yeah… That's up in the air, Brother… Yeah, I'll do what they tell me… And you too. Take fuckin' care."

He ends the call, lets out a long sigh, then turns toward me. When he reaches out his hand, I read that he needs comfort, and place mine in his, going so far as to squeeze it.

"Grumbler and Mary always knew there was a risk, being what their ages are." His brows knit together and draw down.

"What's happening?" I prompt as he falls silent. I hardly dare breathe as I wait for his answer.

Mary had had so much compassion for me, and she was such a sweet lady, I can't bear to think of her going through what had happened to me.

Niran sighs heavily before replying. "Mary's got something called preeclampsia. Apparently, she's been suffering headaches and shit and didn't let Grumbler know. But she got herself checked and was diagnosed." His eyes meet mine. "She's in the hospital, and likely to remain there for the rest of her pregnancy."

"How long's she got left?"

"Eight weeks he says."

"Will they deliver the baby early?"

He shrugs. "They're monitoring her carefully and want to keep it cooking a little longer. But Saffie, Grumbler's been warned they might lose the baby." When he looks at me, I see moisture in his eyes. "Fuck, Saffie. This is all foreign territory to me. I never knew there was so much that could go wrong in a pregnancy."

I, and now Mary, have been an education to him. "She's in the best place," I tell him, knowing it's no comfort.

"Grumbler waited nearly six decades to find his ol' lady. It will destroy him if he loses her now." Niran's eyes crease in pain. "I just fuckin' wish I could be there for him." He pauses, then adds, "Pennywise, Salem and Dart have to go home. Grumbler's stepping back as sergeant-at-arms, and his job should have fallen to me. He suggested Pennywise fill his shoes until his situation is sorted." A flicker of pain crosses Niran's face.

A sergeant-at-arms needs to watch out for the club, even I know that. Niran would have been perfect for the role. I can understand what's got him upset.

"I should be there, Saffie. I should be there for my club."

He'd offered to leave it for me. It's clear what a crazy idea that would have been. "You'll be there," I respond firmly. "One way or another, you'll get back to your club." Once he's back on his feet, he'll take his place once again and will no longer need me.

He slams his fist down on the bed, hitting it repeatedly. "I should be there. I should be with my brother. I should be there, especially now." After the final words, he clamps his mouth shut.

"Why now?" I ask, sharply. Is it because of Grumbler's problems or something else?

He gives me a loaded glance but doesn't say more.

Up to now, I've been focused on me. My escape from Duke,

my pregnancy and the dreadful end to it, my kidnap and return to my husband. Me, me and me. My eyes have been opened. While it doesn't lessen my pain, I start to understand that bad things don't only happen to me. Niran might lose the use of his other leg, and Mary? Well, she and Grumbler might lose their dream. There's another woman today, wondering as I had, about the fate of her baby.

A tear escapes from my eye. As I wipe it away, Niran notices. He grasps the hand he's still holding more tightly. "I'm sorry, babe. I shouldn't talk about Mary. It's bringing everything back to you." His eyes, so full of compassion, land on my face.

"I'm sad for Mary," I tell him, truthfully. "And for you. If you hadn't gotten caught up in my mess, you wouldn't be here."

"What would you have had me do?" he replies, fiercely. "Let that bastard take you, knowing what he would do? Hurt you, rape you—"

"Force me to have another baby," I tell him.

"What?"

The word is echoed by another man entering. It's Bolt back again.

Shrugging, I tell them the story, talking about the legacy and about the chain of inheritance in my family. Both men listen, all the time exchanging glances. Niran and Bolt might not come from the same chapter, but they seem to understand each other's non-verbal communication, with a raise of an eyebrow here, and a clench of the jaw there.

When I've told them exactly what Duke had wanted from me, Bolt speaks, with Niran nodding as if it's already been decided between them.

"I'll check on your dad, see if he's getting treatment for cancer, or if Duke was lying, again."

I'm free. There's no one after me. I could go see my dad, reconnect with my parents. Of course, they might not want to see me, but if Dad is really ill, it could be the time for us to make up.

After a moment, I speak, my voice little more than a whisper. "I'm not sure I'm ready just yet, but especially if Dad's ill, I'd like to go visit them." But what would I say to them, and what would they say to me? If I'd listened, I'd never have ended up in this mess.

"It wasn't your fault," Niran says fiercely, seeming to read my mind. "Duke deceived you. Hell, now we know he had reason to."

"Give it time," Bolt suggests, with a look I can't interpret being sent Niran's way. "I'll find out the prognosis, and we'll go from there." He makes a change of subject. "Now, I came to tell you we're all set. The boys are sorting out a room for you both on the ground floor. I'll be back tomorrow and get you as soon as you've been discharged. Oh, and Saffie, Cat asked me to ask if there's anything that you need. She's a nurse and should be able to help with Niran."

A surprising burst of something akin to jealousy goes through me. *If Niran needs anything, it will be provided by me.*

What the hell? What have I got to be possessive about?

He's my old man in name only.

CHAPTER NINETEEN

Grumbler

"I'm already bored."

"Mary," I growl at her. "Fuck knows I don't want you here, but it's the best place for you to be." Normally she's an active woman. We'd had enough arguments when I insisted she give up her job. And thank fuck I did.

"I know." Sighing, she picks at the bedsheet. "I just miss you, Grumbler. I miss Alicia, and I miss our home, and it's only been a few days."

A few days, it feels like an eternity. Thank fuck Preacher had the plane and had been able to fly me home. I think I aged years on that journey back from Nevada. When I landed, I spied more grey in my hair than I ever had before.

From the moment we knew she was pregnant, we hadn't been blind as to what was in store. But with the scant update I'd received, I hadn't known whether she'd lost the baby, or heaven forbid, there was a chance I was losing her. But while her condition is serious, they're still both with me. And if I have to chain her to this hospital bed to make sure it stays that way, I will.

"I can take care of Alicia. Hell, that kid's of an age she can look after herself."

"There's the nursery…"

Yeah, we've not started on that yet, the risk of tempting fate always on our minds. "Don't worry yourself. You choose colours, and décor, and I'll get it fixed. The brothers will help."

Mary bites her lip. Lying in that hospital bed, she looks so small. I'm used to her being energetic, rushing around, doing stuff, getting involved. The house has seemed so empty since I've returned home. But I'm man enough to suck it up, as long as she does what she's told.

Laying my hand on her stomach, I look into her face, noticing she's got a little more colour than when I first saw her lying in this bed. "You concentrate on growing our baby. Our son." If there's a glimmer of pride in my voice, who could blame me? At fifty-eight years old, I never expected to father a child.

"How's Niran?"

I'd given her the barest details of the rescue in which I'd been involved, but I had to explain Niran's absence. When she'd thought his foot was smashed as a result of coming off his bike, I hadn't contradicted her.

"Niran and Saffie are going to the Utah club today. Bolt's keeping me updated."

"Is it safe for her?" she asks sharply.

I know why she asks. She was the first to meet Saffie, and knows she's terrified of bikers. "They'll be as respectful as any of our clubs, darlin'. Don't you worry about that. And if they're not, I'm sure Swift will do some ass kicking."

I've made her smile. Yeah, Mary was amazed when she met Swift. As we all were.

"There is that." She grins at me. "She's certainly a force to be reckoned with." I glance at the clock on the wall. She notices, of course. "You've got church, you better go."

"I'll go when Alicia comes. She's visiting straight after she's completed her homework."

Mary grins knowingly, and I wonder whether she thinks

Alicia has me fooled. She doesn't know I've bribed my stepdaughter to make sure she keeps her grades up. That will be a secret we keep between ourselves.

Then, she sighs. "I'm okay, Grumbler. Patsy's shared some books from her account, so I'll read."

"Patsy?" I narrow my eyes. "She reads that MC romance shit. You gonna be okay with that?"

"Hmm," she breathes out, then winks. "I'll just enrich my imagination with all those sexy sergeant-at-arms."

I widen my arms and wink. "You don't need your imagination for that. You've got the sexiest one here, sweetheart."

Snorting, she leans forward and pats my arm, saying condescendingly, "I know that."

Another upward look at the hands ticking around the dial, and I grimace. "I really ought to go."

"Scat." She waves her hands. "I'll be fine."

Standing, I lean over and plant my lips on hers. It was meant to be a peck, but I can't help myself, it turns more heated. When I pull back, her face is flushed.

"Go, before you get me all excited."

My face twists as I look down at myself. "Too late for me, darlin'." Shamelessly I resituate my now chubby cock.

I lived without sex for years, now I've got to do it for months. Shouldn't be a big ask, but that was before Mary. Without her, it's going to be hard. And yeah, that's no double entendre, that's my normal state around my sexy wife.

"Behave yourself, Mary." I point at my eyes, then at her. "Don't overdo it, or if you do, when I find out, you'll get a sore ass."

"Go before you make me any more promises you can't do anything about." She laughs.

I leave her with a smile on my face which fades as soon as I exit her room, and immediately stand with my back to the wall, leaning forward with my hands on my knees and taking a deep breath. Fuck. All the fears I had on the plane ride back haven't dissipated. The shock at discovering all wasn't well with the pregnancy had hit me hard. While I keep a brave face on around her, I'm worried sick about where this could be leading.

"Grumbler? Is everything okay?"

At the concerned voice, I raise my head, then straighten my back to reassure Alicia. "Everything's fine, darlin'. Your mom's quite perky today."

"Is she really going to be alright?"

Opening my arms, I pull her into me, holding her close. Of course she'd fucking worry, she lost her dad when she was ten. "Nothing's going to happen to your mom," I reassure my step-daughter, using the words to also bolster myself.

"Is it my fault I didn't notice how tired she was?"

"Not your fault at all," I contradict fast. Mine, perhaps, for leaving even though I'd noticed her looking pale. But what more could I have done? As she'd told me time and time again, she was pregnant, not fucking ill, until she was proved wrong. "Just do me a favour, eh, sweetheart?" When she looks up, her head tilted to one side, I continue, "Your mom's already given me more grey hairs. Just for the next couple of months, behave yourself."

Lightly she punches my arm. "Are you saying I'm trouble?"

No, I wouldn't say that. Yeah, a few months back she was, but having been burned once, her head's now on straight.

"You're a teenager." I shrug. "It's expected."

"There is that," she responds with a grin.

"Now go visit with your mom. I'll be back later." And I will. I'll stay until they kick me out. If Mary's got to be cooped up in this hospital, the least I can do is share that burden with her. Or as much as I'm able to.

Leaving the hospital, I divert to the house that I'd bought years back, but barely lived in and never called a home until Mary and Alicia moved in. I shower, change into a fresh t-shirt, then take a moment looking around our room. Fuck, but it feels so empty.

Invading Mary's chest of drawers, I take out some of her underwear that she'd asked me to take in, taking a moment to run my hands through the items I'm used to seeing her wear. My Mary's got a thing for nice panties and matching bras, not that the latter fit anymore.

Feeling like a perv, I raise the items to my nose and breathe in, but they've been laundered, no scent remains of her.

She'll be back soon, I lecture myself. Seven, eight weeks and she'll be home, bringing my son with her.

Maybe I should make the most of the peace while I can. *Fuck chance,* I admit. *I had too much peace before she came along.* Now I don't know what to do with it.

I want the house to be full of baby's screams, of her bustling around, of Alicia complaining she can't find anything. I want that. Me, an old, seasoned biker who never knew he was missing anything until Mary dropped into my life.

Now what before was enough is anything but.

Don't take her away from me, I plead to the mirror where Mary would sit, putting her makeup on.

Then, realising I'm sinking into the mistake of thinking the worst, I shake myself, pull on my cut and go out to my third most favourite lady. My bike, which had been trailered back from Nevada.

Yeah, this used to be my old lady, now she's been replaced by Mary, and Alicia too. Once I thought she was my everything, now I know there's more to life.

But old habits die hard. I spend a second brushing off invisible dust, before throwing my leg astride the seat, then starting the engine, kick into first, ease out the clutch and twist the throttle gently.

It's not long before I arrive at the club, but the clubroom's empty of all but the prospect. *I'm late.* I shrug. Before it would have bothered me. Now I've more important things to think about, things that take precedence over my club. And that's something I never thought I'd be saying.

Church has already begun when I walk in. I march to my seat next to Lost, and as discreetly as a latecomer can, sit, and try to indicate my interest in the proceedings. I notice Dart, Pennywise and Salem have made it back from Utah.

Lost pauses. "Mary?"

I sigh. "She's good. Well, as good as can be. And the baby's doing okay."

"That's great, Brother." Dart grins at me.

I raise my chin, then thinking now's a good a time as any, give them the rest. "Looks like they'll be keeping her in until the baby's born. I've decided I've got to step down. I can't be sergeant-at-arms while I'm spending all my time at the hospital with my ol' lady."

"I expected this." Lost doesn't seem perturbed. "Just comes at the wrong fuckin' time. We'd already agreed Niran would step up in your place."

"Yeah." I frown. "I've had words with him. He won't be fixed any time soon." *If he can ever ride a bike again.* "We both propose Pennywise step up."

"Whoa, Brother." Pennywise looks startled. "Hey, I'm just along for the ride."

"It's about time you started paying your way." Salem glares at him. "It's not all fun and games, Brother."

Pennywise gives Salem his finger, then a serious expression comes over his face. "I'm a sniper, a darn good one even if I say so. I'm used to acting independently and looking out for myself. It's not the same as watching out for the club. Especially with what we might have coming our way."

"Who else have we fuckin' got?" Salem asks, adding, "No disrespect, Brothers."

"None taken," Bones says with either a sniff or a snort, it's hard to tell. "I'm not cut out to be sergeant-at-arms."

"Nor me." Kink shrugs. "But when you want enemies tied up, I'm your man."

I snort, I can't help myself.

"Me? I'm an artist. A lover not a hater," Blaze states.

"I'm good with a pen," Scribe puts in.

Token indicates his laptop. "Got no time, Brothers."

Dusty sinks down lower in his chair and pulls his beanie down over his head.

"Whatcha all looking at me for?" Brakes widens his eyes. "I'm not doing that shit."

Snips' lips open. As eyes roll when they turn to him, he snaps his gummy mouth shut.

Lost shakes his head. "Deuce, Reboot, Wrangler and Keeper have barely patched in."

"Hey," Deuce nods at Reboot, "we've sat around this table longer than Niran."

"You want it?" I ask.

"Fuck no." They grin at each other.

"We need someone," Dart says in a reasonable tone, his eyes focused on Pennywise. "And I, for one, think you'd do a great job."

Pennywise lifts and lowers his shoulders. "Aw, fuck. I don't know. But I'll give it my all. I'm in. But…" he pauses, and looks around, "only until Grumbler's got more time on his hands, or until Niran gets back."

"Settled." Lost bangs the gavel and looks at me. "Give him your patch after the meeting, eh, Grumbler?"

I nod, but it's stiff. I was proud as fuck to be trusted by my brothers, who, despite what they say, could have done my job. It's gonna hurt stepping back, but my family comes first.

"Now, getting back to the business at hand." Lost pauses, and tugs at his short beard. "Duke, as we know, wasn't in the fuckin' clubhouse we blew up. I thought we'd gotten every damn one of them, but he, and one unidentified other, escaped by virtue of being out on a fuckin' run. So far, none of our info experts have discovered where they've gone to ground."

"You think he's still after Saffie?"

The VP sits forward, answering Salem. "I'd say yes. In his eyes, she's still his property, and in the eyes of the law, his fuckin' wife. Taking her back was his big mistake. It brought down the wrath of the Devils. Can't see how he's just going to walk away and start a new life. And, as it turns out, she was his meal ticket."

"But surely, he thinks she's dead?" Blaze looks confused.

"A mafia hit which left no survivors." Pennywise nods. "I can't see Saffie's got anything to worry about."

Lost glances at Dart and rolls his eyes. When he speaks, his voice is hard. "Duke's got contacts with the mafia. Don't you think he'll soon find out it's a lie that they're responsible? Once he knows that, where will he look next, or do you think he's just going to accept all his brothers have died?"

"And he'll point fingers at us because of Niran." Dart supports the prez. "If he suspects, or heaven forbid, finds out Niran's alive, he'll make the mental leap and assume so's Saffie."

"Utah decided to register Niran under a fake name in the hospital. Fuckin' lucky as it turned out."

"Yeah." Token nods approvingly. "They altered his old medical records to back that up."

"So," Pennywise frowns and sits forward. "We should be prepared for Duke to come knocking on our door." He pauses and seems to consider for a moment. "In my new role, I think I'd be remiss not to suggest going on lockdown."

"Serious step, Brother," Salem remarks.

Around come various expressions of 'fuck that shit' or 'suppose you're right'.

Me? As long as I'm free to go back and forth to my old lady, I tend to think Pennywise is right.

I tap the table. "Pennywise has made a good point. A man like Duke is fuckin' dangerous, and he'll want revenge, and his property back." I realise I'm giving my views as the sergeant-at-arms for possibly the last time. "He can't do it alone though. We need to discover who's likely to be working with him. Who was he meeting in Carson City for a start? Wolves ran pipelines for drugs, guns and women. The loss of that trade might hit hard, and they might support him in starting it all back up. He was VP. He'll have connections, and we can't discount them."

"I've been talking to Snatcher," Lost takes it up. "Our view is that all of our chapters should be on high alert if he's got any idea Saffie is still alive."

"Did we kill Grit?" Token asks, suddenly sitting forward and taking interest. "Was Duke on his own, or did he have back up? If Grit's around, that might make life more difficult for us."

"That's the unknown," Dart confirms. "We didn't stop to ask names, just took down everyone wearing Crazy Wolves cuts."

"You'd have to have dug out some of the bodies to check patches." Pennywise enlightens those who weren't there. "The explosions brought half the clubhouse down."

Fuck. It just gets worse. I'm so torn—torn between working for my club and spending time with Mary.

"We've another possible problem," Dart says with a frown. "Before we left," he jerks his chin toward Salem and Pennywise, "we grilled Niran about how the fuck he was kidnapped and not killed by the Wolves. Duke didn't stumble upon her address by accident. Saffie was betrayed, and Niran knew by whom. His guess was correct and that allowed him to fool Duke into believing the info came from him."

"Well don't keep it to your fuckin' self." Snips looks frustrated. "Who?"

"The main culprit was Susie. But she may or may not have been assisted by Cyn." Dart looks around cautiously.

The table goes silent. Then, "Cyn?" The name's echoed around the table with various expressions of shock.

"His *sister*?" Dusty comments with wide eyes. "She put her brother in Duke's sights?"

"How the fuck would she contact Duke?" Blaze asks, his brow creasing.

"She didn't," Dart states, waving his hand to get them to pipe down. "Susie did. Cyn's role must have been flapping her mouth, spilling everything she knew to the hangaround who's got the hots for Niran. Niran suspects she'd been eavesdropping and hearing things she shouldn't have. Susie's second cousin's a fed, and she got the information that way."

"A fuckin' fed?" Blaze crosses himself.

Token jerks as though he's been hit. "She can't be. I ran a fuckin' background check on her." Token, as though desperately seeking an answer, scrubs at his hair and hangs his head. "I clearly didn't go fuckin' deep enough. With that connection, she should never have been near the club."

"It was a second cousin, if that helps?" Salem tells him.

"No fuckin' help," Token growls. "I fucked up."

"Or," Lost rubs at his nose, "someone purposefully hid the connection so you couldn't find it."

"We need answers. Where the fuck's Susie now?" Wrangler half-stands as though he's going to go get her.

"Not here," Dart says fast, indicating he should retake his seat. "Somehow Duke enticed her to Nevada, probably tempting her with the thought Niran could be hers. Niran spoke to her, that's how we know about the cousin. Their reunion didn't turn out as she intended." Dart gives a twisted grin. "She ended up property of the Wolves instead."

"We didn't kill any bitches." Pennywise scrunches his face as though trying to remember. "Only men were in the clubhouse… oh…" His voice trails off.

Dart gives a sharp nod. "Either we killed her when we razed the clubhouse to the ground, or any sweet butts and she were housed along with the kidnapped women. Assuming they were all unwilling, it makes sense they were kept under guard."

"And what happened to them?" Keeper queries. "If Susie was with them, where would she be now?"

Dart shrugs. "We assume the cops would have called in the feds, and from there it depends on whatever story she told them."

Lost thumps his fist on the table. "Fuckin' hell. She'll guess at the Satan's Devils' involvement."

"Nah, she didn't see any of us," Salem states. "When Mace went in to check them out, he wasn't wearing a cut."

"I still don't like it," Lost growls.

"So now she, too, is in the wind?" Bones snorts and rolls his eyes to the heavens.

"If she has any fuckin' sense, she'll stay well away," Keeper states firmly.

"That's what I hope," Dart agrees.

"Can we get a prospect to keep watch on her apartment?" Pennywise suggests. "If she betrayed Niran and Saffie, then she needs to fuckin' pay."

"Agreed," Prez states firmly. "Though we have to be careful, given her connection to the feds."

Reboot rubs his chin thoughtfully. "If she thinks Niran was killed along with the others, she might even come back to the club."

Salem cracks his knuckles. "Fuckin' hope she does. As long as it's me who gets to talk to her. *Bitch.*" The last is muttered under his breath, but we all hear, and from the nodding of heads, all agree.

"What about Cyn?" Dusty asks. "She's still around."

"Bitch needs a beating at the least, and to be chucked out of the club."

"That's got to be up to Niran," I tell Snip. "I'm not happy about what I'm hearing, but I'm not sure of what she's done other than she opened her mouth, spouting things she shouldn't have done. I'm honestly not certain that girl's all there." I circle my fingers around my temple.

"That bitch is getting on my nerves," Deuce remarks. "I don't even know why she's still here."

"Me neither," Keeper grumbles.

Dart's eyes narrow. "Niran's got enough to concern him without him having to worry about his little sister. She stays until he says otherwise. But," he shakes his head, making his hair fly, "no loose talking around her."

"Fuckin' got that, VP." Blaze makes a show of zipping his mouth shut.

"You want me to talk to her? Get the truth?" Salem offers.

Lost thumps his hand on the table. "No one touches her. Not without Niran's say so."

Scribe's brow creases. "Why don't we just get rid of her?" When Lost glares at him, he adds fast, "Jeez, I mean send her home, not off her."

Prez sighs. "Because there's a risk that Cyn's heard more than she gave to Susie. We can't trust her to keep her mouth shut. Who knows what more she's learned? Nah, Brothers. I want her here where we're in control of her."

"What do we tell her about Niran?" I raise the point. "If she hasn't asked about him already, she will do soon."

"Oh, she's asked." Snips looks up to the ceiling then back down. "It's all I heard when you lot were in Utah. *Where's Niran? Where's my brother?*" He's raised his voice and asked the questions in a falsetto, then adds in his normal tone, "I just told her club business."

"That he's moved temporarily to a different chapter." Lost makes the decision quickly.

"Without him here, she might decide to move on on her own," Reboot suggests.

"Like we'd be that lucky," Wrangler puts in. "She's not our fuckin' responsibility. As far as I'm concerned, she should be fuckin' dead for the part she played."

"Niran's call," Dart says quickly. "And as Lost said, if she's here, we can keep eyes on her."

"I can discourage her from leaving." Salem raises his hand. "She likes her job and is good at it. I'll keep her busy."

"Assign a prospect to tail her, if she goes off compound for any reason," I suggest. "I don't trust her, now I know what part she played in Niran's misfortune."

"Talking of prospects." Prez seizes the opportunity I've given him. "First, we need to discuss fuckin' Kid." He pauses for a solemn moment to descend, then informs us, "Patsy and Alex have agreed to arrange a funeral."

"He got folks, Prez?"

"Nah." Token takes it on himself to answer Scribe. "No fuckin' one."

"I'm patching him in," Lost states, in a voice stating he'll accept no argument. "Kid gave his fuckin' life for the club, we can ask no more."

"Send him out with a big bang?" Keeper suggests. "All chapters sending representatives."

"Kid would have been over the moon," I observe, shaking my head at the useless loss of a promising life. "I'll get in touch with my counterparts once we've got a date set."

A moment of silence passes as we remember the prospect who'd served such a short time with us.

It's broken by the VP. "On the subject of prospects, I was fuckin' impressed with Curtis in Nevada. Can we give some thought to patching him in?"

Salem's happy to back Dart up. "I agree. Not only was he good with explosives, he did some excellent sharpshooting. He handled his shit well, and fuck knows he's been entrusted with enough secrets of this club."

I add my support. "I fuckin' agree."

"Leaves us fuckin' short, VP. It will only leave Connor. No way can we follow up Grumbler's suggestion of tailing Cyn."

"Don't forget Ross." I stare at Wrangler. "Bolt's been talking to him about being able to handle a bike. I suggest we bring him on board."

Lost looks at me sharply, then gives me a raise of his chin. "So the proposal is patching Curtis and bringing Ross in. Let's vote on the first." Lost grins, liking this part of the job. Hell, we all do when a man has proved himself. "Show of hands? Who's for?"

Every brother puts up his hand.

"Motion carried." Prez bangs the gavel. "Curtis to get his patch. We'll get that sorted at the next church. Now on to Ross?"

There are no objections to the ex-Marine becoming our latest prospect.

CHAPTER TWENTY

Niran

She's doing this for me, and I have to admire the hell out of her for it.

As Rascal wheels me in through the door of the Utah clubhouse, I glance over my shoulder at the woman walking behind. She's shaking like a fucking leaf and she's pale. In fact, she stops on the threshold.

"Come on in, honey. We don't bite," a rough voice calls out. It makes her jump.

A pregnant woman comes into sight and walks up to us. "Hey." She stretches out her hand to me. "Welcome." Her attention on me is brief, she seems more interested in the woman hesitant about entering. She steps closer. "I'm Cat," she introduces herself. "Were the clothes I sent for you, okay?"

Saffie's voice sounds forced when she responds, "Thank you. They fit well."

Very well. I hide my grin. Those jeans she's got on hug her ass to perfection. Perhaps it's lucky I'm in no state to do anything about it.

"You coming in or going out? Will ya make ya fuckin' mind up?" a gruff voice yells, making me wince. I'd hoped the brothers here would all be on tiptoes as I'd explained the situation to Bolt.

"Calm your tits, Grinch," Rascal shouts back. Then to Saffie, he says, "Apologies, sweetheart, he's one of the old-timers. They didn't learn about manners."

"Well?" Unrepentant, the voice shouts again. Then its owner appears.

He's the epitome of an old biker—grey shaggy hair, long beard down to his chest, a pot belly hanging out over his jeans. He puts his hand on Saffie's shoulder, moves her aside, then squeezes past the wheelchair.

Halting, he stares down. "So you're what we've had to widen doors for." He looks me up and down, and for a moment I hold my breath, hoping he's going to say nothing to upset Saffie. Then a wide grin splits his face, and he stretches out his hand. "Welcome, Brother."

I reach mine up to take his, but I don't keep his attention for long. His eyes narrow, then open and sparkle as he focuses behind me and on the woman he'd just moved out of his way.

"Well, welcome to you, little lady. Been a long time since we've had someone as beautiful as you grace our clubhouse."

"Ahem." Cat coughs loudly beside him.

"Ah, honey, you don't count. You're taken."

"So's she," I say fast. "This is Saffie, my old lady."

Ignoring me, he reaches out his hand. Saffie shoots me a look. I notice she's even paler. I try to transmit to her that he just wants to shake her hand. So, at my nod, Saffie takes his politely, but he seizes advantage, gripping it and pulling her inside. Once in, he doesn't let go.

"Hey—" I start.

"Shush," Bolt, who's obviously followed the man in from outside, hisses.

"Mystic, Goofy?" the old biker yells out. "Lookie what we got here."

Hearing a squeaked, scared protest from Saffie, ignoring the pain that goes through me, I try to raise myself up. Now it's Rascal who catches my eye and shakes his head.

"Hey. You going to introduce us?" Another older biker steps up, quickly followed by a third.

Grinch puffs out his chest. "This is… er?" He looks at her for help.

When she doesn't respond, or is incapable, I speak up for her, growling, "Saffie. *My* ol' lady."

"Saffie," he repeats proudly, as if he'd worked it out for himself. "I'm Grinch." He points to himself, then adds, "And this here's Goofy, and Mystic." He glances down at her and grins. "I'm thinking of adopting her. She looks just how I'd picture my daughter would have had she lived. Pretty as a fuckin' picture."

I see Saffie stiffen, then she turns her face up to his, her eyes wide and full of compassion. "Your daughter?" she asks hesitantly, adding as we're all prone to do when we hear of a bereavement, "I'm so sorry."

"Nah, don't worry your little head about it. It was way back. She was only given to me for five years, but that time was precious. More than the docs gave her when she was born." He reaches out gently and touches a strand of her hair. "She had dark hair, just like yours." He shrugs. "You're how I imagine she would have turned out."

Saffie seems to be at a loss for words, but more than anything, his words have reassured her as the rigidness of her stance begins to relax. She's not being treated like a prospective whore.

"Ma'am." The equally bearded man called Goofy tips an imaginary hat toward her. "Your man can leave you with us. We ain't like those young bucks."

"Young bucks?" Two men appear. One lays his hand over the other one's shoulders. The speaker snorts. "Young bucks he's called us." He raises his chin toward his companion who chuckles.

"I'm Honor." He turns and pouts as though blowing a kiss. "This 'ere is Duty."

Saffie at last finds her voice, curiosity spurring her to ask, not unjustifiably, given their posture, "Are you together?"

Behind me, Rascal starts choking. Grinch is grinning widely, and Mystic is doubled over.

It's the one called Goofy who answers her. First, he turns, gives a calculated look toward the two men, then one back at her. "Maybe they are, maybe they aren't. Truth is, we've never asked." He turns again, raising an eyebrow toward the pair.

Totally unconcerned, Honor removes his arm from Duty's shoulder, and reaches out his hand. Winking, he tells her, "Well, we don't share a bed if that's what you're asking."

Duty raises his eyebrow at his friend who barks a laugh. Saffie, though, seems more bewildered than scared.

"Whatcha thinking?" Goofy asks, allowing me to see how he got his name. He's got a big fucking goofy grin on his face, making him look totally harmless. Being the hardened man that I am, I suspect it might be an act.

It works on Saffie though. She answers, "You really are a different club."

"To the Crazy Wolves?" Rascal asks. "That we fuckin' are."

"Come on, darlin'." Again, Grinch reaches for her hand, and despite her earlier experience, she allows him to take it.

Once he's got her moving, he tugs her under his arm. "Let's get you introduced to the rest of the fuckers."

"You up to a tour?" Rascal bends his head to my ear.

"Got nothing better to do," I respond, my eyes narrowing. "I want to stay with Saffie." Grinch might be old, but hey, he's still a man.

"Understandable." He begins to push me in the direction Grinch has taken.

"Right, Saff." My eyes narrow. If that fucker wasn't so old, I'd be taking him on. Not only has he appropriated my woman, he's shortened her name. "You know much about our club?" When she shakes her head he continues, "Me, Goofy and Mystic are part of the old guard. We're your typical love riding bikes, bikers. Can't be doing with all this modern tech and fancy stuff. When the chapter changed direction, they built a new clubhouse, all glass and steel. It wasn't for us, so we stayed here, keeping up pretences Utah was an old-fashioned club."

"Yeah, that would have suited you better," Mystic puts in with a nod my way. "Fuckin' elevators in that place."

Grinch gives him a glare as if he's taking away his right to explain. "Most of the club lived there."

"Do they now?" Saffie asks, clearly wondering as I am why we're not being housed in a building more suited to wheelchair access.

"No." Grinch snorts. "There's nothing of it left now. Well, not after Stormy blew the place sky high."

"Fuck it, Grinch. For the last time. How the fuck was I to know how many explosives they brought in?" A man, striking looking, one side of his hair growing out, the other shorn short, comes striding up. He glares at the older man, then winks at Saffie. "He's partly right though, the explosion destroyed the clubhouse. I'm Stormy by the way, and it's good to meet you in person. I was responsible for sorting your paperwork out."

So this is the infamous Stormy that caused so much trouble for the Devils. A sniper to rival Pennywise's abilities, and a total ass. Though I have to admit, he's not acting like one at the moment.

As I look at him curiously, the woman who's not said anything after greeting us at the doorway, nudges my shoulder. "If you're wondering about Stormy, I tamed him."

Stormy tenses, and from what I know of his reputation, I

don't think he'll put up with that. *Fuck it.* Just when Saffie was starting to look more interested than worried.

In two strides he's next to Cat. He puts his arm around her, pulling her tight to him, nuzzles her hair with his nose, and states, "Too fuckin' right you have." He runs his hand over her swollen belly, then gently places his lips over hers. There's a fleeting heated look in his eyes, which fades fast as he glances to Saffie, and asks, "You want to see where everything goes down?"

When she gives a hesitant shrug, he takes it as acquiescence. "This way then."

There's one thing I'm fast starting to hate about wheelchairs, I'm not in control. Rascal doesn't even ask if I want to tag along, he just takes charge of the handles and we're following. Not that I'd object, I want to stay close to Saffie, and am curious myself, but hey, I'd like the choice.

We go down a corridor which morphs from the fifties-style building into something recently built. Stormy stops at a door with a camera above it, looks up and simultaneously touches his finger to a keypad. When the door opens, Saffie gasps.

I can see why. It's like mission control in here. Banks of monitors, computers, workstations seemingly equipped with all types of high tech, some of which I can't even name are all crowded in. There's a background hum, and lights flash on various equipment.

I think of Token back in San Diego and suppress a grin, thinking it's highly unlikely that any of the Utah men would be given blow jobs while they're working. Despite the lack of that perk, Token would be green with envy.

There are two occupants. Swift gets to her feet and comes across. "Saffie. Niran. It's good to see you." She points behind her. "This is Gears."

Gears nods and mock salutes me. "Good to see you again, Saffie."

There's a snuffling sound and a happy looking black spaniel appears. His tail is wagging like crazy. Swift sighs, and bending down, gives him a stroke.

"This is Apollo, or App for short," she informs us. "He's my hearing dog."

Saffie's eyes brighten and at the same time, she looks curious. "Hearing dog?"

Swift claps her hands to either side of her head. "I'm deaf. He's my ears when I don't wear my hearing aids."

"Can I pet him?"

"Sure." Swift beams at her as Saffie bends down and ruffles the dog's ears.

App is obviously in doggy heaven and lapping it all up. Saffie's brow creases. She stares at Gears, looking like something's just clicked.

"What happened to the dogs?"

"Fuckin' dogs," Stormy moans.

Gears grins. "They're kennelled out back."

"You brought them here?" She looks astonished.

Raising and lowering his shoulders, Gears expands, "Sure, they're well-trained dogs. We could use them around here.

"As long as you keep them out of the clubhouse." Swift points a warning finger at him.

"Yeah, yeah." Gears rolls his eyes. "I won't let them eat App." Swift snorts, and I'm half expecting her to say App could take them on, but Gears continues with a shrug, addressing Saffie, "I suppose, technically, you've got more claim to them. You want them?"

"Me?" Saffie squeaks and then looks at me.

When I cock an eyebrow at her, she realises I have no idea what she's talking about. "They're the Wolves' dogs. They sent them after me, but I'd already befriended them, so they took the role of protecting me."

And now I'm grateful to a pair of canines. It does make sense of the words I'd heard when I first knew she was alright. *Dog slobber*. I'd begun to think I must have misheard.

"They're good dogs," Gears says. "Though I suspect they'd tear a man to shreds if you gave them the right instruction."

I try to read her. Does she want the darn things? On my part, I'm not so sure I want to take potentially vicious dogs back to San Diego. As I'm trying to get a bead on her, she's doing the same to me.

Eventually she comes to a decision. "I think they're in the best place, if you can keep them."

Thank fuck.

Swift grins. "Gears is going to bring in a trainer. They might be able to help us on missions." It seems as long as they're no danger to her precious hearing dog, she's got no problem with them.

She's also right. They could be useful. I've seen some of the shit military dogs can do.

"As long as they don't fuckin' shit everywhere," Stormy groans. "One dog's enough. I've had enough of dodging land-mines when I go out back."

"That's what prospects are for," Gears informs him.

His words remind me of doing that task for the Wolves. I don't envy the poor prospect. Inwardly, I chuckle at how things have worked out, and that I could never have dreamed the Wolves' dogs would end up working for the Devils.

Grinch coughs from behind us. "Now you've seen mission control, are you hungry?" He's obviously bored.

Saffie looks at me. "I could do with a coffee," I tell her.

The next stop on our tour is an equal revelation, a kitchen equipped with top-of-the-line very new-looking appliances, and a man called Cowboy leaning over the stove.

"That smells amazing," Saffie can't help but exclaim as we walk inside.

The man turns around and gives her a nod. "Nothing fancy.

Just Boeuf Bourguignon. Done the traditional French way of course."

"Beef stew," Rascal informs us none too quietly.

"Fuckin' heathens." Cowboy slings an oven glove onto one of the worktops. "I don't know why I fuckin' bother sometimes."

"Because you love us?" Rascal suggests. Then, clearly alerted by a text, he frowns. "Okay, let me show you to your accommodation now, then, Niran, Snatcher wants us in church."

"You," Cowboy points a spatula at Saffie, "you're welcome here anytime. You, Rascal, not so fuckin' much." He marches across to a wall where a sheet of paper hangs up, and points to it. "These are the mealtimes. Don't be late."

Mealtimes? Confused, I glance up at my wheelchair handler, who just shrugs, then expertly turns me around, and we're retracing our steps, or tracks in my case, back into the clubroom itself and go straight to a hallway the opposite side to the kitchen.

As we move down the corridor, I remember what Grinch had said, as a doorway comes into sight, one with bare unfinished wood around it. This must be where they'd quickly widened the doorway. That they've done so much on my behalf gives me a warm feeling. More than anything else, it makes me feel welcome.

Rascal reaches around me and opens the new door and reveals our accommodation. "Bathroom through there," he points out. "I hope you'll both be comfortable here."

A soft gasp from Saffie has me realising what he's said. Well, fuck me, there's only one bed, and this room is for both of us.

Oblivious, he continues, "Take a moment to get freshened up, and then come out. Snatcher wants you in attendance." The final sentence is said to clear up any doubt.

He pushes me fully inside, then after waving Saffie in, steps out, closing the door behind him.

Before she can speak, I get in fast, "That's a big fuckin' bed,

Saffie. And I'm in no state to do anything to you, even if that's what I wanted."

She bites her lip and takes a moment to think. "To be honest, I'm kind of glad we'll be together. It makes me feel safer."

I wheel myself in further, checking the bed. It looks brand new to me—mattress, sheets and bedding, all clean and smelling fresh. "This is a very different club," I tell her. "Even to me."

"They seem…" She seems lost for words.

"Odd?" I chuckle. I'd thought that myself.

I wheel over to the bathroom. Disabled handles have been conveniently placed close to the toilet I'm pleased to see, and there's enough room to wheel myself in, and turn around. Glancing at the walls, I see the telltale signs of new sheet rock, and feel overwhelmed at the amount of work they've done just in a day or two, and all to make life comfortable for me.

"I gotta freshen up," I tell her, closing the door, then heaving myself from the chair to the commode. Jeez, I feel like a kid having to sit down to piss.

When I've finished and have made the return transfer back into the chair, washed my hands and splashed water on my face, I wheel myself out, pausing for a moment when I enter the bedroom. Saffie's already put herself to work, emptying the bags that have been brought in. New clothes purchased for the both of us by the Utah club.

I've a lot of thanks to give, and not just for our rescue.

I watch her for a moment, enjoying the view as she bends to her task, then with some regret, tell her, "I better go. You going to be alright by yourself?"

She turns and offers a weak smile. "Sure, I'll just stay here. I'll be fine."

There's no point in me telling her she'd be okay making herself at home in the club, so I don't waste the words. She'll have to learn that for herself. Nothing I could say would convince her.

I exit, and head for the clubroom. A man wearing a prospect cut is waiting for me. "This way."

I'm grateful when he lets me wheel myself then holds open the door to a meeting room. When I enter, I notice enough space has been left at the table for the wheelchair.

"Welcome, Brother." Snatcher lifts his chin toward me. "Some of us you've already met, but I'll go through them again in case you haven't. At my left is Thor, my VP." He raises his right hand. "This here is Preacher, sergeant-at-arms and pilot."

"Medic too," I remember, giving him an appreciative nod.

"Next to him is Swift our enforcer. Opposite her is Rascal our money man. Duty and Honor next to him, then Bolt who, like Swift, you know from their trip to San Diego. Stormy, of course, our resident asshole..." This raises a laugh and a snort from the man himself. "Then Cowboy, and Road, our road captain, and Swift's better half."

Swift responds with a scoff, and a rise of her eyebrows, while Road simply salutes.

"Then we've the trio of has-beens, Grinch, Goofy and Mystic."

With his lopsided grin, Goofy retorts, "I resemble that remark."

"And finally Gears, who's our newest patched member."

"You haven't got a road name?" Thor asks me directly.

I shrug. "Haven't picked one up as yet."

"Lucky bastard," Goofy mumbles under his breath.

"Okay." Snatcher raps on the table with his knuckles. "Let's get started now the pleasantries are out of the way. Just a refresh of the rules for Niran's benefit. Let everyone talk, and no one speak over each other."

Another strange turn to the club, politeness isn't normally stressed. But seeing my head tilt in question, Swift caps her ears, and without any embarrassment reminds me, "I'm deaf, remember?"

Ah yes, I do. But most of the time, you wouldn't notice.

"Moving on," Snatcher states, impatiently. "There's only one item on today's agenda. Duke Marshall. Stormy?"

Stormy's face grows serious. "We've got feelers out everywhere, Prez, but so far there's been no sign of him. We've backtracked and looked into who he could have been meeting in Carson City." All eyes are on him as he pulls a tablet toward him. "So far, no luck. We're looking at it from all angles. We've hacked into the police records of interviews given by some of the women that were rescued from the Crazy Wolves compound."

"Some of whom aren't in any fit state to be interviewed," Honor interrupts. "They're still in the hospital and/or getting counselling."

Stormy's face tightens. "Of those who were, how and where they were taken suggests they've been moved across country."

"Organised crime," Snatcher says.

"Exactly. All handpicked to provide delights to the depraved appetites of Vegas."

"Mafia?"

Stormy nods at his prez. "That's my gut feeling."

Duty sits forward. "The mafia tend to meet in a few different locations. It depends how important the Crazy Wolves' role was as to where he would be meeting them, and with what level of organisation."

"Niran, you sure he was going to Carson City? Could you have misheard?"

"I'm certain."

"We can prove it." Stormy gives me a lift of his chin. "We hacked into the traffic cameras around various locations and put the facial recognition software into use. Came up with this." He turns his own laptop around. Peering forward, I can see two bikers standing at a gas station. They've removed their helmets, and their faces can be seen clearly. "One's Duke Marshall."

"And the other?"

Stormy takes over again, spitting out, "Grit. Aka Jim Hampshire. Aka, ex-fuckin' fed."

Duke's own hacker and information expert.

Swift sums it up aptly. "Shit."

If anyone was worse to escape death in that clubhouse, it couldn't be anyone worse than Grit. Sitting in my wheelchair, I feel at a disadvantage. I raise my hand to get attention. "Getting back to the women and what they told the cops. Any mention of a woman called Susie?"

"Your betraying bitch?" Bolt asks. "Dart told me she might have been herded up with the rest of the women."

"That's her," I agree. "And I suspect that she was."

"She's not listed as being interviewed by the feds." Stormy frowns.

Honor's brow creases. "Could she have been fucked up so badly she couldn't speak?"

"Or," Swift puts in, "she got her cousin to get her out of their clutches."

Do I think she's learned her lesson? I can't see her coming after me again, or certainly not with thoughts of being my old lady, not when I used her so cruelly. But revenge is another matter entirely, and I'd put nothing past her. That no one knows where she is means there's another string loose which could start to unravel. She could be dead of course, but with my luck the way it is, I'd say that's unlikely.

"San Diego are staking out her apartment," Bolt informs me.

But that's not helpful unless she goes back there. "We've got a bitch on the loose," I tell them, through gritted teeth, "who deserves to be dead. She can link the Wolves to the Devils, and more than that, she's got an in with the feds."

"That's what I don't like." Snatcher glares around the table. "With luck, she'll think Niran's dead, and it's safe to go home. But if she doesn't deliver herself on a platter to our SoCal club, then it's up to us to find her."

CHAPTER TWENTY-ONE

Saffie

When Niran leaves me alone, I spend a while just staring out the window, considering the two chapters of the Satan's Devils that I'd met. Neither bear any resemblance to the Crazy Wolves, thank God.

While I keep waiting for the other shoe to drop, for them to prove they're no different underneath, my logical self tells me there's no comparison. *Except for that reference to a girl being tied up in someone's room back in San Diego.* Hmm. I'm not sure how I could have interpreted it wrong. Would a woman allow herself to be willingly restrained? *Some do,* I remind myself, if the books I read are to be believed.

Utah is yet another beast. It has all types for a start. At first Grinch had scared me, but when he'd mentioned he'd had a daughter and that I resembled her, I couldn't help but feel sympathy. I truly believe they don't care whether Honor and Duty are gay. Stormy openly appreciates his woman, and as for Swift, what can I say? The Wolves would never have accepted a woman member, whatever the circumstances.

Mealtimes? I chuckle, wondering whether Cowboy had been serious.

I think here I can feel safe.

From somewhere there's the sound of a motorcycle revving, and my palms start to sweat, my heart kicks up a gear, beating so rapidly it drains blood from my brain. I become so dizzy I have to collapse on the bed. My lungs heave, but I'm starved for air.

Safe? Far from it. I'm in the middle of a motorcycle club.

Recognising the signs of yet another panic attack, I try to get myself under control. Drawing in air through my nose for four seconds, holding it, and then breathing it out through my mouth as slowly as I can. I repeat, and then again, until my heart gets the message I'm not in flight mode.

I'm battling with my own head. However much I tell myself it's irrational, my nostrils seem full of the imagined sense of leather, and my skin itches as though I'm being crawled over by a thousand bugs.

The Devils aren't Wolves.

But how can I tell? I'm the stupid woman who's been wrong so often before. They might not be wolves, but they're dressed in leather. *Sheep's clothing,* my brain tells me.

I fight my own body, trying to calm myself. I was okay until Niran left me. Somehow it's different when he's there, even confined to the wheelchair, he makes me feel protected. For some reason, thinking of Niran is the one thing that calms me.

After a few minutes, my panic attack starts to fade, leaving me worn out and exhausted. Lying back on the bed, I close my eyes, but not to sleep, just to rest. Since the escape from the Crazy Wolves' compound, each night when I sleep, it's only to relive lying shot on the ground, but this time, the bullet hadn't missed. It's then that I wake, sheets tight around me, and covered in sweat. *Maybe tonight, Niran will keep the nightmares at bay.*

Because tonight, Niran will be sleeping next to me.

I hadn't been horrified to see we'd be sharing a bed. Niran's in no state to try anything, and if he holds me like he had back in my apartment in San Diego, he'll keep the monsters in my mind away.

The danger isn't being close to him. The danger is that I'll come to rely on him, and forget he represents everything I hate. I refuse to be an old lady, property, or even a wife again.

Interrupting my thoughts, a gentle tap comes on the door, followed quickly by a female voice saying, "Saffie, are you there? I thought you might like some company."

I recognise the voice, it's Cat. Cat, who's got everything I want—a healthy baby growing inside her. But she's tied to a biker for which she deserves my pity. I ignore the loving way Stormy had kissed her, suspecting it was an act, and that eventually he'll revert to who he really is. Just like Duke.

Nonetheless, I open the door, and stepping back, wordlessly invite her in.

She glances around the room. "You got everything? If you haven't, one of the prospects can go and get anything you need."

"We're fine for now. Thank you." I try to think of something to say, and end up asking the obvious, though I'd really prefer not to know. "How long have you got to go?"

"Three months." Her hand moves to her stomach. "I can't believe six have passed already." The smile drops from her face. "I know you lost your baby. I'm so sorry."

I don't want to hide the truth. "I had a termination."

She waves her hand dismissively. "I heard. And I know the reason. It's the kind of thing any pregnant woman worries about and wonders what they'd do." Her eyes fill. "You've been so brave."

Brave? I think I was anything but. I hate that tears come to my eyes, but I can't do anything to stop them. "I just couldn't… couldn't carry on, knowing there was nothing anyone could do."

"Oh, honey." She approaches me. "I'm so sorry."

I turn away, unable to face her sympathy, knowing I'll break completely if I allow myself to wallow in her compassion.

Cat seems to know what I'm thinking without me saying a word. "Want to get out of this room?"

I don't. Without Niran, I'm nervous, but I don't want to continue talking about things lost to me now, so I give a half-hearted nod.

First, she leads me into that fabulous kitchen and makes us both a coffee. For once, I'm not the one drinking decaf. She takes care cleaning up after herself. Then we return to the club-room. Apollo, Swift's dog, is lying on the couch. He raises his head as we walk in.

Cat scoots him away and then invites me to sit. Noting how new looking the couch is, I remark how it all looks fresh. Chuckling, she explains that it was all part of the renovations, when her man blew the old clubhouse up. She's got a twinkle in her eye when she says it, but that's followed by remembered pain. Then, she tells me the whole story.

"You saw him fall?" My eyes go wide imagining it.

"God, yes." She winces. "I never want to go through that again—Stormy slip-sliding down the building which was on fire and collapsing around him."

She seems so put together, that when she tells me the whole of her story, I wonder how the hell she can appear so serene. My eyes widen with horror as she explains she'd been kidnapped and raped, yet had come through, all down, apparently, to her beloved Stormy. My jealousy of her healthy pregnancy fades. After what she's been through, she deserves everything. I open up a little to tell her in PG terms about where my fear of motor-cycle clubs stems from. This is someone who can understand, though she didn't suffer for five long years.

We also discuss Niran's condition, and I'm pleased to find she knows what she's doing and has some helpful tips on how to make him more comfortable. Which includes making sure he takes his pain meds, however much of a man he tries to be about it.

Cat's good company, and fast becomes someone I could call a friend, and if I do keep stealing wistful glances toward her swollen belly, who's going to criticise me for it.

I'm smiling and laughing when a door slams back against a wall, and men's voices sound. I spin around. Cat shoots out her hand and rests it on my arm.

"Believe me," she says firmly. "These men would rather cut off their hands then harm a woman."

But an ingrained fear is hard to overcome, and my heart beats wildly until I see Niran following the rest. He sees me, and directly wheels himself over. In his path, Apollo gets to his feet with a sigh and moves. When he spies his mistress, he bounds across.

"You want a drink, Niran?" someone yells out.

As he opens his mouth, Cat leans forward, saying primly, "Not on those painkillers."

Niran chuckles, not taking umbrage. "You're right, of course."

Satisfied, Cat gets to her feet and goes to greet her old man. Niran takes my hand. "You doing okay?" His eyes examine me carefully.

"I think so." Then I try to say more brightly, "How was your meeting?"

"Strange," he says, enigmatically. "It's a different bunch of brothers here, and I've yet to get to know them."

Suddenly everyone starts to stand and move off in the direction of the kitchen.

"Hurry," Rascal says, moving past us. "You don't want to miss out."

Niran raises an eyebrow at me, and we start following the others.

Well, colour me shocked. Behind the kitchen is an area I haven't seen, another new construction if I'm not mistaken. It's laid out like a restaurant. A buffet is on the left as we walk in.

In something of a state of shock, I take two plates and put a small portion on mine, and a much larger one on Niran's. *Hot damn, this smells good.* We find a table set out for four, and having placed our food down, I move away one of the chairs. Niran smiles his thanks at me.

I'm too keyed up to be hungry, but as I put my fork to my lips, I know I've rarely eaten this well before. It surpasses the meals my father's live-in cook served while I was growing up.

Swift and her man, Road, take seats at our table, and Road looks across as a soft moan of appreciation escapes my mouth. He chuckles.

"Yeah, I was surprised when I first arrived. Cowboy," he jerks his head toward the man in the kitchen area, "was a top Navy chef. He's used to cooking gourmet meals for Admirals, and now he's cooking for us."

"No starter today though, and this is pretty standard fare," Swift remarks. The two share a satisfied glance which I don't understand.

Standard? I wonder what happens when Cowboy pulls out the stops. Bewildered, I just carry on eating. I so did not expect to be served top-notch food in a motorcycle club.

After our meal, we relocate to the clubroom, and Swift brings us some drinks from the bar, non-alcoholic for us both, Niran, because of his painkillers, me by choice. When Cat, Stormy and Road join us, I realise what's different. I can hear myself think, and conversation is easy.

I become suspicious about how quiet it is. The music plays softly. Men are drinking, for sure, playing pool and darts, and there's a card game going on. But it's tame, and apart from me, Cat and Swift, there are no women around.

I lean toward Cat. "Are they doing this for me?"

"What?"

Circling my hand around, I explain, "They're too well behaved for bikers."

It's Stormy, who, putting his arm around his old lady, barks a laugh and enlightens me. "The music's kept down when Swift's around." He hugs his woman tight for a second then releases her. "It fucks with her hearing aids. As for women," he glances as if to check there's none around, "there'll be enough patch chasers here at the weekend. The work we do, Saffie, needs full commitment and attention. It's actually rare we're all here. Often, a number of us are out on missions. Sure, we let our hair down, but fuckin' isn't the end-all be-all for us."

They might wear cuts, but I start to wonder whether they qualify as bikers.

Changing tack, he addresses Niran. "What are you going to do about your sister?" I notice Road tilts his head, seeming interested in the answer.

Niran brushes his hands over his head, linking them behind him. "Fuck knows. I've been trying not to think about that."

"San Diego's waiting on a decision from you."

"Yeah." He nods. "Lost told me."

"She betrayed me," I remind him. "And nearly got you killed. How could you ever forgive her?"

"If she knew what she was doing, I can't," he says, firmly, pain spreading over his face. "Cyn..." he stares straight at Stormy as though his words are for him, "Cyn's a kid in a woman's body. I'm not sure she knew what she was doing. She might have been lording it over Susie, showing off what she knew."

Stormy shakes his head. "Oh, I think she knew. From what I can gather, Cyn's possessive of you. She hadn't a clue she'd hurt you but didn't give a damn about what happened to your ol' lady. Just wanted her out of the way and knew that Susie would help her."

Niran sits forward, his brow creasing. "But why the fuck's she fixated on me? I barely know her. We didn't even grow up together. She came to see me out of the blue." Pausing, his eyes glaze as though he's thinking back. "She didn't know I was a biker, and when she found out, she took to living at the club like a duck to water."

"Patch chaser?" Stormy's brows rise.

Niran waves his hand dismissively. "None of my brothers would go near her. They got the message to be hands off, loud and clear."

Stormy takes a long sip of his beer, "Would they be interested if you took the reins off?"

Niran snorts. "After she all but got me killed? Maybe crippled me? I doubt they want much to do with her right now."

"See," Stormy puts his bottle back down, "this is what I'm thinking. Cyn sees something she likes and doesn't want to leave. Is it you, her big brother, or the club itself? Could there be a brother she wants?"

Niran chokes on his soda. "Whether she does or does not, none of my brothers would give her the fuckin' time of day."

Stretching out his legs and folding his arms, Stormy asks, "Remind me. Why's she with you, and why's she not heading home?"

"She objected to her parents splitting her and an abusive boyfriend up. Trouble is, it looks like Cyn still wants him, and if she goes back, it's likely it will be to him."

Now I can see why Stormy gets his name. His face grows thunderous and dark. "What's the fucker's name?"

"He goes by the name of Hester, that's all I know."

"Want me to dig into his background? See if there's anything we can use to put some distance between him and her? If we can, then problem solved, she can go back without worries she'll fall back into the same relationship."

While I'm thinking that wouldn't hurt, Niran slowly nods his head. "Sounds like a plan. Hell, Stormy, I feel bad asking the club to keep an eye on her while I'm not there to take the slack."

"They told her what happened to you?"

"Nah. I told Lost to tell her I was away on urgent business."

I tap Niran gently on the arm. "Why don't you call her?"

"You got taken." Niran turns flaring eyes on me. "You could have been killed. I thought you were fuckin' dead, you feel me? And I might never walk again. Yet you want me to talk to my bitch of my sister as if nothing's wrong?"

Shaking my head, I explain my thoughts. "She'll get suspicious if you don't go back. Tell her you got hurt. She'll either deny her involvement or confess. If the latter, she'll be distraught at the outcome."

"At some point you'll have to," Stormy puts in, reasonably.

Niran shakes his head. "I don't know if there's a big enough river to flow under that bridge before I want to hear her voice again." He reaches out his hand, touching me as if to ensure I'm real. "Saffie would have been killed if she hadn't fallen over her feet. That's my fuckin' recurring nightmare, Stormy."

Stormy's eyes darken. For a moment he's silent, then he gives a sharp nod, and getting to his feet, bids us goodnight and leaves us.

"Can't she just go home, Niran?" I wonder aloud.

"No." Swift speaks for the first time. "Keep your enemies close. I think there's more going on with Cyn than it appears on the surface. If you want, I can come back and ask her myself." Apollo jumps on her lap. Idly, Swift strokes him, but on her face is a fixed glare.

Her expression makes me shudder and realise I wouldn't want to be questioned by Swift.

"I'm tired as hell." Niran pushes his chair away from the table. "And you look dead on your feet. Let's call it a day, Saffie, and go to bed."

CHAPTER TWENTY-TWO

Niran

Despite the pain pills I popped before coming to bed, I can't switch off my mind. Whereas normally I sleep naked, tonight I'm wearing a t-shirt and boxer shorts. The unfamiliar clothing is annoying my skin, making me itch all over.

I'm also lying as still as I can, not easy as my foot and lower leg throbs, and I want to change position to ease it. But Saffie has finally dropped off, and I'm loath to disturb her. I know she has to be uncomfortable sharing the bed, but there's not much I can do about it. Even if I could insist on another room, I don't think I would. While she's beside me, I know nothing will hurt her, and will be there to soothe any nightmares.

I snort in my head. Me keep harm away? What could a no-legged man do if someone approached with evil intentions? Fuck all unless I had a gun at my hand. Which, here, I do not. Maybe something to rectify tomorrow.

Saffie being shot is on a revolving loop in my head. I just can't seem to shake it, even when I can hear her regular breathing. *I could have lost her.*

That I came close is all down to my fucking sister who, right now, I couldn't care less if I never set eyes on again. She's fucking lucky there's so much distance between us. While I doubt she intended the outcome, her intention had been to separate me from Saffie. Me, I doubt she had wanted harmed, Saffie, though, she clearly gave no damn about.

Lost had called me before I retired. After checking what I was doing, he'd informed me they were going to keep Cyn close. It was apparently my decision as to what to do with her. To be honest, she's the least of my concerns. Any damage she could do has already been done. I've time to decide what retribution should be coming to her.

It's who I can't find I'm more worried about.

Susie, for one. Where the fuck is she? My hand itches to wrap around her throat. But she only comes third after Duke and Grit who are far more dangerous.

Where are they? Will Duke have gone to ground? Does he suspect Saffie's alive? Does he harbour suspicions that the Satan's Devils were involved in taking his club down? An intelligent man may think it too much of a coincidence that their compound was destroyed so soon after they'd taken me there. Would he believe his mafia contacts if they said they had nothing to do with it?

It would be convenient if the Crazy Wolves had other enemies at whom fingers could point, but with my luck, that would be too much to hope for.

As I'd agreed with Lost, we should prepare for Duke to put the blame on the Devils.

The other question I can't stop thinking about is how the fuck can I make the world right for Saffie if I can never walk again. If I can't ride, I won't be a Devil. I won't have my club behind me. She might prefer that. But hell, I wouldn't.

I might have thought about turning in my patch but that was before every single chapter of the Satan's Devils had ridden to rescue me. How could I give up on them? They hadn't given up on me. How could I make Saffie see this is a life she could lead? What would it take to convince her?

I must sleep eventually as I'm woken by a hand placed gently on my shoulder.

"You okay?" Saffie's eyes are concerned as they stare into mine. "You've been groaning for a while. I didn't know whether to wake you."

I'd been in the midst of that fucking nightmare again—seeing her drop to the ground—and this time Slinger hadn't missed his target. But I don't tell her that.

"My foot hurts like hell." I turn my head toward the bedside table, noticing my tablets aren't there and the glass that had been full of water is empty.

With the intention of getting from the bed to the chair, I start to push myself up.

"Where are you going?"

"I need my painkillers. I left them downstairs." And I need more water. There's no way I'm downing those horse pills without lubricating my throat.

Saffie clenches her jaw, then puts a light pressure on my shoulder. "You stay here. I'll go get them."

Eyeing her warily, well aware of how much an ask for her that is, I check, "You sure? I need water too."

For an answer, she gets out of bed. She's wearing sweats, and like me, a t-shirt. Certainly nothing provocative or revealing. Nevertheless, she hesitates by the door, even from here I can see her shaking. When she takes a breath, then another, and still doesn't move, I think, *fuck this*, and start to rouse myself.

"Stay there," she says over her shoulder as she hears the bedding moving. Without further delay, she unlocks the door, opens it, and steps out.

Expecting her to return immediately, I begin to get worried when a few minutes pass. A couple more later, and I'm inching my way to the edge of the bed. *How long does it take to get one bottle of water and collect my pills?*

Just as I'm about to move painfully to my wheelchair—the effect of last night's medication having completely dissipated by now—the door, at last, reopens.

The first thing I notice is Saffie trying not to laugh. She walks over to me, holding a bottle of water out in front of her which I take gratefully from her hand, then passes me my pills.

"What's up?" I'm pleased to see her smiling, rather than being scared, but am curious as to what happened beyond the door.

"I can't believe this is an MC," she says, still grinning and perching herself on the bed. "Sure, the clubroom's a bit old, but that kitchen?" I nod, having been impressed myself. "You need to take those and get your ass moving."

"What's so amusing?" As I ask, I tap out the tablets I need to take, and swig them down.

"Because eggs Benedict is on the breakfast menu." When she sees my eyes widen, she raises her chin. "I kid you not. That Cowboy is something else."

Sure is an improvement over the sweet butts who cook for us back home. My lips twitch as I imagine Patsy and Eva trying to teach them advanced cookery skills.

"Is there anything normal on offer?"

She chuckles. "Eggs, bacon, waffles, which are homemade, sausage links. Apparently, whatever the," she pauses and puts the next in air quotes, "'heathens' want. But we've got to be quick. He starts serving in fifteen minutes."

Forgoing my shower, that's an ordeal I'll put myself through later, Saffie gets the clothes that I need and leaves me to dress, while she disappears into the bathroom. After her, I make a pit stop there myself.

The first full day in the Utah clubhouse goes well. After a breakfast which puts most I've ever had to shame, and yes, we both tried the eggs Benedict, Saffie seemed to be a little more relaxed. It could be more that there's nothing to worry her. Grinch, Mystic and Goofy disappeared to the attached auto-shop, and the brothers who remain seem ultra-focused, going in and out of their comms room, or pouring over plans in the bar area.

I, myself, feel like a fish out of water. They all wear cuts with the same patch on the back as the one I left in San Diego, which I'd last seen hanging on the back of Saffie's front door. But there the resemblance with our club ends.

With nothing practical to do, I can only focus on healing. Saffie gets out an e-reader Cat had lent her and gets lost in a book, and I play mindless games on my phone. It irks an active man like myself not to be in the thick of things. Even the fuckin' dog, App, has a job. The one thing stopping me butting in and asking to be included is that I feel outclassed. The brothers in Utah all have roles and know what they're doing, whereas I wouldn't have a clue where to start. My way of tracing someone is to get out and start looking, not sitting behind a computer screen.

Despite my boredom, we fall into a routine.

Church, minus the old-timers, takes place every day to make sure everyone is kept updated. It bothers me that not much progress is being made, and Duke, Grit and Susie all remain elusive.

Was Susie dead, or had she gotten away? Honor's concentrating on trying to root out the name of the fed to whom she's related but has so far failed to marry them up. The daily updates at least serve to let me know my new brothers are putting all their resources on it. While I miss the fuck out of my brothers back home, I can't deny staying here serves a purpose.

Being here is doing Saffie good too. She seems to become more at ease as the days pass. Stormy's woman has a lot to do with it. Cat takes her shopping, bringing back necessary but basic clothing and other items for me and her. Gradually, Saffie's starting to come out of her shell and is becoming more confident.

In the evenings when the old-timers come in, Grinch regularly monopolises her attention. The three of them often assing around and making her laugh with some of their outlandish stories, not many of which I believe. But I note her entering an easy relationship of these men wearing leather, and have on occasion thanked Grinch, as I know he's doing it purposefully.

I spend a lot of time on the new phone Utah supplied, calling brothers in San Diego. Mary, Grumbler says, is still hanging on. Bored as fuck being confined to a hospital bed but doing the best she can to keep their son cooking inside. More serious conversations ensue with Lost, where we try to assess the danger Duke poses. Lost tells me the minute he thinks Duke might have the Satan's Devils in his sights, he'll be locking down the club.

Of course we discuss Cyn. I don't know what the fuck I want to do about her. I'm livid that my injuries and Saffie's new nightmares can be laid at her door, and I can't shake my impulse to have her face some retribution. But I want to talk to her first, get to the bottom of what the hell she thought she was doing, and what the purpose was behind it. While on one hand she deserves the truth dragged out of her, I can't ask Salem to question her on my behalf. I hope I'll be returning to San Diego sooner rather than later and can resolve the question of Cyn once and for all.

I concur with Lost that Cyn could be a danger and it's best to have her close. I don't envy him the problem of daily telling her, no, she can't contact me, and he doesn't know when I'll be returning. On my part, I don't trust myself to speak to her, not until we're face-to-face and I can see whether I'm getting the truth out of her.

Time drags heavy, I'll admit that. A week's gone past and we're no closer to finding Duke, Grit or fucking Susie. They seem to have dropped off the face of the earth.

I hate being confined to a wheelchair. So when Bolt tells me he's got me an appointment to get a new prosthesis, I'm elated and eager to get started on the rigmarole to get it ordered. I'm already sick of being pushed around everywhere.

That day, I'm impatiently waiting with Saffie as Bolt seems to be taking his time getting ready to leave, when my phone rings. As she's taken to doing, Saffie steps away to give me privacy.

"You got Niran."

"Curtis here. How are you… Brother?" I knew who was calling having seen the prospect's name on the device.

"I'm—" I break off. There's only one reason for that form of introduction. "*Brother?*"

"Yup." That one word is tinged with pride. "Patched in last church. Picked up a new handle. Sharpshooter."

That's great news. I knew he'd make the grade. "I'm happy for you, but fuck. That's a mouthful." I chuckle.

"That's what *she* said," he responds, making me laugh from my belly.

When I've recovered, I ask the reason for the call. "So what can I do for you?"

"It's about Cyn."

Damn. My good mood is shot. "What's she been up to now?" I growl.

"She's not having a good time. No one wants to speak to her. If it weren't for her enjoying her job, I think she'd leave."

Is it fair on my club to lay this burden on them? Perhaps that would be the best all around. "I'll talk to Lost, Brother. That might be for the best."

"Think about it for a moment, Brother. What if Duke knows about her? What if he uses her to get back at us?"

"How do you figure he might?"

"Susie's in the wind. Don't forget at one time they were tight, and that's where she had to have gotten her information from. Susie might have let something slip, Niran. She might have said anything to try to stop them abusing her. Lost's filled us in on what happened to her, and the hell she probably went through that night. A bitch like her might have thrown your sister's name in to fuck with you. Cyn's a link to the club he might follow if he's sniffing around."

I start to form the words, *let him,* then I shut my mouth. This is my sister we're talking about. Although she deserves some kind of punishment, I don't want her blood on my conscience. Or at least, not until I know whether the situation calls for that.

When I don't speak, Curtis, or rather Sharpshooter, fills the silence. "Look, Niran. I'm ringing to ask your permission to get close to her. Something's wrong, and I don't know what. I think I know a way to find out."

It doesn't take much for me to read between the lines. "You're seriously asking me if you can fuck my sister?"

Sharpshooter snorts. "Well, after some foreplay, perhaps. Look, Niran, prospects get the shit end of the stick, we all know that. Maybe it takes one to recognise one. I just thought maybe, with you gone, she might appreciate some attention."

"I don't give a damn, Brother, do what you want." I can't even tell him not to hurt her, she's done too much harm herself.

"I hear you. I'll keep you in the loop if I find anything out."

"Hey, Niran. You ready to roll?" another voice interrupts.

Hastily I end the call with Curtis, then turn to face Bolt with a genuine smile on my face. I sure am. This is my first step back to normality.

We've assessed the security and the wisdom of the trip we're making, but there's been no trail to link me to Utah, or even anything to say that Saffie or I are still alive. Both of us had been booked into the hospital under fake names.

There's no reason Duke should be on the prowl. Even if he knows I'm alive, there was no one left alive to say what went on when they tortured me, or him to even consider me needing a new prosthesis.

Now he's ready, Bolt doesn't hang around. Ten minutes later, I'm situated in the rear of an SUV, the length of the seat giving me enough room to stretch my injured leg out. Saffie's up front next to Bolt, and there's an air of anticipation, of a new start—things to look forward to, instead of looking back. Of course I won't know how well my foot has healed until the cast comes off, but at least I'll be semi-mobile sooner than that.

Bolt has told me these people are fast, with an in-house lab, they can produce a new prosthesis within days.

The drive, which soon starts to bore me—like any biker, I hate being in a cage—takes four hours, and hell am I glad to arrive. I'm stiff and aching, and by the way Saffie stretches as we get out of the car, I'm not the only one. Bolt's busy removing the wheelchair from the rear, and I'm getting ready to manoeuvre myself into it, when a booming voice sounds.

"Hey fuckers!"

Turning toward the voice, I see a tall, heavy-set, bearded man, with a small blonde woman by his side.

"Peg!" Bolt shouts delightedly, racing forward. He links hands, then exchanges back slaps with the stranger. Then, remembering me, runs back and gets me settled in my chair.

The only man I've heard of with such a name is the Tucson sergeant-at-arms. What the fuck would he be doing here? I'm confused as Peg and the unknown woman come striding across.

"Niran," the stranger states, reaching out his hand. "Last time I saw you, you were un-fuckin'-conscious. It's good to see you kinda up and around. How the fuck are you now?" Automatically, I let his fingers engulf mine, remaining stoic as he grips it tightly. "This 'ere's Sophie," he informs us.

Suddenly things drop into place. "You were there, at the Crazy Wolves compound?" I'm still holding his hand. I give it a hearty pump. "Can't thank you enough, Brother." I've been told how many men from all the chapters had rallied around.

"And you must be Saffie." Peg grins down at her. "Fuckin' glad to see you in one piece, little lady."

"Hi," Sophie says, not shy in coming forward and wrapping her arms around Saffie in an exuberant greeting which my woman doesn't quite know how to deal with. "You're Niran's old lady, yes? I'm bloody chuffed to meet you."

Saffie's eyes widen, obviously surprised at the English-woman's accent and greeting.

I'm still mystified why they're here. "Is this happy circumstance or by design?"

Peg grins. "Your man, Bolt, here asked my opinion on this facility. Guys like him," he sneers, but not in an unfriendly way, "don't go to the usual pleb places like us." He nods at Bolt's bionic hand, certainly well beyond anything I'd expect. Though I doubt I'd have much use for toes which could grip things or any of the other fancy stuff he can do. Just something to allow me to walk is all that I want. Peg continues, "Just so happens both Sophie and I could do with a refit of the sockets for our prosthetic legs, and this is the place we use."

"Are you Peg's old lady?" Saffie asks Sophie, who responds with a loud laugh.

"Nah," Peg answers for her. "My ol' lady's a firefighter who couldn't get off shift. Sophie's man's the VP."

"You've both got prosthetics?" I ask.

"Yeah." Peg nods toward the building behind. "Good place this. They get you sorted damn quick."

Bolt's gesturing to us. He takes the handles of my wheelchair and starts to push.

"You drive up?" I ask conversationally as we move toward the entrance.

Not having to watch where I'm going, I turn as I speak, and notice the look of pain that crosses Sophie's face.

"Nah," Peg informs me. "We flew. Saves time." He casts a look Sophie's way, and his hand lands on her shoulder briefly.

There's a story there, but I don't press.

Instead of being a tedious wait, having company helps the time pass. While I'm talking bikes with Peg and Bolt, and the challenges of riding with various prosthetic parts, Sophie's entertaining Saffie with tales of how she came to the United States, and stayed under the personal protection of Wraith, the VP of the Tucson chapter. When she'd first arrived, like I am now, she was confined to a wheelchair, and picked up the very non-PC handle Wheels. The only time Saffie's smile slips off her face is when Sophie lovingly mentions her two little girls, but that's only momentary, and no one other than me notices.

My visit is quite quick as I need no explanations. Wearing a prosthesis isn't new to me, it's just a case of choosing the style and being measured to ensure the cup will be the correct fit. Peg and Sophie are even quicker, having come to this place before.

With the formalities completed, we stop off in town to grab a quick meal. Peg and Sophie have a plane to catch, and we have a long drive back to the clubhouse.

When we part, Sophie tries to get me to promise to bring Saffie to Tucson.

I could see Saffie was embarrassed at the assumption Sophie made that I was truly her old man, and hard to decline without saying our relationship is in name only. That's a matter I'm becoming more and more eager to change, but without a fucking clue how to go about it.

CHAPTER TWENTY-THREE

Niran

Knowing my prosthesis will be ready in a few days, I returned to Utah feeling much lighter. The wheelchair will soon be a thing of the past, and hopefully I'll only need it when I'm preparing for bed or getting in and out of the shower. It will be a balancing act with the crutch and prosthesis, but I'm certain I can handle that. I'm determined to, I hate not having any independence.

"Niran? Prez has called church. You coming?"

Raising my chin to Bolt, I then turn to Saffie. "You going to be okay?"

She looks up from her book and smiles. "Sure. You go and do your man stuff."

"Oi! I heard that. Bloody cheek." But Swift winks at her as she walks past, pausing by her chair and looking around as though seeking something, then leans down to Saffie, saying in an overly loud voice, "I see no men here. Well, not real ones, anyway."

As Saffie snorts, Road, who'd followed her in, lands his hand down hard on Swift's shoulder. "Not what you were saying just now," he remarks with a wink.

"Yeah, yeah, Swift. You're more man than any of us. All we've got are our dicks," Stormy mumbles as he passes by.

"Might be better if you stopped playing with yours for a moment," Swift retorts.

"Again," Road leans in, "not what you said earlier."

Swift leans back, raising her hand and placing it on his cheek, twisting to look into his face. "Okay, so I'll admit it. Some dicks are alright."

"Better mean just the one, woman," Road snarls, but his tone is counteracted by his fond expression, and by lowering his mouth to hers.

"Come on, Brother. I'll get you in."

I'd like to give Saffie a kiss, show my affection just like Road had shown Swift, but although we sleep in the same bed, we've not progressed any further, and I don't dare broach it. While my broken bones still have a few weeks to heal, a certain part of me is in full working order. Just her lying beside me has me sporting a stiffie more often than not. The more Saffie becomes comfortable here, the more she is gradually embracing the Satan's Devils lifestyle, the more I want to see whether we could work together.

Bolt and I aren't the last to arrive in church. I get myself settled, fastening the brake so I don't embarrassingly roll back from the table, and take a moment just to watch as the brothers around me get themselves seated. I've come to like and respect all of them. I notice two chairs remain empty, those of Preacher and Piston.

Snatcher is the last to arrive. He heads for the top of the table and, once seated, without commenting on the missing members, picks up the gavel. Having banged it once, he looks down the table, stopping when he comes to me.

"What's the latest on Duke Marshall?" He immediately flicks his eyes to his own members, showing the question wasn't directed at me.

I might not know but I'm very interested in the answer.

Honor clears his throat. "On delving into the Crazy Wolves, we've found a lot of ties with some of our other investigations. Like missing women, and an influx of drugs into the market." He pauses and consults the tablet that's in front of him. "We've been trying to link shit together, following leads to pick up a pattern. We've come up with a list of interested parties, people who may have had business dealings with that club."

Duty takes over in a move that's almost choreographed it's so smooth. "To locate Duke, we've got to find someone who knows where he is, or where he might hole up to lick his wounds. We've found definite club links to the mafia, and some of the seedier business types, and have been trying to narrow it down to names. We've come up with a couple that look interesting."

"There's a guy in Carson City. He's not part of the mafia but sometimes works as a liaison between them and suppliers like the Wolves. He might have information."

As Honor finishes speaking, Duty inclines his head and seamlessly takes over. "And a man in Vegas. One of the clubs we're pretty certain took the Wolves' merchandise. Red's said he'll check that lead out."

Snatcher raises his chin. "Yeah, Red was pissed at the thought Duke might be hiding in his town."

"But so far we've got nothing?" I can't be a spectator, I have to ask. "Surely Duke's business links are in the past. With no organisation behind him, he can't set up pipelines again, nor supply them."

"I've been listening to chatter on the dark web," Stormy puts in. "The Wretched Soulz seem interested in filling the vacuum, well, as far as in the drugs and weapons trade that is. Even they wouldn't touch women."

"Maybe not for business reasons," Piston puts in with a wide grin.

"They might," Swift interrupts. "They do run prostitution

rings, but I haven't heard the women are forced, more that they've got no other option."

"Have we asked them about Duke?" I ask.

Snatcher nods and rubs at his forehead. "I spoke to Drummer who's made an official approach. Wretched Soulz' line is that they gave the Wolves their charter but didn't look closely at their business dealings. Now they've taken more of an interest, they've found the Wolves had been stepping on toes. Rather than shelter Duke, I reckon they'd take him out."

"What we should be considering," Swift says, "is Duke's mindset. He's lost his property. Is he going to take that lying down? Any influence he had over Saffie's father is gone with her supposed death."

Rascal sits forward. "I've been checking Winston Bartell's bank accounts. There was a hefty sum going in regularly to Duke's accounts, but that stopped a few months back."

"Presumably as Duke's no longer providing proof of life?"

"Huh," Swift exclaims. "It's probable that her parents were the first people he approached trying to find Saffie. Once he showed his hand, Bartell had no reason to continue the payments."

"Was he paying much?" I ask, wondering what Saffie's worth.

Their treasurer shrugs. "Approximately a million every three months."

I whistle through my teeth. That's enough to keep any club going. More than our auto-shop brings in, that's for certain.

"Small change for Bartell." Rascal shrugs.

Just how loaded are Saffie's parents?

"What the fuck do they do with that money?" Snatcher snarls. "That clubhouse could have had gold-plated fittings with that type of dough coming in."

"Hang on a minute." Something's playing on my mind. My brow creases and I tap my fingers on the table as it comes back to me. "Knife didn't seem upset when he thought Saffie had died. That's a chunk of money to lose."

Stormy raises his chin. "You heard but you're not listening. Most of the money was going to Duke, not directly to the club." As my eyes fill with horror at the assets this man must have at his disposal, Stormy grins. "We have, of course, frozen any monies going out. All Duke will have is the cash he has with him, or what he can beg, borrow or steal from someone else."

"That means he'll be looking into who's blocked his accounts." Road's frowning. "He'll know he's a wanted man."

"He'll know that anyway. Whether it's the mafia, feds or another club who took the Wolves out, he'll believe someone will want to tie up loose ends. Which he and Grit are, by being alive. It's no surprise he doesn't want to be found." Rascal sits back and links his hands behind his head after making his pronouncement.

"What about the support clubs?" I ask. "Could they be giving Duke shelter?"

Snatcher's phone pings at that precise moment. He looks down at the device, reads a text, then he looks at me with a broad smile. "Funny you should ask that."

"Preacher successful?"

"Yeah." Snatcher nods at his VP. "He, Piston, Grinch and Goofy got access to all the clubs. All bugs discreetly placed and…?" He tilts his head and looks straight at Stormy.

Stormy checks his laptop then gives a thumbs up. "All working and reporting back."

"So," Snatcher directs his words to me again, "we've got ears in all the support clubs. If they know about Duke, we'll hear all about it."

I'm impressed. "How the fuck did you do that?"

"Lone biker broken down on the road, near enough to each." Snatcher consults the text again. "They only had one which was a bit dubious about giving sanctuary, but Preacher got around that. It involved a knife and some blood but got him access to the club."

"He cut himself?" Swift's shaking her head.

"Yeah, that man's a raving lunatic. He even bleeds for the club." Thor's grinning widely, and no one seems surprised.

"Anyway, once they had access, it was a simple case of depositing the bugs. Unfortunately only in the clubhouse, but hopefully their members have loose mouths."

Cowboy, quiet up to now, proves his use isn't only in the kitchen. "Why don't we bait them? Anonymously approach them and see if they're willing to work for us. Now the Crazy Wolves have gone, they'll be unprotected."

"And spike their conversations?" Thor leans forward, giving Cowboy a sharp nod. "I like that idea."

"I can get onto that," Stormy states seriously. "Then we'll wait and listen. If they're in contact with Duke, they'll run any approach by him."

Snatcher holds up his hand. "Let's see what they give us on their own first. Don't want to waste manpower if they don't know anything."

There are general murmurs of agreement, while I sit frustrated. I'd rather be doing something than nothing.

Swift's sitting frowning. After a moment, she throws me an apologetic glance. "We need to talk about the bitches—"

"Whoa, bit strong for you, Swift." Road remarks, with his eyebrows rising.

His partner shoots him a grin. "Normally I wouldn't use that term for women, but Cyn and Susie both qualify."

"Cyn's being handled," I tell them. "While I hate what she did, she had no way of directly contacting Duke. That was all on Susie."

"You sure about that?" Stormy raises an eyebrow.

"Absolutely. Susie admitted it." I wonder why we're going over old ground. "She used her cousin in the FBI."

Thor's frowning. "Susie's got no reason to think kindly of the Devils. Not when you literally threw her to the Wolves. Don't like the fed's involvement in any way whatsoever."

"Dig deeper and find the link," Snatcher instructs Stormy after acknowledging his VP's comment with a frown. "I don't fuckin' like anything that puts the Devils on the fed's bad side. Are you no closer to finding out who this fuckin' cousin is?"

"Susie's got a background which we think might be fake." Honor's announcement gets our attention.

Swift is first to react. "She was a fuckin' plant? Niran?"

I sit forward. "Nothing that bitch did suggested anything of the sort. She was a patch chaser pure and simple."

"Or that's what she'd have you believe." Stormy raises his eyebrow.

"But why target me? I wasn't an officer. Why not go after Salem? He wouldn't have turned her down."

"Because she likes Black dick," Duty remarks with a grin.

"I didn't give her fuckin' any. Not voluntarily," I snarl. "Bitch tricked me."

There are grimaces all around. No man wants to admit he had something taken from him he wasn't prepared to give.

After a moment, Swift sums up. "So Susie could be what she appeared. A fake background could simply mean she was running from someone or something. Or she was put in as a plant. But why the Devils? That doesn't make sense. Even the feds know we don't make waves or regularly deal in anything illegal. They'd be wasting their time."

"Agreed." Stormy raises and dips his head.

Swift's eyes now meet mine. "Why are you so certain Cyn's not a problem?"

"Sharpshooter's going to get close to her."

"Sharpshooter?"

"Recently patched in," I explain to her. "Curtis, who you met as a prospect."

Snatcher's head has been moving back and forth as though watching a tennis ball being batted around. Now he raises a hand. "There's one other option." When all eyes turn to him, he expands, "I'm sick of pissing around. We use Saffie as bait. Get Duke to come out of hiding."

"No!" I thump my fist on the table. "No, no and no. She doesn't even know the fucker's still breathing. She's starting to heal. She's even accepting the club. Her knowing will send her straight back to that mental pit of hell she's emerging from. And he doesn't know she's alive."

"Can we be sure of that?" Thor challenges.

I shrug. How would he know?

Snatcher pushes back his chair and stretches out lazily. Apparently, he hasn't given up. "We can use her without her knowing what we're doing."

"So we'll what? Set her up and hope to fuck he doesn't get her?" Not for the first time, I resent being stuck in this chair, seemingly limited to express my rage. Use Saffie? Risk her getting into Duke's hands again? Never.

"You think it's okay to let her keep believing everything's alright?" It's Swift who challenges me. "Niran, I know you want to protect her. But what if she gets to know Duke's alive and you haven't been straight with her? How do you think she'd feel about that?"

Protected? Kept safe? Or betrayed. Unwillingly, I have to admit it's the latter.

"Whether she helps us bring Duke out of hiding or not, I think she's got a right to know." Bolt places both his hands on the table. "You might think you're protecting her, Niran, but it's her life."

Placing my head in my hands, I wonder if I'm right, that Saffie would prefer to be kept in the dark. Hasn't she already been through enough? As she starts to relax in the clubhouse, shouldn't her focus be on moving forward and not looking back?

But what would happen if she found out I've been lying by omission? What would that do to the trust I'm starting to win back. I'm letting her believe she's safe to do and go wherever she wants, when she's not. Not until Duke is removed from the picture forever. She'd never forgive me.

If I want any relationship with her, I'll have to be honest. This is one instance where *club business* won't cut it.

"I'll tell her," I say, at last, my sigh showing reluctance. "But I'm damn well not using her to smoke Duke out."

CHAPTER TWENTY-FOUR

Saffie

Cat walks into the clubroom with Stormy. He kisses her, then goes off toward their comms room. She comes over and sits beside me.

I take the opportunity to ask a question I've been wondering about. "Do you consider yourself Stormy's property?"

She sits forward, and her eyes open wide. "Well, that's an odd opening. You've obviously got something on your mind. But to answer your question, I've got a cut with those words on it, so yeah."

My eyes crease. "I've never seen you wear it."

"Ha. Well, being six months pregnant might have something to do with that. I mainly wear it when we're out on his bike."

That's a good point. Giving her a sheepish look, I continue, "Don't you mind? Being called property?"

Sitting back, she sighs. "It was odd to start with, but no, I really don't mind. To these bikers, having an old lady is more of a commitment than saying 'I do' in front of a judge. It means I'm Stormy's, and he'd kill any fucker who touched me." She meets my eyes. "I feel cherished, cared for and valued."

"What are you two talking about?" Swift comes over and pulls up a chair. Her hearing dog settles down beside her. Her appearance makes me realise church must be out, though some of the men, including Niran, seem to have stayed behind.

"Being property," Cat enlightens her.

I glance at Swift. "You don't wear a property cut."

She snorts. "No, I don't. But that's because I've got my own cut in my own right. Doesn't mean I'm not property, just as Road is property of mine."

I widen my eyes. "Really?"

"Sure. Property is important to us. Road is mine." She shrugs. "It's a word, Saffie. No difference to us than saying you're a man's wife. Both convey ownership. Our way is to have no written contract between us, no spoken vows. Just a commitment, 'til death do us part. A property cut is just a visual sign you belong to your man. Nothing much different to wearing a wedding ring, except it specifies whose you are."

Unable to suppress my shudder, I explain, "It has different connotations for me."

"Only because it was the wrong man," Swift replies sharply. "There are abusive husbands around, Saffie. We've seen enough wives escaping assholes who think they own them and who want to control every aspect of their lives. Duke didn't treat you badly because he was a biker. Even if he didn't wear a cut and ride a bike, he'd have still been an abusive, cruel motherfucker."

"The whole club was like that."

"Like attracts like." When my head tilts as I consider her response, she carries on. "Take the Satan's Devils' chapters. I've no doubt anyone like Duke or his cohorts would soon be weeded out. The men, and woman," she waves to herself with a grin, "treat their partners right. Any prospect showing such disrespect wouldn't get his patch."

"The Wolves only patched those who were ruthless."

Swift beckons to Brute to bring her a drink. "That's because of the trade they were in. What right-minded man would want to flood the streets with drugs that were just as likely to kill as to provide a high, or kidnap and sell innocent women? You'd have to have a cruel streak a mile wide to be involved in anything like that. Anyone with a hint of humanity about them wouldn't have a chance of joining Duke's club. Your problem is, Saffie, you saw the worst, and connected it to anyone who rides a bike."

She's right. "I'm trying to get past that."

Her eyes fill with sympathy. "You've got PTSD, Saffie. And bikers are your trigger. It will take time to get over that."

"You're going to have to," Cat comments, but not unkindly, "if you're going to have a life with your old man."

I want to admit I'm living a lie, that I'm nothing to Niran, but part of me is jealous of what these two women have, something I've never had. A man who openly cares and obviously loves me. When I'd met Clive, I didn't know what love was, and then there was Duke, and what I had with him was all illusion.

Could I find that in Niran?

If I was to list the attributes of my ideal man, I would find more than enough in him. For the first time, I start to think rather than pushing him away, whether I'd be able to draw him in. I wonder what he would say if I suggested I wanted to become his old lady for real.

Could I live this life?

Could I? If the alternative was to say goodbye to Niran and never see him again?

But to be an old lady means not just overcoming the block in my mind about being referred to as property. It would mean giving him all of me. Could I do that? A shiver runs down my spine. Maybe Niran would accept a relationship without sex.

Don't be stupid. What man would?

If I want Niran, I've got to be prepared to go all the way. I'm not sure I'm brave enough yet.

I look up as I hear men coming my way, and smile as I see

Niran, then frown. His mouth has set into a thin line, and there's a tick at the side of his jaw. I can't tell if he's angry or upset.

I still don't have a clue when he says, "Saffie. Can I have a private word with you, please?"

I get to my feet and follow as he wheels himself in the direction of our room. Leaning past him, I open the door, then close it again, after we're both inside.

"Is everything okay?" He's worrying me.

He bows his head, wipes his hands down his face, then glances up. "Sit, Saffie, please."

Had something happened to Grumbler and Mary? Is Niran going to tell me he's fed up with playing this game, that he no longer needs me? Questions start racing through my head, but as he patiently waits for me to obey, I hesitantly perch on the side of the bed.

He brings himself closer, and reaching out, takes my hands. "Saffie," he starts, then swallows and shakes his head. "I don't want to scare you."

I wait for more. When he doesn't continue, I tell him, "You are scaring me. Just tell me straight."

"Duke wasn't in the compound when we killed the Crazy Wolves."

What? "Duke's alive?" If my voice squeaks, who can blame me?

Pulling my hands free, I get off the bed and pace to the window. Thoughts, all resulting in questions, slam into me, and I try to sort out what's the most important to ask.

In the end I settle on, "Does he know where I am?"

"Absolutely not," Niran assures me. "We don't think he believes you're alive. He'll think you died when the clubhouse was attacked. We were registered in the hospital under fake names. There's no way for him to trace you or me."

I snort. "I didn't even realise you were."

He shrugs. "I'm Niran Simpson, not Nigel Rogers. That's what's shown in their records."

Suddenly I'm angry. I round on him. "I should have known not to trust you. You're an expert liar, Niran."

"I didn't lie, I just didn't tell you the truth—"

"That doesn't make it right." I feel like bursting into tears. There I'd been, just thinking about how to make this relationship real, and now he's showing me what a fool that would make me.

"I can't trust you," I repeat, my voice sounding weak.

Niran drops his head into his hands and rubs at his brow. After a second, he raises his eyes. "What can I tell you, Saffie? I'm a man, we fuck up. It's what we do. But I didn't hold back the information for anything other than giving you peace of mind."

I look down at him. "How long have you known?"

The grimace tells me everything. Shaking my head, I turn back to the window again. *He's known the whole time.* Ever since our rescue. "Why tell me now?"

"I should have told you before." He sighs.

"But you thought I'd fall to pieces." I have to admit, maybe he's right. It's hard enough for me to deal with now, but I am stronger since I've grown to have friends in this club.

"We've been trying to find him. I thought we could take him out and you'd never have to know. But he's gone to ground."

Rolling my head back and circling my shoulders, I wonder why the news hasn't triggered a panic attack. Then, I'd lived months knowing he was out there somewhere, and managing to get by on my own. Nothing's changed, except I'm no longer alone.

"Was he the only survivor?"

He grimaces. "Grit and Duke were out on a run."

I shiver and wrap my arms around myself. I've been living in a bubble since I arrived in Utah, thinking Duke was far behind me, that I had a future I could look forward to.

But I hadn't, had I? I'd actually given no thought to what I was going to do. I've been living each day, here with Niran.

Why hadn't I started planning a future? Niran will soon have his new prosthetic leg. With all his brothers around, he's not needed me much anyway. He'd be fine without me. So why hadn't I been thinking where my path led next?

Why have I stayed with these bikers, instead of heading off to new pastures? I could have contacted my parents or gone back to San Diego on my own.

But I hadn't.

Was it because deep down I somehow knew this nightmare hadn't ended? Or was it because I didn't want to leave Niran? And if so, has that changed now I know the truth?

"Talk to me, Saffie. I'm so damn sorry I kept this from you."

He sees me as weak, and why shouldn't he? That's all I've ever been around him.

Suddenly I swing around. "Is this why I'm still here?"

"What the fuck are you talking about?"

I shrug. "If Duke was dead, I wouldn't need the Satan's Devils' protection anymore. I could go home. I wouldn't be your responsibility, Niran." I've been stupid. I should have guessed. That's why he's kept up the pretence that I'm his old lady, else the club would have thrown me out.

Why should I think otherwise? We sleep in the same bed, but he's never made a move toward me. We've never spoken of a future, or what would happen once he gets his new leg.

"Christ, I fuckin' hate this chair!" he exclaims, bashing his hands down on the arms, and swiping a hand over his head. "Why haven't you asked to go home if that's what you want? You thought the threat was gone, Saffie."

That's unfair. "I thought you needed me!"

"I fuckin' do!" Again his hands move, this time to the wheels, but he just rolls forward and back. It's plain to see the frustration that he can't move. "I need you, Saffie. Not as a fuckin' nurse, but as my old lady. Whether Duke's in the picture or not, it's you that I want."

A fresh blaze of anger goes through me, and I'm not even sure why. Annoyance at myself for being unable to commit to him, or at him for keeping me in the dark?

I go so far as to stomp my foot. "How the fuck can you want me as your old lady? We've not even kissed, let alone anything else. You don't have the hots for me, that's easy to tell."

"I don't?" he cries out. "Then why do I have so much fuckin' trouble hiding my hard-on for you each morning? Why is it torture to sleep in the same fuckin' bed? I want you, Saffie. I've always wanted you." He'd sat up straight, now he slumps. "But you're not ready."

Just hearing him say that he's been holding back makes my heart beat fast and my body prepare for flight. My reaction proves he's right that I'm not ready.

I'm annoyed at myself, angry at Duke who's turned me into this half-woman. I don't know what to say, so instead I run, taking sanctuary in the bathroom behind a closed door. I stand with my back against it for a moment.

Niran wants me.

Going to the basin, I stand with my hands pressed down onto the porcelain, and stare into the mirror. I'm the same woman I've always been, yet he's just said he's attracted to me. If I allowed myself to admit it, I'm attracted to him. I'm just so damn scared. I'm also sick to death of feeling that way, of letting Duke still control me.

What would it be like to have Niran's hands on me?

Am I brave enough to find out?

Whether Duke's dead or alive, I no longer want him to have any influence on my life. Why should I expect every man will be like him, every touch painful and cruel? When will I be able to break free? Will I ever be ready or is it something I can force?

Suddenly I come to a decision. Exiting the bathroom, I find Niran with his head again in his hands. I walk over to him.

"Kiss me."

His head shoots up. "What?" His eyes examine me, as if trying to tell my intention.

"Kiss me," I repeat.

One corner of his mouth quirks. "Kind of hard to do with you being up there, and me being down here. Think you'll have to make the first move, babe."

I can do this.

I lean down, brushing my lips over his. He places one hand on the back of my head, holding me so gently, I know I could pull away. Placing a hand against the side of his cheek, I press my lips harder.

Our mouths move together. His is softer than I expected, with only a slight scratching sensation from the rasp of his short beard.

He lets me control the kiss completely. Feeling braver, I press my tongue against his seam, and he opens for me. Again, he leaves it up to me how far I take it, mimicking my actions instead of instigating any of his own. It's nice, pleasant, but doesn't tell me anything about how he's feeling, and how much he reciprocates what I feel for him.

My nostrils are filled of the scent of leather, and a spicy aroma from the soap he's just used.

Leather, leather, leather.

It's the scent I associate most with Duke.

Moaning into Niran's mouth, I press my lips down harder, trying to find the uniqueness of the man himself while simultaneously wanting to tear myself away and run. My heart beats faster, and I grow lightheaded.

If I don't do this now, I never will.

Driven by a need to prove myself normal, that I can move on

from Duke, I suddenly swing my leg over his lap so I'm straddling him. It's awkward as hell on the wheelchair, but he uses his hands to steady me.

He's hard. He's enormous, I can feel, as I grind myself down, my movements getting more and more frantic.

"Saffie, Saffie. Stop." Niran's superstrength arms lift me.

"No," I wail, trying to reclaim my position.

"Fuck, Saffie. If I really thought you were into this, I'd take everything you're offering me. But you're not. I can fuckin' tell."

"I am!" I cry out, though whether to persuade me or him I don't know. If I don't do this, claim him as my man, I'll never be his old lady, and I'll have nowhere to go.

Somehow he's lifted me right off his body, and unless I'm going to fall, I have to stand on my feet.

"Saffie." He's sitting up, leaning forward, his hands still steadying me. "You don't want this. Not yet."

"I do." I feel my face burn. "I thought you wanted me too."

His face tightens as if he's trying to control himself. "Believe me, I fuckin' do. I'd give anything to take what you're offering, but, Saffie, this isn't the way it should be. You shouldn't have to force yourself. I can tell you're not aroused. Or are you going to lie to me?" His eyes blaze into me. "When you're ready, we'll both know it. You'll be begging for my hands, my mouth, my cock. You'll be so turned on you won't be able to help yourself. I won't make a move before then."

He's suggesting I'd be so desperate for him that I'd beg? Sex had never been that important to me, just an act to get over and done with, and preferably without discomfort of pain. It's not something I need, it's all for him.

I pull out of his hold and stand, my chest heaving as though I've just sprinted. I thought I'd gotten up the nerve. Thought him being aroused was enough, then he'd take over. If he fucked me, he'd tie us together.

But he's thrown it back in my face.

Duke's out there, still coming after me. And Niran? How long will he put up with a broken woman and protect me?

Embarrassed, scared, I rush for the door and run out of it.

CHAPTER TWENTY-FIVE

Niran

Jesus. What was that?

For a moment, I'm stunned. I never expected Saffie to come on to me, not that her approach wasn't wanted, it was. But it had been forced, as if it was something expected. Sure, I'd willingly take her to bed, well, try and make it work due to my current limitations that is. But not when I sense it's out of duty.

What had Kink said? That what she wants isn't what she needs.

There'd been no scent of arousal in the air, no flush to her cheeks. No signs that she was physically into me, though her brain was driving her to pretend. It would have been too fucking easy to take advantage, but my honour had prevented me.

This wasn't the way to win Saffie.

She'd tried to give me what she'd given to Duke. That makes me angry.

My first instinct is to rush after her, but I force myself to stay put and get my emotions under control, to work out why she'd make that impetuous offer.

Had it been because I'd told her Duke hadn't died? Placing

my head in my hands, I rub at my temples. Does she think I'll get bored and leave her alone while he's still out there somewhere? Does she think I need to be bribed to stay?

Oh hell. I'm proud to have Saffie as my old lady, even if she's not in my bed in any meaningful way.

Had I held back too long? I've been treating her with kid gloves, hardly daring to touch her. Maybe that's not what she needs.

Oh, Saffie. Internally I cry out in anguish. *What do you really need?*

When I've suppressed my anger, directed at Duke and not at her, I wheel myself out of the room and go in search of her.

I don't need to look far. She's in the clubroom, and so is Grinch dressed in his mechanic's overalls. He's got her curled up by his side, and she's sobbing into his chest.

A tightness comes into mine, a sense of losing what I never had. Then I mentally slap my hand to my forehead. Grinch would never look at her like that.

Indeed, as soon as he sees me, Grinch carefully extracts himself from her, and stomps across to where I've come to a halt.

"You're fuckin' lucky you're in a wheelchair."

"I didn't do anything," I defend myself, while knowing it's what I didn't do that's upset her.

"Grinch! He didn't, he…" Saffie looks up, horrified as she too notices his bunched fists. "Don't hurt him. It's my fault, not his."

Ignoring Grinch who's at least become hesitant, I navigate around him and approach her. "Saffie, darlin'." I don't give a damn we've got an audience. "I didn't reject you." I know she took it that way. Knowing I've been too hands off, I lean so far forward I'm at risk of falling out of my chair, just to take hold of her hands. "I care about you, so fuckin' much, Saffie."

Her eyes meet mine, but she gives me no sign whether I'm saying too much or too little, or whether it's far too late.

I wish I could get out of this chair, sit beside her and pull her close. But I've not so much as a leg to stand on. "I'm not saying no, darlin'. What I'm saying is we take this slow. You have no idea how much I want you. But I need you to want me too."

Grinch clears his throat. "You fuckin' hurt her, and I don't give a damn you're crippled. You'll get a beatdown. You hear me, *Brother?*"

"If I fuckin' hurt her," I say without turning, "I'll let you."

There's a pause before he says, "Then that's my cue to get out of here. Talk to your man, Saffie."

As I hear his footsteps fade, I squeeze the hands I'm still holding. "I want to make love to you. I want to take my time. I don't want a quick fuck to get it out of the way. I want to worship your body."

Her eyes finally meet mine. "Then why haven't you made a move?"

"Because I wasn't even sure we were on the same page. Now, I know, Saffie, let's take this slowly. We'll kiss, touch, explore each other. And only when we're ready, then we'll go all the way."

"I was ready today," she tries to object.

"No, you weren't. You thought I needed something from you, and I don't. Want it? Hell yeah."

She bites her lip. "I'm sorry I've made things awkward between us."

Chuckling softly, I contradict her, "Nah, I think you've cleared the air. I want you as my old lady, but I'm prepared to wait. I was thinking you didn't want me."

"I do, oh, Niran, I do," she cries. "I didn't want you to think it was just for protection from Duke."

"I was taking that as a way to stay close to you," I admit. "But I'd hoped to persuade you to stay. Even when Duke's finally out of the way." I tug slightly and unbalance her. As she comes forward, I pull her into my arms. "I've never met a woman like you before. So fuckin' strong."

"Me strong?" She huffs. "You thought I was too weak to handle the truth about Duke."

"I fucked up." I meet her eyes. "Saffie, I thought it would be easy. Find Duke and put him in his rightful place—six fuckin' feet under. Then time went on, and we couldn't find him. It became too late to admit I'd been leading you on. I can't promise I'll never make mistakes again, as I said, I'm a man."

She sighs. "I can see why you did it. You thought I couldn't handle the truth."

I play with a strand of her hair. "I was wrong. I think you can handle anything, Saffie. You're still standing after all that you've been through. I admire the fuck out of you for that."

When she looks surprised, I let her see the earnestness in my face. She shakes her head, before telling me, "I never even thought there were men like you." She grimaces slightly. "One lesson I've learned is that not all bikers are the same."

I take a deep breath and ask a question, "You going to be able to come back with me to San Diego?" One thing I know is I'll never be able to turn my back on my club. There's nothing I can do to repay them for saving my life, except give them my loyalty. But neither do I want to lose Saffie.

She doesn't answer straight away. Her eyes close briefly, her throat works as she swallows a couple of times. Then what she says surprises me. "Why did one of your brothers have a woman tied up in his room?"

"What?" I reel back, wondering why she's asking.

"I heard that night when I was in the clubhouse. One man asking another if he still had a bitch tied up."

I emit a sound that's halfway between a snort and a groan. "Oh hell, Saffie. That must have been Kink. He's into BDSM in a big way. And anything he does is one hundred percent consensual. I assure you of that. If he had a girl restrained, then it's only because she wanted to be."

"BDSM? Bondage?" Her eyes widen.

"Uh-huh."

"She was willing?"

"Absolutely."

She pushes her face against my chest. "I don't think I'd ever like to be restrained."

Again, I chuckle. "No worries there. When the time's right, there'll be lots more games we can play."

"Games?" She sounds surprised.

"Sure, babe. Sex should be fun."

Without looking up, she shakes her head. "It's never been fun for me."

Oh hell. Well, I've got my work cut out for me. "I'll be sure to make it that way. When the time's right, Saffie." And, I add to myself, *when I've got one working leg.*

She's quiet for a moment, and I just enjoy her being close. Holding her in my arms but this time not for comfort, but with hopes of a future. It's a while before she speaks again, and when she does, she surprises the fuck out of me. "I'll come back to San Diego."

"Yeah?"

"Yeah." She places a hand against my cheek. "I trust you, Niran. I think perhaps more after what happened today. You could have taken what I offered."

"Never think I don't want to." I stare at her intently.

She goes a delightful shade of pink and her eyes become hooded. "Can I kiss you again?"

"Of course you fuckin' can. Only this time, do me a favour. Don't sit on my lap."

Her colour fades. "Did I hurt you?"

Barking a laugh, I tell her the truth. "Nah, but I nearly fuckin' came in my pants just like a schoolboy. Here." I motion her to sit back on the couch and move my wheelchair closer. Then I pull her between my legs.

When our mouths meet, I swear I'm tasting a slice of heaven. This time I'm emboldened and take charge of things, sweeping my tongue into her mouth. After only a second's hesitation, she's following mine when I retreat.

I wrap my hand in her glorious soft hair, angling her head so I can get it just right. She moans softly, showing she's into this as much as I am. With my free hand, I trace her cheek, then her jaw. Her skin's soft, flawless.

Our kiss is gentle, with a wealth of emotion from both sides. It's not a prelude to getting off, but the main event.

Saffie is fucking perfect. Her taste is intoxicating. While our caress is having a predictable effect on my cock, I ignore it, knowing I need nothing more than this and could go on just kissing her for hours.

I probably would have done, or at least for a few more minutes, were it not for the clearing of a throat behind us.

Reluctantly, I pull back, turning to see who dared interrupt. It's Bolt.

He's standing, grinning widely. "The clinic called. Your prosthesis is ready."

"Yeah?" My face splits into a grin much broader than his.

As I'm calculating whether I can call on him again to drive us there and how soon, he gets in first, "Preacher said he'd fly us there if you want."

I fucking want. Oh, how I fucking want. To have a leg back again? I can't think of anything better, even if I'll still have to use crutches.

In almost less time than it took to drive the route one way, I'm at the clinic, and have had my fitting and am now equipped with a prosthetic leg, much like the one ruined in the Crazy Wolves' clubhouse.

As it was only a short trip there and back, Saffie had

stayed behind. She's the first to stand and greet me as I 'walk' into the clubhouse, taking care to balance myself on the prosthesis and crutches while keeping my injured leg off the ground.

Applause and cheers sound as I enter under my own steam, but I don't get long to enjoy my new vertical status, as Snatcher appears and calls out, "Church! Now!"

I take it that includes me, so tossing an apologetic look toward Saffie, I follow the men heading that way, noticing the three old-timers have stayed in their seats. Exchanging a chin lift with Grinch, I know he'll keep Saffie company.

It's great to be able to sit on a chair, though it takes a bit of manoeuvring and a helping arm from Road. I'm used to using crutches, but that's with a flesh and blood leg. Couple that with getting used to a new prosthesis and I'm like an ungainly newborn foal.

When I'm seated, I notice the serious faces of the men sitting opposite me.

Snatcher bangs the gavel, then hands over to them. "Honor, Duty?"

Honor kicks it off. "Niran, we've got some information about your sister. Would have told you privately, but Snatcher wanted it brought to the table so we can decide what to do."

Cyn? My eyes crease. *What the fuck has she done now?*

"Token's been monitoring her communications. She's in contact with Susie."

"The fuck?"

"Yeah," Duty takes over. "I can show you the transcripts, but basically Susie's trying to see whether you survived, and if so, to track you down."

"And Cyn's helping her?" My eyes go wide.

"We don't think so, Brother," Stormy puts in quickly. "Susie's playing her. Came up with a cock-and-bull story about why she hasn't been around. Cyn was a bit cagey, but confirmed you weren't in San Diego, but were with one of the other chapters."

Fuck. That's bad enough. "Susie knows I'm alive." I quickly shake off my despondency. "There's no way she can be in contact with Duke. She knows what he's like. She wouldn't go near him."

Duty opens a folder and shoots something across the table at me. From this way up it's only a piece of blank paper, so I pick it up and turn it over.

"Oh hell," I utter with feeling.

It's an image obviously snapped from a security camera. It shows Duke, Grit and Susie. "Why the fuck has she teamed up with them?" I study the picture, trying to see if somehow she's being coerced. It seems not. "I'd like to know how she caught up with them when we couldn't find them."

"So would I, Brother." Honor's shaking his head. "When did Susie come into the picture? Was it before or after Saffie moved to San Diego?"

"Before," I tell them with certainty. "She's been hanging around the clubhouse for months. And Susie's had no prior relationship with Duke, otherwise I'd be dead. He'd have known I was lying about betraying Saffie to him."

"He could have been toying with you," Thor suggests. "He was torturing you, putting you so close to Saffie. Let's face it, you were never going to be allowed to patch in. It was a matter of when, not if, he ended you."

Rascal's now staring at me. "You say Susie had been hanging around the clubhouse for months. How many? Saffie had been in San Diego long before you met her."

I hadn't thought of that. "On that timescale, maybe it was after then. But she came onto me before I ever knew about Saffie's existence. Unless she's clairvoyant, there's no way she could have predicted how things could have played out."

"What job did she do?" Snatcher asks.

I shrug. "Worked in a dress shop I think."

Honor snorts. "According to Token, she's an independent fashion designer. Works for herself."

Swift's been taking it all in, but not saying much. She changes that now. "Duke might have known early on that Saffie was in San Diego. Rather than sending men to track her down, he sent Susie."

"That doesn't fit," I tell her. "Why did she come to the club? He must have known the one place where he wouldn't find Saffie was in a club of bikers."

"That's easy," Swift tells me. "She's a biker bitch. I take it, it wasn't just your cock she was hungry for?"

"She gave it to just about everyone." I scoff. "But it was me who she wanted for the patch."

Snatcher bangs the gavel. "We can go on and on about this all day. The facts are Susie is now with Duke Marshall. And, courtesy of Niran's sister, Duke knows Niran was rescued while all the Wolves died. He'll guess Saffie's in the land of the living. He's been given four chapters to search to find you and her."

"You think he's got eyes on us?"

"If he can still call on the support clubs, we can't rule it out," Snatcher states. "From now on, neither you nor Saffie can leave the clubhouse."

"For how fuckin' long? I've got hospital appointments for a start." I hate being cooped up. And now I'm mobile of sorts, it's going to feel worse. As for Saffie, it's not fair to keep her locked down. She enjoys those shopping trips with Cat. I also want to take her out and spoil her, make her feel special again.

"We force his hand," Swift suggests. "Get back to Plan A. Use Saffie to tempt him out. Finish this once and forever."

I growl deep in my throat.

But Swift doesn't give me the time to comment. "I'd like to know Saffie's opinion on this. You're trying to control her. What would be her choice?"

"She wants him dead." As he was supposed to be. But I don't want to put her in danger.

Bolt taps the table with his real hand. "Saffie mentioned seeing her parents at some point. Why don't we set that up? We could use Cyn to tell Susie that's what we're doing. If Duke falls for the plan, we'll be there, staking the place out, and making fuckin' certain he doesn't get close to her."

"I like that idea," Stormy says. "Her father's got his own security. If we liaise with them, we can keep her safe."

"No," I say, simply. "It's not happening." I might not have met Bartell, but I don't trust the man. He'd not lifted a finger to save her.

"I can't see any other way," Snatcher states. "Though I think we'd have to work around any security Bartell has in place. Duke might have compromised them." I open my mouth again, but he raps the table. "I'll tell you why we need to make a move. Niran, you don't know this chapter, but it's not often we're all here. We're luckily having a quiet time, but if we get a shout, it's all-hands-on-deck. What if Duke's watching and decides to get closer when we've only got half the fuckin' club here?"

"We can't hang around in case of an attack," Thor backs his prez up.

Swift stares across at me. "Why not ask Saffie? If she says no bloody way, then we'll take that answer. But if she wants to be part of the solution, then we'll set it up."

I can only hope she refuses.

Snatcher starts to wind up the meeting. He's just one more request for me.

"I'll contact Drummer, Demon and Red. Can you speak to Lost and update him?"

I agree, of course.

When the brothers have left, I take out my phone and use the empty room to place my calls. First, I ring the newest member.

"What the fuck you playing at, Sharp?" I don't give him a chance to greet me. "You said you'd keep an eye on Cyn."

"We didn't confiscate her phone. Didn't think Susie might call her. But what's the harm done? So Susie knows you're alive, what of it?"

I'm angry, but still, I realise I wouldn't have seen the danger myself. Who'd have thought Susie would hook up with Duke, or that a conversation with her and Cyn would expose Saffie to danger?

"Susie's been seen with Duke."

"Fuck," he breathes out. "Niran, I'm so fuckin' sorry. I'll tell Cyn not to talk to her again."

I snort. "You'd think she'd do anything you tell her?"

Sharpshooter chuckles. "I think there's a chance."

Good luck with that, Brother. "I've gotta speak to Lost."

"Niran, before you do. Word of advice, before you blame, think rationally about what she's done. She's been kept out of the loop, and quite rightly. She received a phone call from a friend. All she did was tell her what she knew, that you were doing business with another chapter. How the fuck was she to know she shouldn't say anything at all?"

Damn it. He's right. "Point well made, Brother."

We end with the normal salutations, then I tap my phone to my lips for a moment. Sure, Cyn's disclosure puts us right in Duke's sights. I fucked up by keeping shit from her. *She can't be trusted.* No, but we could have told her both Saffie and I had died. But we never expected Susie to contact her.

Fuck it.

My call to Lost lasts longer. Once I've explained the position, he asks for clarification. "So if we assume Susie's been ferreting out info on his behalf, Duke knows she's not in San Diego."

"Snatcher's suggesting lockdown to the other chapters."

Lost's quiet for a moment. "We need to lockdown as well. He

might not take Cyn's word for it, and I don't want to be taken unawares."

I grimace. Lockdown is never welcomed by anyone in the club, but I'd rather my brothers were safe than sorry. We've got women and kids and I wouldn't want them to get hurt.

Which reminds me. "Mary's in the hospital."

"Grumbler's with her most of the time. I'll also put a prospect on her for when he's not," Lost decides. "We'll take care of ours, Niran. You take care of yours."

CHAPTER TWENTY-SIX

Saffie

I've listened, I've thought about it, I've weighed the pros and the cons. I'm scared shitless, but I've only one answer. "I'll do it."

"I don't want you too," Niran tells me, his voice determined and firm. "I don't like it at all."

We're lying in bed. Tonight, though, instead of Niran lying what feels like miles away from me, he's got his arm around me. His closeness makes me feel safe, and therefore brave.

"I wanted to see my parents anyway. And this way, you'll be with me."

"I'd be there anyway. If you want me to."

"Duke's got Grit, and maybe some support club members. But he's not a match for the Devils. I've already seen that."

Niran rolls over so he's looking directly into my face. "The best laid plans can go wrong, Saffie. There's a risk. Sure we'll minimise it, but a risk nonetheless."

Leaning back, I put an arm over my face. "I thought he was dead, Niran. I thought I was free. Now I know he's not, it's like I'm facing a prison sentence all over again. I need this to end."

"You don't have to be there," he decides, suddenly. "We'll set it up. Get Swift to dress like you—"

"Swift?" I huff a laugh. "She's far too tall."

"Well, I don't know. We'll find someone who resembles you better."

"No. It's got to be me. Dad won't play along if it's anyone else." He wouldn't be able to. It's his long-lost daughter he's going to be seeing. He won't fake emotion with anyone else, whatever his reaction is going to be, anger, because of the mess I've made of both our lives, or elation at his prodigal daughter's return. "I'm going, Niran. This time I want to be part of the solution, not the problem."

"You're never a problem."

How can he say that? It's all I've been ever since he met me. "You said I was strong, Niran. Let me prove my strength. Give me a fucking gun and let me shoot Duke myself."

He chuckles softly. "Now you're getting bloodthirsty."

Too true. Duke stole too much from me. Five years of my life and two babies. "Maybe it's Swift rubbing off on me. I won't break, Niran. I'm not as fragile as you think me to be."

"I don't think you're fragile. Maybe needed some gluing back together, but never weak. You're so fucking strong, Saffie. Another woman would be an utter mess, yet you're getting yourself sorted." He pulls himself up on one arm, and with his free hand, brushes strands of hair off my face. "I thought you'd refuse. I didn't expect you to want to put yourself anywhere near Duke."

"I don't want to, but I want this to end. You'll be there, and your club. They're the people that I owe my life to. They took out the rest of the Wolves. I'm sure they can handle two men."

"As I remember," he huffs, "I nearly got you shot."

"You saved me. Got me away from Slit." He knew his chances of getting away from the Crazy Wolves had to be zero if his brothers hadn't come for him. Yet he did what he could to go to Nevada with Duke, then blow his cover to prevent me being raped. How could I have ever lost my faith in him?

With Niran lying beside me, I believe I can do what they want of me and come out the other side. While just a short time back, I thought I had nothing to live for, I now want a life. The pain of losing my baby is still there, that will never be gone, but it doesn't make me want to give up, not like it had done at first. Perhaps in the future there'll be another baby for me, one that's healthy and given the best start in life. Maybe even with Niran.

A few weeks ago, it would have been easy to sacrifice myself, now I have something to lose, the future that Niran is offering. Instead of making me want to take the easy way out, I want to deal with my problems head-on. If that means facing Duke, then I'll do it.

With Duke in the world, I'll only be able to live a half-life, always looking behind me.

"There may be other ways to get Duke." I speak my thoughts, "But the quickest way is to tempt him out of hiding, and to do that, you need me. I hate him, Niran. Hate the influence he's had over my life, the legacy of the five years with him which I still bear. He's there in my thoughts. He's telling me never to trust you or your club. He's dragging me down every day, even though I try to fight it. He's coming between you and me. I want him *gone*, Niran. And if I have to risk myself to do it, I will. I need this. I need to be involved. Up to now, I've been a pawn, now I want to take charge." Pausing, I turn my head to face him. "I need him out of my mind. Which means I need him out of my life. Out of all our lives."

"You're so fuckin' strong," he whispers, bringing his face down to mine, the action causing our lips to brush together.

His body's so close I can feel his warmth on my skin. Feeling brave, I sneak my hand under the t-shirt he wears to bed, and rest it against his chest. His heart beats heavily under my palm, and my touch makes him hiss.

"Fuck, Saffie, you're killing me."

Hesitantly, his eyes on mine, he lowers his hand from my face, and rests it lightly on my shirt-covered breast. Such a gentle touch, it's almost not there. Despite that I can barely feel it, my nipples tingle, and begin to peak.

Clive's movements had been deliberate and followed a set pattern. A preparative kiss, a quick fumble at my breasts, then moving on to the main event which didn't last very long. I pretended enjoyment and was thankful for his lack of stamina and when the cuddling part came around. That I couldn't respond the way he expected was obviously my fault.

Duke took what he wanted, and knowing I was lacking in that department, it hadn't worried me. At the start, he'd used lube to make up for my lack of natural lubricant.

Niran, though, he's barely touching me. My body reacts without any instruction from my brain as I push up into his hand.

With his eyes fixed on me as though cataloguing every reaction, he brushes his fingers across my nipples, then pinches one lightly. My back arches as I feel a zing from my breast to my very core.

I wonder if my touch will have the same effect on him?

With my hand still on his bare chest, I find one of his nubs, and apply the same pressure as he did on mine. He groans and briefly closes his eyes.

"Fuck, Saffie, you've no idea what you're doing to me."

Tempting the beast, I think to myself, but it's without fear. Even if Niran was mobile and whole, I instinctively know he'd never hurt me, or force me to do more than I wanted.

He moves his hand from my chest and with it removes mine from under his shirt. Grasping my hand firmly, he focuses on my eyes.

"If you want to play, Saffie, I'm happy to oblige. I want to see your glorious tits. I want to suck them, play with them, and if you want, you can do the same to me. If you want to go further,

I'll touch you, play with you, get you off. But that's as far as it will go tonight. I am not giving you my cock."

It's said in a deep growly voice which goes straight to my lady parts, but when the words filter through to me, I frown. "That doesn't sound very spontaneous."

Niran's eyes darken. "You've been abused for years, darlin'. I want you to understand exactly what's going to go down, and have your chance to agree or object to it. I don't want to inadvertently trigger you or do anything you don't like. So for now, we'll agree limits upfront, and that includes you having a safeword. Something you can use to stop me if I accidentally go too far."

Pressing my lips together, I feel like we're negotiating a business transaction, not letting our base desires run wild. "I'll just say no."

"Sometimes no can mean yes, so you need to be specific." He chuckles as though it's a hidden joke.

"What?" When he doesn't speak, I encourage him again. "Tell me."

"It's sick, Saffie. But I was thinking your safeword could be wolf."

He's right. It is sick. It's not funny at all. But nevertheless, I laugh. "Okay, then, I'll cry wolf if you do anything I don't want you to." Then I grow serious again, my body urging me on. "Can I touch you?"

There's a sharp indrawn breath, then, "Touch all you fuckin' want. I'm all yours."

With those words, he pushes himself upright, and rips his t-shirt off over his head. My eyes feast on his body. He's muscular, his skin smooth, unmarked by tattoos, and gleams with a sheen from the bedside light. My hands reach out of their own volition as I want to see if it's as soft as it looks. He's a contrast, hard muscles covered with silky velvet.

He doesn't move, just lets me explore. When I finger his

nipples, he shudders, his muscles rippling under my touch. It makes me feel powerful.

"I've shown you mine," he mumbles. "Now show me yours."

I'm not perfection like him. My boobs which had swelled during my pregnancy are less firm than they were before. My ribs still show after the weight I've lost and not yet put back on, and my stomach is decidedly pouchy. When Niran raises an eyebrow, I wince, then sit up and slowly pull my shirt over my head, then half turn, partly to throw my tank top down and partly to avoid looking straight at him.

His fingers touch my lower back and I freeze as he sucks in a sharp breath.

"Duke made me," I tell him quietly, while in my head it all comes back. Me being held down while Weasel, the club's tattooist marked me, *Property of Duke*.

Niran traces the wording, and I wonder how angry he'll be. No man wants to see another's name on his woman's body.

But when he speaks, it's not to admonish or blame me, nor indicate he's turned off. Instead, he informs me, "Club's got a great tattoo artist, Blaze. He'll come up with something to cover this. It might be a cliché, but I can see a phoenix rising from the ashes, or something like that. Something beautiful, instead of this ugly reminder."

"I think I'd like that." I want every physical trace of Duke erased, and eventually, hopefully, to expunge him from my brain.

"Now turn and show those tits to me." Hesitantly, I do, only to be rewarded by him breathing out, "Fuck me, you're gorgeous."

Embarrassed by the lust in his eyes, I want to hide myself, so I move against him, pressing my chest against his. The feeling of skin on skin and the heat exchange between us makes my clit twinge. *He feels so right.*

He holds me tight for a moment, his hands stroking my back. Then, applying a little pressure, he pushes me back and lifts his hands. His heated eyes are the only thing touching me, but I feel my skin burn. He lowers his mouth and so gently mouths the tip of my nipple.

Another zing shoots through me.

He begins to lavish attention by massaging my breasts, sucking and pinching my nipples. All the time his eyes keep checking in to see the expression on my face. Eventually I give in to sensation, rolling my head back and closing my eyes and just allowing myself to feel.

I don't think I've ever been so turned on in my life, and he's only touching my breasts. I begin to wonder whether I'd survive being touched anywhere else. My breathing speeds up, and I feel warm.

My hands have dropped. I've completely forgotten I'm supposed to reciprocate. All I'm capable of doing is lying back and letting myself enjoy his talented hands and mouth.

When he resituates his cast-covered leg, and manoeuvres his body down, I'm treated to a trail of kisses descending my stomach.

"Oh God," I breathe out in anticipation as his mouth moves back to my breast once again, but his fingers continue the trail down.

He circles my clit, making my body involuntarily flinch, then his fingers continue to explore, delving inside me before returning to my clit. His touch is both firm and gentle. I moan, and my muscles clench once again as he does something my body seems to like.

He chuckles softly, then repeats his action, moving his fingers and strumming my clit. The whole time his mouth is sucking, and his other hand fondling my breast.

As I tighten again, he raises his head, and now moves his lips over mine, delving his tongue inside my mouth as though making promises of things to come.

Oh God, I'm so close. I moan, wriggle and move my hips up as his fingers continue to work.

His mouth is now at my ears as he demands, "Come for me now."

It's as if I was waiting for his instruction. My muscles ripple and tense, my legs go taut as I reach a peak higher than I've ever been before.

"Niran!" I cry out as I lose control, then forget to breathe as wave after wave of sublime ecstasy goes through me, prolonged by his expertise.

It seems to take forever before he gently lets me down.

I reach up my arm, encircle his neck and pull his head down. He doesn't disappoint, taking my mouth in a scorching kiss.

When he eventually draws back, all I can say is, "Wow."

Then I start to sit up, pushing him back, but he stills my movement. "That was for you, Saffie. I don't need anything."

His cock is rigid, I can feel it against my hip. "But you—"

"We agreed, Saffie."

This is a new one on me. Sex has been tit for tat, with more tat in my experience if I'm honest. It's never been completely for me.

I feel a bit disappointed, a little as though I'd been rejected. But if I'm truthful, also relieved. The thought of a man's cock going anywhere near me still makes me tense, and not in a good way. Duke had used it to punish me. Any pleasure I'd gotten from the act has long been forgotten. Though I wouldn't object to Niran pushing his advantage, it's something to be gotten through and I don't expect to enjoy.

"Not tonight," Niran says softly, moving himself again until his head is on the pillow and he's lying on his back. He pulls me close so I'm half on his chest. "We've got time, Saffie. No need to rush into anything."

It's for the best, I tell myself. He won't be prepared. Anticipating that time in the future, I murmur softly, "We'll have to get lube."

He half raises and turns his head. "Lube? Why?"

Embarrassed, I jerk my head to indicate downwards. "For there."

He snorts. "Babe, you don't need lube. Not with me." He takes my hand and forces it down between my legs.

Jeez, I'm so wet it's embarrassing. When my mouth opens into an O, he takes advantage and kisses me again.

When we pull apart, he draws back his head and chuckles, taking the opportunity to stress the point. "No lube required, babe." I snuggle against him, less embarrassed now as hopeful. With him, maybe sex will be different. That orgasm certainly was.

As his breathing shallows, the rise and fall of his chest lulls me into complete relaxation. But before I allow myself to succumb to sleep, I vow I'll play my part and free us of the nightmare following us around. Niran's someone I want to hold on to, and to give us a chance means taking out Duke.

Then I'll be free to truly be his old lady, and he'll be my old man.

With a shock I realise I'd wear his property patch if he asked me to, and I'd wear it with pride.

CHAPTER TWENTY-SEVEN

Niran

I hate this. Absolutely fucking hate it.

"You sure you want to do this, Saffie?" I cast a look at the woman beside me.

Her lips are pressed together, her eyes staring out in front and there's a determined set to her shoulders as she turns and simply says, "Yes."

It has taken two weeks to arrange. Fourteen days to get everything in place. One delay being a kidnapping which the Utah team had been called in to resolve. It had been interesting to see how they worked, how they pulled together, and how their expertise was employed. They'd successfully foiled the plot and got the victim back unharmed. Just another day in Utah apparently, but to me the life-or-death situation handled so calmly came as a surprise.

Then, for our part, what we were going to do wouldn't work if Duke was oblivious to our plans. The only way we could think of to let him know, was to work on the assumption that he was in tight with Susie for some unfathomable reason. Despite my intention to keep Cyn in the dark, Stormy had come up with the idea to use her.

Contradicting my earlier instruction that Sharpshooter was to lock all contact down between Cyn and the queen of bitches, I'd asked him to encourage it, fostering the friendship while feeding Cyn only information we wanted passed along,

Not knowing anything about the arrangement between Duke and Susie, we'd then have to leave sufficient time for the message to get to where we wanted it.

Of course, we could be completely wrong. Duke's meeting with the ex-hangaround could have been entirely accidental. But the photo had showed two people speaking amicably, and she hadn't looked like she was running for the hills. My gut tells me I'm right. For some inexplicable reason, she's thrown her lot in with him, and it's a fair bet that information will be exchanged between them.

Having failed yet again to dissuade Saffie, seeing her staring out of the window as though lost in her thoughts, in my head I return to that conversation with Sharpshooter.

"My sister driving you crazy yet?"

He'd gone quiet as though thinking. "We'll need to have a chat about Cyn when you're back, Brother," he'd told me, a little ominously. "But as for the business in hand, I told her exactly what you wanted me to. Token recorded the conversation." He'd chuckled. "Susie had a few choice words about you being with Saffie but seemed interested when Cyn passed over the information that you were going to visit Saffie's parents this weekend."

"She told her, just like that?"

"As I said, there are things you need to know, Brother, but I don't want to go into it now. But yeah, in the midst of a girly chat, she gave the update just as we planned. You can't criticise her for doing what you wanted. She doesn't know what the fuck's going on."

He's right, she doesn't. But I'd have thought she'd have shown some sense and some loyalty.

Fucking Cyn. As soon as I get back to San Diego, I've got to sort her out. She's trouble to me, and the club. If she was anyone else, I'd take her out for the part that she'd played. But she's my fucking sister. She might only carry half of the same blood, but how could I condone killing her? Conversely, sending her home without her making any recompense doesn't feel right. Her betrayal nearly got both me and Saffie killed, and she's got to atone for that. *Maybe sending her back to that abusive fuck of a boyfriend would be punishment.*

I relegate that problem to the back of my mind, and concentrate on the now as the brr-ing sound indicates a call coming in. It's Snatcher.

"Red's got brothers in place around the perimeter." As we're in Nevada, Red had offered his support, and we'd gratefully accepted. "Stormy and the other snipers are in position. Thor and Rascal have just taken over from the guards in the gatehouse."

I smile to myself. Our initial view against warning Bartell in case anyone on his staff was on Duke's payroll was reinforced for different reasons once we'd hacked into his security cameras. Having studied the behaviour of his security staff, we'd determined they were unpractised, lazy and used to being a deterrent rather than capable of any action. Hence, Thor taking control of the guardhouse without a shot being fired. We'd have heard if he'd run into trouble. We're just coming up to the entrance now.

"Swift, Preacher, Piston, Road and Cowboy are inside the grounds at any possible points of entry. Gears is managing the drones. Honor and Duty are back at base, watching the monitors and analysing activity from CCTV in the area," Snatcher continues. He pauses, waits a beat, then advises, "Niran, Saffie. You're good to go."

This is it. I turn to Saffie, taking her hand and tightening my fingers around hers. She looks worried, but when she turns to face me, she gives me a brave little nod.

As the gates open, Bolt drives the car disguised as a cab through. Gazing ahead, I watch as we traverse the long driveway, and as the mansion appears ahead. I knew Saffie's parents had money, but this is beyond anything I expected. I cast another look at the woman beside me.

She's changing in front of my eyes. I'd left Utah with a biker babe, not that she'd appreciate me describing her that way, but her tight jeans, t-shirt, and the way her hair hangs loose, screams to me she was dressed to be riding up behind me.

Now she's in the same clothing, but she's combed back her hair, taming it, and there's a new poise about her. It's in the raise of her head and in the set of her shoulders, as if she's morphed into a different persona.

For the first time since we met, I don't feel worthy of her. What am I, but a damaged vet? She's a socialite and heir to a fucking fortune.

I thought I'd be the one to offer reassurance, now I'm not so certain it won't be me needing it from her. I'm so out of my depth.

They're monied but they're still human, I try to convince myself.

Bolt catches my eye in the rearview mirror and gives me a chin raise. It's a reminder that we're not on our own. He'll be waiting outside.

We've set it up carefully, fully believing that if Duke's going to take the bait, he'll be watching. We want him to think Saffie and I have come on our own. If I'm really lucky, he'll believe we think he's dead, put down with the rest of the Wolves in the clubhouse, and that we won't be on our guard. Chances are he won't bank on it, but however well he comes prepared, we're better. He's heading straight into a trap he won't be able to get out of.

Bolt brings the fake cab to a halt, then he steps out and opens my door. I grin as I see it's his prosthetic arm he's using to help me out, but it does so more than adequately. He holds me until I'm balanced on the prosthesis with a crutch under each arm.

"I'll keep you updated," Bolt mumbles into my ear. "Your earpiece on?"

With a tiny raise of my chin, I confirm it, then hop around to Saffie's side, but she's already getting out without waiting for any gentlemanly action from me.

The steps to the front door take some negotiating, but I manage them without falling on my face or otherwise making a fool of myself. By the time we've traversed the small terrace, the door has been opened.

A man in a smart suit stands waiting, his eyes open wide as they land on the woman by my side. He opens his mouth to say something but gets no chance as he's suddenly pushed to one side.

"Sapphire. Sapphire?" An older man takes his place. He's got grey hair and watery eyes. "Is it really you?"

"Dad," Saffie replies, hesitantly, unsure of her welcome.

"Who is it, Winston?" comes a female voice.

"It's Sapphire!" Saffie's father calls back excitedly. Then remembering his manners, waves her inside. "Come in, come in."

Saffie puts her hand on my arm. "This is my friend, Niran." She hasn't moved, clearly waiting for me to be included in the invite.

Bartell narrows his eyes, but nevertheless, nods his head. His, "This way," is directed to both of us.

My crutches make thudding sounds as they hit the wooden floor, the sound echoing in the large space. With Saffie alongside, we follow Bartell across the large hall and into a room on the side.

Bartell can't take his eyes off of his daughter as he indicates we should take a seat. I ignore the chair he points me to, and instead sit beside her on the couch. Just as our asses hit the cushions, a woman rushes in through the door, her hands busy pinning her hair.

"Sapphire!" she exclaims immediately. "Where have you been?"

Saffie draws in a breath but isn't given time to answer.

Bartell turns, sends a warning glance toward his wife, and poses a different question. "Have you finished with Duke?"

"Winston. Marriage vows remember," she hisses.

"Clarissa. We've talked about this," her dad growls. "Marriage vows be damned when it comes to that reprobate. If Sapphire's left him, then it's about time."

"I didn't leave him," Saffie starts in a small voice. As her father narrows his eyes at her, she continues, her voice getting stronger with every word. "He tricked me into marrying him, then held me captive for five years. When he nearly killed me, I had to go to the hospital. There, a nurse took pity on me and set me up with some people who could get me free. That was about six months ago."

"Captive?" Her father seems to have difficulty processing this.

"Oh don't be so dramatic, Sapphire." Her mother huffs. "Duke kept in touch with us, sent us photos and everything. Such a good son-in-law even though you didn't want anything to do with us. In the photos you always looked happy." She sends Saffie a stern look. "Many women feel trapped in marriage, but holding you captive? You were always prone to exaggeration." While Saffie stiffens at my side, her mom continues, "And who's this?" Belatedly, she turns to me.

"I'm Niran Simpson, ma'am," I start politely. "And I'm the man who rescued her from the captivity she was held in. I killed the man who was going to rape her with her *husband's* permission." By the end of my statement, I'm speaking through gritted teeth.

Clarissa gasps. Her hand covers her mouth, and her piercing eyes stare as though trying to work out whether I'm telling the truth.

Bartell's expression is different to that of her mom's. He doesn't appear shocked, just devastated, as if he'd known there was something wrong all along.

He steps closer and takes the chair he'd previously offered to me. His position puts him opposite her. He links his hands between his spread knees.

"Why didn't you come to me, instead of relying on strangers?" His quick glance my way shows he's numbering me one of them.

Saffie shrugs. Raising her hand, she wipes a tear from her eye, then looks at the moisture on her hand as if it's betrayed her. "Duke told me you hated me. I didn't know if you'd help, or if you'd send me back to him." She gives a stern look at her mom, who has the grace to turn away and not meet her eyes.

Bolt's voice sounds through the device in my ear. *"All clear out here."* Having the confirmation Duke hasn't yet turned up, I focus back on the scene playing around me.

"Sapphire, I don't know how to believe what you're saying. You chose Duke, you married him." The reminder comes unhelpfully from her mom. "Marriage vows—"

"Fuck marriage vows, Mom," Saffie cries out. "Duke tricked me. He wasn't a businessman, he was a member of a motorcycle club, and that's where he took me. He abused me and gave me no freedom. But you knew where I was." She addresses the final comment to her father.

"Winston?" his wife asks sharply.

"It's business," he tells her, equally abruptly.

"Is this true what was happening to Sapphire? Did you know? Is Duke a criminal?"

"I knew." Bartell gets to his feet and rubs at his balding head. "I didn't know she was being abused. Duke sent us pictures. As you said, she always looked happy." He looks at Saffie. "If you'd come to me, I'd have given you protection. But you didn't, and I swear to you, I never knew."

"She's still married to him," her mom says as if she's got a one-track mind. "But I suppose you're thinking of getting another divorce?" She makes it sound as though that's worse than what Saffie's been through.

Bartell looks a little unsteady and reaches his hand to the back of a chair to steady himself.

"Winston, sit down. You shouldn't be overdoing it," his wife scolds.

"Dad. How are you? Duke said you were ill."

"He's got cancer." Her mom doesn't sugarcoat it.

"I'm alright." Bartell brushes it off. "I've got years in me yet."

But the expression on Clarissa's face says he has not.

Maybe it's to get the subject off of himself, but Bartell turns to me. "And why are you here?"

"I'm Saffie's man." Might as well bite the bullet.

Clarissa covers her mouth. "She's *married*."

"Not for much longer," I tell them. "Then, when she's free, I'll be hoping your daughter agrees to marry me."

Saffie turns to me with wide eyes, but her mouth curves, and I take it she's pleased. Although it's been two weeks, in the bedroom department we've messed about, but not taken that final step. I won't, not until I'm absolutely certain the ghost of Duke won't come between us. We've talked of a future though, and of her being my old lady, but this is the first time I've mentioned marriage.

"And who are you?" Bartell asks. "What do you do?"

I could tell him I work as a mechanic, could embellish it by saying I work for myself, which is kind of true in a way. But I don't. I give it to him straight. "I'm a biker. I'm in a club."

"No!" Bartell shouts. "No. Just no." His anguished eyes find Saffie. "Sapphire, leave Duke, yes. But come home to us."

"Duke will just come in and take her again," I tell him.

"I've got security. He'll never get past them."

"I served as a Marine," I snap. "I could tell you exactly what I think of your security. Within days, hours even, of Saffie coming home, Duke would have her back again."

"And you think you can protect her?" Winston throws at me. "You?" He sneers as he waves at my crutches.

"My club's offered her protection." I shrug.

"Your club?" He rolls his eyes, then points his finger at me, waggling it furiously. "You're after her inheritance like everyone else."

As he's still standing, I want to be upright myself. Awkwardly, I struggle up and balance on the prosthesis, and with the aid of the crutches walk closer to him. "Saffie doesn't want your money, and neither do I. I understand there's another relative. Alter your will and leave it to him."

"It wouldn't go to you or her anyway," Bartell sneers.

"No," I agree, letting him know she keeps no secrets from me. "It would go to a son. But I'll be damned if we're going to breed just to keep a lifeline going. Any children Saffie and I have will be free to live as they want, with no ties to an antiquated family stuck in the past, nor have the responsibility of running a criminal enterprise."

"I'm no criminal," Bartell objects.

"No?" I glare at him. "Money laundering is okay? Tax evasion?" Yeah, Rascal had found out some shit for me.

"Winston?" Clarissa looks worried.

"Everyone does it." Bartell brushes off my comments. "Don't worry yourself, we're clean."

Saffie lowers her head into her hands, then looks up with a sad expression. "You admit it, Dad? Duke wasn't just paying you for me, was he? You were working with his club."

"I never wanted you caught up in it, Sapphire. That was all on you. I warned you, didn't I? I knew what Duke was like from my business with the Crazy Wolves. But no, you had to go and marry him."

Saffie stands. She takes a step closer to her father. "No, you didn't. You could have told me exactly what he was, but that would have exposed you, wouldn't it? That might have soured your *business* arrangement."

"You come first, Sapphire."

"Do I?" She tilts her head to one side. "I've been wondering why you lent Duke your private jet to come and take me."

Hmm. I've been wondering that myself. I watch with interest as Bartell's face goes bright red.

"He told me you'd been visiting friends and wanted to come home." But his shifty glance to the side belies the innocent words.

Saffie huffs a laugh completely lacking in mirth. "I don't believe you. It was part of your deal with him, wasn't it? It makes me wonder just what business you were doing with the Crazy Wolves that you'd do anything for them."

"I didn't know, Sapphire," Bartell cries out. "I didn't know he was hurting you. If I had…" his voice trails off.

"What?" Saffie jumps in. "If you'd known, what?" When he doesn't answer, she says sadly, "Money was always more important than me."

Bartell opens and shuts his mouth, but in the end, he says nothing. Clarissa's gone red in the face. I guess she thought their money was all legit.

Saffie places her hand on my arm. "I think we're about finished here, Niran."

"Still no sign of Duke." I hear Bolt's update.

"You've only just gotten here, Sapphire."

"Mom." She swings around to address her mother. "You'd prefer me married to a monster than leave him and be free. And as for you," she turns to her father, "you only want me to breed so I bring an heir to the family. Not once have either of you asked how I am, how I'm feeling, or how badly Duke hurt me.

Niran's a good man. He's all that I need." She turns to me. "Come on, let's leave."

"Where will you go? Where are you living?" Clarissa seems to realise she's losing her daughter again.

"I'm sorry I can't tell you that. I can't risk anything getting back to Duke." With parents like these, I'm glad she's being cautious.

For a moment I tune out as they ask her to stay longer and her rebuttal that there's really no point.

I hadn't needed Bolt's confirmation. I'd heard no shots, no commotion at all. The lack of an overt move from Duke worries me. I'm so fucking certain he's out there, somewhere, just waiting for us to emerge. Will we be ambushed on the way out? On the grounds, or out on the road?

I know my brothers have got it covered, but still, I'm nervous. I'd hoped he'd make his move while we were safe inside, and by the time we emerged, he'd be taken care of.

Now I'm facing the prospect that Saffie's going to be exposed.

He's not getting near her, I silently promise.

CHAPTER TWENTY-EIGHT

Saffie

During the five years I lived under Duke's control, I'd often fantasised about getting away, wondering what reception I'd receive from my parents when out of the blue I'd turn up. In my dreams, they'd welcome me home with open arms and provide a sanctuary for me. In my nightmares, they'd tell Duke exactly where he could find me.

In the end it hadn't been one or the other of the extremes, but something in between. Mom had been disgusted at the idea of yet another divorce, while Dad was more worried about his business than me. I do wonder exactly what his ties are to Duke's MC, but as Niran had said, I couldn't give a damn if no part of his fortune would be coming to me. I didn't want myself, nor any future child, to be part of dirty money.

Of course I'm upset that my father's got a terminal illness, but it doesn't shatter me. I've not seen them for five years, and though it hurts, I know there was more they could have done to rescue me. Instead of paying Duke, they could have used the money to get me away.

As we walk to the front door, I clutch at Niran's hand as though it's a lifeline. He's my future now. No looking back, no more regrets. I'd rather be his biker babe than Duke's little socialite any day.

Had money made me happy growing up? I'd had a nanny, the house was run by the housekeeper, and food was prepared by a cook. My mother's time wasn't dedicated to me, my father tied up with his work. I'd had everything I could ask for, except for attention.

Freedom, feeling alive. Being part of the everyday world held far more attraction than any wealth handed to me. Having enough to live on would be welcome, but I don't need the trappings of a rich life. I have no regrets turning my back on the opulence that had been my life.

Maybe, when Duke's no longer after me, I'll reconnect with my family. But not today. It's Niran who's got my best interests at heart, not them. I'm surprised how little that thought hurts me.

I'm not stupid. I'd expected that meeting to be interrupted by gunshots and shouts. I'd hoped to exit with the news that Duke had been captured or was dead. That nothing had happened was worrying. I now feared we'd exit into a hail of gunshots. As such my heart's beating fast, I'm inhaling double the normal number of breaths.

I can feel Niran's tension in the way he's holding himself, and much of my fear is for him, knowing Duke would kill him to get to me.

"Bolt says it's all clear," he bends his head to whisper to me. "A flea couldn't get onto the grounds without being seen."

"He's waiting for us to leave," I softly say back. "He has to be."

A dip of his chin shows he agrees.

"Sapphire. Don't leave like this." My father's voice comes after me.

Turning, I have one last word. "What's here for me, Dad? A chance of an inheritance I don't want? You've no welcome for the man I want to be with."

"Him?" He approaches and moves in front of us, momentarily blocking our way. "Sapphire, you've got poor judgement in men. He's another only after your money."

"Money?" I snort. "I've none to my name, remember? Niran wants nothing but me."

Dad throws up his hands. "You're doing it again, Sapphire. Making the same mistake again. Look, stay here with your mother and me. We'll put this to rights."

"How?" I round on him. "How the fuck can you put this right? I've been brought up with dirty money, you've just admitted that. At least Niran's no criminal." When his lips purse and his cheeks flush, I shake my head. "Come on, Niran, there's nothing for me here." Navigating past him, we continue our path to the door.

Recovering, Dad cries after us, "Can't you see? He'll use you just like Duke. Well, if his club asks me for money, if they want a slice of my business, they'll get nothing from me."

Niran swings around at this, losing his balance slightly, but fast finding it again. "We want nothing from you, Bartell. We wouldn't touch your money if you wrapped it up in a bow and handed it to us. We earn our living honestly."

Dad snorts.

We've reached the door. Instead of a reply, I give Niran a gentle push to get him out to where Bolt is waiting, the cab door held open for me.

"Go ahead." Niran gives me a little push.

I know he wants me to get to the safety of the car first, but he's the one at most risk. Taking a gamble that Duke wouldn't shoot me, I position myself in front of him instead.

Tuning out my father's protestations, I focus only on getting to the vehicle just a few steps away, mere yards, but it could be miles. As though in the throes of a nightmare, time seems to stop. Each step I take, I brace for the shots I expect to hear.

When we reach the doors and all I hear is birdsong, it's only then I feel I can breathe.

"Nothing?" Niran checks in with Bolt, as he first seats me, then goes to help Niran get in the other side.

"Nothing," Bolt confirms. "But he's out there somewhere. I know he is."

We don't delay. Bolt starts the engine immediately, and as we begin to proceed down the driveway, I don't look back.

A voice comes through the car speakers immediately. "Gears has the drones up. Honor and I are into the local CCTV cameras. There's nothing suspicious that we can see."

It's Snatcher's voice we hear next. "Exit the gates. There's a parking lot up the street. Pull in there and we'll regroup. We'll escort you from there."

"Got my boys checking it out. It's safe," comes another voice I don't recognise.

"Thanks, Red." Bolt inadvertently gives me the name.

My hand trembles as I reach for Niran's. He glances quickly at me. "Don't be scared, Saffie. We've got this."

"The car's got bulletproof glass." Bolt catches my eyes in the rearview mirror. "It might not look like it, but it's built like a fucking tank. Red knew what he was doing when he hired it."

We pull up where Snatcher had instructed. It's only a moment or so before we set out again, this time escorted by trucks carrying the Utah members, and bikes with those from Vegas.

Christ, it's nerve-racking. We know somewhere out there is Duke. *How will he stop us?* Will I hear bullets bouncing off the car, or will he ram us? I worry about the men on bikes. They must be so much more vulnerable than us.

"He might have given up seeing how Saffie's protected," Bolt suggests, his eyes constantly moving, looking ahead, then in the mirrors to the side and our rear. "There's only two of them against all of us."

Niran huffs. "That's why I expected a hit on the parents' house. That's where he knew we'd be, and we were discreet. Nothing would have looked out of the ordinary. I don't know why he didn't choose to play that hand."

"He's got Grit, remember?" Bolt sounds thoughtful. "We tried to be careful, but something might have shown up on the CCTV. Grit might have noticed something didn't look right."

"So you think he might have given up today?" I ask, half hoping, half fearing the answer. If not today when the situation is under control, when will it be? Then more optimistically, I offer, "Maybe he's given up on me?"

Catching Bolt's expression in the mirror, I see him frowning. "Could be he's given up."

"You believe that, Brother?" Niran asks, his voice laden with incredulity.

Bolt snorts. "Well, if there was an investment attached, I wouldn't place money on it."

"Maybe he thinks I'm dead?" I don't know how they were so sure Duke knew where I'd be today, but maybe that's the part of the plan which fell through.

"We could have fucked up," Niran, says, half to himself. "Made assumptions and leaps."

"Maybe," Bolt agrees, obviously catching the meaning that eludes me.

"He's out there." Niran clenches his teeth. "Somewhere."

Somewhere. But it seems, not here. We reach the airport and the plane without incident. Preacher checks with Grinch and Goofy who'd come along to provide security for our mode of transport home. There's been no sign of anyone, and no attempted interference.

"Hey, adopted daughter, com'ere." When Grinch holds out his arms, I pull away from Niran and run into them. "I'm fuckin' glad you're safe," he says as he hugs me. "I've been worried out of my mind. You okay?" He pushes me away and examines me carefully.

"I'm fine, Grinch." Though I hate to admit it, in a few short weeks, Grinch has become more of a father to me than my real dad's ever been. This wizened, battle-scarred biker has wormed his way in and has become family.

A lone biker rides up to the plane, making me realise the others have peeled away from our escort at some point. He walks up to Snatcher, and they do that man hug thing.

"Got my boys surrounding the airstrip." He explains the other bikers' absence.

"Thanks, Red. I owe you."

Red brushes that off, then walks over to Niran and me. Niran balances both crutches under one arm to allow Red to shake his hand, then Red reaches around him, careful not to push him off balance, and slaps his back. "Good to see you back on your feet."

"Getting there," Niran says, with a grin. "Thanks for—"

"Thanks for fuckin' nothing. You're a brother," Red says, almost violently. "We ride for each other, remember?" He waits a beat for that to sink in, then turns to me. "Hey, little lady. I've been wanting to meet you." As I take his offered hand, I muse the reason for his name is more than apparent. His hair is flaming red. "As no one's fuckin' bothered to introduce me, I'm Red. I'm the prez of the Vegas club."

Prezes to me are people like Knife, cruel with the power of life or death, or intense, like Snatcher and Lost. Red though, there's a hint of mischief about him, and a boyish grin as he smiles at me. But there's also something, a depth in his eyes, which warns me to keep on his right side.

"I used to love going to Vegas," I tell him, conversationally.

"Well, once all this is put to bed, you and Niran will have to come visit. We'll always find room for you both."

"I'd like that." As I respond, I realise I'm being genuine.

Hey, look at me, a woman scared to death of bikers, accepting an invite from yet another chapter of an outlaw MC.

But how could I not, when he and his men have put their lives on the line a second time for me. And all because I'm Niran's old lady.

"Come on," Snatcher barks, looking around nervously. "The sooner we're home, the happier I'll fuckin' be."

Red waves his hand theatrically in the direction of the plane and steps back with a flourish.

Preacher's standing by the gangway, head bowed just as he was on the way out. I notice Road glancing at him apprehensively as he reluctantly walks up the steps into the Satan's Devils' jet. I smile, it's already been explained to me. Preacher offers up a prayer every time he pilots the plane. I wouldn't be surprised to learn he does it to fuck with people like Road, who are nervous about flying.

Being in the air has never bothered me. I've been flying on my dad's private plane since I was three.

Soon, I'm got my safety belt on with Niran seated beside me. Experienced as I am, I can acknowledge Preacher's obvious expertise as we zoom down the runway, lift into the air so smoothly it's only the ground dropping away that gives it away, and gain cruising height.

When the seat belt light flicks off, there's movement all around me as the men congregate near the front of the plane. Niran, balancing himself on the backs of the seats, joins them.

I sit back and close my eyes. They may be having a private meeting, but their voices come clearly to me.

"What the fuck was that?" Stormy asks disgustedly.

"That was a visit to Saffie's parents going without a hitch," Thor reminds him.

"But it shouldn't have fuckin' gone without a hitch. Where the fuck was Duke?"

"Must have had a warning. Or he didn't fall for a trap,"

Snatcher says, reasonably. "Or, could he have bigger fish to fry than getting his wife back?"

"He's not going to give up." That's from Niran.

"Maybe he didn't want to make his move near the Bartells," Swift offers. "Perhaps he didn't want to take on their security."

"Or perhaps he didn't get the message. Maybe our math was wrong, and two and two didn't add up to anything." Piston suggests exactly what I'd been thinking. Maybe today was all for nothing, except for me reuniting with my parents.

"So, we set it up again."

"I'm not having Saffie baiting another trap." My eyebrows rise as I hear Niran speak for me. "Once was more than fuckin' enough."

"What else do you suggest? Brother, you want to go home. I want to get back to focusing on my club. Unless we can get Duke to come out of hiding, there's fuck all chance of any of those things happening." Snatcher sounds exasperated.

Could Duke have given up? I ask myself, tuning their voices out. Is he building his business back up? Working with another mafia or another club? Sure, I'm his wife, I'm his property, but maybe he's decided I'm too much trouble for him.

Would it be a relief to think he's given up?

I shudder. No, it wouldn't. I'd never be able to believe it. Even evidence wouldn't convince me. I'd live my life in fear, always thinking he was waiting around the next corner.

CHAPTER TWENTY-NINE

Niran

"It was a bust, Prez." To relieve pressure on my arms and shoulders as much as what remains of my leg, using crutches can be a bitch, I'm perched on a low wall outside the Utah clubhouse. To my right, I see Mystic greeting Grinch and Goofy.

"I heard," Lost replies drily. "I was sure that plan was going to smoke him out."

Me too. "I don't know what to do next, Prez." Save using Saffie, exposing her to danger again, and I'm not prepared to do that.

"Could he have given up?"

"That's Snatcher's way of thinking, Prez. But I'm not so sure. The only reason for him not turning up must be that word hadn't gotten to him."

Lost's quiet for a moment. "Any other sign of him at all?"

"Not since that sighting of him with Grit and Susie. He's dropped back off the radar."

"You know, you were making a lot of assumptions that Susie had teamed up with him. Perhaps it was a chance meeting?"

"No fuckin' chance, Prez. Last I saw of her, Duke was

making her a club whore, and not one where she was willing. That image of the three of them together? They looked cosy as hell. There has to be something in it for her."

"Always liked biker cock, that one. Maybe his punishment didn't have quite the effect you were thinking. Maybe she enjoyed it and wanted more."

Lost may have a point, but I'd met most of the Crazy Wolves. All I'll say is the club wasn't misnamed.

"How did Susie find him?"

"Fuck knows," I reply. Then, when the silence stretches out, I add, "Hell, Lost. You've got a point. If she could find him, why can't we?"

"Her cousin, the fed," he suggests.

But surely Honor and Duty can get into the same databases? I make a mental note to check.

"You thought about coming home?" All the fucking time. The brothers, and Swift, here are okay, but it's not like having my own family around me. "And how's Saffie?"

"Saffie's doing great." I answer his second question first. "She's far less jumpy. And Lost, she's agreed to be my old lady."

"That's fuckin' great." He sounds genuine. "We'd love to have you both back."

"But Duke's the unknown," I tell him. "Utah's better equipped to look after themselves, and there are no kids around. I don't want trouble to follow us home."

"What the fuck, Niran? You don't think we can handle shit?"

"Nah," I step that back fast. "That's not what I meant. It's the old ladies, the kids—"

"That means we protect all the harder. It's no reason for you not to come home. In fact, as your Prez, I'm ordering you to."

He's not making it easy. Now I've got my prosthesis sorted, the only reason I'm staying away is out of respect for my club. I'd be elated to go home. There's no medical reason for me to stay. In three more weeks, all I'll need is the cast to be removed, and an assessment of how the bones have fused.

But as he's insisting, I have no choice other than to agree. "Okay, Prez. I'll get things moving from my end."

"See that you do. Can't wait to welcome you back, Brother."

"How's everyone, Prez? What's the latest on Mary and Grumbler?"

"Mary's doing well, the baby's hanging on in there. Two more weeks and they're going to induce her. They just want to leave him cooking as long as they can."

"Looks positive, then?" I ask him, pleased as fuck it seems to be working out for them.

"Looks that way."

I hesitate before asking, "And Cyn?"

He chuckles. "Sharp's got her under control."

Well, good for him. But I can't quite believe it. And being her brother, I'm not sure I want to ask how.

I end the call but stay where I am for the moment, wondering how Saffie's going to take the news. She knows we'll eventually be returning to San Diego, but she'll miss Cat, Grinch, and the other members here too. They've helped her overcome her fear of bikers which will hopefully bode well for the San Diego chapter.

When I make my way back into the clubhouse, Honor's standing by the bar. I go straight over. In a few seconds I've summed up the query Lost had asked, about how Susie had known how to contact Duke. I really can't write that off as a chance meeting.

Honor stares down into his bottle of beer for a moment, as though expecting to find answers. Then he looks up. "The feds aren't actively looking for him. There's nothing in their database. Grit was ex-fed, wasn't he? What's the bet he knew this second cousin of hers? The cousin knew enough about the Crazy Wolves to direct her there in the first place."

I raise my chin. "Makes sense."

"Yeah." Honor drains his beer and places the empty bottle on the bar top. "We've not found the fucker yet. But now you've mentioned Grit, let me track back, see who he used to work with. Might have more luck if we find a connection there." He slaps me on the back. "Thanks for that, Brother."

I watch his back as he goes. Could I have given him a lead? Possibly. Turning, I scan the room, seeing Saffie deep in conversation with Cat. If I'm not mistaken, they've got a baby equipment catalogue in front of them. Anxiously, I study Saffie's face. She looks at ease, but deep down I know how badly she'll be hurting.

Saffie's come a long way in the last few weeks, but however much she buries her pain, it's always there, lurking just beneath the surface. I think about what I'd said to her father, that I was going to marry her as soon as she was free. She hasn't questioned me on that, but I'm determined. She'll be wearing my patch and having my name as soon as I can achieve it. Then, if she wants to try for another baby, I'll be all in. I'd give that woman everything.

But first we have to find Duke, and I have to kill him.

Accepting a beer from Brute—now I'm off the horse painkillers, I'm allowed to drink—I wonder if that's best achieved by staying here or going back to San Diego as Lost demanded. But what can I do here that I can't do there? Sure, I attend church, but news can be communicated in any way.

Do I doubt these brothers would still have my back if I was out of sight?

Nah. I trust them to do what's right. They'll keep looking, I know it.

"What you thinking so hard about?" Saffie joins me and hops onto the bar stool at my side.

Avoiding her question, I ask instead, "You okay?"

She grimaces. "Yeah. I was just helping Cat choose some stuff for her nursery. I can't help wishing that was me."

Placing my hand behind her head, I draw her toward me, resting her cheek against my chest. "I know, darlin'." Gently I smooth my hand over her hair. "You ever think about having another baby?"

She glances up, startled. "Of course I do."

"See me as the father?"

Her eyes widen. "What are you saying, Niran?"

Shrugging, I explain, "You're my old lady. I want you to be my wife. Doesn't seem too much of a leap to say I want a family with you. If you want that sooner rather than later, I'm all in."

"Niran!" She sounds shocked. Various expressions cross her face, and for a moment I think I may have overwhelmed her, especially when a look of disgust fills her face. "I can't do anything while I'm married to Duke."

Of course she won't risk it. Even though there'd be visible proof the baby was mine, not his.

I sigh with relief that it's not me as the father she's objecting to and just can't help myself. Leaning down, I whisper into her ear, "I'm going to enjoy trying to make babies with you."

"Niran!" Again she uses my name, this time there's a quirk to her lips. Then, fuck me, she raises herself up, "Think we'll need to get some practice in first."

"Yeah?" Carefully I examine her face. We've fooled around a lot, but never gone all the way. I haven't wanted to push her. Now I'm wondering whether it's time, and I can take the risk. "I've never tried to get anyone pregnant before. You're going to have to tell me what to do." I wink.

She bats at my arm and rolls her eyes. "Somehow I don't think you'll have any problem."

I glance at the crutches propped by the bar. "Problems, I do have, Saffie. With no legs to speak of, it's going to have to be all down to you. I'll just have to lie there and take it."

Her brow furrows, then smooths again, and her cheeks become flushed. "You mean, ride you?"

I chuckle softly. "Yeah, I do." It doesn't help that I get the mental image, and my cock's reaction is predictable.

She squirms on the stool, and I notice her eyes are dilated. *Fuck me, is she turned on?*

She rests her hands against my chest, her fingers curling into my shirt. She stares at the material, then raises her eyes. "Do you want to try a practice run?"

Fuck yeah, I do. But... My elation fades. I can't get her pregnant yet, and I haven't anything to use. I grimace and start to explain, "I do, but Saffie, I've not..."

At that moment, the prospect, who'd been crouched out of sight behind the bar, places a box by my hand. When I glance at it, Igor steps back and salutes, then whistling tunelessly, walks off to serve Rascal a beer.

Picking up the condoms, I bark a laugh and narrow my eyes at his back. That's one prospect I wouldn't be surprised soon patches in.

Saffie peals with laughter, then slides off her stool. "Seems we've got all that we need."

I hold her back. "You sure? I thought you'd be upset after what happened today."

"Seeing my parents?" She bites her lip. "I hadn't built it up in my head, so I wasn't disappointed. Over the past couple of weeks, I've come to realise my family is you."

"And all my brothers," I tell her.

"And a proxy dad." She laughs.

I've checked in, she's not distressed. When she pulls at my hand, I let her lead me off into our room. Once there, she immediately takes off her shirt, and lets her bra fall to the ground.

"Fuck, woman," I growl. "You get better all the time."

She shimmies out of her jeans, and soon her panties fall too. We've gotten used to being naked with each other, wearing clothes to bed now a thing of the past, and I thank fuck for that as I rip off my own tee. Wearing only my jeans, I hop my way toward her, placing one of my hated crutches down, and pull her to my chest.

"Cowboy's cooking has been good for you," I tell her, caressing her smooth skin.

"A little too good. It's gone straight to my ass."

"An ass I fuckin' adore," I respond, palming said attribute.

"Sit on the bed," she instructs.

When I do, she folds to her knees, undoes my button and zip and starts to remove my jeans. Usually I wear sweats, but today I wanted to dress normally again. One leg is easy, it slides over the prosthetic. The other is slit up to the knee to accommodate the cast, and she gently eases that down too.

Saffie then starts to remove my prosthesis. The first time she'd done it, I was as embarrassed as fuck, but she'd just asked me what to do, and got on with it as if taking a leg off a man was the commonest thing in the world.

"You need cream?" She eyes my reddened stump with a critical eye.

"I'll do it later."

"Don't forget."

I chuckle. "No, Mom."

But levity fades as she removes my boxers, and my cock comes into view. She pushes me back, already taking charge, and places her mouth over the tip.

Even that had been hard for her. The first time she'd tried to take my cock in her mouth, she'd vomited, as memories of Duke had invaded her mind. Of course I'd insisted her sucking me off wasn't something I needed, but unwilling to let that monster rule her life, she was equally adamant that she wanted to try.

My Saffie is a strong woman, and I'm just a man, so I lay back and let her do whatever she wants to do. Normally, I'm quite happy to let her play just as she wants.

When her lips close around me, this time, though, I stop her. "My turn first. Come up here and sit on my face."

It's the easiest way for me to get my mouth on her, without me awkwardly trying to get into position, manoeuvring on my stump down the bed while trying not to jostle my injured leg.

Fuck but I love that she likes oral sex as I'm addicted to her taste. My dedication to her pleasure seems to have taken her by surprise. Each orgasm I give her is still met by her astonishment, and the admission it just keeps getting better and better.

Her indrawn breath shows she's totally into my suggestion, but before she places her knees either side of my head, she lowers her face.

I grasp at her, holding her lips to mine like a man in a desert would do a glass of cool water. I devour her, sweeping my tongue into her mouth, loving how she responds. Her perfume, both of her and her arousal, fills my nostrils. Her silky strands of hair cover my hands, the sensual touch of her tongue gliding across mine sends me wild.

It's perhaps lucky that I'm immobilised, if I wasn't, I'd be hard pushed to prevent myself throwing her down, going caveman on her, shoving my cock straight inside and claiming her as mine.

As it is, I'm impatient. I've waited more than enough time. Pulling back, I gasp. "Here, Saffie. Now." With my hands on her waist, I lift her.

It's not the first time we've done this, she knows what to expect. She places her knees either side of my head and lowers herself down. I position her where I want her, then get to work.

How the fuck can this gorgeous woman ever think she didn't get wet enough? My face is already drenched and I fucking love it. Her taste is sublime, and I can't get enough. I lick, lap, suck, and all the time she's writhing above me, grinding down until I almost suffocate. I grin into her pussy, feeling on top of the world that I can make her lose control like this.

I circle my tongue around her clit, probe it inside her, mimicking what I'll shortly be doing with my dick, then attack that tender nub again.

"Niran, God, Niran."

Yeah, my baby likes that. Her thighs start to tremble and close around my cheeks.

I growl, the vibration hitting her pussy making her clench.

"Niran, I'm…."

She doesn't have to tell me, I fucking know. She opens her mouth and screams, her body pulsing, grinding into me as she finds her release.

I continue to use my tongue, sustaining her pleasure until she rolls off me, collapsing down at my side, breathing heavily. It's only a moment before she curls into me.

When her heart rate slows, she pulls up and looks down at me. "I think it's your turn now."

She's handled my dick, brought me to orgasm, watched in fascination as my cum shoots out. Even tried her best at giving me head until the memories get too much. But she's never had me inside her.

Mindful of that, I'm content if she just wants to fool around. "It's your show, Saffie. Do what you want. Just remember, if you need to, you can cry wolf."

She rolls her eyes at the reminder of her safeword. The last thing I want her to do is to use it, but I want her to have the security of knowing it's there.

Having to be so damn careful of my foot in its cast, the missionary position, or any dominant role for that matter, is beyond me. Normally I could balance on my stump, but not with only a damaged limb to support me.

She sits up, eyes the pack of condoms, opens them and takes one out. With a cocky grin, she begins to slide it on me.

I suck in air. Her hands feel too fucking good and the anticipation of what her actions mean put me on a hair trigger. I begin to count backwards to prevent disgracing myself.

Some primal part of me wishes I was taking her bare, putting my baby inside her. Without conscious thought, I voice the idea. "I'd fucking love to make you pregnant, see you grow round with my baby."

She pauses and stares at me intently. "I love you, Niran."

Raising my hand, I reach for her cheek, and she lowers her face into my palm. "I fuckin' love you, Saffie. I think I always have."

It's then she sets out to seduce me. I could tell her she couldn't get me more aroused, but as she puts her mouth on my nipples, teasing me the same way I do her, I give into the sensation of my woman, my old lady, making love to me.

This is what she needs.

"Fuck, Saffie," I groan, letting her know exactly what she's doing to me. My body's in her control, not mine, as I jerk and writhe under her ministrations. As she fondles my balls, teasing my perineum, I almost shoot my load.

"Saffie," I cry out warningly, rolling back my head and biting my tongue.

"Are you ready for me?" she asks, seductively.

Fuck yes.

Our eyes lock as she positions herself, takes my cock in one hand and gently lowers down.

I'm big, she's tight. From her tortured expression, I know she's feeling the burn. "Fuck, that's it Saffie," I encourage her, though she's not taken much of me yet. "You feel like fuckin' heaven." That's the absolute truth.

"You feel big," she complains with a gasp.

"Your pace, Saffie. You're in charge."

She rises, then lowers herself again, her copious lubrication easing the way. I use gentle murmurs of praise until, finally, she's taken all of me.

Pausing, with a grimace on her face, she acclimates herself to my size.

I want to move, take hold of her hips, thrust myself into her, but I refrain. She's been fucked over enough. There'll be plenty of time in our future when I can introduce her to the fucking I like. This time, it's all down to her.

Experimentally, she rises so my cock almost leaves her, then takes me back in again. She repeats it, slightly changing the angle. After a moment, she finds something she likes as her muscles squeeze down on my dick.

"God, Niran, you feel so good," she cries out when she finds her rhythm.

Her face is reddened with exertion, so I take her hips in my hands, helping her as she moves.

I'm trying to hold back, determined not to come until she does, but it's fucking hard as she feels so good.

"Niran," she wails, her face contorted in frustration.

I reach out my hand and let my fingers find her clit. After I start strumming, it doesn't take long before she's clamping down on my dick.

"Niran!" This time it's a screech and my dick becomes strangled as her pussy convulses around me.

I lose it, I can't hold back. I come with a roar, pumping jet after jet into the condom. I may be imagining it, but I swear it's never felt this good. Never this perfect. Nothing compares with shooting my cum into my old lady.

"You're fuckin' mine, Saffie," I groan out when I'm capable of speaking again. "Fuckin' mine, and always will be."

She eases herself off my dick, then lies over me, placing her cheek against my wildly beating heart. "I'm yours, Niran. Because I want to be."

"Works both ways, Saffie. I'm yours. If you left me, it would fuckin' break me."

CHAPTER THIRTY

Saffie

I suppose it could be third time lucky, but how on earth, after the disasters in my life, could I have even dreamed of meeting a man like Niran, let alone ended up with him?

He hasn't taken from me. He hasn't pushed me. He'd waited patiently until I was ready. Until I believed that sex wasn't the end-all be-all. It was an addition to our relationship, a physical extension of what we feel for each other.

My love for him has been growing each day, the realisation I was ready to make the admission culminating as he threw my father's suggestion of money back in his face. I was so glad he did.

While I'd only recently learned that a son of mine would inherit, I'd immediately baulked at the idea of how much responsibility that would be on a child, especially as my suspicions have been confirmed that my family's business is partly, at least, not made from honest endeavours.

I lie with my face against his chest, feeling the beating of his strong heart. He's claimed me but has also given me himself. Clive was supposed to be mine, but he'd shown no reciprocal commitment. As for Duke, the thought that I had any equal ownership over him was laughable.

Niran's admission I had the power to break him if I were to leave is exactly the way I feel about him. As an old lady, I'm property in his brothers' eyes, but for once, that word doesn't hurt, doesn't suffocate, and isn't anything I want to run from. I want to be his, as much as he wants to be mine. If I'm his property, then I'm equally possessive about him.

Not that I think he would stray. How would he when he's waited so patiently for me to be ready? Even when I'd been pushing him away, he was always there waiting in the wings.

"You okay?" His voice rumbles under my cheek.

"More than okay."

He taps my back. "I've got to deal with the condom."

Reluctantly, I ease myself away. When he sits and removes the very necessary item, knotting the end, to save him from having to move, I take it from him. Going into the bathroom. I flush it away, relishing how easy things are between us. There's no embarrassment over the tiniest of things.

When I return to the bedroom, I can see he's fallen asleep. I smile at his sleeping form, acknowledging how vulnerable a man looks at rest.

It's been a long day. I, too, feel drained, but am still too hyped up. Instead of returning to the bed, I sit on the chair with my head propped on my hand, watching my man sleep.

I'm disappointed Duke didn't turn up and wonder why he didn't. Had he not known? Or am I no longer important to him? Without knowing, I'll never fully be able to move on. As long as Duke's alive, I'll never be totally free of him. I'm still married for a start. Niran and I would be happy living in sin, but he wants to marry me, and I'd proudly wear his ring on my finger. A sign to even civilians that I belong to him.

The thought reminds me of my parents. Why am I not distraught over my father's diagnosis? I suppose I was prewarned, Duke having already told me. The little girl inside is upset at the thought of losing one of the first influences in her life, but the woman I've become wonders how much he knew and when he knew it about my relationship with Duke, and why he hadn't done more to save me? I tend to think his business with the Crazy Wolves was more important than my happiness and well-being.

As they hadn't been able to have another child, their legacy would only continue if I gave birth. That's my only value to them.

As a child you don't think too much about how you were brought up. Things that might be out of the norm for other people seem natural for you. It's only with an adult's hindsight, you look back and realise perhaps things weren't how they were meant to be. Looking back, I seldom spent time with either of my parents.

But I'd loved them, hadn't I?

Now Dad is dying. Do I care? Of course I do. I'd not wish death on anyone—with the exception of Duke. But am I beating myself up about the time we've spent apart? No, I'm not. Dad had known where to find me, he just hadn't bothered to launch a rescue.

Will I miss him when he's gone? I will. But more because he's a man not there anymore, and not like losing a dad. Do I wish him to go through pain and suffering? No, I do not. His only crime was not caring.

My mind circles back to Duke.

I'd started the day wound up on adrenaline, scared as hell Duke would turn up, but excited too. My fears were for the men protecting me, but my elation was for myself. I was going to be free. Now I've come down to earth with a bump and regretting that Duke lives to darken another day.

But his chains on me have been loosened, as evidenced by

what had just taken place with Niran. I smile to myself, shifting to ease some of the delicious ache that I'm feeling.

It's the first time a man's allowed me to be in charge. I don't think I could have done it any other way. Not for the first time at least. It might have been expediency on Niran's part, but I don't believe that was all. *He'd given me what I needed.* And I've certainly no regrets, how could I? I've just had the best sex of my life.

Unable to stop myself yawning, I realise I'm tired at last. When I slide under the sheet next to my man, his arm comes around me, as though even in sleep he was waiting for me. I snuggle against him, my last thought before closing my eyes is that in the morning, I want a repeat. Just to check my amazing orgasms weren't flukes, of course.

Smiling, I join him in sleep.

Niran's the first to wake when his phone sounds like it's going to vibrate itself onto the floor. His hand snakes out to grab it.

Sleepily he answers, "Prez?"

The voice on the line is shouting at him, but I can't make out actual words.

"You're fuckin' kidding me!" Niran shouts, throwing back the sheet. "When did this happen?… How the fuck's Grumbler taking it?… Yeah, okay. I understand…" He casts a look my way, his eyes flaring with both anger and sadness. "I'll talk to Snatcher and Saffie. I'll do anything, *anything,* you hear me, Prez?"

He ends the call and puts his head in his hands. "Can you grab me my clothes, Saffie?"

"What's going on?" He'd told Lost he'd talk to me. Surely this must be something he can share? As I speak, though, I'm out of bed, and gathering up his underwear, sweats and a fresh t-shirt. I hand them to him and for good measure, put his prosthesis and crutches close at hand.

"Talk to me, Niran."

He puts his head through his shirt, then slides in his arms. He's breathing heavily. I slide to my knees, helping him to put his cast through his boxers and pull them up over his stump. I then pick up the prosthesis. He takes it from me, strapping it on, but he allows me to take charge again as I help get him into his sweats.

"What's happened?"

This time he looks at me. "Saffie," he starts, his eyes creasing and filling with more pain than I've ever seen. "Fuck, Saffie. Duke didn't come yesterday as he had something else planned. He must have fuckin' guessed he was walking into a trap."

When his voice trails off, I prompt, my voice monotone, my gut roiling with dread. *What has Duke done?* "What else did he have planned?"

"He's trying to force us to go to him," Niran says, blankly, as if his brain's too busy trying to process what he's heard to divulge it to me. "He's taken Mary from the hospital. He wants to exchange her for you."

My legs give out from under me. For once it's not fear for myself, it's fear for her. Mary, trying her best to bring her child into the world, should be on bedrest and being cared for, not in the hands of a homicidal maniac like Duke. As I fall to the floor, I wail. All my own hopes and dreams are coming back to me, as I know that's what Mary will feel.

"No, Niran!" I try to protest that what he's said is wrong, but when he reaches down and his strong arms pull me up to sit beside him, I know it's only the truth that I heard. I swallow, then ask, "What time do we leave?"

"Saffie, you're going nowhere—"

"No, Niran. This is down to me. Grumbler must be beside himself. Duke wants me. It's not fair that anyone else is involved."

"I'm not going to let you give yourself up to that bastard," he snarls.

"What else can we do? Mary's not well, she needs care. She could *die*, Niran, or lose the baby at least." My eyes widen and fill with tears at the thought of all that could go wrong. At least I'm young and have another chance. Grumbler and Mary won't have that luxury.

"I need to talk to Snatcher," he states, his brow creasing, his jaw working as if he's trying to get control of himself. "See if we can come up with a plan."

"There's no plan other than to go to San Diego and I'll do whatever Duke asks."

Niran takes hold of my hair and uses it to position my head so I'm looking straight into his eyes. "You think Duke's just going to give her up? You think he'll make the exchange? You know him better than anyone, Saffie. He'll take the easiest way out, which might mean he'll kill her." That horrific thought hadn't occurred to me.

"What can we do?"

"Get brains on this for a start." He pulls his crutches toward him and gets himself upright. "Wait here."

"No." Standing too, I take his arm. "This involves me, Niran. You're not leaving me out. Whatever I need to do, I will. But we've got to do what we can to rescue Mary, and fast."

He gives me a sharp look, then a raise of his chin. When he opens the door to exit the room, Bolt's standing there with his hand raised.

"You heard?" he asks grimly, reading our faces.

"Yeah."

"Snatcher's convening church." Bolt glances at me.

"She's coming," Niran informs him, his eyebrow rising in challenge.

Bolt grimaces, then nods and seems to agree.

It's early. At another time I might be amused at the state of the men who arrive in the meeting room and take their places around the table. Most are dishevelled, some just woken are yawning and wiping sleep from their eyes. The one thing lacking is one word of complaint, and all look sympathetically at Niran and me.

Honor raises his hand. Snatcher nods down the table at him.

"Right. We've got the security footage." He does something, and a screen descends behind their prez. Snatcher moves to the right and turns his head. "See that black ambulance?" Honor uses some sort of laser pointer to indicate the vehicle he means. "That arrives about 2am, and two men descend, both wearing white coats."

"That's Duke and Grit," I interrupt, without asking permission.

"You can tell?" Duty questions me.

"It's the way they're walking." Their faces might be turned away from the camera, but there's no fooling me.

"Right. We've also got footage from inside. There's a waiting area outside Mary's room."

"That's Ross," Niran tells them. "He's a new prospect for the club."

"Well, apparently he was on Mary's guard duty. This is from shortly before."

And not doing a good job, obviously. But watching him, my observations are at odds with my thoughts. Despite the late hour, he's wide awake, getting up and patrolling, and scanning the corridors.

"How did they get past him?" Thor wonders aloud.

"Watch," Honor insists.

I stare at the screen, feeling my jaw drop as a nurse comes out of the door of the room opposite where Ross is waiting.

"That's fuckin' Susie. Damn it. Ross wouldn't have known who she is." Niran bangs his hand on the table. "He didn't come around the club before I was taken, and she's dressed as a fuckin' nurse."

"Yeah, and she's a right flirt," Swift puts in, observing the screen.

"But he's not falling for it," I speak again, pleased he seems to be turning his back on her.

There's no sound, but presumably she asks him something, and his answer is an affirmative nod.

"Oh no," Niran groans, as Susie reappears with a cup of what looks like coffee. "Drugged?"

Honor shrugs and moves his pointer again. Ross drinks the coffee. Whatever's been put in it doesn't take long. He sits, violently shakes his head, tries to stand, but falls back and slumps in his seat.

Susie reappears and taps on her phone. Within moments, Duke and Grit, dressed as orderlies, appear. They go into Mary's room where there doesn't seem to be CCTV, presumably for privacy.

"Is she asleep?" Stormy wonders aloud.

"I'd say drugged." Duty doesn't sound happy. "Courtesy of Susie I would think."

My hand goes over my mouth. Whatever drugs have been given to her can't be good for the baby. But Duke wouldn't have given a damn.

"How the hell do they just wheel her out?" Niran asks. "Wouldn't they be stopped?"

This time Honor just nods toward the screen where Grit is showing some paperwork to a nurse.

"It would be easy for Grit to hack in and fake a transfer request, or hell, permission to transfer a body to the morgue," Stormy says through gritted teeth.

CHAPTER THIRTY-ONE

Niran

So that's how they did it. I'm fuming so much I can barely speak. I'd rather they'd taken me and tortured me again than getting their hands on Mary.

"Does San Diego have this footage?" Piston asks.

Honor raises his chin. "Yeah, I sent it to them before we came in here."

In one of our updates, Lost had told me Ross had come on board as a new prospect, so that wasn't a surprise to me. But if it had been anyone else, Susie would have stuck out as suspicious. I wonder whether they would have tried to enact their plan if it had been anyone else, or whether they'd had alternatives. Whatever, him being there had played straight into their hands.

I hope it was just a sedative they'd given to him, else Duke will have more blood to answer for. Just one more item to add to his growing list of crimes.

Questions are going on around me, while the only answer seems as clear as day. Suddenly, I bang my hand on the table. "I've got to get back to San Diego. Saffie will stay here."

There's a gasp at my side. "You are not leaving me here. It's me Duke wants."

"He's not going to get fuckin' near you," I growl.

"Preacher. Can you fly me to San Diego?" Saffie asks, making me regret she's overcome her fear of bikers.

"Sure." Preacher grins.

"Over my fuckin' dead body," I snarl.

"Niran," Snatcher snaps. "Think. Duke's not going to be swayed by some lookalike or whatever your fuckin' plan is. You're going to need Saffie to pretend to make any exchange. An exchange, I doubt he means to go through with." That catches my attention. It was my thought as well. "You and she need to be in San Diego to set this shit up. I'll send some of my boys down with you. Saffie won't be put into danger. We'll have her back, same as the rest of your brothers. But if Grumbler's woman means anything to you, Saffie has to be involved."

"I'll go!" Stormy's the first to put up his hand. "I can understand what Grumbler's going through. It would fucking kill me if anything happened to Cat."

"I'll go too." Swift raises her chin at him.

"And me," Road offers. "Just in case you need anyone for fast riding."

"We'll stay here, work the back end," Honor suggests, presumably speaking for Duty too.

"I'd like to go. Get some sea air." Bolt winks at me across the table.

Thor waggles his hand. "Preacher will obviously be there. Want me along too?"

Snatcher considers for a moment then grins. "Yeah, why not. The more the fuckin' merrier and we can put this thing to bed once and for all. Preacher, get the plane equipped with any toys you might need. Stormy, you work on the comms end."

Stormy nods his head.

"Wheels up in an hour? Will that do?"

All heads but mine nod at Preacher.

"I'm still not happy about Saffie."

"Niran," she rests her hand on my arm, "this is something I need to do. I trust you and your brothers. They took out the whole Crazy Wolves' club to get us back. You've shown me how I can trust the club, and I have faith that if it's humanely possible, they'll keep me safe now. I'll do anything you ask, but I won't stay here."

What can I say? She's no longer the timid mouse I first met, no longer scared of men on motorbikes wearing leather. I just hope that means she hasn't forgotten how dangerous Duke is.

Snatcher bangs the gavel. "That's it then. Ready to leave in an hour. Gears, get Brute to drive Niran and Saffie to the plane."

As men get up around me, Saffie leans her head on my shoulder. "It's going to be okay, Niran. We'll get Mary back safely."

She can't say that. Grumbler deserves to have his old lady, but I deserve to have mine. Trading one for the other is unacceptable. But how could I be so selfish as to put my needs above his?

I turn to her, telling her fiercely, "You do everything I fuckin' say, Saffie."

"Of course I will. I'm not stupid, Niran. The last thing I want is for Duke to take me again. But we have to do this, can't you see? Mary doesn't have much time. She needs to be back in the hospital. They wouldn't have kept her in if she didn't need to be there."

Yesterday, I was all set to return to San Diego with Saffie, thinking she'd be the one I'd need to persuade. Now, I'd do anything to stay here and not expose her to danger.

Wordlessly, I follow her back to our room and watch as she empties the closet and drawers. We've accumulated more than I expected staying here. She puts the clothing onto the bed, and I pack the duffel bags Bolt dropped off for us. When everything which shows we've ever occupied this room has been removed, I hold out my arms.

She comes straight into them. The tension I feel in her belies her confidence that she'd just expressed. I'm not stupid. I know she must be terrified at the risk she's proposing to take. But if I'm completely honest, using her is the only way I can see of getting Mary back, and quick enough before being held captive causes harm to her and the baby. I'm more than aware we've got no time.

Trying to find Duke on our own is like looking for the proverbial needle in a haystack of immense proportions. If we're going to save Mary, we have to move fast.

"You ready in there?" Bolt's voice shouts through the door.

Saffie's there and opening it before I can get to my feet. "We're ready."

He comes in, hefts both duffels over his shoulder, then gives me a chin lift. "Brute's out front with the truck."

Standing, I raise my chin back, then follow my woman and Bolt out.

The clubroom is full of all the brothers not going to San Diego. Grinch steps forward and envelopes Saffie in a bear hug.

"You take fuckin' care, little lady," he growls at her, then glances toward me. "You'll answer to me if any harm comes to her."

"I'll miss you," Saffie replies with a catch in her voice.

"You need me, and I'll be there. You got me?" Saffie's nod shows that she has.

Mystic is missing, but Goofy's here and he hugs her too. But when Honor and Duty step up, my barely suppressed snarl means they're satisfied with just shaking hands.

One by one I'm subjected to man hugs and, considering my crutches, gentle, *thank fuck,* slaps to my back. When Piston, Rascal, Honor, Duty, Cowboy and the old-timers have finished with me, Snatcher steps forward holding out his hand. As I take it, he pulls me in.

"You're welcome in Utah anytime, Niran. Both you and Saffie."

"Thanks." I feel a bit choked up myself, so clear my throat and try again. "Thanks for everything, Snatcher."

"Are we going or not?" Preacher yells impatiently.

Swift passes App into Gears' care, then heads to the door. As Stormy, Swift, Road, Bolt and Thor follow her out, Saffie and I, both taking one last look back at our temporary home, go to the door. I know I'll have bittersweet memories of this clubhouse. It's been a place where I've more often than not been in pain, but also the place that finally brought me and Saffie together, and where these men have removed that final obstacle, the one where she'd sworn never to get involved with another biker.

The journey to the small airfield is short, and there I find the missing member as Mystic steps toward Preacher and updates him on the condition of the plane. Apparently, it's been fully serviced and checked after yesterday's outing to Nevada. A last round of goodbyes, then we're seated on the plane, and before I really have time to process, are landing in a private airfield just outside of San Diego.

Two trucks are waiting for us, one driven by Ross wearing his new prospect cut, and one by Connor.

"Fuckin' glad to see you," I tell Ross. "Thought for a moment you'd been poisoned."

He looks sheepish. "Nah, just ketamine, thank fuck. I'm sorry as fuck about that, Niran. I let you all down."

"No, you did not." I grimace. "You weren't to know that bitch Susie."

"Tell that to Grumbler," he mumbles, ruefully rubbing at the reddened patch of skin I now notice on his cheek. In a day or so that will turn purple.

I'm itching for news, but there's no point asking either him or Connor. Club business isn't shared with prospects. So I take my seat in the truck, arranging my cast so it's comfortable, and impatiently watch the scenery go past.

Saffie holds my hand tightly, her tension seeming to mount the closer we get to the clubhouse.

"You don't need to do this," I tell her quietly. "Fuck, after all you've been through, everyone will understand."

"I do," she replies, her voice shaking. "It's the quickest way to get Mary."

"Duke might not give her up," I warn and not for the first time. She might not even be alive. She's a means to an end and may have already outlived her usefulness. I hate to fucking think it, but I wouldn't put anything past Duke.

"I've got to try, Niran. How could I live with myself, otherwise?"

"We'll look out for her." Bolt leans over from the passenger seat. "We won't let anything happen to you, Saffie."

He's trying to reassure her, but when his eyes meet mine, I can see he's not as confident as his words sound.

I try not to think of all the ways this could go wrong. What if he wants to kill Saffie? What if he believes she was the reason why his club was taken out, and hates her so much he doesn't want her to keep breathing and no longer gives a damn about his plans for her? What if we fuck up, and he gets her in his clutches again? Or, does he still think he's got a chance of getting her family's money? *Which would mean he'd literally fuck with her again.* My hands clench. *I couldn't bear it.*

Saffie's sharp intake of breath shows I'm squeezing her hand too hard. Making an effort to relax, I try to release my tension. But it's fucking hard. The only relief I can find is when I picture myself getting vengeance, not just for Saffie, but for Mary, and all the women who Duke's fucked up.

I'll make him hurt.

I curse my damaged foot, knowing I'll be side-lined for whatever's ahead. Unable to walk properly, I can't charge in. My tension rises again.

"I love you," Saffie says quietly, her hand leaving mine but only to rest on my thigh and squeeze it. "I've made mistakes, but the only one with you was not being able to see what a good man you were before I did. I want everything with you, Niran. I want a family. I want to live your life. I want to ride behind you. We've got so much ahead of us. I swear to you, I'll do nothing to fuck that up."

It's a reassurance I need, but not one I think she can make. So my only response can be, "I fuckin' love you too, Saffie."

I thought we were quiet, but it seems we were not, as Bolt again leans over the front seat as the gates of the familiar compound come into sight. "This is Duke's last stand. I'm sure of it. You'll get your vengeance, Brother."

All I can do is hope that he's right.

I can't lose Saffie. I couldn't bear it.

CHAPTER THIRTY-TWO

Grumbler

"They're here," Salem calls out, quite unnecessarily as a deaf man would be able to hear the trucks as they approach the clubhouse.

As I rise from my stool, Prez reaches out his hand and grabs my shoulder. "Easy, Brother."

Shrugging him off, I make my way to the door and step out into the sunlight. The trucks pull to a halt. The one Connor is driving is first, and I eagerly watch the bodies getting out. I recognise Stormy, Preacher, Swift, Road and Thor, but not the man I'm looking for.

I stomp to the next, smaller, truck. Bolt's out first and is going to the back door. He takes a pair of crutches in one hand and offers his arm to the man I'm looking for. When Niran's standing, balanced on one leg, he passes the crutches to him.

My rage can't be contained. I take the next steps at a run and place my fist in Niran's face. "This is all your fuckin' fault!" I roar.

"Grumbler!" Salem's there, holding my arm tight, preventing me punching him again.

At least my first found its target and did its job. Unbalanced,

Niran's fallen to the ground. He's shaking his head and wiping blood from a cut lip.

"Deserve that, Brother." He looks up into my face.

"And fuckin' more," I tell him, spittle coming out of my mouth. "My fuckin' old lady's gone because you brought that bastard down on us." I struggle to try to get out of the enforcer's hold, but it seems I'm going nowhere.

"It's not his fault," a new voice says, as Saffie places herself between me and Niran, her hands on her hips. "If you want to blame anyone, it's me."

"Fuckin' touch her and I'll kill you," Niran growls, as Bolt once again helps him get to his feet.

What? They think they need to warn me not to hit a woman? I'd never dream of doing such a thing. The very idea pulls me up, changing my anger into grief in a split second. My face becomes wet with soundless tears as I face the woman in front of me down.

"It's not your fault, Saffie. You asked for none of this. But Duke's got my woman, and it's tearing me apart inside."

"I'm so sorry," Saffie wails, throwing herself at me. Taken by surprise, I hug her tight. "I'm going to give myself up so you'll have her back by your side. Right where she's meant to be."

I clutch at her, hearing her suggestion and immediately knowing that's not right.

"No one's going to be giving themselves up to that fucker!" Lost's voice booms. "Now Niran's back, we'll have church."

"Welcome home." I see Pennywise going to Niran and slapping him on the back as I turn and almost run after Lost, but such pleasantries are beyond me.

I barely know which way is up. I never want to get a call like I got in the early hours of this morning.

"Mr. Winslow, your wife isn't in the hospital. Have you any idea where she might have gone? Is she with you?"

What the fuck? "No she's fuckin' not. What do you mean, she's not in the hospital?"

"A nurse just checked her room."

"What about the man who was there?" Who was it? Oh yes, the new prospect, Ross. I'd left my old lady in his hands.

"He appears drunk," the anonymous voice told me. "We're trying to rouse him now."

My initial snarl of rage was suppressed as my brain kicks into gear. A man who wants a patch doesn't get drunk on the job. "I think you'll find he was drugged. Check your fuckin' security tapes. If my old lady is gone, it wasn't her fuckin' choice." My Mary is sensible. She might not like being confined to a hospital bed, but she'd do nothing to risk our kid.

Having put the phone on speaker, I was already halfway dressed.

"We'll do that, of course, Mr. Winslow. I just needed to check whether she went home. Have you any idea where else she would have gone?"

"She didn't leave of her own fuckin' accord," I screamed at her.

"If that's the case, the police will need to be involved."

"Well fuckin' involve them!" I was screeching now.

"I'll call you back after I've viewed the footage," the voice told me.

"Who am I speaking to?" I belatedly enquired.

"My name's Jean Robes. I'm the maternity ward supervisor."

Mentally I stored that away and ended the call.

"Grumbler? What's going on?" Alicia came into my room rubbing her bleary eyes.

How could I tell her, her mother's gone missing? I couldn't. Not until I knew what was going on. "Club business," I told her roughly. "I've got to go to the club."

"Okay." She seemed to accept that easily. "When you see Mom in the morning, give her my love."

I fucking hoped I'd be seeing her mother in the morning. Aware there could be a wealth of hurt coming our way and wanting to save her from that for as long as I could, I gentled my voice.

"Go back to sleep, sweetheart. I'll speak to you later."

I stepped out of the house, locked the door behind me, then went to my bike. Glancing back, I saw Alicia's bedroom light switch off. Content she was out of earshot, I placed my call.

"D'you know what fuckin' time it is?"

"Mary's gone from the hospital. I think she's been abducted."

"Fuck. Grumbler. Get your ass here now."

"On my way, Prez."

I made it to the compound in record time and had just backed my bike into my normal spot when my phone rang.

"Grumbler, it's Ross. I'm so fuckin' sorry, man. I must have been drugged." His words sounded slow and slurred.

"You goddamn sorry waste of space. You're never getting your fuckin' patch!" I yelled down the phone. "Who was it? Who got her?"

"I don't know. I drank coffee, and that's all I remember."

"Fuckin' asshole. Get your ass back to the club."

"Grumbler? What the fuck's going on?" Salem, still pulling his t-shirt over his head, ran up to me.

I ended my call and turned to him. "Mary's been taken."

"Shit." He looked at me with disbelieving eyes. "Let's get inside."

Christ, the last few hours have been a nightmare, I think as I take my seat in church for the second time today, and wait while the rest of the brothers come in.

It hadn't taken long for a call to come in. When it had, Lost had put it on speaker.

"You've got something of mine, and I've got something of yours. We'll make an exchange and put things back in their rightful places."

"To whom am I speaking?" Lost had asked.

"You want to play it like that? Well, I'm Duke, VP of the Crazy Wolves."

"Not sure I've heard of that club." Lost tried to toy with him.

"Like that is it? Guess you don't want the woman back. Can't say I blame you." Duke actually chuckled. "She's too old for my liking, and about ready to pop. Guess I'll be doing you a favour—"

"Listen you motherfucker!" I screamed. "You touch one hair on her head—"

Lost waved me down. "So we've established you've got something of ours. I don't know what you think we have in return?"

"Well let me prod your memory. My wife, Sapphire. My old lady. The Satan's Devils have got her, and I want her back."

"I don't know what you're talking about. She's not at my club."

"I'm aware of that, but you know where she is. Or you had better. Else the woman I do have is dead. Maybe I'll cut her open, take the brat out first…"

I launched over the table, Dart blocking me as I reached for the phone. "Get him out of here," he hissed.

"No, I'm staying," I protested, but Pennywise and Scribe took me by the arms and dragged me out and into the clubroom.

"Calm yourself the fuck down. You're not helping," Pennywise told me, his fingers pinching his brow. "It's fuckin' shit what's happened to Mary but shouting ain't gonna help."

"I've got to get back in there."

"No," Scribe interjected. "You're going to sit out here and wait. Lost can talk to him calmly."

I got in a punch. Scribe was ready to fight back, but Pennywise took hold of my arms and pinned them behind me.

I fought, how I fought. Now I risk a look at Pennywise as he takes his seat and see him rubbing his jaw. Yeah, I back headed him one, left my mark on him, but still I hadn't been released. Not until Lost had finished his conversation. Even after that, they'd had to calm me down.

It hadn't worked.

One by one, the brothers come in. My brothers take their usual seats, the newcomers bring in extras from outside, Niran, the slowest, walks in last. Or, not last. Saffie is behind him. Bold as brass she steps up to a chair and sits down. She's grown some balls since we last met, walking in amongst a group of bikers acting as if she belongs there, especially given all the raised brows.

Lost takes his seat and bangs the gavel. "Welcome, Brothers from Utah. Let's kick this off. Any updates since we last met?"

"Hold up," I ask. "What's she doing here?"

"She's got as much right as anyone," Niran states. "She's got to understand any plan if she's going to take part."

Since I hit him, I've come to my senses. "Saffie's not getting anywhere near Duke." This is a man's war, I'm not trading one woman for another.

"I am." With just one wary glance toward Lost, Saffie speaks for herself. "It's me Duke wants. Using me is the only chance of getting your old lady back."

"Since when do we let bitches do our work for us?" I rasp.

A cough draws my attention. *Fucking Swift.* It's followed by a snort from Road.

"Saffie's staying," Prez says, overriding my objections. "Let's move on."

Token raises his hand. "I've got a location for the phone call. It came from somewhere down by the beach."

"Reckon he'd probably not call from where he is," Blaze remarks. "Grit would make sure it couldn't be traced."

"But he wouldn't be too far away." Stormy, from his place at the back of the room, sits forward. "Honor and Duty are looking into any new rentals or abandoned buildings close by. Should get a list through any moment."

"Then we can get up the drones. Take a look from the air," Preacher states, explaining some of the equipment he'd arrived with. "One of our new models has infrared. It can seek out heat images within buildings." At my raised eyebrow, he adds with a smirk, "Military spec. Absolutely top secret."

"Any more news from Duke?" Niran asks. He seems to take whatever Utah's got access to in his stride.

Lost shakes his head. "Not since he told me to wait by the phone. Reckon he wants us to sweat."

"He'll know Saffie was in Nevada yesterday," Niran states. "If so, he'll know she's not in San Diego, and is giving us time."

Swift raises her hand. "We've been doing some digging since the no-show at Saffie's parents yesterday. Honor's been listening in on the ex-Crazy Wolves support clubs. Seems like they're vying to take over the empty top spot, and don't have any particular time for the one-man band that's Duke. If that's true, that could explain why he didn't walk into an ambush yesterday, and why he's not coming directly for the club."

"So he takes his war to a defenceless and heavily pregnant lady?" Snips shakes his head.

"You were on lockdown, and quite rightly," Swift notes. "She was the only one unprotected."

Unprotected. Yeah right. The prospect we had on her is a useless waste of space. "I want Ross's prospect patch." I can't hold back any longer.

"Not up for debate, Brother," Lost says deceptively calm. "He took a cup of coffee from a woman dressed as a nurse. Could have happened to any of us. Even you, Grumbler."

I wouldn't have been so stupid. And being intelligent, I hold any further words on the matter. I just make a promise to myself not to vote Ross in when the time comes.

"What's the plan when we get a locale?" our newest member, Sharpshooter asks.

Preacher glances at me, but I've taken a step back. Pennywise is in my seat now, and it's him who answers the question. "We've got Swift here, she's an experienced negotiator."

"I am that," she says without any false modesty. "But I can't see Duke wanting to talk or be open to a bargain. It's Saffie or nothing as far as he's concerned. Our best ploy is to attack once we know where he's hiding."

Lost taps the table. "There could be a problem. Where he collects Saffie might not be where he's holding Mary."

"Which is why we need to find him now." I thump my fist down hard.

"Okay," Stormy says, glancing down at his laptop. "Info's starting to come in. I've got some locations to check out. I'm happy to get the drones flying, but I need to be closer. I need someone to point me to the locality."

"I'm coming." I start to stand.

"Grumbler, sit the fuck down. We need you here for when Duke calls. It may be he'll let Mary talk."

Stay to hear my Mary's voice? Or be out doing something just because it's better than doing nothing at all? It's a hard call, but I plonk my ass back down.

"I'll go," Snips offers. "I know the city."

"Or at least the back streets and where to pick up whores," Salem jokes, and gets a finger raised toward him.

I'm pleased to see Salem's the only one assing around. Stormy and Snips waste no time leaving their seats and the meeting.

CHAPTER THIRTY-THREE

Saffie

I've had to pinch myself a couple of times during this meeting. For five years I was an old lady with the Crazy Wolves. Never was I allowed to be involved in club business, let alone invited into church. I'd have got a fist in my face for even the suggestion.

Yet here I am, seated in yet another members' only meeting.

If the reason wasn't so serious, I'd be enthralled at the insights into the dynamics. Both Utah and San Diego have similarities, but each are different, much down to the personality of the presidents. Snatcher rules more with a rod of iron, Lost has an edge, don't get me wrong, but there's also something about him that suggests he listens as much as commands.

The more I think on what Duke has done, the more I don't see any other way out than to sacrifice myself to him. Mary doesn't deserve what's happening to her, and Grumbler deserves his old lady and his son back where they belong.

My first introduction to this club had been Mary being so determined to help a fellow woman in distress, so how could I abandon her now?

While it would kill me to lose Niran, and while I'd kill

myself rather than return to Duke, it's the only thing that will mean Mary will be returned unharmed.

My reasoning? Well, if the support clubs aren't behind him, as Stormy had just suggested, who's Duke got on his side? Only one man, Grit. Duke might be impetuous, but he wouldn't take on a whole club on his own. And harming Mary would make him a wanted man, by not only this chapter, but all the Devils, whatever territory they come from.

On the other hand, if he's trapped like a cornered rat, he's going to fight back. And rather than lose a bargaining chip, if he's going down, he'll take anyone with him, including Mary.

"You got that, Saffie?"

Having tuned out, I jump when I hear my name. "Sorry." I feel my cheeks burn. "Could you repeat that?"

Niran takes my hand and links his fingers with mine. "We'll arm you, Saffie, so if Duke gets close to you—which he won't —" he breaks off then warns everyone with a scowl, "then you'll be able to defend yourself."

"We'll have snipers around the vicinity," Pennywise puts in. "While we'd prefer to take Duke unharmed, I'd prefer him dead than have a chance to take you."

I notice Lost's eyes keep returning to the silent phone in front of him. I take it we're just waiting for a call from Duke now. Or, hopefully, contact from Stormy, to say that the drones have done their jobs.

"I think that's all we can cover for now," Lost says. "As soon as I hear from Duke, we'll reconvene."

As the men start to stand, Niran leans into me. "I'll take you up to our room. Hopefully a prospect has taken our bags up already."

Why unpack? I'll probably be gone in a few hours. But I know better than to say that to Niran.

I wait while he gets his crutches beneath him, then follow him out.

The clubroom is busy with all the men hanging around, but for once the smell of leather is comforting, knowing as I do, they'll all put their lives on the line to save Mary, and if possible, me.

The club whores are passing plates of sandwiches around, and Patsy, catching sight of me, gives me a finger wave.

I'm wondering whether I should go over and talk to her when someone comes barrelling up.

"Niran! Oh my God, no one told me you were back." Cyn launches herself at her brother, almost bowling him over.

"Cyn," Niran says sharply, getting his balance again.

Cyn seems to notice he's got one leg in a cast. "No one told me you were injured!" she screeches. "You come off your bike?"

"Something like that," Niran says grimly.

His sister seems to notice me for the first time. "And what the fuck are you doing here? No one wants you here."

"I fuckin' want her," Niran starts to growl.

"Hey, Cyn," another voice interrupts. "What have I fuckin' told you." The Black man who's now wearing three patches on his back, and who I remembered as a prospect, marches up. Without breaking stride, he picks up Cyn, tosses her over his shoulder, and gives her ass a resounding slap. Instead of thinking *abuse,* inside I'm cheering.

With Cyn batting at him with her hands, looking like a mouse trying to fight off a cat, the man walks away, just calling a, "Sorry about that, Niran," over his shoulder.

"What the fuck was that?" Niran asks no one in particular.

It's Salem who enlightens him. "That, there, was Sharp. He's brought Cyn to heel. Well, mainly." He barks a laugh, then grows serious. "You do know your sister's a lying cunt, don't you?"

"Are you talking about that business with Kid?" Niran grimaces as he mentions the prospect who I'd seen killed, reminding me if I ever get close enough to sink a knife into Duke, I'd do it without a second thought.

"Nah. Worse." Salem shakes his head from side to side. "Sharp could give you the details, but the long and short of it is, her boyfriend's no fuckin' abuser. She took an awkward tumble down some stairs and blamed her injuries on him."

Niran's brow furrows as he tries to process the information. "But her father beat him up, or well, got some of his friends to."

With a dismissive shrug, Salem just tells him, "Well, he didn't lay a finger on her. She made it all up."

"What the fuck for?" Niran rages. "Why the hell—?"

"Sharp will tell you when there's a minute," Salem assures him, then with a look toward me, reminds him, "We've got far more to worry about."

"Church!" Lost shouts.

There's a stampede toward the meeting room. I hang back with Niran so we don't get trampled, and then we follow the rest of the men.

Once we're all seated—Keeper late because, he informs us huffing and out of breath, he was in the heads—Lost wastes no time.

"Two pieces of info. Stormy's had some success. There's an abandoned warehouse, four bodies in close proximity inside. Three wandering around, one staying in place.

"A heat signal tells us she's still breathing," Grumbler breathes out. "But four? You reckon Susie's still with them?"

Looking around, I see another couple of seats that are empty. Have they all got weak bladders?

But I'm enlightened when Lost continues his update. "Preacher and Blaze are headed out to the location with a directional mic. Might be hard to pick up anything, but hopefully they'll be able to get close enough."

"Anything from Duke?" Grumbler asks.

"Yeah. I just got a call from him. He wants to make the exchange in two hours." Lost's eyes meet mine, and his mouth twists.

My heart drops into my stomach, and I risk a glance to the man at my side. Just two hours, one hundred and twenty minutes, and then I'll be leaving Niran. Maybe forever if their plans don't work out.

"Where's the exchange?"

Dart, their VP, takes over. "A shopping mall to the west of San Diego. It'll be crowded as fuck. Huge place, two separate parking lots. The plan is apparently that Duke will bring Mary, and will exchange her for Saffie, but only once he sees she's alone. With the number of people around, we can't fire at him, and will need to be careful about how we take him down."

"In a crowd we could lose him. He'll disappear as we won't know where he's parked," Salem says grimly.

"He'll make a diversion." Pennywise is thinking aloud. "He'll try to snatch Saffie. Maybe he'll leave Mary somewhere, maybe he won't."

"Maybe he'll use her as a distraction. Pregnant woman having a baby would cause a crowd."

"He better not use my ol' lady!" Grumbler roars.

In my head, I'm picturing a crowded mall. He's asked for me not to be accompanied, which means my protection will have to stay away from me. He could take me anywhere, pull me into the restrooms, or into a busy shop.

"We'll hack into the CCTV." Bolt must see that my face has drained of blood and tries to reassure me. "We can track him from the first moment he appears."

"You don't know him." It occurs to me suddenly. "Only Niran has seen him. He could come in disguise. I'd know his gait, the way he walks, his mannerisms, but you would not."

That I've made a valid point is confirmed by the sudden silence.

"I'll stick close to you, Saffie," Swift offers. "He won't be expecting a woman. I'll act like a friend you bumped into. If he tries to take you, he won't know what's hit him."

"I don't like it," Niran states, giving me a look as worried as my own. "It would be too easy to lose both Duke and Saffie."

Swift glares at him, but in the end, all she can do is say she'll try.

Dart's looking at me strangely, then he turns to Lost. "Niran's right. It's hellishly risky."

Lost drums his fingers on the table. "Then we come up with a new plan. If it's confirmed we know his location, we take him there."

"We've got one hour fifty-five minutes," Grumbler points out. "Not long enough to see the lay of the land and organise an attack. *And,* if we attack, he might kill my old lady."

Lost furrows his brow. "I don't like leaving it until we're at the mall. We risk losing him, even if we keep Saffie safe and get Mary back. We know he won't give up. And there's always a risk he'll pinch Saffie and keep Mary as well."

It seems we're at a standoff.

Lost pinches his nose, then rubs his forefinger of both hands against his brow, then he toys with his beard. Suddenly his face brightens, and he looks up. "If it looks like we've found the right location, we'll go stake it out. Duke won't go to the mall without backup, so he'll be taking Grit along, maybe leaving Mary with Susie. We can take him on the road."

"But if he's true to his word, he'll have Mary with him. How are you proposing to stop him? Crash the fuckin' car? She's pregnant, goddamnit!" Grumbler's understandably upset.

"So we'll get Stormy's drones to monitor the building and see who's fuckin' left there." Lost seems to be getting frustrated.

Tentatively, I raise my hand. It takes a moment for anyone to notice me. When they do, I swallow nervously as I prepare to propose my idea. I mean, who am I to offer advice to bikers?

"What is it, Saffie?" Lost prompts me, his eyes settling on me gently.

"You'll know what car Duke will be driving if you watch

him leave the warehouse, right?" Dart's eyes widen, then he makes a gesture to me as if to say, *carry on.* "You can find it in the parking lot and put a tracker on it or something."

"Then what?" Niran growls beside me. "What's on your fuckin' mind?"

Knowing he's going to hate this, I rush my idea out fast. "We do exactly what Duke says. Go to the mall. If he's true to his word, he'll exchange Mary for me. Then you can track his car and come get me."

"No." Niran's hiss is somehow worse than a shout.

"Let her continue," Lost orders.

"If he's left Mary at the warehouse, you can swoop in and take her while he's gone."

"But you'll be in Duke's hands," Salem states.

I shrug. "Hopefully not for long. You'll be able to track his car and then intercept it. But this time, Mary won't be in danger."

"She might," Pennywise says, shaking his head. "What's to say he wouldn't leave her immobilised in the car when he takes you, and keep you both?"

"Whatever we do, there's a fuckin' risk." Lost wipes his hands over his face, drawing down his eyes. "We're damned if we do, damned if we don't."

"And we're running out of time. One hour forty-five now," Grumbler says, his voice vibrating with anger. Though that's what I assume before I look at his face. *He's terrified.*

Lost's phone pings. Pressing a couple of keys, he answers and puts it on speaker.

"Talk to me."

Preacher's voice comes over loud and clear. "Managed to get the mic working. Got a direct line of sight, so hearing them is a breeze. There's some dissent in the enemy camp."

"What are their plans?" Lost asks, while Grumbler interrupts.

"Can you hear Mary? Is she alright?"

Preacher snorts. "She's currently tearing Susie a new one." For the first time today, I see Grumbler smile. "The plan was to leave Susie behind to watch Mary, but she's refusing. Mary's water has broken. She's been having pains and Susie doesn't want to be left delivering a child." Grumbler's smile is completely wiped away.

"It's too early," he rasps. "She needs to be in the hospital—"

"Just hang on," Dart tries to reassure him. "She's still got time. We got this, Brother."

But Grumbler looks frantic, his eyes are wild. "Mary..." he wails.

"Grumbler, man. We've got a plan," Preacher says fast and loudly. "Duke and Grit will leave shortly, and they'll be leaving Mary behind. She may or may not have Susie with her."

"Is Susie armed?" Pennywise asks, his brow creased.

"I think that's the plan."

"Stormy can take her out. As I said, there's a direct line of sight."

"We take Duke when he's driving to the mall," Lost states firmly. "You give us the make and model of his car, give us the nod when he leaves, and we'll take it from there. Grumbler will head down to where you are so he's on hand when you rescue Mary. Thanks Preacher."

"Sure thing, Brother. Take care."

Lost ends the call and starts grinning. "You know, thanks to our Utah brothers I think we've got a plan that will work. And Saffie, you won't need to be part of it."

"Thank fuck for that," Niran states.

Suddenly the door to the meeting room bursts open, and Connor unapologetically all but falls through.

"Prospect!" Dart shouts. "What the fuck?"

"Thought you'd want to know," Connor huffs out, his chest heaving as though he's been running. "There's a drone hovering over the gate to the compound."

"Fuck it!" Niran roars. "Grit's using the same toys we are."

Lost purses his lips, looks down, then says calmly, "Change of plan. Let's give them a show. Saffie, you and Swift will head out in a car to go to the mall. Half of us will follow, Duke will expect that. Grumbler and the others will hang behind, and then when we're clear, set out to rescue Mary."

"Using the back exit," Salem suggests.

Lost's rise of his chin shows he agrees.

"I want to hear about Plans B and fuckin' C, Prez." Niran spits out.

"That would be me." Swift raises her hand. "I'm Plan B. If you can't stop Duke, I won't let him near Saffie. Nothing will happen to her." She looks at Niran earnestly. "He's not getting through me."

I shiver and my hands start to sweat at the thought of how many things could go wrong.

I find myself sympathising with Niran when he shoots a look toward Swift, then asks, "What's Plan C?"

CHAPTER THIRTY-FOUR

Grumbler

Sitting in church it's hard to concentrate on the discussions going on around me. My head's a complete mess. *I can't lose Mary or my baby.* Then I'm torn, glancing at Saffie, knowing all she's been through, and listening to how she's going to be exposed to danger in the only chance we have to save my old lady.

Mary's alive. That's the only positive I can hold on to. The rest of the news causes me to go into a blind panic. That she's got pains doesn't come as a surprise. She's only four weeks off her due date, two from the time she's going to be induced as they want to deliver the baby early. I'm hopeful they're only the Braxton Hicks that I know she'd had with Alicia. She'd told me to prepare me for false alerts.

I was rushed into the hospital, Grumbler. It was so embarrassing to be sent home again. Yeah, I hope that's all it is. The alternative doesn't bear thinking about.

But it's not a false alarm, I remind myself, going back over the conversation that takes away any hope. *Her water has broken.* This is the real thing. My baby is on its way, and there's nothing to stop it.

Being held captive in an abandoned warehouse is not where she should be when the baby comes, her only support being that bitch, Susie. On top of that, she shouldn't try to give birth naturally. That was one of the things we were warned about from the start. She's due for a caesarean, as at her age her muscles would probably no longer be strong enough to push a baby out, or not before he got distressed. We're not going to take any chances, planning to help nature along before the natural process gets started.

I glance at the clock on the wall. The minutes are ticking off, and I just want to get moving. I estimate it will take about forty-five minutes to get to the warehouse. Anxiety makes my leg bounce and twitch.

Lost is talking, but I'm only half listening. "Swift will accompany Saffie. Once they're on their way, Dart, Blaze, Dusty and Deuce will head for the mall. Bolt? You okay to join them?"

"I'm going with Saffie," Niran snarls. "You're not leaving me out of this."

"They'll be on bikes," Lost patiently points out. "And you can't go in the car with Swift. Duke will be on the lookout for you."

"He'll expect us to send someone with her. I'll take Swift's role." Niran won't give up. In his position, I wouldn't either.

"I know this is fuckin' hard." Road's eyes fill with sympathy. "I've been where you are. Fuckin' sucks to be grounded. But, Brother, Duke can knock you over with a fuckin' feather. And if he runs with her, you'd never be able to keep up. Swift on the other hand…" His voice trails off. Yeah, we all know how good Swift is. I doubt many can outrun her, and as for hand-to-hand combat? Well, few would take her on.

Best part? Duke will have no idea that Swift's anything other than a female companion sent for support. The misogynistic prick will expect her to be an airhead and no threat at all.

"Got a role for you, Brother." Lost's eyes focus on the

disabled man. "Kink and Bones will be in a truck ready to pick Duke up. You can go with them."

If they pick Duke up that is. I hope we fucking do. He's escaped retribution one too many times already. I've had enough of that man to last a lifetime, and I've not yet met him.

"Salem, Pennywise, Wrangler and Reboot," Lost lists, then his eyes land on the newcomers to our table, "and Thor if you're agreeable, well, you'll be tasked with stopping Duke on the road. Preventing him getting anywhere near the fuckin' mall."

The Utah VP agrees, sitting forward as if more engaged now he's got a task assigned to him.

"We best make a start now. Get in position before he leaves the warehouse." Salem starts to stand.

Swift sits forward. "You say you've got a back way off the compound?"

Salem grins. "Sure have. Bit rough, but useable." He salutes her, then the brothers going with him get to their feet.

"Here." Kink throws the keys to his bike to Thor, and Bones does likewise to Bolt.

There's a moment's pause in proceedings as the six men file out, with *"good lucks"* and *"fucking take him down"* calls following them.

Then Lost resumes, "I'll go with Grumbler, Brakes and Deuce to get Mary. Stormy and Preacher as well as Snips are already in place. Scribe, you'll bring the truck to transport Grumbler's ol' lady. Once we've got her, take her straight to the hospital." I raise my chin in approval. "Token, you stay here and liaise with Utah. Now, any questions?"

There are none. It seems everyone knows what they have to do.

Pennywise, in my old seat, remembers his duties. "Use the time before we leave to check your fuckin' ammunition." He adds another few things, but I tune out.

I'm just pleased he's taken over. I'm incapable of thinking about anything other than getting to my old lady.

"Okay. That about wraps it up. We'll also take the back way. Dart, you'll be expected, you go out the front."

"Yeah," the VP agrees. "We'll let Saffie get a good start, then we'll follow."

As soon as Lost finishes speaking, I vacate my chair. *Hang on, Mary. I'm coming for you.*

"Grumbler?" A soft voice stops me in my tracks. "I hope Mary's okay."

Looking down, I see Saffie biting her lip and remember the part she's got to play. If it all goes tits up, she might be back in Duke's hands by the end of the day. It goes against everything I am to let a woman fight my battles, but I've no choice if I want to see my old lady again. "You take fuckin' care, you hear me?" I growl.

Why does it have to come to this? One old lady versus another, when I want them both safe.

"Just concentrate on Mary," Niran says, his arm going around Saffie.

I can tell by the pain contorting his face that the situation is killing him, but not once has he suggested we sacrifice Mary to keep Saffie safe. Not that I'd expect that, but in his position, it has to be tempting. "Brother…" I start, unable to continue. I pull him in for a hug. As we exchange heartfelt back slaps, all my anger at him being responsible for Mary being abducted fades away.

"We'll keep them both safe," he assures me when at last we release each other. But the look in his eyes belies any certainty he might have.

"You coming, Brother?"

I swing around and jerk my head up and down in response to Lost. I've been ready for hours.

Three quarters of an hour later, I'm pulling up next to the

other bikes in a vacant lot not far from the warehouse. Scribes pulls the truck in behind. Getting out my phone, I calculate the quickest route to get Mary to the hospital from here. I can't let my mind dwell on the idea we might not rescue her as anything other than uninjured and alive. *I'm coming for you, Mary. Just hang on.*

It seems an age until Lost gets a call. I race to him as the others gather around, but from the look on his face, he's not hearing good news.

"What the fuck is it?" I demand.

"Duke and Grit have left the warehouse." *So?* That was what we knew they had planned. But again, they seem to be one step ahead of us as Lost shakes his head and relays, "In two separate vehicles. Both windows blacked out."

A text pings, Lost reads it, then says, "Hot fuckin' damn. They've taken different routes. Utah's hacked into the CCTV, but we don't know who's in which car, or who to stop."

His phone rings again. "Yeah, I'm hearing this, Salem. Yeah, split the fuck up. You'll have to follow both cars."

That's bad news, but what I'm focused on is that Mary's only got that bitch Susie with her now.

"What if Grit turns back once he's happy he's created a diversion?" I grab at Lost's arm. "We've got to get in there and get her out."

Lost gives me a sharp nod, and signals. Without delay, we get back on our bikes and ride toward the warehouse, pass it, me turning my head and praying for Mary's safety under my breath, then park further up the road where Snips and Preacher are waiting.

Snips stubs out a cigarette, then points to the roof of a building opposite. "Stormy's up there. He's got Susie in his sights."

"There are three entrances to the warehouse. The front is chained and locked, but there's also one at the back and one at the side. Duke and Grit came out of the side one," Preacher informs us.

"Any eyes in the sky apart from ours?" Lost asks.

"None. We've been keeping an eye out seeing as Grit is also into his toys."

I'm getting impatient. "What's the delay? Let's go in and get Mary out." There's only a fucking bitch between me and her and I'm not going to let Susie get in my way.

Preacher raises his chin at me, while Lost pulls at his chin and shoots me a warning look. "We've got to do this quietly, Grumbler. Susie will probably be armed, and we don't want to back her into a corner where she tries to shoot her way out. Too much risk she'll either shoot Mary, or your old lady will catch a stray bullet." At his chilling warning, I nod once, showing I understand. While I'd rather rush in with all guns blazing, that isn't the way to do it. When he sees I've got the message, he continues, "Be on the lookout for booby traps. One thing Duke isn't is stupid. Grumbler, you, me and Snips will take the side door, Preacher, you, Brakes and Deuce come in from the back."

"You want the bitch alive?" Preacher asks.

"Preferably," Lost decides. "I want to know more about her fed cousin. But if she has to be collateral damage, so be it. Mary's who we want."

At fucking last, we're on the move.

The windows are at the front, so we circle around as quietly as men in motorcycle boots can, and soon come across the side door. As Snips approaches it, he kicks at a stone, and it skirts across the ground and hits up against a metal pipe.

As I shoot daggers at him, he looks contrite. We wait a beat but there's no sound from the interior.

Lost places his hand on the door handle and carefully presses it down. *It's unlocked.* Utah's done their job and disabled any alarm system.

I tap his back, then indicate myself. I want to be the first to enter, and the one who rescues my old lady.

He nods and steps aside.

Carefully, so fucking carefully, with my back to the wall, I inch down the corridor in the direction of where Mary's being held. I hear her voice before I can see her.

"Duke's gone. Please, Susie, get me to the hospital now. Or call 911 and disappear."

"Oh shut your moaning," the unsympathetic voice replies, and I hear footsteps walking back and forth.

"Oh!" A gut-wrenching exclamation of pain comes, accompanied by audible heavy breathing. "Susie, if you've any humanity in you, get me some help now. I'm in labour." My Mary sounds desperate as I inch closer, having to fight my instincts to run straight in.

"Duke told me to stay here. Anyway, women have had babies since the beginning of time. You've got a daughter. You must remember the mechanics."

"That was eighteen years ago! Oh hell, here's another one." A suppressed groan reaches my ears. I take advantage and move nearer.

No rushing now, I tell myself. *Susie will be armed.* But everything in me just wants to get to my old lady and damn any consequences to myself.

Lost, so close behind me I can hear him breathing, taps me on the shoulder. As I turn, he points first to me then jerks his head left where Mary's voice had come from, then to himself and his head moves to the right indicating he'll go for Susie. He then holds up three fingers and counts down. Three… two… one.

I burst in, throwing myself in front of Mary as Lost, taking advantage of her surprise, kicks the gun out of Susie's hand. He's been none too gentle about it.

"You broke my fucking arm!" she screams out.

Vaguely, I'm aware of the room filling as Preacher, Scribe,

Brakes, Deuce and Snips rush in, but I've only got eyes for my old lady.

"About fucking time, Grumbler," is her greeting to me. "I thought you'd never turn up. The baby's coming."

No thanks for saving her life. I'd roll my eyes if the situation weren't so dire. Instead, I lean down, grimacing when I see the reddened mark on her cheek. *Duke's going to pay,* I think, as I go to pick her up.

"Wait!" she cries out. Her face contorts and her breathing comes fast.

I fucking hate seeing her hurting. I wait only for that contraction to pass, then gently lift her into my arms, carrying her bridal style. I've got to get her to the hospital.

"I'm too heavy."

It's true, with the weight of the baby she's heavier than she was, but that's not going to stop me. "Clear out of the way!" I shout, as I manoeuvre my way through the now crowded room. "Scribe, you need to drive us."

Scribe runs ahead, pausing to hold the street door open for me, then does the same to the back door of the truck. I have to pause before putting Mary in, as another contraction hits. *Surely they shouldn't be coming this fast?*

I hate the way her face twists with the pain, how her hands clutch at my cut. She hadn't been meant to feel any of this. Birthing for her was meant to be easy.

When the strong muscle movements that had made her so tense start to fade, I lift her into the truck and slide in beside her.

"Drive," I instruct Scribe.

Not more than a few minutes later, Mary screams, "Stop!"

Scribe does so, screeching to a halt at the side of the road.

"What?" I turn to her. "Mary, there's no time, we've got to—"

"The baby's coming, Grumbler. Take a look. Tell me I'm wrong." Mary's body goes rigid again.

Take a look? I'm no fucking doctor. What do I know what I'm looking for? But as her hand grips at me, and her eyes widen in panic, I know I've got to step up.

"Lie back, let me see." Scribe's got the door open. I get myself out so she can have the whole of the back seat.

When she's manoeuvred herself leaning against the opposite door, and has her feet on the seat with her knees drawn apart, I lift the skirt of her maternity nightgown she was wearing when she was taken. Using my knife, I slice off her panties. And oh, fuck me. Her vagina is bulging. When she starts to scream, a nightmare commences in front of me when a fucking alien starts to come out.

I'm going to be scarred for life.

No, I fucking won't. *That's the head of my baby*, I realise, coming back to my senses.

I've no idea what to do. "I can see the baby," I tell her, excitedly. "I think you're supposed to push."

She screams again, and her pregnant belly goes taut.

"Push, Mary. Push. That's it. His head's fuckin' out. That's it, babe. Just one more time."

"I can't, Grumbler. I'm too tired," she cries. "It hurts."

"You can, Mary. You fuckin' can." My gruff voice is sterner than I wanted it to be, but it seems to have an effect as she proves me right.

Another strong contraction has her wailing in pain, but she huffs her breath and bears down, and in the next second, I'm looking down at the messy bundle of miracle baby I'm holding in my hands, forgetting for a moment to breathe.

He's fucking perfect. Bloodied, covered with some unknown substance, with a shock of hair the colour of mine before it went grey. I fall in love immediately.

"Is he alright?" Mary's voice is weak, but full of concern.

The baby twitches his arms and legs, and then as if already fed up with the world, lets out a wail.

"Let me hold him." Her hands beckon to me.

I leave the umbilical cord attached and grab the quickest thing I can take off. My cut. Nestled in the leather, I hand my son to his mom.

"I'm so fuckin' proud of you, Mary."

It's only then I become aware of voices outside.

"Hey, don't blame me, Officer. I had to stop. My brother's baby's being born in there."

"Yeah, right." The disbelieving comment comes from a stranger. Then the door behind me is opened wide, and I pull down Mary's skirt fast. "Fuck me," the cop breathes. "Fucker outside was right. You need an ambulance?"

I don't want to waste any time. "We need to get to the hospital fast. He wasn't supposed to be born yet."

"Okay then." The police officer sums up the situation fast. "You better follow me."

After I make sure Mary's comfortable, Scribe gets back behind the wheel. The police car moves ahead of us and puts on the blue and red lights. To the sound of sirens, we're escorted to the hospital.

Mary, looking up from the precious bundle in her arms, tiredly smiles at me. "This will be a story we'll have to make sure he never forgets. Being born in the back of a truck and already coming to the attention of the cops."

I can't help it. I laugh. After all the tension of the last few days, fuck, all the long months when we first found out Mary was expecting our child, leaves me in a rush. My laughter turns to a sob, and I, Grumbler, outlaw biker and sergeant-at-arms, am brought to my knees by my old lady and newborn son. Tears roll down my cheeks and I do nothing to stop them.

CHAPTER THIRTY-FIVE

Niran

We're in Bluetooth connection with Salem's team who've split up trying to rendezvous with the two trucks. The enforcer's leading one, Pennywise the other.

"How far is the comms channel good for?" I ask Kink.

"I'm told about two miles." He casts me a look which I interpret as we'll lose touch with one or the other in too short a time.

"Following them on the traffic CCTVs. The Ford seems to be the one taking the direct route to the mall." Honor's voice sounds from the car speakers.

"Too fuckin' obvious," Kink states.

"He doesn't know we're following." Or so I desperately hope.

"He's got Grit, remember. Grit will plan for technology even if he doesn't think we've got access to it." Kink sounds patient as thought talking to a child.

He could be right. "He's running out of time, though," I point out, for some reason literally indicating the digital clock readout. "He's meeting Saffie in thirty minutes and he still has to park."

"So that could be him." Kink casts a sideways look my way. "You want to put money on it?"

It's not money, it's my old lady's life.

Honor updates us again. "The other car has turned. It's also heading toward the mall. Different entrance."

Shit. Shit. Shit.

"I got a chance to take this one out," Salem's voice interrupts. "He's turned onto a side street. Go Road!" His statement is shortly followed by, "Fuck that man can ride."

"What's happening?"

"Road's headed toward him. It's a fuckin' game of chicken. He's making him swerve. Yeah! Fuck, Road, that was some riding. He's out. Repeat. The hostile is out. Smashed into a streetlamp."

"Who the fuck is it?" I cry.

The roaring of engines is all I hear for a minute until the engines shut off. "Grit." Salem tells me, sharply. "Duke's in the other one."

"On it," Pennywise says.

"The one fuckin' coming in from the north." Kink wrenches the steering wheel around and does an abrupt U-turn. "I knew we shouldn't have gone for the obvious."

I can't blame him. "Just drive as fast as you can."

"I know a shortcut."

Kink does, it would seem. Unfortunately, there's a breakdown and traffic's backed up trying to get past.

"Goddamn it!" Kink bangs the steering wheel.

"Fucker's disappeared into a tunnel," Honor informs us. "He hasn't appeared back out."

"He can't just stop," I exclaim.

"It's alright," Pennywise says. "We're waiting for him. We're ahead of him and will pick him up once he comes out."

"There he is!" Duty butts in, shouting. "He's tricked you,

Pennywise. He's two miles ahead. He must have put pedal to the metal and shielded himself with that massive trailer."

"We're too fuckin' far away. We're playing catch up." The new sergeant-at-arm's voice sounds agonised.

And so are we, now we're past the car with its hood up. We're moving, but too far away.

I dial a number on my phone. "Swift?"

"What you got?" Her voice is calm.

"They used two vehicles. Grit's being handled. Duke's heading your way. We've got no eyes on him."

"I've got this," she confirms, with no sign of panic.

I hope she has. *Saffie, I promised I'd keep you safe.* I end the call as a voice comes over the car speaker again.

"Kink? Swing by and pick Grit up, will you? Can't keep him here for long. Someone's going to investigate the accident."

"Don't you fuckin' dare," I warn him. "I've got to get to Saffie."

"Dart's on his way," Kink answers in a reasonable tone. "And we've got to get the brothers out of trouble. If we want to question Grit, we've got to get to them before the cops turn up."

All fair points, but logic holds no sway at this point. My hand twitches and inches toward my gun, but at the last moment, I come to my senses.

Instead of threatening my brother, I call Swift back. "Swift, you've got my fuckin' life in your hands. If anything happens to Saffie—"

"I won't let her out of my sight," the Englishwoman promises.

Damn it, Saffie. Why couldn't you have still been afraid? Why didn't you let us dress up a sweet butt in a wig as a decoy? Though maybe that wouldn't have fooled a man who'd intimately known her for five years. But it might have bought us some time.

Kink makes a final turn, and we pull up beside a crashed car, and a group of onlookers. An unconscious Grit is lying on the sidewalk.

Salem walks up and leans in the window Kink has just lowered. "Had to punch the fucker unconscious when this lot turned up." He jerks his head back toward the crowd.

"Well, let's get him loaded."

Kink signals for me to stay put and gets out. The back doors are opened, and I hear the sounds of a body being put inside, and a voice protesting, "Shouldn't you wait for the ambulance?" That's followed by the snick of handcuffs being applied, and a tearing of duct tape.

Then a welcome sight appears in front of my eyes—Curtis and Ross with the tow truck. Hopefully by the time the cops arrive, all signs of an accident will have disappeared, except for the slightly crooked streetlight.

Come on. I drum my fingers against my leg. *This is taking too much time.* I'm so anxious to get to Saffie, my worry is eating me alive, bile churning in my stomach.

I can't lose her now. Not when we're so close to starting our future together. I try to imagine us buying a house, starting our own family, but it's impossible. My brain keeps summoning up images of her dead by Duke's hand, or stolen away by him, and me never being able to find her.

At fucking last, Kink gets back into the driver's seat, and we leave our brothers hoisting up the damaged car.

Jerking his head toward the back he tells me, "I've restrained him. Hopefully he won't cause too much trouble. I would prefer to return to the compound and drop him off, but if we get lucky, he'll soon have company."

Then, finally, we're heading in the right direction again—to the mall.

Dart's voice tells us that with Utah's help he's found the truck Duke had been driving in the parking lot and gives the location details to Kink.

After navigating the traffic, trying to get in and park, we get to the lot and pull up beside Duke's truck. When Kink helps me out then hands me the crutches, I hear a whistle.

Turning, I spy the VP.

"If we head inside, we risk Duke getting wind that we're around," he tells me. "Thought it best to wait here and be the last line of defence."

On one hand the plan's sound, on the other… "What if he's got another vehicle stashed nearby?" Dart's expression is all I need. "Shit, we're fucked." I bang a crutch against the side of Duke's truck, hard enough to dent it.

There's a banging from the rear of our vehicle, and Kink's mouth turns up at the same time as Bolt's does.

"I think there are ways we can find that out." Bolt's eyes light.

"Torture Grit?" While I'm not averse to the idea, we're in a very public parking lot. Shoppers are going to and from their cars all around me. Full bags one way, empty hands the other.

Dusty cottons on fast. "One scream and all hell will break loose." He jerks his head toward a security camera.

"I've duct taped his mouth," Kink tells them.

"So how's he fuckin' supposed to talk?" Deuce rolls his eyes and looks around warily.

Blaze shrugs. "Yes or no answers only."

"He'll be a fuckin' hard nut to crack." I'm certain Grit won't betray the last remaining Crazy Wolf lightly.

Bolt's still grinning. "You got water in there?" He nods to the truck.

Kink looks startled, but opens the rear door and peers in. "Whatdya know?" he asks rhetorically. "A five-gallon container, looks full."

I'm not surprised, this truck is known for having a leaky radiator. "What you thinking, Bolt?" But while I ask, I've got a good idea.

Dart's now got a grin which splits his face ear to ear. "Waterboarding," he says quietly. "It's hard to scream when you're drowning."

Ah yes. My mind goes back to the demonstration Swift had given to us.

Bolt asks, cracking his knuckles, "He conscious?"

Kink nods. "Yeah, he's moving, trying to get free." But he won't. If Kink knows anything, it's how to restrain somebody.

"I might only have watched," Bolt informs us, "but how hard can it be? Wanna help, Brother?"

I wish he was asking me, not Kink, but it would be awkward as fuck for me to get into the truck and help hold Grit down. Once again, I curse my injury.

"Give us some cover," Bolt instructs, then takes off his bandana, as he and Kink get into the back of the truck.

"Cover," Dart muses. Then, reaching into the truck, he turns on the radio, tunes to a channel playing heavy rock, and dials up the volume. "Come on, Brothers, let's party."

Blaze gets out a pack of cigarettes. Deuce is the only taker, but they both light up and sit on the hood of the truck. Dusty starts jiving to the beat. Taking my cue, I balance on my prosthesis, and tap one of my crutches on the ground to the beat, and all the time the San Diego sun beats down.

"Hey, pretty lady, want to dance?" Dusty holds out his hand to a young woman walking by. She blushes, but hurries on past.

"Your charms aren't working," Dart informs him, chuckling.

There's movement from the truck behind us, and muffled cries. A husband and wife—her pushing a stroller, him holding the hand of a toddler—are heading toward us. They give us a filthy look and divert their path so they don't come close.

One braver man, his back ramrod straight like he's got military experience, is braver. "What the hell's going on?" He points to the truck where the suspension is bouncing up and down.

"When the truck's rockin', don't go a knockin'," Blaze drawls with a wink.

"Brothers having fun," Dart informs him.

"You got a woman in there?" The man looks on suspiciously.

Grit chooses that time to get out some words, "Oh God, no—"

"Nah, not a woman." Blaze grins knowingly. He nods at Dart. "What he said, just brothers having fun."

"Fucking perverts," the man says with outrage on his face.

"Fuckin' homophobe," Dart responds quickly, his face becoming vicious.

The man backs off immediately. "Hey, each to their own, but here, man? Where there are kids?" He throws up his hands and walks off.

"Fuck," Deuce says quietly, stubbing out his cigarette. "There's security."

Following the direction of his eyes, I see two uniformed men approaching.

"What's going on here?"

"We're just waiting for our old ladies to finish their shopping," Dart tells him.

"Yeah, and we could be here all day." Dusty gives an exaggerated roll of his eyes.

Faced with four men wearing cuts, and me, the security guys don't look too sure of themselves. That's probably why one says politely, "Keep the noise down, will you? We're getting complaints."

"Sure," Dart agrees amicably, reaching into the truck and turning the music down just a notch.

We give mock salutes, then the security guys leave.

Shortly after, Kink gets out of the back, water dampening his chest. He glances around before beckoning us close and saying quietly. "Duke's got a car stashed in the southern parking lot. I've texted the license plate to your phones."

"Grit?"

Kink grins. "Bolt's knocked him out again. He's staying with him to make sure he doesn't come round."

Dart's already checking his phone. "We'll find it." He looks at Dusty, Deuce and Blaze. "Party's over, let's move this on."

Within moments, there's a roar of engines, and the four bikers ride off.

"You wanna go with them?" Kink walks back around to the driver's door.

That was my first instinct. I do, but I don't. Something's stopping me. "It might be a decoy." I rub the bridge of my nose. "Duke might be keeping both options open."

"He'll know Grit's gone radio silent by now," Kink agrees, his intelligent eyes sharpening. "I'm with you, Brother. He might abort his Plan A, and return to Plan B. We'll stay here and ensure all his options are covered."

CHAPTER THIRTY-SIX

Saffie

Glancing to my left as we leave the compound behind, I watch Swift driving. Like everything she does, she's handling the car with precision and confidence.

Despite the circumstances, I have to smile. "I almost didn't recognise you."

Swift had emerged from the clubhouse in her customary jeans, but instead of her boots, had sparkly sandals on instead. And rather than the plain black or camouflage t-shirts she normally wears, today hers is bright pink and adorned with the slogan picked out with diamante, *Girls just wanna have fun.* But the biggest change is her face. I've never seen her with makeup before, not once in those weeks spent in Utah. Today, eyeliner, mascara and eyeshadow make her eyes stand out and seem much larger. But it's the bright red lipstick that draws the eye.

Swift chuckles. "I had a little help from Cindy," she explains. "These are her shoes and top." She pauses to indicate she's moving out into the next lane. "Arsehole," she says under her breath as the driver in front does the same, causing her to brake. She continues the conversation as if she'd never stopped. "I don't think the sweet butts know what to make of me. When I went to Cindy, she asked if I wanted her to go down on me."

I snort, so very unladylike, and so much so I have to get out a tissue and blow my nose. "Did you take her up on it?"

"Nah," Swift replies seriously. "Road's good enough in that department."

Feeling more relaxed in her company than I have before, probably due to her looking feminine for once, I tease her. "So, if it wasn't for Road…?"

Swift barks a laugh. "I prefer the old-fashioned game of hide the salami. Muff diving isn't for me. Though Cindy did seem to be interested."

I giggle, I can't help myself. "They see the cut and think you're a member."

"I *am* a member," she retorts. "I'm just a brother without a dick. Well, except for Road. He's my dick."

I snort again. "He's not going to know it's you when he sees you like that."

"Oh, he will. He'll have ideas about my lipstick." She glances at me and winks. "And I might just oblige."

It's probably that I feel comfortable with her today, that the words just tumble out. "I can't give head to Niran. Not after Duke—"

Swift shoots a look of compassion my way. "Bloody hell, Saffie, you've come a long way. Just look at you. You've become comfortable with bikers, and I know you're dancing the horizontal tango with Niran. Don't be too hard on yourself. After what you've been through? I'm fucking amazed at you. Niran won't push you to do anything you don't want to do."

"But men expect that."

"It's not a failing, Saffie. In time, you may want to, if you don't, there's no foul. Lots of women don't like sucking dick."

"Duke—"

"Duke's a fucking wanker, and he's going down today." She

cracks her knuckles on the steering wheel. "I'm looking forward to meeting this arsehole of yours."

I'm most definitely not. My mood sours as what-ifs go through my mind. *What if Duke manages to capture me? What if he kills me on sight? What if, what if, what if...*

The car speakers come alive with an incoming call.

Swift presses the button to connect.

"Swift?"

Instead of confirming, she just asks, "What you got?"

"They used two vehicles. Grit's being handled. Duke's heading your way."

"I've got this." It's said with one hundred percent confidence, unlike the near panic I hear in Niran's voice.

As she ends the call, I ask, "What does it mean?" I'm trying to translate the information we've been told.

"It means they followed the wrong vehicle, and Duke gave them the slip. It's you and me, girl, against him."

At my gasp, she says confidently, "You don't need anyone else, Saffie. Not when I'm around, and certainly not dressed like this. Duke will underestimate me, men always do. That's my advantage."

The phone rings again, and once more, it's Niran.

"Swift, you've got my fuckin' life in your hands. If anything happens to Saffie—"

"I won't let her out of my sight," she promises patiently.

My hands are trembling. When Niran's off the line, I admit, "I'm scared."

"Of course you are, Saffie. Fear helps, it makes you sharp. It makes you more observant. Adrenaline makes you faster on your feet. Embrace it, don't fight it."

If she'd told me to calm down, it wouldn't have worked. The thought of using the pent-up terror inside me actually helps, as long as I don't have a full-blown panic attack and fall at Duke's feet.

"I hate him." All that passion comes out in my voice.

"Hold on to that, Saffie. Hold on to that."

We're in stop-start traffic as we queue to get into the parking lot. Once through the barrier, we easily find a spot to park.

"We need to head through that door there," Swift points out as we get out of the car.

"How do you know?" I've never been here before, and as far as I know, she hasn't either. I thought we'd have to find someone and ask how to find the meeting spot Duke had chosen.

"Honor sent me the floor plans."

Of course he did. I should have known the brothers in Utah would have our backs.

Swift clicks the button and locks the car, then hefts a sparkling jewel-studded purse over her shoulder, I believe that too is courtesy of the sweet butt. As she starts striding away, I run after her, suddenly realising.

"What's your name? I mean, I know you're Swift, but if we get into conversation and Duke asks who you are...?"

She hesitates, then tells me, "Karen."

I have never met anyone more unlike the proverbial Karen in my life. Shaking my head, I follow her into the mall.

As soon as we're inside the entrance, Swift links her arm through mine. It looks casual, but her grip is firm. It gives me the confidence it will be hard to part us.

We go to the area Duke had instructed. I scan my surroundings, but I can't see him anywhere. Swift seems preoccupied with a mannequin display, but I'm sure she's using the reflective glass as a mirror.

"He's not here," I whisper.

"He probably is," she says, getting a firmer grip on my arm. "He'll be checking there are no bikers with us."

"Where is Dart?" I hiss.

Swift checks her phone. "Held up," she says, reading a text. "But they're on their way."

"I wish we knew more about what was going on." I'd heard that all the others were linked on different comms channels, but when it came to us, I was to be ignorant of what was happening. That way I couldn't inadvertently give away the bikers' plans to try to rescue Mary. I hate it, but even I know I'm not that good of an actress, and if, heaven forbid, they find Mary dead, then my face would probably give that knowledge away.

I'm trying to spot Duke when a voice behind me makes me jump.

"My lovely wife," he starts, sarcastically. "I really didn't think you'd have the guts to turn up today."

My mouth opens and shuts. I'm speechless as fear paralyses me. I thought I'd be prepared to see him again, but instead I'm just as terrified as I ever was. The rest of my life seems to flash past me—me being tortured, molested and imprisoned by Duke again.

"Mary's my friend," Swift says from beside me. "Where is she?"

Duke looks my companion up and down and sneers, "I expected her man to come with Sapphire. Who the fuck are you?"

Swift shrugs. "Grumbler would have torn you apart. So," she looks around, "where is Mary?"

"Mary's safe. She'll be released when I'm out of here with Saffie."

"That wasn't the plan," Swift says sharply.

"No?" Duke gives that evil grin he's so practised with, and leers as he eyes her. "Tell you what, why don't you come with me and Sapphire, then you can see Mary for yourself?"

As Swift has taken over the talking for me, she's given me time to calm my breathing and try to relax. Her taking charge and Duke's reaction has reminded me how misogynistic he is. In his world, no woman is a challenge, and none ever fight back.

It also doesn't surprise me when he starts to flirt. "What's your name, darlin'?"

"Karen," Swift all but simpers, responding to Duke's change in body language. While inside his core is rotten, on the outside he's an attractive man and used to women falling at his feet. It doesn't surprise me he doesn't suspect she's acting.

"Well, Karen, I don't know what rumours you've heard about me, but all I want is a divorce from Sapphire, and she won't give it to me. She hid so I couldn't serve papers. Now I have her attention, and I'm here, and so's she. We'll soon be ending our alliance. Maybe you and I could have something?"

I don't know whether to be enraged by his lies and his blatant approach to the woman standing beside me or laugh at his underestimation of Swift.

Instead, I play along. "I'd have given you a divorce anytime, Duke."

"Would you?" he pans. "You never served papers on me."

It's true I had not, but then, that would have given him a way to find me.

"She aborted our baby. She tell you that?"

Swift gives a gasp. "She did not." She looks and sounds completely horrified but doesn't let go of my arm.

Duke, constantly scanning his surroundings, looks around again. He appears to be getting nervous. "Let's get out of here and go to my car. Sapphire can sign the paperwork, and I'll take you to your friend."

He dares to put his hand on the small of Swift's back, and one arm over my shoulder. "I've got a gun, Sapphire," he says, directly into my ear. "I'm leaving here with you, dead or fuckin' alive, got it?"

What's Swift's plan? I wonder, fear making it hard to breathe, as Duke pushes us both in the direction he wants us to go.

Duke doesn't just smell of oil and leather, he's got a unique perfume that's pure evil. Different from the rich, earthy and slightly sweet aroma of Niran's cut or those of any of his brothers. It makes me question how I'd made the comparison. But the scent affects me, his closeness making it suffocating, wiping rational thought from my mind, replacing it with sheer terror.

I've a knife in my bag, but I'm incapable of using it. I'm just Duke's toy, returned to its master. My feet step forward one after the other, propelled not just by his pressure on my shoulder, but by his presence.

Obey or be punished.

Paralysed by horror, my mind jumps to conclusions. *Swift's a biker. She's helping Duke. It was all a set up.*

I glance at the happy shoppers around us. No one takes one bit of notice. No one comments on a woman whose blood has drained from her cheeks. People step to the side as though not to impede the progress of one man and two women, not even looking into our faces.

There's no security, no one to whom a call for help could be addressed.

We walk through the main shopping area, and out into the vestibule. Outside, the sun is still shining.

"Come on, ladies. My car awaits." Sensing victory, Duke speeds up. I try and pull away, and he drops his hand from Swift. Swift seems to stumble, falling into him, her hand going up to his shoulder.

Immediately, Duke slaps his hand to his neck. "Bitch," he hisses, pushing her away hard. "What the fuck have you done?" He tries to raise his gun, but it wavers in his hand.

Swift twists his wrist, disarms him, and puts his weapon into her glittery purse before anyone notices.

When he starts to slump, she takes his weight. Without missing a beat when someone walks in the door and looks at her, she tells them, apologetically, "Man can't hold his drink."

Then she's semi-carrying him, semi-pushing him out the door and into the parking lot.

"What was that?" I ask, my head spinning. "And why didn't you act earlier?" Mentally I'd given up, thinking she had to have been working with him. My mind now spins as it quickly does a one-eighty, acknowledging in no way is Swift the enemy.

"GHB." She shrugs. "It's dangerous to inject it, but while I'll be sorry if it kills him, I won't waste any tears. Hey, over here."

The last is directed to someone behind me. Swinging around, I see Dart has got his phone to his ear but puts it away as he approaches.

Glancing at Duke, he smirks, then says loudly to a couple walking past. "Asshole's had one too many." He goes and helps Swift with the near deadweight of her load. "Truck will be here shortly," he tells her, then looks at me. "Your man will be fuckin' pleased to see you."

As disbelief and relief send a wave of dizziness through me, I bend over, placing my hands on my knees and breathing deeply. Now Duke's in the hands of the Satan's Devils MC, he'll no longer be a problem to me. It's going to take more than a minute for that to sink in. I straighten as I remember today's not all about me. "What's happening to Mary?"

Dart begins to shake his head, but at that moment his phone rings. "Lost." He greets his prez.

"We've got Mary." Lost's voice booms so loud even I can hear it. *Oh, thank God.*

Dart's more cautious. "She okay?"

There's a snort on the line. "She's fine, but I'm not so sure about Grumbler. He just delivered his son by the side of the road."

"Say again?" Dart splutters out while Swift and I shoot looks at each other.

"Yeah, you heard right. Grumbler's a fuckin' midwife. They're on their way to the hospital now to get checked out, but Theodore Jack appears to be fine."

Theodore Jack? That must be the baby. What a cute name.

"It's good to hear some good fuckin' news, Prez. What about Susie? You got her?"

"Sure have. She's on her way to the brig."

Swift grins at Dart, then at me. It takes a moment for the implications to set in. Duke's been captured, and so too has Susie.

As tension leaves my body, tears prick at the back of my eyes as I start to believe it's over and I'm finally free. And, of course, I'm overjoyed about Mary.

Am I jealous of her and her baby? Of course I am. But I can't feel resentful of every pregnant woman and baby that I see. Mary and Grumbler deserve their happy ending.

Dart had ended the call after he'd had a few more words with Lost.

"What did he weigh?" I'm genuinely interested, a sign I'm beginning to heal.

Dart shrugs as if to say, why ask me?

"He was six pounds," Swift informs me, putting away her own phone. As Dart looks curiously her way, she raises and lowers her shoulders. "Honor hacked into the hospital database."

Dart snorts. "Does Utah do anything the easy way, you know, like texting Grumbler and asking?"

His question starts me laughing, finding his comment far more amusing than it warrants. As the sound coming out of my mouth surprises me, I realise it's a relief of tension, a feeling that from this point on, everything's going to be okay.

CHAPTER THIRTY-SEVEN

Niran

*S*affie's okay.

Those words echo in my head as Kink drives from one parking lot to another. *Saffie's safe.* And now they've got Duke, that's the way she's going to stay.

I won't fully believe it until I see her for myself, or him in our custody. My hands flex as I imagine getting my fists on him.

Today could have ended in so many different ways. But Saffie's now going to be free, Duke will soon be dispatched to meet Satan, and Grumbler's wife and son are doing great. I can allow myself to think of that future at last, with my old lady beside me.

As soon as Kink's got the truck parked, I open my door, and start to get out. Bolt's there before I can fall on my face, helping me get my prosthesis under me. My eyes search for Saffie, only to find her watching for me. She breaks away from… *Swift?*— hell, I wouldn't have recognised her—and runs straight for me.

Balancing on my prosthesis, I hold my crutches out to the side as she barrels into me, stopping just before she hits, then wrapping her arms around my waist. "It's over."

"It is," I confirm. My eyes leave hers for a moment, and land on a man sprawled on the ground. He's acting weird, as if he's tripping or something. Duke. Brought down by the Satan's Devils MC. If I was more mobile, I'd go over and kick him.

Instead, I watch as Swift leans down and jerks him up with one arm, and then Dart lends his none-too-gentle support. They sort of steer, push and pull him toward the truck, open the back doors and shove him in.

"Let's get going." Dart waves to the bikes.

Oh no. I realise Saffie's going to have to come with Kink and me, which means travelling with Duke and Grit in the back.

When I see the moment it dawns on her too, I take her by the arm. "Swift's coming as well," I reassure her. "Just a short ride, then you'll never have to see Duke again."

Saffie looks up at me, her eyes narrowed, and her brows drawn down. "I want to see him die. I want to make sure for myself that he's gone."

Which gives me a problem, as I don't want her to see the violence I'm capable of. "Saffie—"

"Why don't we let Saffie see the end?" Swift interrupts, sending a meaningful look my way. "She does need to know he won't be able to bother her anymore."

"I—"

This time it's Saffie who doesn't let me get more than a word out. "I've seen Duke torture people, Niran. I've been tortured by him. Now it's my chance, I want him to hurt. You think I'd be squeamish? That was knocked out of me five years ago." She jerks her head toward the back of the truck. "There's nothing you can do to that man that would sicken me."

"Let's get moving," Kink calls out. "They're both restrained. They won't be a problem on the journey."

Kink's right. He's an expert with knots and handcuffs, and duct tape it would seem. Neither man makes much noise except for rolling around as we drive back to the compound.

We're the last to arrive home, and as we draw up—except for

Grumbler who'll be with his old lady—everyone's waiting outside. When Saffie and I step out, cheers sound from all around, jubilance created by relief, the knowledge the last of the Crazy Wolves are about to be put down.

"Swift!" comes a shout, and Road pushes through the throng. He takes one look at her, winks and leans in. "I can think of where I'd like that lipstick, darlin'."

Swift catches Saffie's eyes and both women start giggling. From Swift it's an uncharacteristic sound. Then throwing off her badass persona for once, Swift jumps at her man who catches her expertly as her legs go around his waist. "We've got time for a quickie," she tells him.

Behind me, Curtis and Wrangler are dragging our captives out.

"Swift?" Lost calls out, catching sight of Duke for the first time, his voice stopping Road's progress toward the clubhouse. "How long before whatever you gave him wears off?"

"Fuck knows," she responds, and by the look she's just given to her man, she's hoping it's long enough.

Bolt chuckles by my side. "Road's fuckin' good for her," he observes.

"Yeah, she's not so much of an asshole anymore."

Bolt swings around and mock punches Stormy. "You can fuckin' talk. It was a good woman who brought you down."

Stormy grins widely. "Very true. You okay, Saffie?"

"More than okay," she answers him, her arm tightening around my waist. "I feel my life's been given back to me."

And I feel Road and Swift have the right idea. I want my woman naked. There were times today I'd feared I might never see her again. "Lost?" When Prez turns to me, I shout, "Saffie and I are just—"

"Going to fuck!" Dusty yells.

Saffie goes bright red, but I couldn't give a damn. "What he said!" I agree. She makes no protest as I lead her off.

After an hour or more of life-reaffirming downright-pleasurable lovemaking with my woman, I leave her sated and sleepy as I come down to find everyone milling around with drinks in their hands having a celebration.

"Duke come around yet?"

Salem raises his glass to me. "Prospects are using a water hose on him. He's getting the message."

"Ross okay with that?"

Salem frowns. "Ross heard about Saffie. He was disappointed that prospects were only involved with warming them up. Susie's there as well, by the way."

Susie. The bitch I hate almost as much as Duke.

"She hit Mary, ya know?" Salem adds.

Christ. It will be down to me to make her hurt on Grumbler's behalf. My problem is, however provoked, I'm not sure I can hit a woman.

"Fuck," I breathe out.

"I hear you, Brother." From his tone, I know Salem's views coincide with mine. "Maybe let Swift handle it?"

It's a tempting idea, but something tells me this is something I should man up and do for myself.

"A word, Brother?"

Turning, I raise my chin. "Sure." When Sharpshooter leads the way to a free area at the end of the bar, I follow him.

"Cyn," he starts, glancing at me to make sure I'm listening.

Damn it. I came down from making love to my woman and he's brought me back to earth with a bump. I don't want to think about my sister. She's a problem that needs solving, but that will come after I've dealt with Duke. But now he's approached me, I can't see how I can avoid it.

When I give an exasperated sigh, Sharp shifts, his eyes falling away from mine for a moment, then says awkwardly, "I'm not sure about your relationship with your mother."

I get the feeling that whatever he says is going to be difficult, both for him to say and me to hear it. For that reason, I give his question some serious thought. "She was a great mom, up until my father died. They'd been happy. It broke something inside her when he was killed. She came back to life when she met Grover." I pause, thinking back, then add, "Though I think that was convenience rather than a love match."

"Grover's Black, yeah? Like your father?" When I raise and dip my chin in confirmation, he resumes, "Hester's White. You know that?"

I'd assumed from the name that he'd been Black. Don't ask me why. Stormy's revelations about the man hadn't told me his skin colour. But I set that aside, instead querying what I'd been told.

"Is it true he never hit her?"

Sharpshooter sighs. "Seems that way, Brother. He loved her and wanted her back. Even after he took the punishment that he didn't deserve."

"I thought Cyn wanted to return to him?" That's what I'd been led to believe. She was here, wasn't she, to keep them apart?

Sharp shakes his head. "No, she did not. Cyn didn't reciprocate his feelings."

"Then why the fuck was she with him?" I don't understand.

He draws in a breath, holding it for a second before letting it out. "Your mother."

"Mom?"

"Your mom's got dark skin, yeah?"

Shrugging, not understanding where he's going with this, I tell him, "Yeah. I inherited it from her."

"Same as Cyn," he agrees. "Unlike her younger sisters, who resemble their dad, and are lighter." I raise an eyebrow but keep listening. "Cyn got into a lot of trouble growing up. She was picked up for shoplifting a few times, when she was totally innocent because her skin was so dark. One time," his eyes glaze slightly, showing he's relating a memory of hers, "she was in a mall with a mix of White friends and a couple of Blacks who were lighter skinned than her. One of the White kids stole a lipstick, it was Cyn who was pulled up for it. Cops didn't even search in their bags, only hers. They didn't find anything, but they still took her in and made her parents pick her up."

I grimace, knowing there's always bias, and not in a positive way. "What's this got to do with Mom?"

"Your mom lives for her kids. You, she counts as a success, but Cyn? She impressed on her from an early age that her problems were down to her skin. And if she had kids, she should make sure they were different. When she hooked up with Hester, your mom encouraged it. When Cyn wanted to walk away, she was pressured to stay with him."

My brow creases as I try to work it out. Mom's prejudiced? I didn't expect that. She'd told me Cyn was trouble, but from what Sharp is saying, trouble seemed to come to her, when she was innocent.

Not totally though. Sure, the cops might have made her life difficult, while never stopping her White friends, but that's not an excuse for the other things she's been up to.

"So she made up a lie to get out? You think that excuses her?"

Sharpshooter shakes his head. "There's no excuse for a man getting a beating he didn't deserve, nor for all the other untruths she's told. But Cyn grew up feeling she had to apologise for being what she was. It's complicated as fuck, Brother, and perhaps you and I are the only ones in this club who'd understand."

I glance around at my brothers, all of whom I'd love and would die for, confident in the knowledge they'd give their lives for me in return, as had been proven only recently. White Privilege isn't something they'd fully understand, not having been subjected to what it's like to be Black. To be the one always looked on with suspicion, to be the one most at risk when picked up by the cops.

Even less comprehensible would be the prejudice that's still inherent in some of the Black community, a spectrum where the darkest skin comes out at the bottom, and the lightest at the top. Where having the colour that could pass for a tanned White was the most valued.

I cast my mind back to when Cyn had gotten off the plane all those weeks back, my initial thought of how she'd disguised her natural hair with a wig. Not down to her boyfriend as I'd assumed at the time, but more likely down to her mother.

"Your mom wanted grandkids who'd fit in," Sharpshooter confirms.

"So Cyn's fucked up?"

"Six ways to Sunday," he agrees. "Can you imagine what it was like to grow up, never thinking you were good enough, and not being able to do anything about it? She's admitted she bought cheap skin lightening products, but they only fucked her complexion up."

"How did Grover treat her?" Why didn't he step up?

"He encouraged her to embrace her heritage, but it was her mom who had more influence."

I recall the phone call with Grover, how he endorsed sending her to me. Maybe I could have helped more if I'd known the background, or maybe not. If Cyn's grown up with the knowledge she was born into a world where she'd never fit in, maybe that was enough to send her off the rails.

Sharpshooter breaks into my thoughts. "Susie took advantage without knowing any of that."

My eyes snap to him. "What do you mean?"

"She represents everything that Cyn is not—proud and confident in her own skin. Susie was into you before Cyn came along, you know that. When she found out you had a sister, she manipulated her. Cyn found a confidant who'd listen to everything. The more attention Susie gave her, the more she craved. Susie allowed her to feel she fit in, so Cyn gave her everything she wanted."

I'm silent as I try to process what he's saying. It makes some kind of warped sense, but doesn't get Cyn off the hook. "She hates Saffie."

"She's White, Brother. You're the man she looks up to, the man who, disregarding the age gap, could, on looks, be her twin. You hooking up with a White woman just reinforced everything. You abandoned her for the very thing she'd grown up accused of not being."

"Susie's White. Yet she encouraged me to have a relationship with her." I point out the holes in his explanation.

"Because Susie made out that she valued her. Cyn doesn't know Saffie. All she could see was her taking you away."

"So where do you come in, Sharp? Come now, you can't want my sister. Not with the baggage she's carrying around."

He gives an uneasy grin. "Can't say I don't want her either. As for fixing her? I'm not sure where to begin, but I'm trying."

Well, I'll be fucked. I didn't expect that. I narrow my eyes. "You intend on her sticking around? That might be a problem for me, Brother. And for the club."

He snorts. "Well, I'm nowhere close to asking for a vote to give her my patch, but I'm up to giving her a chance. She sure appreciates a Black dick."

My eyes go wide and my nostrils flare. My hands fist, and I try to calm myself, but still it comes out as a growl, "That's my fuckin' sister we're talking about."

He chuckles. "Just wanted to let you know how the land lies. She needs a firm hand, Brother, and just so happens, I've got the time for her. And," he winks at me, "I know not to touch her hair."

I snort.

"We ready for this?" Salem, standing by Lost's side, shouts out, his hands rubbing together as if he's eager to begin.

Calls start to ring out.

"Fuck yeah!"

"What are we waiting for?"

"Let's go skin us some Wolves."

As brothers indicate that they sure are, I brush all thoughts of my sister to the back of my mind.

____

CHAPTER THIRTY-EIGHT

Niran

____

Before I leave to follow the others, I go up to my room and check on Saffie. She's still sleeping. I stand watching her for a moment, thinking how right she looks in my bed as though she was always meant to be there. This is the first time she's been able to relax properly for literally years, and I'm not surprised her mind and body are taking advantage.

Back downstairs I spy Eva.

"Hey, can you keep an eye on Saffie for me?"

Eva gives me a kind smile. "Sure, Niran. I'm so happy for you. I knew you'd find your someone, eventually."

There's a smile in my voice as I reply, "She's good for me, Eva."

"Go on." She prods me. "Go do what you men do." She winks. She's been around long enough to guess exactly what goes on in the brig, my assumption confirmed when she adds, "And make him hurt for what he did to your old lady."

That's exactly what I intend to do, I think, as I follow the stragglers into the second hangar, weaving my way past half built and finished custom motorcycles which Salem has been

374

working on. The door at the back lets me into a completely different area, this one well soundproofed, the floor sloping down to the middle where a drain is conveniently located. From the struts overhead hang chains and attached to those currently are Duke and Grit.

Salem and Swift approach me.

"We were waiting on you, Brother," Salem says, lifting his chin. "You've got more skin in this than any of us, well, both you and Grumbler."

Grumbler's with his old lady and baby which is exactly where he should be. But I'll be sure to make him proud when he eventually hears all the details.

"Where's the bitch?"

It's Swift who answers me. "The prospects are keeping her out of the way to deal with later. Thought you might prefer to get the main event over with first."

Susie's going to be hard.

Reading my mind, Salem tells me, "She's club business as much as yours, Brother, considering her connection to the feds."

Parking that thought for later, I notice brothers have parted for me, leaving me a clear passage to approach the two Wolves. An air of anticipation hangs over the space. Although initially Saffie was the only person affected by his existence, increasingly the Satan's Devils had been pulled into his orbit. When he'd taken me and her, he'd declared war on us. Even then it hadn't been over. That he'd escaped retribution at the combined chapters' hands meant all our chapters had gone into lockdown. That inconvenience pales into insignificance compared with stealing an old lady, a pregnant and vulnerable one at that, and holding her hostage. For weeks, if not months, Duke has been the epitome of the bogeyman to this club.

My role today is, on behalf of my brothers, to serve vengeance for his many crimes. A quick bullet to the head is not going to make amends.

My tours in the Marines had hardened me to the harsher side of life. Having seen good men blown apart by roadside bombs, I wasn't one to flinch at the sight of blood and guts now. I may not be an enforcer, though I may possibly, if my foot heals, become sergeant-at-arms. But I've a few tricks up my sleeve before I hand them over to the experts.

Duke sees me approaching and spits on the ground. "Fuckin' nigger." Then he throws back his head and starts laughing. "Oh, my boys got you good, didn't they? They fuckin' crippled you." He jerks his head toward the cast on my leg and lets out a belly laugh.

Around me I hear my brothers stirring, disgruntled murmurs come to my ears, but I make a cutting motion with my hand to show I've got this under control.

"You hate that a Black bettered you, don't you, Duke?" I casually ask, my crutches clattering on the cement floor as I make my way toward him. "I bet you can't fathom why, not one chapter, but all five charters of the Satan's Devils MC rode out to save a *nigger*. That loyalty between brothers trumped your pissant little club."

"Any one of the Crazy Wolves is worth ten of you," he snarls.

I snort as chuckles come from around me. "Evidence says otherwise, fucker."

"Call yourselves a fuckin' MC?" he roars out, his eyes raking over the assembled men. "What do you know about loyalty? My only crime was to want my property back. Property that had been stolen from me. The code of the brotherhood says she should have been returned as she wears my patch."

"Yeah?" I step closer. "Our rules are that property is to be cherished, not abused."

"Bikes, yeah," he agrees. "But women? Fuck no. They'd be nothing without their men."

A very unladylike growl comes from behind me, even though

it's emitted by the member without a dick. "Fuckin' arsehole," follows it up, then, "Who does this prick think he is? What fuckin' century is he living in?"

Duke's eyes narrow and look around, but Swift's keeping to the shadows for now. "What the fuck type of club is this? You allow women into men's business? You're a bunch of fuckin' pussies."

All of a sudden I realise the best vengeance I can have is not doling out the pain myself, but letting Swift loose on him. Pain to his body a man like him would probably be able to handle, but having it dished up to him by a woman would damage his pride.

Turning around, I catch Swift's eye, and quickly find the signs I used in the Marines are universal in the military, or at least so far as we can understand each other. The outcome of our silent conversation leaves me grinning.

"Get him down," I instruct.

"What the fuck?" Salem is beside me in seconds.

I whisper into his ear, causing him to beam. He slaps my back. "Nice one, Brother." He gives a thumbs up to Blaze and Snips who are closest to the winch.

They just let the darn thing free and Duke crashes to the ground. He gets to his feet shaking his head as though stunned, both physically and mentally by his swift release.

"You fight one-on-one." Salem approaches him, indicating his still-shackled hands which remain attached to the chain.

"You let me go free if I win?" Duke seems cautious, but there's a new confidence about him too.

"Nah," Salem tells him not sugarcoating it one bit. "You win, you die quickly. You lose, well, I think you can guess."

"I'll fight the whole fuckin' lot of you," Duke sneers. "You were right in one thing, nigger. This is a pansy fuckin' club."

I hide my smile, knowing he's soon going to be eating his words.

I hear bodies moving behind me, as Salem unlocks and

removes Duke's cuffs. Brothers reposition themselves so they're standing on the edges of a square.

When Swift appears, Duke snorts a laugh. "Got your sweet butt as a referee? Well, I tell you now, I ain't playing by MMA rules."

Swift's still wearing that fucking sparkly pink t-shirt, and she might not often put makeup on, so when she does, it seems she forgets she's wearing it and that maybe, to look badass, she should take it off. The lipstick isn't looking as fresh as it was, but considering Road's grin, I reckon he's wearing some of it himself.

"I'm not a referee," she says deceptively sweet as she approaches Duke. "I took your arse down once already today, just so happens I get to do it twice."

Duke's face is a picture. "You're seriously putting me up against a bitch?" He holds his arms out and turns around, viewing us all one by one. "Are you fuckin' crazy?" Then he turns back to Swift. "The only fighting you're going to be doing is when I put my cock in your ass."

"Nah," Swift's done playing as she gets into a fighting stance, "my ass is reserved for my man." Without taking her eyes off Duke, she manages to send Road a wink.

Her man, though, is looking unconcerned, leaning back with his arms folded. He gives a sad little shake of his head, as though having sympathy for the idiot who dares taunt his woman.

Duke swaggers across the makeshift ring, then his nonchalance disappears as he decides to put Swift in her place. He launches himself at her but finds his fist meeting air, and then stumbles forward as her kick hits him straight in the back.

With a roar he recovers, but Swift's too fucking fast. With a right punch, then left, she gets him straight in his face. Blood spurts as he howls with rage.

It's like watching a cat playing with a mouse. Each move Duke makes is countered before he lands a single hit. The more he fails to leave his mark on her, the more infuriated he gets, while Swift just calmly keeps out of his way and gets in blow after blow.

Winded, he drops to his knees, trying to recover from a direct strike on his kidneys. As he rasps in air, Swift grabs his hair and pulls his head up, exposing his throat. "Remind me what it was you were saying about women needing a man? Mind you, I'm not sure that word applies to you, even if you have a dick."

"You bitch!" His arms break her hold, and he leaps for her again.

This time she goes straight for the money shot and hits him squarely between the legs. Now when he lands on the ground, he stays there, hands covering his junk and his reddened cheeks puffing as he pants for air.

A giggle comes from behind me. Spinning, I turn and see Saffie. *What the fuck?*

Dart shrugs. "I thought it would do her good to see Duke being put in his place."

Saffie's grinning widely, but her face grows serious as she looks around the room. I wince seeing the various implements that we so often use. Fuck, I didn't want Saffie to see this side of me.

Swift catches her eye, and they seem to have a moment of silent girl talk. Then the Utah enforcer holds out her hand in invitation.

"Think you should get in on this, Sister."

I go to hold Saffie back, but she neatly sidesteps and evades me. Her head tilts to one side as she watches Duke, still recovering from the agony of Swift's last shot.

"He broke my legs with a baseball bat," Saffie says sneeringly as she looks down.

It suddenly hits me. Fuck me, but Saffie hadn't been looking around in disgust, she'd been looking for something to use.

Dusty, who'd cottoned on faster than me, helpfully gets the bat she must have seen, and brings it over to her.

Duke, at last, manages to get oxygen into his lungs once again. As he looks up, Saffie's in front of him, holding tight to that bat.

"Look who it is," he sneers. "My property."

"I think the tables have turned, Duke. I'm not yours anymore." Saffie's voice sounds strong and I'm proud as fuck of her.

"You haven't the fuckin' guts," he mocks.

But seeing Saffie's face, I think he's being optimistic as he underestimates her.

I'm in two minds. What she does here will never be able to be undone. Should she be anywhere near this, or kept far away? If she lets loose her demons, will they haunt her forever, or does she need this? Does she need to take control and destroy the man who once tricked her into thinking she was in love?

I'm still undecided when Saffie takes the first swing with the bat. It's not half-hearted, she's put every ounce of heartache in it.

Duke's head whips to the side and I'd be surprised if she hadn't broken his jaw. But he's hardly able to bellow in pain before she swings again.

"That was for me, you bastard. For tricking me."

The bat now meets his skull with a sickening crack.

"And that was for my baby you kicked out of me."

She widens her stance and takes a breath. "And this is for my son who never knew life." The bat rises, falls, then rises again. Blow after blow is dealt until Duke's unconscious, his face nothing but pulp, his skull crushed for certain.

"Saffie, Saffie." It's Swift who stops her, holding her arm mid-swing. When Saffie turns to her, I'm worried by the expression on her face. It seems to take a moment before she comes back to herself.

It's Bones who pushes forward and crouches by the thing that barely resembles a man and places his fingers on his neck. "He's gone."

All this time I wanted to be the one who took him out. My months of planning and hoping for vengeance, my thoughts of it being by my hand that Saffie became a widow, and now my chance has gone. Am I pissed? Hell no. A more fitting ending there could never be. A misogynist taken down by two women. I'm proud as fuck of Saffie. My only fear is that what she's done today will haunt her.

At Bones' words though, Saffie raises her chin. Then her gaze turns to land on the other man, Grit. He's been silently watching the proceedings without saying a thing, probably knowing there was nothing he could say in defence of his ex-VP.

Saffie with a strength that surprises both me and Swift, wrenches back control of the bat, and approaches the ex-fed.

"You, Grit. You stood by and watched everything he did to me. You helped him to find me, knowing what he'd do when he was successful."

"Sapphire," Grit starts. "Duke made me—"

"Duke made you?" she screams. "You're a fuckin' man. You could have stood up to him. You and the rest of the club. He forced you to submit when he made me give you that blowjob? You know, the one where you came all over my face?"

Oh fuck, Saffie. I realise that five years is a fucking long time and I'll probably never know everything that happened to her. I'm not even sure I could stand it if I did.

As brothers growl and swear from all directions, Saffie takes a firm hold of the bat once again. Putting all her might into a swing that would hit a ball not just out of the park, but probably out of the city, it lands between Grit's shackled legs.

The scream is ear piercing. But Saffie's not finished yet. She starts swinging again, first on the ribs, then his legs, then his face. Each hit is accompanied by a name. "Take this for Slit... for Knife... for Croak... for Slinger... for Stoat... for Weasel..."

Grit is a complete mess, but still not dead. Moans are coming from his throat, a gurgling sound coming from his lungs.

Saffie turns away, hands the bat to Swift and turns pleading eyes to me. "Finish him for me, Niran. Do it for Jude and for Kid."

I don't know who the fuck Jude is, but I certainly know Kid. Grit might not have personally killed him, but he was in the room.

I push myself forward, examining the remains of the man hanging in front of me, satisfied to see he's still conscious.

"This ends now, with you," I tell him. "You're the last of the Crazy Wolves. No man who rode with them deserves to live or to die pain free." Reaching out my hands, I undo his belt, then his button, then finally lower his zipper. His scrawny white dick is shrivelled and small, almost hidden by the size of his swollen scrawny balls.

"No, please…" Somehow he manages a piercing scream.

I take out my knife. "What better vengeance on a bunch of dicks, then cut them off at the root?" With that, I cut that organ right off.

Blood spurts out. "Leave him to bleed out," I suggest. "He's not a man. He never fuckin' was. Let Satan have him."

Wiping the blood off the knife on Grit's loose hanging trousers, I make my way to Saffie.

"It's done," I tell her, staring down into her eyes.

Her warrior-like expression starts to soften. Her shoulders lose their tension, and some of the darkness leaves her eyes. "It's done," she replies.

"Come." I start to make my way through the brothers, confident she's following me.

"Hey," Lost calls out. "What do you want to do about Susie?"

I pause, turn around, eye my old lady who's got no remorse in her eyes—no it's something far hotter, and full of promise for our new life. After any ending, there's a new beginning, and I can't wait another moment to get started on ours.

I tilt my head in question, and she gives me a smile and a nod.

"She's all yours," I reply to Lost. "Club business."

"Hey, brother?" Dusty's voice reaches me as I reach the door.

Swinging back, I see him cupping his junk with one hand, and at the other he's pointing at Saffie. "Word of advice? Don't piss her off."

A raucous wave of laughter follows us as we walk out.

I'm grinning widely. I didn't intend to before, and certainly not now that I've seen what she's capable of.

CHAPTER THIRTY-NINE

Niran

"Got a moment, Niran?"

Reluctantly, I pull myself away from Saffie. It hurts to let her out of my sight. Even though Duke is dead and gone, some part of me refuses to believe that she's safe and we can focus on our future. A future I've got many plans for.

"Sure, Prez." I get my crutches under me, stand, then follow him into his office.

In deference to my current physical state, he holds the door open, then closes it behind me, before taking a seat behind his desk. He leans on his elbows and steeples his hands, regarding me for a moment.

"I expected you to be breaking my door down this morning to hear what happened with Susie."

Giving a half-shrug, I explain, "I knew you'd deal with her, Prez. I trust my brothers to have my back. Saffie's my highest priority."

"I get that." He grins, then lines crease his brow. "I was fuckin' impressed with her yesterday. But how is she after that?"

"Killing Duke?" I grimace, remembering how I'd seen a different side to my old lady. A side that I fully admire, the final piece dropping into place, showing she's going to be okay with this life. "I doubt her parents would have recognised her. But Saffie's been through hell and back over the past few years. It's shaped her, made her the woman she is today. She could have been broken and cowered, hell, for a time, I thought she was. But it's hardened her, made her stronger. I was shocked, Prez." I break off to shake my head. "Wanted to save her from any more violence, but she needed to have that control. I read it wrong, but thank fuck, Swift read it right. She needed to see Duke was dead and have a hand in his retribution."

"She did," he confirms. His serious expression fades, and he smirks. "Wouldn't like to be you if you get your old lady riled."

I grin back. "I think I'll try not to, Prez."

His levity fades. "If she needs help—"

"I'll get it for her." I've already thought she might need counselling, but after last night, I wasn't so certain. Killing Duke had seemed to bring that chapter of her life to a close, and she's the better, not the worse for it.

Lost undoes his hands and raps his knuckles against his desk. "Susie," he starts, capturing my interest.

"You get her story?"

His mouth twists. "We did, yes." Leaning back in his chair, he takes a deep breath. "Turns out she was exactly what we thought she was—a biker bitch chasing a patch."

"Her cousin?"

"Second cousin." He emphasises the relationship. "I'll get to that in a bit. But what you should know is she homed in on you from the start."

"Why me?"

"She thought you'd be easy. She'd noticed you didn't go with the club girls, and thought if she forced your hand, you'd patch her." He breaks off, his face looking pained as he informs me, "She used GHB on you that night."

Dropping my head, I rub at my temples. I'd always suspected

she had. I'd never gotten so drunk I'd lost a chunk of my memory and had never understood how she'd taken me to bed. I couldn't even remember being attracted to her.

"She raped you, Brother."

What man likes to hear that confirmed? What woman for that matter? It might be months in the past, but I feel dirty as though it happened yesterday. *It hadn't been my fault*, I lecture myself. But still I wonder whether it was something I'd done, or something I'd said.

"She played on your guilt, Niran. When you didn't fall into her plans and make her your old lady, she didn't give up. I think it became a challenge to her. She saw you as hers."

"So when Saffie came along?"

"She hated her. Saw you as stepping out on her." Lost pinches at the bridge of his nose. "You're too fuckin' honourable, Brother. Salem, Pennywise, yeah, they fucked her, but she knew it meant nothing. You though? You're not indiscriminate as to where you stick your dick. She thought in time you'd give in and be with her."

"But that meant getting rid of the competition." I slam my hand on the desk. "Fuck it, Lost, she never had a chance."

"Of course she didn't," he agrees. "But the woman was twisted as well as single-minded. She got close to Cyn, played on her insecurities, made her believe Saffie would take you away from her." He breaks off and grimaces. "She used her, Niran. Flattered her, told her how once she was your old lady, she'd be her sister."

"And Cyn fell for it." My teeth grind together.

"Hook, line and fuckin' sinker."

"She got Saffie running from the clubhouse, then followed her." Up to now, it had been my belief, but with no concrete evidence.

"She did. Cyn had told her everything she'd overheard that

night. Once she learned of the Crazy Wolves and that Saffie was Duke's old lady, she immediately got in touch with her FBI contact."

"Why did he fuckin' help her?" I spit out.

Lost smirks. "Well, I doubt she told him the truth. But I suspect when he found out his cousin had an in with not one but two outlaw MCs, he went all out to help her. Can you imagine how much credit a lowly intelligence officer would get by bringing in info that would allow the feds to shut down two infamous biker *gangs*?" Lost sneers as he uses law enforcement's term for us.

"He was using her?"

"Let's just say, I don't think loyalty runs in that family. But yeah, he got her the Crazy Wolves details right away."

"Did Susie know he likely wanted to bring us down?"

Lost snorts. "No fuckin' way. She was a patch chaser, like I said. Her cousin's plans would have worked against her."

My brow creases. "Why the fuck did she meet back up with Duke? And how did she find him when we couldn't?"

"You know Grit was ex-fed?" At my nod, he resumes, "Grit used to work with the second cousin."

Now I'm confused. "But why would Grit retain contact if the fed was working to bring the Wolves down?"

Lost raises and lowers his shoulders. "Who the fuck knows? Maybe he underestimated his old work contact. Maybe he thought the Wolves were safe. But yeah, they spoke, and that's how Susie was able to make contact."

"Why the hell would she? The last I saw of her was when Duke was setting her up to be raped."

Now Prez gives a lopsided grin. "She likes her sex rough. What more can I say?"

I snort. "Then I'd never have been able to satisfy her."

"She came to that conclusion herself. She'd decided that if

Saffie was out of her way, she'd have a chance with Duke. She was freed with the other women, but again, courtesy of her cousin, she was whisked away, under the protection of the feds. That's why we never found mention of her."

So that was then. But I want to know more of the now. "What's happened to her?" For her to have given all that information away, she must have had encouragement.

"She raped you. Set Saffie up to go back to her abuser. She slapped Mary and was fully prepared to see her die in childbirth. What the fuck do you think happened to her?" He pauses, but not long enough for me to respond. "Swift took the lead in questioning her. Hell, her methods, Niran." This time his head shake is in admiration. "I think even Kink might have learned a few things about how to torture a woman. Not to those extremes, of course."

Despite myself, I give a quick grin. Growing serious, I ask, "She's dead?"

Lost slowly raises his chin. "I put a bullet into her. Did it for you, Brother. And for Grumbler."

Lifting my jaw, wordlessly I show my thanks.

Lost shakes himself, as if he's closed the book on her. "Now we've got to discuss Cyn."

"Do we have to?" I'd rather forget she exists, but I know we can't ignore the part she played. But hell, how could I condone killing my sister?

Instead of answering me, Lost picks up his phone and for a few seconds, taps into it. After a moment, the door opens and Cyn comes in, Sharpshooter behind her.

"Sit." Sharp points at a chair, luckily discreetly placed a few feet away from my own and out of reach of my fists.

Lost opens a drawer, takes out a gun, and lays it on the desk in front of him. Cyn's eyes are drawn to it. They widen and fill with horror while my gut churns. *Am I going to witness my sister's death?*

Suddenly, Prez rears up. He half-stands and looms over her. "We took you in," he spits. "We trusted you in this clubhouse. And how did you fuckin' repay us? By almost getting your brother and his old lady killed."

Her eyes come to me, but I keep my features fixed. She turns to look behind her, but Sharpshooter's standing with his arms folded over his chest.

"I didn't know that was what Susie was planning," she cries out. "I didn't want to hurt Niran. I just wanted my brother."

"If you were a man, you'd already be dead," Lost states coldly.

"I'm sorry," she wails. "I never meant for anyone to get hurt." Tears fall from her eyes as she shakes her head. "I thought maybe Niran might get into a fight over Saffie, but tortured and almost killed? If I'd known that, I'd never have said anything."

"An MC runs on loyalty and respect," Lost informs her, his voice monotone as he retakes his seat. "You betrayed us."

Cyn again looks behind her to Sharp, but his face gives nothing away. "I didn't know I wasn't supposed to talk to Susie. She was my only friend here."

For the first time, Sharp speaks. "And why was that, Cyn?"

Cyn's openly crying now, tears running down her cheeks. I don't have any sympathy for her. "Because I'm a brat," she sobs. "I was thinking of myself, not anyone else." Her words sound practiced, I wonder if Sharpshooter has schooled her. She becomes fascinated by the gun once again. "I'll go home."

"It's a bit late for that now," Lost tells her.

She gulps, wipes her tears with the back of her hand, sniffs loudly, then turns to me and says pleadingly, "Niran, I'll do anything. Anything."

I stare at her impassively.

"Please." Her voice has become a whisper. "I didn't know. Honestly. I didn't know I was putting you in danger. It was the last thing I wanted."

Suddenly, I can't stay detached anymore. I sit forward, accidentally knocking my crutches to the floor. They crash as they land as if for emphasis. "Saffie and I were this close to death." I hold my forefinger and thumb a fraction of an inch apart. "I might still lose my foot, Cyn. If I can't ride, I lose my club. Have you any fuckin' idea of the damage you've done?"

She swallows rapidly. "I don't know how I can make it up to you."

"I can't stand to look at you." I turn my head pointedly, instead staring at the Satan's Devils' insignia hanging behind Lost's desk.

"Nevertheless," Lost states, bringing my attention back to him, "she's your sister. It was you who was wronged. You get the final say in what happens to her."

Fuck it. Fuck it to hell and back. How can I say kill her?

Lost gives me a moment, then takes his eyes from me, and they land on the man standing behind Cyn instead. "Sharp? Take her out of here. Get a prospect to watch her."

Sharp nods and puts his hand on Cyn's shoulder. "Come."

"Niran," she says, pleadingly. "Niran, please…"

I refuse to look at her.

"Come," Sharp repeats.

He pulls her up and takes her out. I hear her sobs slowly fade as he leads her down the corridor. Within moments, he's back.

As he takes the seat Cyn vacated, Lost raises an eyebrow toward him.

"Cyn's a civilian," he starts in her defence. "She has no fuckin' idea how an MC works. At most, she expected Niran to get a beatdown, and Saffie to return to her ex. I believe she's truly contrite."

"Fuckin' contrite?" I scoff.

Lost raps the table. "I've had it up to here," he raises his hand to his chin, "with bitches. Make your decision, Niran. We end her or send her home. Your choice."

I cannot sanction the death of my sister. "Send her—"

"Or I keep her," Sharp interrupts.

"That's a big ask, Brother."

"I know, Prez." Sharpshooter sits back and stretches out his legs. "But I think everyone deserves a chance. She's broken, but that doesn't mean she's not fixable. If you send her home, she's not going to get better."

"And we'll be sending her away with fuck knows what secrets she's learned about us. She listens at doors," Lost reminds us.

"A habit I've broken her of," Sharp states, confidently.

"What's in it for you?" I suddenly ask, not understanding how anyone would want to be near Cyn.

"Really?" He raises an eyebrow. "You want me to spell out the advantages of having a warm, willing woman in my bed?"

My eyes widen. No, I do not. That's my fucking sister.

"If she stays, you take full responsibility for her." Lost stares at Sharp.

"And keep her out of my fuckin' way," I throw at him. Cyn stay? Her betrayal thrust in mine and Saffie's face every day? At the least, she should be banished. But both Lost and Sharp have made good points. At home, she'd be made to think she was nothing again, and who knows what she would say about us?

"Your choice, Niran." Lost spins the gun on his desk.

Even after everything she's done, I can't say I want her dead.

I take in a deep breath. "If Sharp's serious and thinks he can control her, she gets one more chance."

"I've got her." Sharp exhales a breath, and his face starts to relax.

"You want to patch her? 'Cause I'm not certain she'd get any votes."

Sharp snorts. "One step at a time, Prez. No, I'm not of the mind to patch her, even if she would be accepted. But let's see where this goes. Right now, I kind of like her."

Prez huffs loudly. "Fuck, I'm not into killing bitches. One was enough. But Niran's right. She gets one more shot at fitting into the club. And Brother?" He stares at Sharp. "Her behaviour is on you."

Sharp nods. "I accept that."

CHAPTER FORTY

Saffie

THREE MONTHS LATER.

"Come to Auntie Saffie," I say in a singsong voice, taking little Theo from his mother's arms. "Who's a clever boy then?" He beams and giggles at me.

Mary flops back and huffs air so heavily it makes her bangs fly up. "I'd forgotten how exhausting looking after a baby is. I mean, I know they poop, pee, sleep and feed, but it's a never-ending job."

"Aww, you keeping your mom running around?" For an answer, Theo blows a spit bubble at me.

Grumbler comes over and places a bottle of soda next to his wife. "You getting in practice?" He nods at the baby in my arms. As I blush bright red, he leans into Mary. "Fuckin' called it, didn't I?"

As his old lady's eyes widen when she looks at me then beams, I know she's guessed.

"We were keeping it quiet." I pout. There's no point in denying that I'm six weeks pregnant. And deliriously happy I might add. It's just that I didn't want to tempt fate by making an announcement so soon.

"She doesn't need practice," Mary points out, prodding her man. "She's been helping out with Theo ever since we brought him home. I couldn't have done it without her help." I have. I'd started while she was still in the hospital. Mary's blood pressure hadn't immediately come down, and Theo had developed some breathing problems. But they were both home just two weeks after the delivery that had found them unprepared, so Niran, his brothers and I had pitched in to get everything ready.

"Hey, what about me?"

Mary looks at me and rolls her eyes, then pats Grumbler on the hand. "You've been a great help, dearest."

I grin. Grumbler's proud as fuck of his son and the part he played in delivering him, but tends to like to show him off and retell the story, each time with more embellishments than to get involved in the details of rearing him. Though I have seen him changing a diaper from time to time.

"I can't fuckin' feed him, I haven't got the right equipment." Grumbler plumps up his flat chest to make sure we get what he's saying. I roll my eyes, *typical man.*

"Where's my brother?" Alicia, appearing at the clubhouse door, calls out.

I sigh, knowing I'm going to have to give him up. Before I do, I nuzzle his down-covered head and breathe in his scent. *This time I'm going to do everything right.*

As I pass Theo over to his big sister, I ease back my head and close my eyes.

Despite Niran being so worried, I hadn't had nightmares about what I'd done to Duke, in fact, the opposite. I don't have nightmares at all now. Ending Duke has erased him from my mind. I'd felt I was selfish in wanting another baby so soon, but Niran had insisted there was no point in waiting. After what we'd been through, we'd lived more in a few months than most people experience in a lifetime. We'd seen each other more at our worst than our best, and that had not only strengthened our relationship, it had given us a solid grounding for the future. As soon as I'd got the all clear after my third period had come and gone, we'd dispensed with the condoms. I'd fallen pregnant immediately.

I'll never replace the son that I lost or forget my earlier baby, but I've been given another chance, new life growing inside me, and this time, a good man by my side.

As if I've conjured him up, when the clubroom door opens again, it's Niran. He makes a beeline for me, his mouth landing on mine, his hand touching my belly. If Grumbler hadn't already guessed, Niran would soon be giving the game away. He can't hide his delight at my pregnancy, even if he complains we should have had more practice.

"Good ride?" I ask him, noticing Sharpshooter coming in behind him, taking off his gloves and tucking them into his helmet.

"Great." Niran breathes in and breathes out, his eyes creased in bliss at the memory.

That day when Niran had had his cast removed is etched in my memory. I'd been all but paralysed by the fear that his foot wouldn't have healed sufficiently and wouldn't be weight bearing. But the surgeons had done their job right, and though he jokes he shouldn't stand near a strong magnet, his foot, while not pretty, is serviceable. The first time he got back on his bike, he looked like a child at Christmas.

He straightens and tugs down his cut, the one now embellished with the new sergeant-at-arms flash. Grumbler's stepped back permanently, wanting to dedicate his time to being a dad. As he says, this is his one chance, and he wants to make a go of it.

"Glad you remembered how to keep shiny side up, Venge,"

Grumbler says snidely, but his lip curls. "And I hear congratulations are in order."

Yeah, my man's at last picked up a handle. Seems he wanted revenge for so long, it kind of stuck to him. Shortly after Duke's demise he entered church as Niran and emerged as Vengeance. As it was all on my behalf, I'd had no problem with it. Vengeance, as the saying goes, is all mine.

Vengeance narrows his eyes. "You told them?"

"I did not. He," I point to the offender, "guessed."

"Does everyone know?" Vengeance plops down beside me and puts his arm around my shoulders.

"Started a book already. I've got twenty on it being a boy," Blaze shouts out.

Hearing his voice reminds me I'm pleased he'd covered my tattoo with an amazing image of birds and flowers. Luckily, we hadn't delayed else I wouldn't be able to do it now.

"Brothers!" Vengeance huffs, but he doesn't seem particularly put out about it.

"So when are you due?" Mary asks me.

"Due?" Eva's passing by. "You pregnant?"

I don't know why I blush, but I do. "Uh-huh."

Vengeance, however, says proudly, "We are."

Mary leans forward. "I love that 'we'. Women do all the heavy carrying and men just bask in it as if they do all the work."

"We do," Grumbler protests. "Ever thought about the effort that goes into producing that baby-making goo?"

I can't help it, I snort.

Vengeance barks a laugh and touches fists with Grumbler. "Too fuckin' right, Brother."

"Hey, that's enough." Alicia breaks off from baby talk with her brother and frowns at her stepdad. "I know how babies are made, I just don't want to think of anything like that between you and my mother. Or," she narrows her eyes at her mom, "worse, walking in on it."

It's Mary's turn to flush. "My baby-making days are over. I made sure of that."

"Thank fuck." Grumbler shoots a fond look at her. "I couldn't go through that again." He looks my way and gives a wide grin. "Saffie, when the time comes, remember, I'm an expert at delivering babies. No need for fancy hospitals."

"Thanks for the offer," Vengeance says drily. "But I think we'll be good, Brother."

"I'm not kidding," Grumbler says seriously. "I told you when to push, didn't I, Mary?"

Mary smirks. "I thought he was going to pass out on me."

"Hush, woman," Grumbler says grumpily. "I was fuckin' nowhere near it. I did good." He raises his eyes to the man by my side. "Offer's still open, Brother."

Vengeance face has hardened, and he says deceptively casually, "Just so you know, Grumbler, I'd have to kill you if you get one glimpse of my woman's pussy."

I snort.

Eva had wondered off. Out of the side of my eye I'd noticed her talking to the sweet butts, and now Cindy, Tits and Pearl come over. Tits leans over and tickles Theo, then looks at me. "Hear we'll soon have another kid to fawn over."

Eva's got a big mouth, I realise.

I don't mind the club girls, they're not forced to be here and certainly not like Duke's captive whores. The only problem I'd have is if they set their sights on my man. Not that they'd have any success. I trust him implicitly, and this time, believe I have a good basis for doing so. If only because he's seen me wield a baseball bat.

The main door opens again. Glancing up, I lean into my old man. "Watch out, it's trouble." I glance up and wave. "Hi, Cyn."

She gives a waggle of her hand back, then goes to Sharpshooter who's standing by the bar. Casually, he puts his arm around her. He bends his head down and says something to her. She steps back and gesticulates. He nods his head.

After a pause, she swings around and stalks over, her hands on her hips. "I'm going to be an aunt, and nobody told me?"

"Nobody was supposed to know. Not yet," Vengeance retorts, glaring at Grumbler.

"You are." In a soft voice, I give her the confirmation.

I've made an effort to get to know Cyn. We eventually bonded over family of all things. Like mine, her mom had pushed her one way, while her inclination was to go another. It had taken a lot for me to forgive her for the part that she'd played, but Susie had been the one most in the wrong. She'd held out the promise of friendship to a girl who was trying hard to fit in, and Cyn had fallen for her lies. Like how she and Niran would have given her a home when they finally lived together. Susie had been clever and had known just how to play her.

What happened to Susie comes under the heading of club business, and apart from the men, no one else here is supposed to know what happened to her. Vengeance had told me she's no longer a threat to me or the club, and I can add two and two together.

Cyn beams and claps her hands together. "I'm going to be an aunt! I'll be the best one ever."

Sharp comes straight over and pulls her into his arms. "You better fuckin' be," he warns her.

Vengeance stares at them for a moment. He still hasn't completely forgiven her, but Cyn's been trying her hardest to make amends, and he's softening toward her.

Like now when he throws her a bone. "Aunt Cyn does have a good ring to it."

She lights up at the gesture of approval from her brother.

For a moment I sit pondering how things have worked out. "You're quiet."

I take Vengeance's hand. "Just thinking."

"We could go think together." He waggles his eyebrows.

We could indeed. Pregnancy hormones are making me horny, and at least this time around, I've someone I can take advantage of.

We've no need for safewords, no need for anything other than ourselves and what we do with each other. There's no fear in my life, just a longing for my man and hopes for our future.

The permanent aroma of leather no longer bothers me, I've come to crave it. The club doesn't scare me. I'm more worried about civilians nowadays, people who judge me for being with a biker.

But what do they know of the family and commitment that binds the Satan's Devils together? What do they know of the love between brother and brother, or of brothers with their old ladies?

How could they imagine the lengths bikers will go to keep each other safe, and their property happy and secure?

I take the hand of the man sitting beside me. *Vengeance is mine, thank the Lord.*

"Saffie? That your phone?"

It is indeed. I lean against Niran as I sit up and awkwardly reach into my back pocket to extract it.

"Daughter!" a voice roars. "You keeping something from me?"

I hold the phone away from my ear. "Grinch," I say delightedly. "And what—"

"I'm gonna be a granddaddy."

I look around suspiciously. "You got this place bugged or something?"

A full-throated chuckle comes down the line. "Nah, Token just texted Stormy."

I narrow my eyes at the computer geek, but grin down at the phone. "It's early days, Grinch. But yeah, you're getting a grandkid."

"Well hot damn, little lady. That's made my fuckin' day. You take care, you hear me?"

Vengeance rolls his eyes at me.

"You heard?" I ask him.

"Think the whole damn clubhouse heard, Saffie." His eyes are twinkling.

I take his hand, holding it tight. "When you first wanted me to come to the clubhouse, I really didn't know what I was getting into."

"Nope." He pops the p. "More family than you've ever dreamed of."

He's not wrong there.

I don't even mind that they're all up in my business.

How could I have ever compared the Devils to the Wolves? It now seems ridiculous.

"I love our crazy family," I confide to Vengeance quietly.

Leaning over, he places one hand on my stomach, and with the other, he cups my face, then kisses me gently. When he pulls away, he says softly, "Not as much as I love you."

Red

When I was young I had no desire to become a member of a motorcycle club.

If I envisioned a future, it would be a replica of the family life I'd had, finding a wife, getting married, and spitting out a couple of kids. I'd do some kind of blue collar job just to put some money in my pocket and food on our table.

But fate had other plans, and drove me into the arms of the Satan's Devils MC.

From then, I never looked back.

Now I'm the prez of the Vegas Chapter and I've achieved more than I ever expected, respect and loyalty from my brothers. The only thing missing is the woman I'd always thought would end up by my side.

I live for my club. That's more than enough. Isn't it?

Cheryl

Oh, the decisions we make when we're young which with age we regret.

At the time fear had me turning my back and walking away. There were men in the sea aplenty, surely a special one would turn up?

But as time moved along and I grew older, I couldn't forget the man I'd been unable to get out of my mind. What would my life have been like is I'd been braver? What if I'd said yes?

Would I have ended up a weary almost forty-year-old croupier in a Vegas casino with no man by my side?

Do we get second chances? How I'd love the answer to be yes.

OTHER WORKS BY MANDA MELLETT

Blood Brothers – A series about sexy dominant sheikhs and their bodyguards

Stolen Lives (#1) Nijad and Cara

Close Protection (#2) Jon and Mia

Second Chances (#3) Kadar and Zoe

Identity Crisis (#4) Sean and Vanessa

Dark Horses (#5) Jasim and Janna

Hard Choices (#6) Aiza

Satan's Devils MC - Arizona Chapter

Turning Wheels (Blood Brothers #3.5, Satan's Devils #1) Wraith and Sophie

Drummer's Beat (#2) Drummer and Sam

Slick Running (#3) Slick and Ella

Targeting Dart (#4) Dart and Alex

Heart Broken (#5) Heart and Marc

Peg's Stand (#6) Peg and Darcy

Rock Bottom (#7) Rock and Becca

Joker's Fool (#8) Joker and Lady

Mouse Trapped (#9) Mouse and Mariana

Blade's Edge (#10) Blade and Tash

Heart Mended: A Satan's Devils MC Novella

Truck Stopped (#11) Truck & Allie

Satan's Devils MC Boxset 1 Books 1-5

Satan's Devils MC Boxset 2 Books 6-8

Satan's Devils MC Boxset 3 Books 9-11

Satan's Devils MC - Colorado Chapter

Paladin's Hell (#1) Paladin and Jayden

Demon's Angel (#2) Demon and Violet

Devil's Due (#3) Beef and Steph

Devil's Dilemma (#4) Pyro and Mel

Ink's Devil (#5) Ink and Beth

Devil's Spawn (#6)

Satan's Devils MC - Next Generation

Amy's Santa (#1) Wizard and Amy

Hawk's Cry (#2) Hawk and Olivia

Twisted Throttle (#3) Throttle and Gwen

Satan's Devils MC - San Diego Chapter

Being Lost (#1)

Grumbler's Ride (#2)

Avenging Devil Part 1 (#3)

Satan's Devils MC - Utah Chapter

Road Tripped (#1)

Stormy's Thunder (#2)

ACKNOWLEDGMENTS & AUTHOR'S NOTE

So now you know how Niran and Saffie's story ended. I do hope that you think I did them justice and forgive me for leaving you hanging after the end of Part 1.

Now you've read the whole story, I hope you can understand why this had to be written in two parts. I really wanted to update you all on Grumbler's and Mary's story, so there was a lot to fit in.

I wasn't quite sure how Part 1 would be received, but I've been blown away by all the reviews. Thank you all for taking the time to tell me how much you enjoyed it (even if you berated me for the ending).

Now like I normally do, I have some people I need to show my appreciation for. Firstly, a massive thank you to my beta readers, with particular mention to Sheri and Danena who both have a large input to my books. Honestly ladies, I couldn't do this without you. Mention, of course, to the other betas, Jo, Tami, Alex, Nicole, Terra and Zoe. It's so encouraging to know at an early stage that the plot works and that you enjoy the book.

Maggie Kern, what can I say that hasn't already been said? Again, I've enjoyed working with you.

Once again, massive thanks to Darlene Tallman who's proof-read Avenging Devil Part 2. I am embarrassed at one particular spelling mistake that you picked up!

For the second time, the cover features Curtis Presley, and the image was provided by Golden Czermak of Furious Fotog. The cover was again brought to life by Dar Dixon of Wicked Smart Designs.

Finally, last as always, but definitely not least, thanks to all of you, my wonderful readers who've taken a chance on this book. If it wasn't for your encouragement, I wouldn't keep writing. I have recently received messages and emails telling me how much you like my books, and I love reading everyone. A positive message inspires me to write more.

This book, like all of my works, has been to beta readers, through editing twice, to a proofreader and then to ARC readers, but there could still be the odd typo that's crept through. Please message me if you've found anything so I have a chance to correct the book. I love to hear from readers, even if you're pointing out something I've got wrong.

If you've enjoyed this book, please consider writing a review. Reviews are essential to us authors, and I appreciate and read them all.

I'm now writing Red's Peril, the first in the Satan's Devils MC Vegas chapter. I know many have great expectations of this book, so I hope I do it justice.

Another Devil will be along very soon.

ABOUT THE AUTHOR

Manda's life's always seemed a bit weird, starting with a childhood that even today she's still trying to make sense of, then losing her parents in the late teens. Going from the tragic to the bizarre, who else could be unlucky enough to have had two car accidents, neither her fault, one involving a nun, and another involving a police woman?

There isn't enough space to list everything that's happened to Manda, or what she's learned from it. But by using the rich fabric of her personal life, psychology degree, varied work experiences, and amazing characters she's met, Manda is able to populate her books with believable in-depth characters and enjoys pitting them against situations which challenge them. Her books are full of suspense, twists and turns and the unexpected.

Manda lives in the beautiful countryside of Essex in the UK, the area's claim to fame being the Wilkin's Jam Factory at nearby Tiptree. She can usually find jars of jam which remind her of home wherever she goes. As well as writing books and reading, Manda loves walking her dogs and keeping fit. She lives with her husband of over 30 years, who, along with her son, is her greatest fan and supporter.

Manda is thankful that one of the more unusual, and at the time unpleasant, turns her life took, now enables her to spend her time writing. Confirming, in her view, every cloud has a silver lining.

Photo by Carmel Jane Photography

www.ingramcontent.com/pod-product-compliance
Lightning Source LLC
Chambersburg PA
CBHW070345170726
48291CB00001B/187